Robert Bryn 'za is the author of the international #1 bestselling Detective Erika Foster series and the Kate Marshall series. Robert's books have sold over 3 million copies and have been translated into 28 languages. He is British and lives in Slovakia.

ALSO BY ROBERT BRYNDZA

COLD BLOOD
ROBERT BRYNDZA

sphere

SPHERE

First published in 2017 by Bookouture, an imprint of Storyfire Ltd.
This paperback edition published in 2020 by Sphere

13 5 7 9 10 8 6 4 2

A CIP catalogue record for this book
is available from the British Library.

ISBN 978-0-7515-7132-5

Printed and bound in Great Britain by
Clays Ltd, Elcograf S.p.A.

Papers used by Sphere are from well-managed forests
and other responsible sources.

Sphere
An imprint of
Little, Brown Book Group
Carmelite House
50 Victoria Embankment
London EC4Y 0DZ

An Hachette UK Company

www.hachette.co.uk
www.littlebrown.co.uk

For Mum and Dad, with all my love

Hell is empty and all the devils are here.
— *William Shakespeare,* The Tempest

CHAPTER 1

MONDAY, 2 OCTOBER 2017

Detective Chief Inspector Erika Foster shielded her eyes from the pelting rain as she and Detective Inspector Moss hurried along the South Bank, a paved walkway lining the southern bank of London's River Thames. The tide was low, cutting a brown swathe through the silt, bricks and rubbish littering the exposed riverbed. In the pocket of her long black jacket, Erika's radio gave a tinny burst and she heard the officer at the crime scene asking their location. She pulled it out and replied: 'This is DCI Foster. We're two minutes away.'

It was still the morning rush hour, but the day was already darkening, with a gloomy fog descending. They picked up the pace and hurried on past the tall IBM headquarters, and the pale squat ITV Studios building. Here the South Bank curved sharply to the right before widening out to a tree-lined avenue leading down to the National Theatre and the Hungerford Bridge.

'It's down there, boss,' said Moss, slowing breathlessly.

On the exposed riverbed, ten feet below, a small group of people gathered on a man-made beach of pale sand, Erika massaged her ribs, feeling where she was getting a stitch. At just over six feet tall, she towered over Moss, and her short blonde hair was plastered to her head by the rain.

'You should ease off the cigarettes,' said Moss, looking up at her. She pushed wet strands of red hair away from her face. Her plump cheeks were flushed from running, and her face was covered in a mass of freckles.

'You should ease off the Mars Bars,' Erika shot back.

'I am. I'm down to one for breakfast, one for lunch and a proper dinner.'

'I'm the same with the cigs,' smiled Erika.

They came to a set of stone steps leading down to the Thames. They were stained at intervals with tidemarks, and the last two steps were slippery with algae. The beach was four metres wide and ended abruptly where the dirty brown water churned past. Erika and Moss pulled out their warrant cards, and the huddle of people parted to let them through to where a special constable was attempting to protect a large, battered, brown cloth suitcase, half buried in the sand.

'I've tried to move them all up, ma'am, but I didn't want to leave the scene unattended,' said the young woman peering up at Erika through the rain. She was small and thin, but had a determined glint in her eye.

'You on your own?' asked Erika, glancing down at the suitcase. Through a ragged hole in one end two pale bloated fingers were poking out.

She nodded. 'The other special I'm on duty with had to go and deal with an alarm going off in one of the office blocks,' she said.

'This isn't on,' said Moss. 'There should always be two specials. So you're coming off the night shift in central London, alone?'

'OK, Moss—' started Erika.

'No, it's not okay, boss. These people volunteer! Why can't they pay for more police officers?'

'I joined the specials to gain experience to become a full-time officer—'

'We need to clear this area before we lose all chance of forensic evidence,' interrupted Erika.

Moss nodded and she and the special started to herd the gawking people towards the steps. Erika noticed at the end of the small beach, next to the high wall, two small holes had been dug out by an older man with long grey hair, wearing a multicoloured poncho. He was oblivious to the people and the rain, and carried on digging. Erika pulled out her radio and called in for any uniformed officers in the vicinity. There was an ominous silence. She saw the man in the coloured poncho was ignoring Moss, and carrying on digging.

'I need you to move up there, back up the stairs,' said Erika, moving away from the suitcase towards him. He looked up at her and carried on smoothing his pile of sand, which was saturated by the rain. 'Excuse me. You. I'm talking to you.'

'And who are you?' he asked imperiously, looking her up and down.

'Detective Chief Inspector Erika Foster,' she said, flashing her warrant card. 'This is a crime scene. And you need to leave. Now.'

He stopped digging and looked almost comically affronted.

'Are you allowed to be so rude?'

'When people obstruct a crime scene, yes.'

'But this is my only income. I'm allowed to exhibit my sand sculptures here. I have a permit from Westminster Council.'

He rummaged in his poncho and retrieved a laminated card with his photo, which rapidly spotted with rain.

A voice came from Erika's radio. 'This is PC Warford, with PC Charles…' She could see two young officers hurrying towards the crowd of people by the steps.

'Coordinate with DI Moss. I want the South Bank closed off, fifty feet in each direction,' she said into her radio, then stuffed it back in her pocket. The man was still holding out his permit. 'You can put that away.'

'You have a very unfortunate manner,' he said, squinting up at her.

'I do, and it would be very unfortunate if I had to arrest you. Now go on, up there.'

He slowly got to his feet. 'Is that how you talk to a witness?'

'What did you witness?'

'I uncovered the suitcase when I was digging.'

'It was buried in the sand?'

'Partly. It wasn't there yesterday. I dig here every day; the sand gets shifted by the tide.'

'Why do you dig here every day?'

'I'm a sand sculpture artist,' he stated pompously. 'That is usually my spot. I do a mermaid sitting aloft a rock with fish jumping; it's very popular with—'

'Did you touch the suitcase, or move anything?' said Erika.

'Of course not. I stopped when I saw… When I saw the suitcase was split and there was… fingers, protruding…'

Erika could see he was scared.

'Okay. Go up to the walkway, we'll need to take a statement from you.'

The two officers and the special had cordoned off the walkway. Moss joined her as the old man staggered off to the steps. They were now the only two people on the beach.

Pulling on latex gloves, they moved to the suitcase. The fingers poking through the hole in the brown material were swollen, with blackened fingernails. Moss gently worked the sand away from the seams, and exposed the rusted zipper. It took Erika several gentle tugs, but it yielded, and the suitcase sagged open as she unzipped. Moss moved to help, and they slowly lifted it open. A little water spilled out, and the naked body of a man was crammed inside. Moss stepped backwards, putting her arm up to her nose. The smell of rotting flesh and stagnant water hit the back of their throats. Erika closed her eyes for a moment, then opened them. The limbs were white and muscular. The flesh had the appearance of raw suet and was starting to flake away, in places exposing the bone. Erika gently lifted the torso. Tucked underneath was a head, with black wispy hair.

'Jeez, he's been decapitated,' said Moss, indicating the neck.

'And the legs have been chopped off to fit inside,' finished Erika. The bloated, badly beaten face was unrecognisable. A swollen black tongue protruded from between large purple lips. She gently placed the torso back over the head, and closed the suitcase. 'We need forensics down here. Fast. I don't know how long we've got until the tide comes back in.'

CHAPTER 2

An hour later the forensic pathologist and his team were at the crime scene. The rain continued to pour, and the fog thickened, obscuring the tops of the surrounding buildings. Despite the rain, crowds had gathered at each end of the police cordon to gawk at a large white forensics tent which had been erected over the body in the suitcase. It glowed ominously against the murky water rushing past.

It was hot inside the tent. Despite the cold, the bright lights in the small space were causing the temperature to soar. Erika and Moss had changed into blue crime scene coveralls, and were with Forensic Pathologist Isaac Strong, who was crouching down by the suitcase with his two assistants, and the crime scene photographer. Isaac was a tall, lean man. His soft brown eyes and thinly shaped eyebrows were the only things to identify who he was through his hood and face mask.

'What can you tell us?' asked Erika.

'The body has been in the water for some time; you can see this yellow and green discolouration on the skin,' he said, indicating the chest and the abdomen. 'The cool temperature of the water will have slowed decay—'

'That's decay *slowed down*?' said Moss, putting up a hand to her mask. The smell was overpowering. They paused, all staring at the battered naked body, at how neatly the pieces had been packed inside: a leg each side of the torso; the knee joints folded into the top right and bottom left corner; arms crossed over the chest and the decapitated head tucked neatly underneath. One of Isaac's assistants unzipped a small pocket on the inside of the suitcase lid and pulled out a small clear plastic ziplock bag containing a gold wedding band, a watch, and a man's gold chain necklace. She held it up to the light, her eyes wide over her protective mask.

'They could be his valuables, but where are his clothes?' said Erika. 'It's like he's been packed, not dumped. Is there any ID?' she added hopefully.

The crime scene photographer leaned in and fired off two shots. They winced at the flash. Isaac's assistant searched the pocket with a gloved hand. She shook her head.

'Dismembering the body in this way, the precision, and packing in the valuables shows forward planning,' said Isaac.

'And why pack in the valuables with the body? Why not take them? It's almost like whoever did this is taking the piss,' said Moss.

'It makes me think it could be gangland or drug related, but that's for you to find out,' said Isaac. Erika nodded as one of his assistants lifted the torso and the photographer took a shot of the victim's decapitated head.

'Okay, that's me done,' said the photographer.

'Let's get the body moved,' said Isaac. 'We've got the tide to contend with.'

Erika looked down and saw one of the footprints in the sand was beginning to fill with swirling water. A young guy in overalls appeared at the opening of the tent with a fresh black body bag on a stretcher.

Erika and Moss stepped outside, and watched as Isaac's assistants unzipped the body bag, spread it open, then gently lifted the suitcase towards the stretcher. Four feet off the sand it caught, and they almost lost their footing.

'Hang on, stop, stop, stop!' said Erika, moving back into the tent. A torch was shone onto the underside of the dripping suitcase.

A length of pale rope had become entangled in the material, which was starting to bulge and fray under the weight of the body inside.

'Scissors, quickly,' snapped Isaac. A pair of sterile scissors were quickly unwrapped and handed to him. He leaned underneath and neatly clipped off the rope, allowing them to lift the suitcase clear. It disintegrated as it was laid on the stretcher. He handed over the scissors and rope, and they were bagged up and labelled. Then the body bag was zipped up, enveloping the suitcase.

'I'll be in touch when I've completed the autopsy,' said Isaac. He left with his two assistants as they started to push the stretcher, wheeling it awkwardly across the sand, leaving deep tracks.

When Erika and Moss had handed over their coveralls, they came back up onto the paved walkway of the South Bank and saw Nils Åkerman, the head of forensics, had just arrived with his team of five CSIs. They would now attempt to gather forensic evidence from the scene. Erika looked back at the water encroaching on the beach and doubted they would have much luck.

Nils was a tall, thin man with piercing blue eyes, which today were a little bloodshot, and he appeared fed up and exhausted.

'Nice weather for ducks,' he said, nodding at them as he passed. He spoke excellent English with a faint Swedish accent. Erika and Moss were handed umbrellas and they watched as Nils and his team moved across the shrinking beach. The water was now less than a foot from the tent, and was speeding past, swollen by the rain.

'I never get his sense of humour,' said Moss. 'Can you see any ducks?'

'I think he meant ducks would enjoy this weather, and who says he meant it as a joke?'

'But he said it like it was a joke. It's the Swedish sense of humour, I've heard it's really weird.'

'Anyway, let's focus,' said Erika. 'The suitcase could have been dumped further upriver and got snagged on the rope as it was carried by the tide.'

'There's miles of riverbank where it could have been chucked in,' said Moss. Erika looked up at the buildings and across the busy water. A barge was chugging past, belching out black smoke, and two long, low Thames Clipper water taxis were slicing their way against the tide in the other direction.

'This would be a pretty stupid place to chuck in a body,' said Erika. 'It's overlooked by offices, open round the clock. And you'd have to carry it all the way along the South Bank, past all the bars and offices, CCTV, witnesses.'

'Stupid is as stupid does. It could be a shrewd place for a ballsy person to dump a body. So many back roads where they could disappear,' said Moss.

'That's not helpful.'

'Well, boss, we shouldn't underestimate whoever did this. Or should I say, *misunderestimate?*'

Erika rolled her eyes. 'Come on, lets grab a sandwich and get back to the nick.'

CHAPTER 3

It was late afternoon when Erika and Moss arrived back at Lewisham Row Police Station, and they were both drenched from the rain, which hadn't let up. The construction work around the station, which was just beginning when Erika was first assigned to south London, was almost complete, and the eight-storey police station was now dwarfed by several high-rise blocks of luxury apartments.

Sergeant Woolf sat behind the front desk in the shabby reception area. He was a large man with pale blue eyes and a jowly white face with several chins which spilled over onto the front of his neatly pressed white shirt. A thin, horse-faced girl stood in front of him at the front desk, cradling a pudgy baby boy on her skinny hip. The baby had a huge bag of boiled sweets in his grip and was chewing nonchalantly, watching his mother's exchange with Woolf.

'How long you gonna keep us waiting?' she demanded. 'I got stuff to do.'

'That depends on your boyfriend, and the 300 grams of cocaine we found up his bottom,' said Woolf, cheerily.

'You lot. I bet you've stitched him up,' she said, jabbing at him with a long, pink manicured fingernail.

'Are you suggesting we *planted it* on him?'

'Fuck off,' she said.

'Your mother wasted all that money sending you to finishing school.'

The girl looked confused. 'What you talking about? I finished school, like, years ago.'

Woolf smiled amiably and indicated a long row of faded green plastic chairs under a board of leaflets. 'Please take a seat, madam. I'll let you know when I have more information.' The girl looked Erika and Moss up and down and traipsed over, taking a seat under a noticeboard swamped with community information leaflets. Erika recalled her first day in London after being transferred from Greater Manchester Police. She had sat in the same seat and harangued Woolf about how long she had been waiting, although her circumstances had been different.

'Afternoon, ladies. Raining outside, is it?' said Woolf, seeing them both with wet hair plastered to their heads.

'Nah, just spitting,' grinned Moss.

'Is she in?' asked Erika.

'Yes. The superintendent is warm and dry in her office,' he said.

The girl sitting with the baby shoved a handful of the boiled sweets in her mouth and made a sucking noise, glowering at them.

'Careful you don't choke, madam; my recollection of the Heimlich manoeuvre is a bit hazy,' said Woolf, buzzing Erika and Moss in through the door. He lowered his voice and leaned forward. 'Retirement is so close I can almost touch it.'

'How long?' asked Erika.

'Six months and counting,' he said.

She smiled at him, and then the door clicked shut behind them. They moved down a long, low corridor, past offices where phones rang and support officers worked. It was a busy station, the largest south of the river, serving a large swathe of London and the Kent borders. They hurried down to the locker room in the basement, saying hello to some of the uniformed officers who were coming in to start their shifts. They went to their lockers and pulled out towels to dry themselves off.

'I'm going to hit up missing persons,' said Moss, scrubbing at her hair and face and then stripping off her wet jumper and unbuttoning her blouse.

'I'm going to beg for more officers,' said Erika, drying herself off and sniffing a white blouse which she'd found at the back of her locker.

When Erika had dressed in dry clothes, she took the stairs up to the superintendent's office. Lewisham Row was an old dilapidated 1970s building, and with the cuts to police budgets, the lifts were now something you avoided, if you didn't fancy getting stuck for half the day. She hurried up the stairs two at a time and then emerged into the corridor of the eighth floor. A large window looked out over south London, stretching from the gridlocked ring road running through the heart of Lewisham, past rows of terraced housing, to the green of the Kent borders.

She knocked on the door and went inside. Superintendent Melanie Hudson sat behind her desk, partially obscured by a mound of paperwork. She was a small, thin woman with a bob of fine blonde hair, but looks could be deceiving and she could be a tough cookie when the situation warranted. Erika glanced around the office. It was just as shabby as the rest of the building. The shelves were still empty, and even though she'd been on the job for several months, Melanie still hadn't unpacked a row of boxes against the back wall. Her coat hung neatly by the door on one of three hooks.

'I've just come from a crime scene on the South Bank. Male, violently beaten, decapitated and dismembered, and then packed neatly in a suitcase.'

Melanie finished writing and looked up. 'Was he white?'

'Yes.'

'So you wouldn't say it was racially motivated?'

'You can be white and still be killed in a racially motivated attack.'

Melanie gave her a look. 'I know that, Erika. I just need to be kept in the loop. Top brass is carefully watching racially motived crime since Brexit.'

'It's still early days. It could be gangland, racially motivated, homophobic. It was brutal. He was packed in the case naked, with a watch, ring and chain. We don't know if they were his. I'm waiting on the post-mortem and forensics. I'll let you know which box you can tick when I have more information.'

'What's your caseload like, Erika?'

'I've got an armed robbery murder I've just wound up. There are a couple of others bubbling away in the background. I need to get an ID on this body but it's not going to be easy. The face is badly smashed up, and he's been in the water a long time.'

Melanie nodded. 'Was it a big suitcase?'

'Yes.'

'You can't buy big suitcases anymore. I've been trying to get a family one for when we go away at half-term, but they don't do them cos of the weight limits. Anything over twenty-five kilos they charge you a fortune.'

'You want me to see if I can get you the suitcase when forensics finish up?'

'Very funny. It's a valid point though. Not many companies make suitcases big enough to fit two weeks' worth of beach gear, let alone a full-grown man.'

'What about staffing? How many officers can you give me? I'd like Moss and DC John McGorry; Sergeant Crane is a good team worker.'

Melanie blew out her cheeks and searched through the paper-work on her desk,

'OK. I can give you Moss and McGorry… and a civilian support worker. Let's see how this plays out.'

'OK,' said Erika. 'But there's something weird about this. I have a feeling I'll need a bigger team.'

'That's all you're getting for now. Keep me in the loop,' said Melanie, and she went back to her paperwork.

Erika got up to leave and stopped at the door. 'Where are you off on holiday?'

'Yekaterinburg.'

Erika raised an eyebrow. 'Yekaterinburg, Russia?'

Melanie rolled her eyes. 'Don't ask. My husband is obsessed with out-of-the-way holiday destinations.'

'Well, you won't need sun cream in October in Yekaterinburg.'

'Close the door on your way out,' she snapped.

Erika suppressed a grin and left her office.

CHAPTER 4

Erika grabbed a coffee and some chocolate from the vending machine, then took the stairs the fourth floor where she had a small office. It was nothing more than a box, with a desk awash with paperwork, a computer, and a set of shelves. The rain rattled against a small window looking out over the car park. She closed the door and sat at her desk with her chocolate and steaming cup of coffee. She could hear distant phones ringing, and there was a creak as someone walked past in the corridor. She missed the open-plan offices she'd worked in over the past few years in Bromley Station and West End Central. The four walls closing in on her were a reminder it had been eight long months mid-thirties since she'd last seen the inside of an incident room and had a big case to sink her teeth into.

There was an old map of the Thames on the wall in front of her desk, and she hadn't paid it much notice until now. Tearing open the bar of chocolate, she took a large bite and moved around the desk to peer at it. It wasn't an operational map, it was one of those arty ones, a black-and-white line drawing taking in the full length of the river. The source of the Thames is near Oxford, and it runs 215 miles, through London, before emerging out to sea at the Thames Estuary. Erika traced her finger along its route to where it became tidal at Teddington Lock, and on, as it wound through Twickenham, Chiswick and Hammersmith, on to Battersea, and then through central London, where they had discovered the body in the suitcase.

'Where was that suitcase thrown in?' she said, through a mouthful of chocolate. She thought of the places along the river where someone could throw it in without being seen: Richmond? Chiswick? Chelsea Bridge? Battersea Park? She then thought of the South Bank, heavily overlooked and there was CCTV everywhere. She shoved the last of the chocolate in her mouth and turned, looking around the tiny office. The polystyrene ceiling tiles above were stained with brown watermarks, and the small shelves were packed with the crap of previous occupants: a small furry cactus; a green plastic hedgehog which held pens between plastic spines on its back; a row of dusty operating manuals for long-extinct software. A niggling voice piped up in her head: *was I wrong not to take the promotion?* Everyone had expected her to accept the promotion to superintendent, but it had dawned on her that she would be stuck behind a desk ticking boxes, prioritising, toeing the line, and worse, making others toe the line. Erika was aware she had a healthy ego, but it was never going to be massaged by increased power, a fancy title, or more money. Being out on the street, getting her fingers dirty, solving complex cases and locking up the bad guys: these were the things which got her out of bed every morning.

Also, feelings of guilt had stopped her from taking the promotion. She thought of her colleague, Detective Inspector James Peterson. He wasn't just a colleague; he was also her… *boyfriend?* No. At forty-five years old she felt too old for boyfriends. *Partner?* Partners worked in legal firms. Anyhow, it didn't matter, she'd screwed it up. Peterson had been shot in the stomach during their last big case, the rescue of a kidnap victim. As his senior officer, it had been her decision to go in without backup. He had survived the gunshot wound, just, and they had saved a young woman's life, and arrested a crazed serial killer but, understandably, it had affected their relationship. Peterson had lost seven months of his life in painful recovery, and it was still unclear when he would return to work.

Erika screwed up the chocolate bar wrapper and pitched it into the wastepaper basket in the corner, but she missed, and it landed on the carpet. She moved over to pick it up, and as she bent down there was a knock at the door and it opened, bashing into the side of her head.

'Jeez!' she cried, clutching at her forehead.

Detective Constable John McGorry peered around the door; he was holding a file.

'Sorry, boss. Bit tight in here, isn't it?' He was in his early twenties and had a handsome face and smooth, clear skin. His hair was dark and cropped short.

'You don't say,' she replied, dropping the wrapper into the bin and straightening up, still rubbing at her head.

'Moss just told me about the body in the suitcase, and said I'm being reassigned to work with you on it.'

Erika went back round her desk and sat down.

'Yeah. If you could talk to Moss, she's started on identifying the victim. Where have you been working for the last few months?'

'On the second floor, with DS Lorna Mills and DS Dave Boon.'

'Mills and Boon?' she said, raising an eyebrow.

McGorry grinned. 'Yeah, but it's done nothing for my love life. I've been working late on cataloguing racially motivated Brexit-related crime.'

'Doesn't sound very sexy,' said Erika.

'I'm pleased to be reassigned. Thanks, boss.'

'I'll email you later, if you can crack on with Moss with the ID.'

'That's one of the reasons I came up. I've seen a load of case files over the past few weeks, and one stuck in my mind. A dog walker who found a suitcase by the Embankment, Chelsea, when the Thames was at low tide. Inside was the body of a white female, mid-twenties. Decapitated, dismembered.'

Erika sat back and stared at McGorry. 'When was this?'

'Just over a week ago, September 22nd. I pulled the case file,' he said, handing it over.

'Thanks, I'll be in touch later today,' she said.

*

She waited until he closed the door, then opened the file. The crime scene photos were just as grizzly as she had seen that morning, but the body was in a much better state, with little decay. The victim was a woman with long, filthy, ash-blonde hair. The legs had been dismembered just below the pelvis, and tucked in the two ends of the suitcase. The arms were folded against her chest; with a female victim, this looked as if the corpse was being modest, crossing her hands over her bare breasts. Her severed head had been tucked in under the torso, and like the male victim from the suitcase at the South Bank, her face was so badly battered it was unrecognisable.

Erika looked up at the map of the Thames on the wall. So many places to dump a body.

Or two.

CHAPTER 5

AUGUST 2016

Eighteen-year-old Nina Hargreaves heard about the summer job at Santino's fish and chip shop from her best friend, Kath. They'd just finished high school and, whereas Kath was leaving for university in the autumn, she had no clue what she was going to do with her life. Nina was a pleasant-looking girl with a strong nose, pale freckled skin, long brown hair, and slightly bucked teeth. She wasn't academic, and her careers advisor had suggested she might try office work, or train to be a hairdresser's, but Nina hated those ideas. She hated the thought of being stuck in an office – her mother, Mandy, worked as a clerk in a local solicitor's and complained constantly – and the thought of working in a hairdresser and being stuck with a load of bitchy women made her feel sick. She'd been picked on enough at school.

Nina was already frustrated with the world and her place in it. Her beloved father had died of a heart attack ten years earlier, and while she and her mother weren't the closest, they'd stuck together. It had been a shock to Nina when Mandy had knocked on her bedroom door and said she wanted them to go out for lunch the following Saturday.

'I want you to meet my new friend, Paul,' she'd said.

'A bloke?' Nina had replied, confused. Mandy had shifted awkwardly, and perched on the end of the bed. They looked alike, but Nina wished she'd inherited her mother's small nose and perfect teeth.

'Yes, Paul is a *special* friend; well, more than a friend. He's a solicitor at the firm,' said Mandy, taking her hand.

'You mean a boyfriend?' said Nina, pulling it away.

'Yes.'

'Your boss?'

'He's not my boss. I work for him.'

'What? So he chased you around the desk and now you're a couple?'

'Don't be like that, Nina. I've been seeing Paul for a few months now, and I didn't want to introduce him to you until I knew it was going somewhere.'

Nina stared at her mother, horrified. She'd teased her over the years about getting a boyfriend, even telling her she should date their handsome flirty postman, but Mandy had always shrugged this off saying it was still too soon.

'Where is it going?'

'Well, I hope, at some point, he'll move in.'

'What?'

'Nina. You're eighteen now, you won't be at home for ever.'

'Won't I?'

'Is that what you want? To stay in this bedroom for the rest of your life, still with the Hannah Montana wallpaper?'

''Course not.'

'There we go then. I'm not chucking you out, I'd never do that, but you need to make your own life.'

Those words had hung in the air long after Mandy had left her bedroom. So, with nothing else on the horizon, Nina went for an interview and got the job working at Santino's chip shop.

Santino's was an old school British chip shop tucked at the end of the busy high street in Crouch End. It had a cracked green Formica counter, lined with jars of pickled eggs, and there was a long row of deep fat fryers where the battered fish, sausages, and scraps were cooked and kept in the glass-fronted warmer above. A few tables were dotted about inside, but Santino's mainly did takeaway, and it was always busy. Shifts lasted eight hours, and four girls worked flat out, taking orders and wrapping fish under the watchful eye of the elderly Mrs Santino, a fearsome woman with a gravelly smoker's voice. Mr Santino was quiet, in comparison, and fried the fish helped by a couple of lads.

Nina didn't meet Max until her third shift. She was at the counter, taking an order, when he staggered up to the fryer with a huge bowl of chipped potatoes.

'Get back!' he growled, and as he tipped in the raw chips, boiling hot oil splashed her arm, making her cry out in pain. 'I told you to get back!' he said and stomped back to the kitchen holding the empty bowl.

Mrs Santino saw the large blister rapidly forming on Nina's arm and pulled her through to the kitchen, shoving her arm under the cold tap.

'I've told you, watch the hot fryer!' shouted Mrs Santino. 'I haven't got time to spend filling in the accident book for stupid girls like you! Keep it under the cold water for fifteen minutes, and you'll take it as your break!'

Mrs Santino went back into the front, and Nina felt tears prick her eyes. The huge potato chipper in the corner began to roar as Max and another lad emptied a giant sack of potatoes into the top. She watched Max as he heaved the huge 50 lb potato sacks from the loading bay, piling them up beside the chipper. He wasn't like the other skinny spotty lads. His body was muscular and filled out. He had a rugged beauty, emphasised by a thin white scar running along his jawline, from his left earlobe to the cleft in his chin. His eyes were beautiful, a strange mix of orange and brown. The sleeves of his T-shirt were rolled up to the shoulder and the sweat glistened on his tanned skin. He caught her looking and glared at her.

'I'm not stupid! You didn't give me the chance to step back from the fryer,' Nina shouted above the noise of the chipper, but he ignored her and went out to the loading bay to take his break.

Nina carried on working at Santino's throughout July. She hated the job, but she had become infatuated with Max. She discovered he had a bit of a reputation as a bad boy, once coming in to work with a huge black eye and a split lip. The more he ignored her, the more Nina rose to the challenge to try and get him to speak. She swapped her Santino's T-shirt for a smaller size and stopped wearing a bra at work, and she started to time her breaks to coincide with his, but he continued to ignore her, grunting the minimal response to her questions, and not looking up from the newspaper or his phone.

As August came to a close, a gloom descended over her. She had been introduced to her mother's new boyfriend, Paul, during dinner at a local Italian restaurant. He was alright looking, a little fat with a bald patch, and a bad sense of humour, but she could see her mother was completely in love, and that Paul would soon be moving in.

On a Wednesday night in early August, Nina left the chip shop after a long shift and got in the car to drive home. It was a short journey from Crouch End to Muswell Hill, and the roads were quiet. At the junction near the end of the high street, Nina stopped at the traffic lights. She was waiting as an old lady with a shopping trolley slowly made her way across the road, when a figure she recognised stepped off the pavement in front and stared through the windscreen. It was Max. He glanced around and then moved to her passenger door and knocked on the window, indicating to her to unlock the door. She found herself pressing the button to release the central locking.

Max climbed in and sat beside her. He wore blue jeans, a white T-shirt and a brown leather jacket. His dirty-blond hair hung down to his shoulders and he had a small cut above his left eye. He smelt of beer and sweat.

The lights at the crossing flashed amber then green.

'It's green. Drive,' he said.

She pulled away, and through the back window saw a couple of police officers come running out of an alleyway, and look around. Max sank down a little in the seat, pulled a packet of cigarettes from his pocket and lit up. Nina glanced at him, wanting to say that he couldn't smoke, that this was her mum's car, but she was unable to speak. Max was in her car, and it made her incredibly excited. He looked at her and then wound down the window, resting his arm on the edge. She realised she was just driving, and she'd passed the turn-off leading home. She glanced across and tried to think of something to say to him. His eyes were scanning the road. She'd never seen such incredible eyes. They had depth, and glowed, almost as if they had embers burning behind them.

'Where are we going?' she said, finally breaking the silence.

'It's your car. You're driving. Why the hell are you asking me where we're going?' he said, flicking his cigarette butt out of the window. She saw him look around the car – at the stack of old Westlife CDs under the stereo, the KEEP CALM AND HAKUNA MATATA sticker on the dashboard, and she suddenly felt embarrassed and uncool. He opened the glove compartment and started to rummage through.

'What are you doing?' she asked.

He pulled out a pink square of cloth with blue polka dots, and raised an eyebrow.

'Is this yours?'

'No. It's my mum's car. It's hers,' she said, leaning over to grab it, but he held it out of her reach.

'She keeps her knickers in the glove compartment?'

'It's for wiping the window!'

He laughed. 'Look like knickers to me. Did she forget them after date night with your dad?'

'My dad's dead,' she said.

'Oh. Shit. Sorry,' he said, stuffing the cloth back in the glove compartment.

'It's okay. She has got a boyfriend, though. He's a real dick.'

Max smiled and shook his head. 'The world is full of them. You haven't got any gum, have you?'

'No.'

He closed the glove compartment and looked out of the window at the road moving past.

'It happened a long time ago,' said Nina.

'What did?'

'My dad, dying. It was a heart attack.'

He peered up at the street signs. Nina could sense he was losing interest, and she was annoyed that she had mentioned it.

'Drop me here,' he said, pointing to a pub on the corner. Nina pulled up at the kerb, and watched as he put his hand on the door.

'Where are you going?' she blurted.

'The pub.'

'I've never been in The Mermaid,' she said. It looked rough, with a boarded up window out front.

'I wouldn't expect a girl like you to go there,' he said, opening the door.

'How do you know what kind of girl I am? You seem to spend all your time at work judging me, and giving me dirty looks, and then you jump in my car and expect me to just give you a lift!'

'I thought it was your mum's car?'

'It is. But all I mean is that you shouldn't go around making assumptions about people, because they are almost always wrong.' She felt her face flush in the silence after she spoke.

He looked at her with a wry smile.

'I'm only gonna be a couple of minutes. I've got some business to do. Why don't you wait?'

'Here?'

'Yeah. Where else were you thinking of waiting?'

Nina opened her mouth and closed it again.

'Do you have to be somewhere?' he asked.

'No.'

'Okay then. Hang here for a minute. I'll be back in a bit, and then you can tell me what kind of girl you really are.' He gave her that sexy smile again, and Nina felt her legs go weak.

She watched as he went into the pub then pulled out her phone and dialled Kath's number to tell her what had happened.

'You think he was running from the police?' asked Kath with concern in her voice.

'I don't know.'

'And what kind of business is he doing in The Mermaid? It's well rough and they keep getting raided for drugs.'

'Are you trying to spoil this for me?'

'No. I'm just a concerned friend. You'll call me when you get home?'

Nina could see Max was coming out of the pub.

'Yes, I promise,' she said and hung up.

Max got into the car pocketing a large wad of £50 notes.

'I'd like to buy you a drink, but I need to swing by The Lamb and Flag on Constitution Hill. Is that okay?' He placed a hand on her knee and smiled. She felt a jolt of electricity.

'Yeah, of course,' she said, smiling back.

She drove him to The Lamb and Flag and waited outside for thirty minutes. When he returned to the car he was holding two bottles of Heineken. She started the engine.

'Straight ahead,' he said.

She started off up the road. It was getting dark and the street-lights were out.

'This is for you,' he said, offering her one of the beers and taking a chug from the other.

'I don't drink and drive,' she said, primly, keeping both hands on the wheel.

'Then don't drive,' said Max, raising an eyebrow. Nina could see the road was a dead end, the streetlights were out, and the houses on each side were dark. He leaned over and stroked her hair. 'Pull over. Let's have a drink,' he said, with a smile.

'Okay,' she said, smiling back. He smelt delicious, a mixture of aftershave and damp sweat. The V-neck of his T-shirt gave her a glimpse of the taut tanned skin of his muscled chest. She felt as if she could burst with excitement as she guided the car into a spot by the kerb and turned off the engine. Max handed her the bottle, and as she took a swig the beer foamed up. She held it over the footwell and wiped her mouth with the back of her hand.

'Dammit, what a mess.'

'I dunno, I like a girl who tastes of beer.'

Max leaned over and pulled Nina's face to his, their lips touching. He kissed her softly, then more intensely, parting her lips with his tongue. The bottle fell from her grip, but she didn't notice. She was lost, intoxicated with lust and desire. It would be a long time before she found herself again. And then, it would be too late.

CHAPTER 6

TUESDAY, 3 OCTOBER 2017

Erika woke early to a message from Isaac Strong. The post-mortem on the male victim was complete, and the body of the female victim found in the suitcase had been transferred over to the mortuary in Penge.

Moss was appearing in court to give testimony on a knife murder, so she took McGorry with her. He was excited at the prospect of seeing the results of the post-mortem, but this soon evaporated when they entered the morgue and he saw the pieces of the two victims assembled on the gleaming stainless steel post-mortem tables.

Isaac moved to the male victim first, and gently turned over the head. 'There are extensive injuries to the back of the skull which were inflicted with a large, heavy piece of concrete. Some of the brain tissue was forced out of the skull cavity by the force of the blows, and amongst this we found fragments of cement. Both cheekbones are broken, as is the nose, and the jawbone in two places. Again, there are fragments of cement in the skin, indicating the same large, heavy piece of concrete.' Isaac moved to the left arm. 'You can see the skin is starting to flake away from the bone after being in the water for so long. The radius bone is broken, and the ulna fractured in two places. There are almost identical injuries on the right arm.'

He noticed McGorry creasing his forehead in confusion. 'There are two bones in your forearm,' he explained, pulling up his sleeve to indicate. 'The ulna is the long bone that stretches from the elbow to the smallest finger. The second is the radius, which runs parallel, and is the larger of the two.'

'He put up his arms to protect himself?' asked Erika, lifting hers and crossing them in front of her face.

'That's for you to confirm, but the injuries are consistent with that theory,' said Isaac.

McGorry cleared his throat and took a deep breath, and put a hand to his mouth.

'Are you okay?' asked Isaac.

'Yeah, fine,' he gulped. Erika saw he was now an odd green-grey colour under the harsh lights.

Isaac went on. 'Apart from these injuries, he was a healthy young male. No discolouration to the lungs; he didn't smoke; he had very little fat on the liver; a strong heart; very little body fat.'

Isaac moved to the second post-mortem table, and the body of the young woman. He turned over her head. Her long straw-coloured hair was parted to show the injuries to the back of her skull.

'Her injuries are almost identical. Blows to the back and the crown of the head with a blunt heavy object, which would have been fatal. The face has been badly battered: jaw, nose, and cheek-bones all have multiple breaks and fractures. Again, fragments of concrete were found embedded in the skin and surrounding tissue, *but* there is one difference to the male victim. She was stabbed in the chest with a long, thin blade.'

'And this could have been what killed her?' asked Erika.

'Yes, but I can't be sure. The fragments of concrete will now be analysed against samples from the male victim, to see if we can link the piece of concrete found in the suitcase with her.'

'Whoever did this went crazy on them,' said McGorry. 'Battering them, stabbing her.'

'Although, the single stab wound is more precise,' said Isaac.

Erika nodded. Not only had they suffered painful deaths, but even their identities had been taken from them.

'Whoever did this wanted to make it difficult for us to identify them. There is still no ID on the female victim after two weeks,' she said with a shudder.

McGorry suddenly retched, and clamped a hand over his mouth.

'Toilet is outside, first door directly on the left,' said Isaac calmly. McGorry made a dash for it, both hands over his mouth. They heard the door to the toilet slam and then heaving.

Isaac went on. 'With the female victim, her left arm is broken in five places; the right collarbone is broken twice. There is also evidence she was sexually assaulted prior to, or even after, she was killed.'

Erika closed her eyes against the harsh lights, but when she did she could still see the outline of the two bodies lying battered and dismembered, side by side. So many questions were running through her mind: *Did they know each other? Were they a couple? If so, which of them died first? Were they together when it happened?*

When she opened her eyes, Isaac had moved to a storage unit at the back of the morgue.

'I also found fifty condoms filled with cocaine in the stomach of the male victim.'

He returned with a clear plastic bag and handed it to her. It was filled with small packages, each the size of a large peanut in its shell. She looked up at him in shock.

'These were in his stomach? He swallowed all of these?' she said.

'Yes. Each one contains around ten grams of cocaine, packed in a condom, then wrapped in a layer of latex. In this case, the finger of a latex glove. It's very well packaged, and has to be, so that nothing leaks into the stomach.'

Erika looked back at the two bodies and the long stitched-up y-shaped incisions on both the torsos. 'Was there anything in the woman?'

'No. Nothing in her stomach; a little partially digested food.'

'Do you think he was a drug mule?'

'That's for you to find out.'

Erika shook her head. 'It doesn't make sense. Why would someone go as far as killing him, and chopping him up, only to leave the drugs in his belly?' She looked at the packages and did a quick calculation. 'This is about thirty-thousand pounds' worth of cocaine.'

'The person who killed him might not have known. Again, that's—'

'Yes, I know, Isaac. That's for me to find out,' snapped Erika. 'Do you know how long the bodies were in the water?'

'Difficult to tell. The male victim could have been in the water for a couple of weeks. You can see with him there is maceration; loosening of the skin on the fingers, palms, and soles of feet, and there is discolouration on the chest and abdomen. With the female, it's different, she was in the water for a few days, at most. Her fingers were in good enough shape to print, and they ran them through the system, but nothing came back. It says on her post-mortem that a large piece of concrete was found in the suitcase with the body; this has been sent to forensics.'

'And the cause of death?'

'In both victims, it was a blow to the back of the head. The lungs were filled with water, but with decapitation, the body cavity would have filled up.'

They stared for a few moments in silence.

'Okay, thank you,' said Erika.

They came out into the corridor, where John was waiting on one of the plastic chairs with a cup of water from the cooler. He stood up.

'I'm really sorry, Dr Strong, boss. I'm okay with bodies, but when they're in pieces...' He put his hand to his mouth again.

'Go on, get some fresh air. I'll see you out in the car park,' said Erika.

Isaac cocked his head to one side and watched as McGorry walked off down the corridor, and out of the main entrance. The door clanged shut.

'He's straight, Isaac. Has a girlfriend. I think she wears the trousers.'

Isaac grinned and sat in one of the chairs. 'I'm sure she doesn't wear them as well as he does. How old is he?'

'Twenty-four.'

'Oh to be twenty-four years old again...' Erika smiled and nodded in agreement. 'How's Peterson?' With the change of subject, her face clouded over.

'On his way back, but it's been a long, slow recovery.'

'It will be. People don't often pull through from a bullet wound to the stomach. He's been very lucky, even having had two nasty post-operative infections...'

'I know what happened, Isaac.'

'Do you know it's not your fault? Because it isn't. He didn't have to follow you into that crime scene.'

'I am his senior officer...' Her voice trailed off, and she tipped her head back against the wall.

'How does he look?'

'Still very thin. His mother has been looking after him, and she's not my greatest fan.'

'Erika. You know the score with mothers and sons.'

'Yeah. It didn't help that we first met when James was wired up to all those machines in intensive care.'

Isaac put out a hand and squeezed her arm. 'Are you sleeping?'

'I manage a few hours a night.'

Isaac's thin eyebrows knitted together with concern. He got up and went to the water cooler, filling a cup with water.

'Do you want me to prescribe you something?' he said, handing it to her.

'No way. I can't start a double murder investigation acting like a zombie.'

He looked at her for a long moment. 'OK, but don't be a stranger. You should come over for dinner soon, you look like you could do with a good meal.'

'When I have an ID on these victims,' she said, draining the last of the water and chucking the cup into the bin, 'I'll be in touch.'

Isaac watched Erika as she left, concerned for his friend and the way she pushed herself so hard. He was dreading the day she would break in two.

CHAPTER 7

McGorry returned to Lewisham Row, and Erika drove over to the offices of Forensic Science in Vauxhall. It was housed in one of the large glass office blocks overlooking the Thames. She pulled in at the ramp down to the underground car park, and then took the lift up to the sixth floor. She buzzed at the door leading into the laboratory, and watched through a small glass window as Nils Åkerman emerged from a door at the end of the corridor. She'd worked with him on three high-profile cases, all of which had resulted in convictions, but he was still a bit of an enigma to her. He was in his thirties, with almost translucent skin, and his usually bleached blond hair was today dyed a bright blue. The little she knew about him was ambiguous: he liked both men and women (Isaac had heard rumours he had fathered a child back in his native Sweden) and Erika had no idea if he was left or right wing in his politics. None of this mattered, of course, as he was an outstanding forensic scientist.

'Good morning, Erika,' he said, opening the door. 'How is your investigation going with the dead man in the suitcase? We now have a woman in a suitcase too.'

'Yes. And that's why I'm here. I figured a visit in person is always better than an email,' she said.

'Of course. Let's go to my office,' he said.

She followed him along the corridor, past windows into laboratories where CSIs worked, and smaller offices where support staff sat at computers. Police incident rooms were noisy, stressful places whirling with the stale smell of sweat and takeout food; this was the polar opposite. The atmosphere in forensics was quiet and studious, and there was a delicious minty smell of disinfectant.

Nils's office was clean and smart, with a desk, a large bookshelf, and a tall fridge. Under a window, looking out over the river, were two elegant armchairs in dark purple and a small marble-topped coffee table. In the centre of the table was a small orange-and-black speckled Murano glass paperweight.

'Would you like a coffee? And a piece of cake, perhaps?' He went to the fridge and took out a large moist carrot cake, turning to her with a grin. The snow white icing had been shaped into glistening peaks. Erika felt torn between the need to press on with the investigation and her belly kicking off at the heavenly sweet smell of the icing.

'I haven't eaten all day,' he said.

'Nor have I.' She grinned.

'That's settled then. It's harder to work on an empty stomach.'

He placed the cake on the coffee table, cut two pieces and placed them on plates, and put the cake back in the fridge.

'Espresso? Macchiato? Cappuccino? *Al Pacino*?' he deadpanned, moving to a coffee machine on his desk.

'Cappuccino. Thank you,' she said.

He fussed about with a couple of china cups he pulled from a drawer, and Erika went to the small window, which was open a little and letting in a cold breeze. A large boat was travelling upriver, fighting against the current. Nils finished their coffees and they sat down. She watched him tackle his cake, sawing off a huge hunk and shoving it in his mouth. His skin was a little sallow against his blue hair, and his nose was running. He pulled out a tissue to blow his nose.

'Sorry, allergies,' he said, through a mouthful of cake. 'Even this late in the year.'

'My sister has a terrible time with them,' said Erika. She went on to quickly outline the case, and finished by saying that the large piece of concrete found in the suitcase with the female victim could be the murder weapon used on one or both victims.

'I know you'll be running the victims' DNA through the national crime database,' she said.

'Yes, we have samples that are due to be processed shortly.'

'I came here to ask if there is anything you can do with the piece of concrete? I've heard in some cases fingerprints have been lifted from concrete?'

'Yes, it's difficult, but possible,' said Nils, swallowing the last big piece of cake. 'There's a process called superglue fingerprint fuming. Whenever we touch a surface, we leave fingerprints,' he said, indicating his fork before licking off the icing. 'A fingerprint consists of various chemicals; moisture, water, amino acids, fatty acids, and proteins. On a flat surface it's easy to dust for prints, but with an uneven or porous surface it's more difficult to get a print, so we use superglue fuming, in particular using the chemical cyanoacrylate which is found in most superglues. We place the object, in this case the piece of concrete, in a sealed container along with a small well of superglue. It's then heated, the vapours react with the chemicals that are found in fingerprints. This reaction leaves behind a white film that can be photographed, or copied onto tape strips, and the chemical cyanoacrylate in the superglue reacts with the acids left by the fingerprint on the object, leaving a visible, sticky white material that forms along the ridges of the print. We can then photograph this or enhance it to get a print.'

'Would it hold up in court?' asked Erika, suddenly feeling hopeful.

'It's a reliable method. The issue we have here is that the object has been in moving water for several days.'

'But with forensics you can work with the tiniest amounts of DNA and evidence?'

'Yes,' he said, taking a sip of his coffee. 'We will endeavour to try; I can promise that.'

'Thank you. There is another thing. The male victim was found with cocaine wraps in his stomach.'

Nils suddenly looked very interested. 'He was a drug mule?'

'That's what it looks like. There were around fifty of these capsules. I'd like to know if we can lift any kind of evidence from these.'

'Prints?'

'I doubt that whoever packed these capsules would have left prints, but there could be some DNA trapped within the layers of wrapping.'

'That would take some work.'

'As I said, Nils, that's why I came in person. I'm looking at a potential double murder. I need to prove a link, find a suspect, and there is also a dealer out there who is searching for his thirty grand's worth of gear. It's a complex case which could yield more than one arrest.'

'OK. I can start conducting the superglue fuming tests in the next day or so.' He rose and went to the computer at his desk. 'I would need to schedule in the work on the cocaine capsules… Friday at the earliest?' he said, turning to her.

'Thank you. I can imagine how busy you are here.'

'Well, take your imagination and triple it,' he said.

'And thanks for the coffee and cake.'

'Coffee and cake in Sweden is like religion. You've now helped me worship at the altar!' He grinned, and his nose was running again. He pulled out a tissue to wipe it.

'You should keep the window shut, if it's allergies,' said Erika, and she left his office and made her way back down to the car, hoping Nils would deliver her a breakthrough in the case.

CHAPTER 8

Late afternoon Erika met with her small team in one of the conference rooms in the basement of Lewisham Row Station. It was dingy, with a large square table and a grubby whiteboard on a stand. Moss was the first to arrive, still dressed in her smart suit for court. She took off her long coat and slung it over one of the plastic chairs.

'How did it go?' asked Erika.

'Depressing. He had a good lawyer and got off on a technicality. I'm glad there's something else to move on to. Another chance to get the bad guy.'

'This could be plural. Bad *guys*.'

McGorry then entered carrying a tray of Starbucks, and with him was a woman in her early sixties with huge glasses and shoulder-length grey hair. She was very slim, and wore a bright red shirt dress, rolled up at the sleeves.

'I heard you lost your lunch in the morgue,' said Moss to McGorry.

'Ha ha, it was my breakfast, actually,' he said, his cheeks flushing. He handed Erika and Moss each a coffee and offered one to the woman.

'Oh, thank you, I was going to use the machine,' she said, taking it with a smile.

Erika introduced herself, Moss, and McGorry.

'I'm Marta Chapman,' said the woman, sitting beside McGorry and taking a legal pad and pen from the large bag slung over her shoulder. 'I'm still quite new to the civilian support team here at Lewisham Row.'

'Glad to have you on the team,' said Erika. She and Moss sat opposite, and Moss gave Marta a smile and a nod. 'Okay, our number one priority is to identify the male and female victims,' she said, opening a file and placing it in the centre of the table. 'Nils Åkerman will shortly be running their DNA through the national database, but this is dependent on either of the victims having been arrested previously.'

'I've now got all the Greater London missing person reports from the past month,' said Marta. 'It's a very broad swathe of data, but I can focus in on white males and females in the twenties to thirties age group.'

'I've got a contact on the Marine Unit,' started McGorry. 'The bodies were thrown in the Thames two, two and a half weeks ago. I could ask if they can do something with tidal patterns; they might be able to pinpoint exactly where the suitcases were thrown in.'

'Just put out some feelers with the Marine Unit. At this stage we have a limited budget and I need to concentrate on identifying the victims. I've already requested forensics fast track a range of tests which will no doubt be expensive, and I'll get it in the neck for blowing budgets,' said Erika.

'My big question is why didn't whoever killed him cut out the drugs at the same time as chopping him up?' asked Moss.

'Exactly. This makes me think there's someone out there looking for him, the same as we are,' said Erika. 'Let's not forget dental records; shit, I forgot to mention it to Nils.'

'I can follow that up,' said Marta.

'No, I'll do it. You concentrate on the missing persons.'

Marta shifted awkwardly. 'I wanted to ask about overtime? I'm happy to put in the hours on this, but there's a freeze on overtime for civilian support staff.'

'After this meeting I'm going up to talk to the superintendent about it all; I'll get it okayed.' Erika checked her watch. 'Let's push through for another couple of hours, and then we'll reconvene tomorrow at nine. Thanks.'

They all got up and gathered their things. Marta and McGorry left, but Moss hung back and waited for Erika as she collected up the case files.

'Boss. I haven't heard from Peterson, he said he'd call. Are you two...?'

'Are we what?' asked Erika.

'I mean, is he okay?'

'I don't know... No, not really,' said Erika. 'He's still taking a lot of meds, not sleeping much. I've tried to keep up regular visits.'

'Me too,' said Moss.

'When was the last time you saw him?'

'A week, ten days ago. I've been busy,' she said guiltily. 'I thought by now he'd be back; at least doing a few hours of desk-based work. It's been over six months since the accident.'

'The doctor says he needs to gain eight pounds before he can come back to work. He's finding it hard with the surgery he had on his stomach, and he had the post-operative infections which screwed things up even more. It's the psychological stuff which takes longer to heal, and it doesn't help that he's stuck at home all day with the four walls closing in on him...' Erika bit her lip and put her head down. She could feel tears pricking at her eyes and as a distraction she started to check through the case files. There was an awkward silence.

'I wish I could help him. I can gain eight pounds on an average Sunday lunch,' said Moss. 'Okay, well, I'll be in my office. On the end of the phone and email if you need me.'

'Thanks,' said Erika. She waited until Moss had gone before she looked up from the pile of files. She moved to the door and closed it, flicking off the lights. Only then, in the darkness, did she allow herself to cry.

CHAPTER 9

AUGUST 2016

Nina started to see Max regularly after that first kiss in her car, but he didn't want to come to her house, and he never invited her over to his place. He would only ever meet her in the evenings, or after work, and it was always in her car.

She knew she was making headway after a few weeks when he let her pick him up outside his flat. He lived in a small block next to a housing estate in a dodgy area of Crouch End, and he was already waiting for her outside when she drove up. So she never got the opportunity to see inside.

Their dates were always the same. First, she would drive him to a pub or club where he would vanish inside for twenty minutes and do some business. She never asked what he had been doing inside, although she suspected it wasn't anything good. After this they would stop at an off-licence or a Chinese, then drive up to Hampstead Heath and sit staring out at the setting sun.

Then they would have sex. It was mind-blowing, uninhibited sex, and Nina had never experienced passion like it before. Max had a remarkable body and knew exactly what he was doing. Amongst all of the uncertainty in her life, these nights with Max were the only thing that kept her going and made her feel excited.

One evening, at the end of August, they were parked up under a low bank of trees on the edge of the heath, and had just had sex when Max asked her if she wanted to go away. The question took Nina by surprise.

'Away? You mean on a holiday? Together?' They were lying naked on the back seat of the car. Nina was resting her head on his chest.

'Yeah, where else do you go away?' he said.

'I don't know. I've heard of people going away to the convent,' she said, tracing her fingers over his chest.

'No, you get sent away to the convent,' he laughed. 'And that certainly wouldn't be you.'

'You cheeky bugger! People go away to prison all the time. Do you know anything about that?'

There was a nasty silence. He pushed her hand away from his chest and sat up.

'Max, I was joking!'

'It wasn't fucking funny,' he growled, grabbing his T-shirt and yanking it over his head.

'Sorry. I didn't think you'd been to…' she started.

He leaned into her face. A dim orange glow was coming from a streetlight further down, but his eyes seemed to glow in the darkness.

'What do you think I am? You think I'm some fucking low life?'

Nina crossed her arms over her naked breasts and shrank away from him.

'No! No! I think you're gorgeous… you're the best thing in my life right now, and I would never think that of you! It was just a joke!'

Max stared at her for a long moment. All the warmth had left his eyes, and it made goosebumps stand up on her arms. 'Max. I'm really sorry, it was honestly just a joke.'

He raised his arm, and she flinched, but he leaned across and retrieved her T-shirt from the footwell.

'Sit up,' he said. She sat up, not taking her eyes off him. 'Lift up your arms.' As she did the shadows played across the inside of the car, and Nina felt a shift in the atmosphere. Max shook the T-shirt out and placed it over her head. 'When I was fifteen, I got caught up in some shit,' he said. She lifted up her arms, and let him hook them through the sleeves. He smoothed the material, running his hands over her breasts, breathing heavily, squeezing them through the fabric.

'It's okay, Max. It's all okay…' She felt afraid, but didn't want him to know this. She kept eye contact as he kneaded her breasts through the material. He went on, his voice low and even.

'I was working in Camden Market, selling T-shirts on a stall, and this guy asked if I could give him and his mates a hand loading up some boxes in the back of a van. It was early on a Saturday and quiet, so I did. There were about twenty-five boxes. They weren't heavy; I think they had clothes inside. Just as we finished, the police showed up and arrested all the guys and me. Turns out they were stolen goods from a nearby warehouse.'

'Did they let you go? Obviously you didn't know?' asked Nina in a small voice.

'No. They booked me and banged me up in a cell. I'd been nicked a couple of times before, stupid stuff, shoplifting, breaking windows at a youth club but all I ever got was a caution. I got a solicitor for the police interview and I told them the truth: I didn't know, I was just helping out. Turns out it wasn't the first time stuff had been nicked from this warehouse in Camden, and it went to trial. As I'd told the truth in my interview I was told that I should plead guilty and I'd just get a few hours' community service.'

'Max, you're hurting me,' said Nina quietly as his hands were now gripping her breasts tight through the material.

'Sorry,' he said, lifting them off her. He sat back on the seat and stared out of the window. Nina relaxed a little, feeling his attention had shifted.

'What happened?' she asked.

'I got two years in Feltham Young Offenders. Fucking brutal it was. Locked up for twenty-three hours a day; there's fucking gangs. There were young lads there, like me, who got the shit kicked out of them. One bloke was in for nicking a phone from a little kid in the park. He got a year. Is that justice? And I was left to rot for what I thought was doing some lads a favour… I tell you, the people in charge in this country think they've got it sussed, they think justice works, they think they're in control. But I want to make it my mission to bring them down. They threw me in Feltham to make an example of me. But I want them to know they created a monster…'

He was quiet for a long time. Nina sat very still. She was now shivering in just her T-shirt. The seat underneath felt cold against her bare skin.

'Thank you for telling me,' she said. 'I love you.'

He looked up at her, and she could only see his profile in the dark.

'You do?'

'Yes.'

'I think I love you too,' he said. He put out his arm and she snuggled under it, glad of the warmth coming from his chest.

'It's me and you, Nina. Me and you.'

'Yeah, me and you,' she said. She had been scared by his outburst, but understood what he had been through. And in her naivety, she thought she could be the one to help him. To change him.

CHAPTER 10

TUESDAY, 3 OCTOBER, 2017

Erika knocked softly on the door of Detective Inspector James Peterson's flat. The communal hallway was empty, and when there was no answer, she put her key in the lock and opened the door, heaving two shopping bags inside. The hallway was in darkness and bathed in the light of the TV, blaring out the evening weather report. She moved through to the small open-plan kitchen/living room. On the TV, the weather map was showing that heavy rain would continue over the next few days. She put the shopping bags on the counter, and went over to the sofa. Peterson was fast asleep under an old blue blanket. The blue and green light cast by the television played over his thin face. His high cheekbones jutted out, and she could see the outline of the bones under his forehead. She put out a hand to wake him, when her phone began to ring in her pocket. Peterson shifted under the blanket, but slept on. Erika moved quickly into the hall and answered. It was Nils Åkerman.

'Sorry to call so late,' he said.

'No problem.'

'I'm afraid there's no match on the DNA samples we took from the male and female victims. They're not in the national crime database.'

'Shit,' she said.

'I'll keep you informed about the superglue fingerprint fuming, I'm hoping to schedule it in the next few days.'

'Any chance you can do it earlier?'

He sighed. 'I'm sorry, no, we have a huge caseload and I'm working through as fast as I can, but I have you as a priority.'

'Okay, thanks, Nils. I really appreciate it.'

Just as she hung up her mobile, Peterson's landline began to trill beside her on the hall table. She grabbed it and answered, not wanting to wake him up.

'Is that you, Erika?' said a voice. It was Peterson's mother, Eunice. She spoke with a very faint West Indian accent, which gave her voice warmth. But it was a commanding warmth.

'Yes. Hi, it's me…' There was a pause, and Erika could almost hear the sound of the old woman's lips pursing.

'Can I speak to James, please?'

'He's asleep, alone. On the sofa.'

'Has he eaten the beef stew I made him?'

'I don't know. I've just got here.'

'Erika. It's nine thirty!'

'I had a long day at work.'

'He needs his rest. You being there means he's not sleeping.'

'I stopped by at Tesco to get him some food—'

'What did you buy?'

'Potatoes. I got him skimmed milk, and Ready Brek. The doctor said cereals and milk are good for his stomach.' Erika could hear her voice getting flustered. How was it that she could hold her own with serial killers and violent offenders, but seventy-five-year-old Eunice Peterson scared the crap out of her?

'Erika, he needs vitamins, lots of vitamin C. You see I have oranges there for him?' Erika could see a fresh towering pile in the fruit bowl on the counter. Eunice went on. 'And Erika, when you visit, get there a bit earlier, please. James needs to be sleeping at this time…'

Erika was about to tell Eunice that phoning James at this hour would wake him up, but he suddenly appeared at her side, wrapped in the blue blanket.

'Who's that?' he mouthed.

'Oh, James has just woken up, Eunice, here he is,' said Erika, handing him the phone.

She started to put away the shopping and saw yet more oranges were piled in the salad drawer in the fridge. She could hear Eunice's loud voice on the other end of the phone.

'You need to tell that girl to let you sleep… Does she still have a key?'

'Yeah,' he replied awkwardly.

'It's very easy to give out your door key to a woman, but much harder to get it back.'

'Erika has been good to me,' he said.

'Eight hours, James. You need to sleep eight hours. People these days think you can get by on less, but I swear by eight hours and I never have to see the doctor. And I eat lots of vitamin C. Are you running low on oranges?'

'No, Mum,' he said, looking at the huge pile in the fruit bowl.

'Be sure to offer Erika some of my stew; there's plenty in the pot and she's so pale and skinny.'

'Yeah. I will.'

'Now you get to bed, and God bless.'

'Night, love you,' said Peterson, putting the phone back in its cradle on the counter.

'Your mother doesn't really need to use the phone, does she? She could just shout across London.'

'Sorry about that,' he said.

'You hungry?' she asked, taking the lid off an earthenware pot on the stove and seeing the beef stew, rich with a spicy tomato sauce. 'What about some stew, washed down with orange juice?

Or perhaps I can whip you up a nice bedtime drink of hydrogen peroxide?'

'Very funny,' he said, tipping out some Ready Brek into a bowl and adding milk. He put it in the microwave and pressed start.

'Why don't you just tell your mum you can't eat acidic food like spicy pot roasts and oranges?'

'I don't want to hurt her feelings.'

'That's very British of you.'

The microwave beeped. She chucked him a tea towel to take the bowl out, and he gingerly carried it back to the sofa. Erika heated herself a bowl of the pot roast and joined him. *Newsnight* began on the TV.

'Do you want my key back?'

He shook his head and blew on his cereal.

'Moss was asking about you today… is there any more news from the doctor?'

'They need to get my metabolism sorted; I'm still losing weight,' he said, not taking his eyes off the TV. They ate in silence for a few minutes, then Erika started to tell him about the bodies in the suitcases, and the cocaine found in the male victim. He shook his head, his thin face reflected in the light from the TV.

'There's this girl who sees my gastroenterologist,' he said. 'She had a cocaine wrap burst and leak inside her. She's had to have the same operation as me, partial removal of the stomach.'

'She was a drug smuggler?'

'Yeah.'

'British?'

'Yeah. Smuggled between here and Curaçao.'

'What's her name?'

'Zada.'

'What does she look like?'

He shrugged. 'She's normal. Pretty.'

'Is she now?'

Peterson's eyes left the television and he turned to face her.

'You really think I'm cruising the gastroenterology clinic for chicks?' he deadpanned.

Erika laughed. 'No.'

'It's not a very sexy place.'

'So, this Zada. How long was she smuggling?'

'I dunno.'

'Was she charged?'

Peterson shook his head. 'She'd already dropped off the stash, if you know what I mean. But one of the packets burst and left her with poisoning. So, technically, she was classed as an overdose.' He saw the gleam in Erika's eyes. 'And let me guess, you want to speak to her?'

'Does she know you're a copper?'

'Yes. Are you ever not at work, Erika?'

'I'm only asking about this Zada because it's relevant to my case. I don't usually talk about work when I visit you.'

'Oh, you *visit*?'

'You know what I mean.'

He got up off the sofa and threw the bowl in the sink. Erika followed.

'You've hardly touched that. And one thing your mother is right about is that you need to eat.'

'I'm not hungry.'

'You have to make yourself eat, James, or you're not going to get better!'

'I feel sick the whole time, constant nausea. I could cope with actually throwing up, but it's the terrible nausea. Everything I eat tastes wrong and makes me want to heave. That cereal tastes like onions, onions that've been cooked and are on the turn. So give me a break about not wanting to eat it!' he shouted.

He went back to the sofa and lay down. Erika took the bowl from the sink and scraped the contents out into the bin. He spent a few minutes shifting under the blanket, and then he was still. She quietly tiptoed around, washing up and tidying. She checked his medication was ready in its little daily dispenser. She boiled some eggs, and peeled them, leaving them in the fridge with a pack of plain cooked chicken, and a loaf of wholemeal bread.

When she went back to the sofa she could see he was asleep, and she knelt beside him. When they first met during a murder investigation a few years ago, he had seemed so tall and vital and full of life. He was six feet tall, but he now looked so small under the blanket, his legs tapering away to nothing. She leaned over and gave him a kiss on the forehead, but he didn't stir.

'Please, God, help him to get back to the person he was,' she said to herself. Then she tiptoed away, and let herself out of the flat.

The air was clear and cold when Erika arrived home, and the car park outside her block of flats was empty. She took a long hot shower, and then wrapped herself in a towel and came through to the living room to pour herself a glass of wine, filling a small tumbler. She pulled open a drawer, where a framed photo lay on top of a sheaf of utility bills. A handsome blond man grinned back at her. In the picture he was sitting in an easy chair by a window. Sun streamed behind and caught in his fair hair. It was her husband, Mark, who had died three years before. She had been his senior officer when they had taken part in a drug raid in outer Manchester. The intel had been bad and Mark, along with four other members of Erika's team, had lost their lives. Feelings of guilt and remorse threatened to overwhelm her, and she took a long drink of her wine. The photo of Mark had been on the dresser in her bedroom, and when Peterson started to stay over, she had moved it into the kitchen drawer.

Peterson, another man who had followed me into danger.

Erika closed the drawer. She picked up her tumbler and went over to the sofa. The living room was neat and functional; a sofa and coffee table both faced a small television. She went to pick up one of the case files when her phone rang on the coffee table. She saw it was a withheld number. When she answered, it was a young woman's voice with a cockney accent.

'Is this Erika Foster?'

'This is she.' Erika could hear a television in the background.

'James just rung me up. He said you wanted to talk to me, to help with a case you're working on… Oh, I'm Zada Romero, by the way.'

'What did he tell you about the case?'

'Not much. You've found a body with a stash of coke in its belly. Look, I don't want to talk on the phone. I can meet you tomorrow morning, at nine thirty, in the Caffè Nero in Beckenham.'

'Yes, that would be very good.'

'James said you usually pay people to talk off the record?'

'Did he?'

'Yeah, he said I'd get two hundred quid. Plus, coffee and a bit of cake.'

'Yes.'

'Great. See you then.'

When Erika came off the phone she couldn't help but smile.

CHAPTER 11

The next morning, as agreed, Erika met Zada Romero in the Caffè Nero in Beckenham. She was a small, delicate woman in her late twenties, with a poker-straight bob of dark hair.

'You don't look much like a copper. More like one of them foreign tennis players,' she said when Erika returned to their table with coffee and cake. She spoke precisely, with a strong cockney accent.

'I was born in Slovakia, but I've lived in the UK for twenty-five years.'

Zada blew on her coffee and took a sip. They were sitting beside a large picture window, looking out onto Beckenham High Street where people hurried past in the rain.

'And this is all, you know, informal and off the record?' she asked.

'Of course,' said Erika. It was busy inside the coffee shop, and a group of well-dressed women at the next table were cooing over a Birkin bag.

'Four grand they cost,' said Zada enviously.

'I know. My sister, Lenka, called me last week from Slovakia, in a complete lather. Her husband had just bought her one.'

Zada raised an eyebrow. 'Lucky sister. What does her husband do?'

'He runs an ice cream parlour.'

'He must have had to sell a lot of Mr Whippys to get her that.'

Erika shook her head. 'The ice cream parlour is a front. He works for the mafia.'

'But you're a copper?' she said, scooping up some of the milk froth from her cappuccino with a spoon.

'Not in Slovakia.'

Zada sucked the froth off the spoon, tilted her head at Erika, and seemed to decide she could trust her. 'James filled me in on your case, as much as he could. There's gonna be someone looking for that amount of coke.'

'I figured that part,' said Erika. 'I worked in narcotics in Greater Manchester Police for six years.'

'Yeah? I think they should just legalise drugs. You're never gonna win the war.'

'Really?' bristled Erika. 'If ordinary freight vans delivered legal merchandise then people like you wouldn't make a living.'

Zada leaned in and tapped the spoon on the table. 'It's not my "living", Erika. It was survival. My beauty salon went under in 2009 and I lost my house and all my savings. I managed to get a small flat and claim benefits, but it had a tiny extra bedroom, so they threatened to cut my money. I then found a lodger, one desperate enough to rent a tiny airing cupboard, but she would bring men back at all hours. One of whom tried to rape me in my bed. So that was the end of lodgers for me, and I lost that flat and ended up in bed and breakfast. The only reason I smuggled that gear is because I was desperate. It was either that or prostitution, and something told me that it was the lesser of two evils. So don't you judge me. We're all a few pieces of bad luck away from having to make horrible choices to survive.'

She sat back, silent, and carefully wiped a tear from her eye. Erika pulled out a tissue. 'I don't want it,' she shot back, taking the small serviette from the saucer of her coffee and dabbing her eyes.

'Okay. I hear you,' said Erika. She let Zada compose herself, then asked: 'How many times did you do it?'

'Three. Swallowing the gear, boarding a plane, delivering at the other end.'

'Where did you smuggle it to?'

'I took stuff out to Spain, twice. And Curaçao. It's the devil's work. I've never felt fear like it. You fear being caught; you fear the time bomb you having ticking inside you. And them packets are so huge, I practised swallowing using chunks of carrot. I thought to myself, I'm a drug mule, but at least I'll be able to see better in the dark.' She smiled and shook her head. 'The first time I did it, it all went like clockwork. The second time, I got ill from the food I ate at the airport before the flight.'

'What did you do when that happened?'

Zada shifted uncomfortably. 'I had to wash them all in the toilet on the plane, and swallow them again.' She forced herself to look Erika in the eye, but she looked ashamed.

Erika put her coffee down, feeling queasy. 'How did you get into it?'

'I bumped into this bloke outside the jobcentre in Catford. He could tell by the look of me that the wolf was at the door. He took me out to lunch. Mind you, it was at the Wetherspoon's, but it was a free lunch, an extra meal before I had to break into my giro. He told me all about smuggling gear and said I could earn ten grand in cash each time.'

'Our victim was found with a belly full of drug wraps. How soon would he swallow those before leaving? That's what I need to establish: if he was leaving the UK or if he had just arrived back.'

'You would do it as close to leaving as possible. He could have been straight off a flight, but he would usually have to deposit what he'd swallowed pretty fast.'

'What happens when you get to the other end, to your destination?'

'You meet with whoever it is you have as a contact. They take you to a place where you can pass the merchandise. And they check it's all there; they check through the packaging to make sure it's all intact. When I made my last delivery, they discovered one of the wraps had burst in my stomach.'

'What did they do?'

'They took the drugs and they left me,' she said, matter-of-fact.

'They left you. Where was this?' asked Erika.

'At this office block, an old office block near Heathrow. I was found unconscious by a cleaner in the corridor outside.'

'I'm sorry.'

'The police took the second part of what they'd paid me. Five grand. What do they do with the money?'

'The police have it.'

'I know, but what happens to that money?'

'It will be held until the case is closed, and then the police force could go through civil proceedings to have it used for public projects, to pay down public debt.'

Zada shook her head. 'No one gives you a break in this world.'

'What can you tell me about the people you worked for?'

'First names, that's all I know, and even then I don't know if they were real. But they know me. They have my passport details.'

'I promise you, no one will know we met. How did they contact you?'

'They phoned, always withheld numbers. One guy called himself Zoot, he sounded quite hippyish, another guy was Gary.'

'Would you be willing to work with an e-fit artist, to give us likenesses of the people in this smuggling gang?'

'I thought this was off the record?'

'It is. But I'm looking for a murderer. And you might have information that can help the investigation. You can come into the station, or we can send someone to your flat. Again, it's confidential.'

'No, sorry, I don't want to take the risk. I've just got myself settled in a good place.'

Erika nodded and took a sip of her coffee. 'Did they get the guy who tried to rape you?'

'No.'

'The person we are looking for has killed two people that we know of.'

Zada wiped another tear with the little serviette, and then nodded.

'Thank you. I'll set it up,' said Erika, and she pulled out her phone to make a note.

'You know he loves you. James,' said Zada.

Erika looked up at her. 'What?'

'James.'

Erika was taken aback,

'He's talked about his private life when he was at the hospital?'

'When you meet on a hospital ward, both wearing stoma bags, there isn't much embarrassing stuff you don't want to talk about.'

'Oh.'

'He wasn't indiscreet, or nothing. But we talked about wanting to live life to the full, after nearly dying. He's almost forty. He wants to settle down... He really wants kids, and you don't. You probably know this already.'

'Do you want children with him?' Erika hit back.

'I can't have kids,' she said. 'So you're safe.'

Erika picked up her bag and pulled out an envelope, sliding it across the table.

'It's all in there. Two hundred. And I hope you will stick to what you said, about working with the e-fit artist.'

Zada took the envelope. 'I didn't mean to upset you.'

'Thank you for meeting with me,' said Erika, trying to keep her voice even, and she left the café.

It was only a short walk to where she'd parked her car at the Marks & Spencer round the corner, but she was soaked. She got in and slammed the door. *He really wants kids and you don't.* The words rang in her head, hitting her just as painfully. She tipped her head back against the seat and looked at the blur of rain on the windscreen, distorting the grey sky and the surrounding cars.

Her phone rang and she saw it was Nils. She took a deep breath and answered.

'Is this a bad time?' he asked.

'No,' said Erika, feeling the irony.

'I have an ID on your two suitcase victims,' he said triumphantly.

'What? I thought you ran their DNA through the national crime database and nothing came back?'

'I did, but I've been trying something new, which could be seen as a little unorthodox; however, it's given us a considerable hit rate in the past couple of years.'

'What is it?'

'I contacted the private DNA database used by several genealogy websites. People tracing their family trees can now apply for a DIY DNA test kit. It arrives in the post, and they do a saliva swab, and send it back. The genealogy database gave us a positive hit on the DNA from both of your victims. I'm emailing all the details over to you now.'

CHAPTER 12

Erika returned to Lewisham Row Station, and went to see Superintendent Hudson in her office, explaining she had an ID on the two bodies. Melanie leafed through the case file on her desk and picked up the passport photos they now had of the two victims.

'I need a bigger team. This is a double murder. I need more officers,' said Erika.

Melanie held up the photo of the drug wraps taken from the male victim, neatly packed like unshelled peanuts in the plastic bag.

'Erika, it's the amount of cocaine involved here. The male victim was a drug smuggler. I think we should pass this over to the narcotics unit. This looks to me like a dealer who has pissed off his boss,' she said, sitting back in her chair.

'What about the woman?' said Erika.

Melanie shrugged. 'She's the girlfriend that got in the way.'

'No! He wasn't killed for drugs. The drugs are nothing to do with this,' said Erika, exasperated. 'And we can't just *assume* she was the girlfriend. These murders took planning. Whoever did this needed to lure them to a place where he could kill them and chop them up without being seen. Their faces were battered to avoid identification. And after all that, whoever did this left the drugs. If this was drugs related, a rival dealer, or the head of the smuggling operation would have taken them.'

Melanie sighed and looked at the two sets of crime scene photos: the bodies in the suitcases. Erika picked up the enlarged passport ID photo of a thin young woman with large green eyes and a small sharp nose. Her skin was clear and shiny and she had long blonde hair.

'The female victim is twenty-four-year-old Charlene Selby. She comes from a rich middle-class family.' She picked up the second passport ID photo of a man with dark hair, olive skin, brown eyes and a round acne-scarred face. His thinning dark hair was greasy and combed back from a high forehead. 'The male victim is thirty-four-year-old Thomas Hoffman. He's a widower, with no criminal record.'

'Erika, I've just been looking at the same photos as you—'

'They're a white, middle-class, hard-working couple. You know how these things play in the press. This has *Daily Mail* headline written all over it.'

'You're threatening to go to the press?'

'No. I'm saying that you don't want to kick this case into the long grass with hundreds of others that the narcotics team are trying to solve. It could bite you in the arse, ma'am.'

Melanie raised an eyebrow and looked at the photos again. She shook her head.

'Okay, fine. I'll give you an expanded team, incident room, and uniform resources with further approval.'

'Thank you,' said Erika, gathering up the photos and stuffing them back in the file.

'But I want to know the moment anything changes, and if this crosses over into a case for narcotics you won't be obstructive, you will hand the case over. Understand?'

'Absolutely. I won't obstruct you, or anyone,' said Erika.

Melanie saw the light shining in her eyes, and the rush of excitement as she left the office, slamming the door. 'Famous last words,' she said.

An hour later, Erika's expanded team assembled in the large open-plan incident room in Lewisham Row Station. Sergeant Crane, a young sandy-haired officer in his mid-thirties, was moving through the crammed-in desks to give out copies of the case file. McGorry was sitting opposite Detective Constable Rachel Knight, a dark-haired officer in her mid-twenties who Erika had worked with before, and Detective Constable Brian Temple, a handsome red-haired young Scotsman who was new to the team. Three civilian support workers – two young men and a young woman – were working with Marta Chapman to assemble all of the evidence on the large whiteboard on the back wall of the incident room. Moss was sitting at a computer and finishing up on a phone call. Erika went to the whiteboards at the back of the room.

'Okay, good afternoon everyone. Our male victim is thirty-four-year-old Thomas Hoffman,' she said, indicating his passport ID photo pinned up next to the crime scene photo of his badly beaten face. 'He's a British national, born in Norwich. No family or siblings. The last known address we have for him is in Dollis Hill, north-west London. He's been married twice. His first wife, Mariette Hoffman, is still alive, but his second wife, Debbie, died two years ago. He has no record, not even a parking ticket. I want to know everything about him, financial, mobile phone records, and all social media.'

She moved along the whiteboard to the second passport ID photo. 'The second victim is twenty-four-year-old Charlene Selby. She is also British. Her parents, Justin and Daphne Selby, are registered as shareholders of Selby Autos Ltd, which is a very successful car dealership in Slough.'

'Do we know if they were reported missing?' asked Moss.

'No. Neither of them have been reported missing, which is rather odd,' said Erika, tapping both of the pictures. 'We need to see if there is a link between Charlene and Thomas. Did they know each other? Were they mixed up in something similar? Were they dating? Was Charlene Selby living with Thomas Hoffman? If she's registered as living at home, why haven't her parents reported her missing?'

Erika moved to a large map of the Thames dominating the centre of the whiteboard. 'The suitcase containing Charlene's body was found two weeks ago by a dog walker at low tide below Chelsea Bridge. This is a residential area; there's flats all along here. We found the suitcase with Thomas's body two days ago, 2.8 miles further down the river, close to the National Theatre. In both instances, the suitcase had snagged onto something which prevented it from moving any further down the river. McGorry, you mentioned talking to the Marine Unit about tidal patterns?'

'Yes. I'm waiting to hear back from Sergeant Lorna Crozier who works for the dive unit. I sent her the dates and coordinates yesterday, and she says it can take a couple of days to look at the tidal patterns.'

'OK. We're waiting on toxicology results for both victims, and Nils Åkerman over at forensics is working to try and lift prints from the concrete block found in the suitcase with Charlene Selby. I believe this could be the murder weapon, and a link between the two murders. We need to follow up every lead,' finished Erika. 'It's all up for grabs at the beginning, and remember—'

The team finished her sentence in unison: 'There are no stupid questions.'

Erika grinned. 'Glad to know you actually listen to what I'm saying.'

'I think it would be a good idea to put out some feelers to the narcotics unit and see if they are aware of any ripples running through the drug dealing community,' said Detective Knight, 'if there are rumours of a missing thirty grand stash.'

'Agreed,' said Erika. 'I'll leave that with you. Sergeant Crane will take things from here.'

The room sprang to life as Crane stood up and started to allocate tasks to the officers and support staff.

Erika went over to Moss. 'You're with me. I want to inform the next of kin today,' she said.

'Thomas Hoffman doesn't have any living relatives,' said Moss.

'But he has an ex-wife, and I think ex-wives are often a great source of information.'

'Hashtag no filter,' grinned Moss.

'Let's hope so.'

CHAPTER 13

Erika and Moss took the train from Lewisham to London Bridge, and then a Northern Line tube up to Old Street. A police car was waiting for them by Moorfields Eye Hospital, and it was a short drive out to the Pinkhurst Council Estate. It always struck Erika how the landscape in London could change in the space of a few roads, from multimillion pound flats and office buildings to a virtual ghetto.

Mariette Hoffman lived in a tall grey tower block, one of five towers making up the Pinkhurst Estate in north-east London. They pulled into an empty, potholed car park, where a gang of lads stood in a circle next to a burnt-out car. Their brightly coloured hoodies and tracksuits were a menacing splash of colour against the grey sky and concrete.

'I'll let you down as close as I can,' said the officer driving, a squat middle-aged man with a greying beard. 'I've been to these flats before. You usually have to wipe your feet on the way out.'

'Good job we've got an unmarked car,' said Erika, seeing the group of lads were looking around and taking notice.

He parked next to a row of three large rubbish bins. Mariette lived on the second floor, and Erika and Moss took a set of stairs up to a long concrete corridor, open to the air. As they passed the flats, there were sounds of babies screaming and people shouting. The kitchen windows were to the side of each front door, and Erika slowed as they passed a tiny girl in pink sitting on the draining board, pressing her tiny hand against the grimy glass. Behind her was a young woman, smoking a cigarette. When she saw them pass, she moved forward and let the blind down.

'She thinks we're social workers,' said Moss, in a low voice.

They came to the door at the end of the corridor and knocked. After a moment, a large bedraggled woman, in her early fifties, with a halo of messy black curly hair, opened it. She wore a faded red tracksuit and Marigold gloves, and in one hand she held a yellowing toilet brush. Next to the front door, they could just see the inside of a small grubby toilet.

'What?' she said, looking Erika and Moss up and down.

'I'm Detective Chief Inspector Erika Foster; this is Detective Inspector Moss,' said Erika as they flashed their warrant cards. 'Can we come in, please?'

'Woss it about?' she said, wiping her forehead with her sleeve.

'It's about your ex-husband, Thomas Hoffman,' said Erika.

'Let me guess. He's dead?' she said, still clutching the toilet brush.

'Please can we come in?'

'Alright. But wipe your feet, and take off your shoes,' she snapped, standing to one side to let them in.

They found it hard to get their shoes off in the cramped hallway, and were mindful of Mariette standing over them with the filthy toilet brush. She lined their shoes up neatly on the mat and replaced the brush, closing the toilet door. She took them down a small hallway, past a staircase, a closed door, and into a small living room. It was beautifully clean, but the furniture was dated. A low sideboard of pale wood was dotted with fussy doilies and ornaments. A small box television sat in the corner with a bowl on top filled with seashells. Through a white net curtain, a window looked out over the estate. The faded worn carpet bore the marks of a fresh vacuum, and the room had an overpowering tang of pine air freshener. On the wall above a beige sofa hung a black and red military-style majorette's cap, with a shiny black peak, red velvet pillbox top and gold braiding. Underneath were two hooks which held a silver baton.

'Have a sit down,' said Mariette.

Erika and Moss sat on the sofa. She perched gingerly on a small armchair beside them. Still wearing the rubber gloves, she took a pack of cigarettes from the pocket of her tracksuit and lit up, exhaling with a loose phlegmy cough.

'So, what is it?'

'I'm very sorry to tell you that your ex-husband was found murdered,' said Erika.

'You could have told me that on the doorstep,' she snapped.

'This doesn't seem to be a shock to you?'

'Oh, doesn't it? You don't know what I'm thinking. Anyhow, are you telling me that every time you inform someone that their relative is dead, they break down in floods of tears?'

'No.'

'There you go then.'

'How did you know we were here to inform you of your ex-husband's death?' asked Erika.

'It was a guess, obviously. I'm not psychic. If I were, I'd make a fortune and leave this bloody estate.'

'If it was a guess, you must have suspected something?'

'He told me he was gonna smuggle some drugs,' she said, tapping the cigarette ash into a heavy crystal cut ashtray on the coffee table. 'How did it happen?'

'We don't know all the details. Two days ago, his body was washed up on the banks of the Thames. It was stuffed into a suitcase,' said Moss.

'A suitcase?' repeated Mariette.

'Yes.'

'You sure?'

'Yes, we attended the scene.'

Mariette shook her head. 'He was such a large bloke. Someone got hold of a suitcase big enough to fit him?'

Moss looked to Erika, who nodded and took over.

'I'm sorry to say that Thomas's body had been dismembered, and placed in the suitcase.'

'That explains it.' Mariette nodded, tapping the ash off her cigarette. 'You can't buy big suitcases anymore. I went to Benidorm last year and we were allowed only ten kilos! If you wanted extra you had to pay a fortune.' She took another drag on her cigarette and stubbed it out in the ashtray. Erika went to ask her a question, but Mariette heaved herself out of the armchair.

'I need a cup of tea after hearing that. You two want one?'

'Er, yes, thank you,' said Erika.

She headed off into the kitchen, pulling down the hem of her sweater over her backside. They listened as she moved around the kitchen, and the kettle boiled.

'What the fuck?' said Moss in a low voice. 'She finds out her ex-husband has been chopped up and stuffed in a suitcase, and all she can talk about is how tough it is to go abroad with the weight limits?'

'He *was* her ex-husband.'

'I know, but most people at least pretend to care.'

'Is it really that hard to buy big suitcases? The Superintendent said the same thing.'

'Yes, it is.'

'Shows how rarely I go on holiday,' said Erika.

A few minutes later, Mariette returned with a tray of tea things and set it down on the coffee table. She noticed Moss looking around at the majorette hat and baton on the wall.

'I was a spinner for five years,' she said, pouring tea into china cups. 'Then I got too old. You could only be in the troupe until you were eighteen. They bent the rules and let me stay until I was nineteen, but then I outgrew the uniform and they said they didn't make them any bigger. The bastards.'

She passed Erika and Moss each a delicate china cup and saucer. They took a sip, unsure of how to respond.

'When did you last see Thomas?' asked Moss.

Mariette lit another cigarette and sat back with her tea, exhaling smoke.

'Three weeks ago.'

'Today is the 4th of October, so three weeks ago would make it Wednesday, 13th September?'

Mariette thought for a moment. 'No, it was the day before, a Tuesday, cos I'd got me giro that day and I bought cake for when he came. I get me giro every two weeks, on a Tuesday.'

'So Tuesday, 12th September you saw him. Is this when he told you about the drugs?' asked Erika.

'Yeah. He'd been signing on for a long time. They'd made him attend one of them job training clubs.'

'What was he being trained in?' asked Erika.

Mariette gave a loose phlegmy laugh. 'Bugger all. The government call it training. In reality, they pay some private company a fortune, who lock them up in a room for three months searching for jobs, and bully them into signing up for factory jobs with zero-hour contracts… That's where he met, er this, er…' She hesitated.

'Met who?' asked Erika.

'Some bloke or other. He asked Tom if he wanted to make an easy ten grand. Who wouldn't turn that down? Tom was desperate to get out of the shit and pay off some debts. He'd had a rough few years.'

'Did he tell you this bloke's name?' asked Erika.

'No. He wasn't gonna start naming drug dealers.'

'So this bloke was a drug dealer?' asked Moss.

'I suppose so.'

'Why would a drug dealer be signing on?'

'I presume for the money, and as a front. I don't know the ins and outs.'

'So this bloke asked Thomas if he wanted to earn ten grand smuggling drugs?'

'That's what I said!' Mariette was becoming flustered.

'Did Thomas say where he would be going, and how this smuggling would work?'

Mariette put up her hands, and cigarette ash fell on her legs. 'I didn't want to know! Okay? Look at where I live. There's bloody druggies everywhere. I've got that shit on my doorstep. I didn't want him talking about it in here.'

Erika could see she was shutting down on them, so she changed tack.

'Can I show you a photo?' she asked, balancing the cup and saucer on her leg to reach into her pocket. It rattled in the saucer, and Mariette leaped up from the armchair, and grabbed it.

'Please watch the spills. This sofa is very pale and it shows everything,' she said, placing the cup and saucer deliberately on the coffee table with a coaster.

'Sorry, of course,' said Erika. She retrieved her notebook, and passed Mariette a photo.

'She's pretty,' said Mariette. 'Who is it?'

'Her name is Charlene Selby. She was also found dead, her body dismembered and stuffed in a suitcase.'

They watched Mariette's face, but she remained impassive and passed the photo back.

'That's awful.'

'You never saw her with Thomas?' asked Erika.

'No.'

'He didn't talk about her?'

'No. Was she involved with this smuggling?'

'We can't share that information. Do you know if Thomas had a girlfriend?'

'He didn't. He'd have told me; he'd have boasted about it.'

'Do you mind me asking why you two divorced?'

'He was obsessive. I felt suffocated by him. He was jealous, and he could be violent. I thought I was better than that,' she said.

'Why did Thomas have a rough few years?'

'He got married again. Debbie, her name was. Nice girl. A bit plain, bit of a doormat, but she took the edge off him. She worked in the office of a haulage firm in Guildford. One day she went out into the yard to talk to one of the drivers, and didn't see a lorry coming. Poof. Died instantly, so did the baby; she was pregnant. Tom went to pieces. He couldn't afford the mortgage on his own. Lost his job. He came back to London hoping that he could get a fresh start. I let him stay here for a bit, but we fought, so when he found some work he got a flat in Dollis Hill. Then the work dried up, so he had to sign on.'

'Didn't you think it was strange that you hadn't heard from him in three weeks?' asked Erika.

'We weren't in each other's pockets.'

'Did you know his family?'

'His mum and dad died when he was eighteen; he didn't have any brothers or sisters.'

Erika and Moss exchanged a glance.

'I'm having a hard job putting his life together. We've drawn a blank on Debbie's relations. Her parents are dead; she was also an only child,' said Erika.

'Drawn a blank, have you? I'm sure you two live happy lives with plenty of cash, a comfortable home in a safe area? Your neighbours probably lean on the fence to chat to you when you mow the lawn. Look around, this is what happens when you don't get a good start in life,' she said, jabbing her finger on the arm of the chair, 'and no bugger gives you a break. I don't have a circle of friends, or go for dinner parties, or to book clubs. I grew up in children's homes, shunted between foster parents.'

'I'm sorry,' started Erika.

'Oh, I don't want your pity. I'm just telling you why you can't find evidence of Tom's full and happy life. It didn't exist... Now are you going to drink that tea I made for you?'

They drained their cups and placed them back in the saucers.

'Would you be willing to come and formally identify Thomas?' asked Erika.

'What? In bits?'

'Yes. It's a formality.'

'Go on then,' she said.

'Thank you. And we may have more questions.'

'Oh, may you? What do you expect me to say to that? If you've got questions, you'll ask them!'

Mariette watched from behind the net curtains in her kitchen window as Erika and Moss walked across the car park. The group of lads were still huddled around smoking, and they turned to look as they climbed into the waiting car. Even though it was unmarked, and they were in plain clothes, they could smell coppers a mile off. When the police car had driven away, Mariette went to the landline in the hall.

She picked up the receiver and dialled a number.

CHAPTER 14

'What did you think of Mariette Hoffman?' asked Erika when they were in the car and heading away from the estate.

'She was honest, brutally honest,' replied Moss. 'But we shouldn't be disarmed by her apparent honesty and willingness to talk.'

Erika nodded. 'Interesting she kept Thomas's surname, even though they were only married for a year and it ended acrimoniously.'

'Is it? Maybe she couldn't face the bureaucracy, especially if she's long-term unemployed and it could have stopped her benefits. Why did you keep yours?' asked Moss.

Erika was taken off guard.

'Shit, sorry, boss. I wasn't thinking. It was a genuine question.'

'It's okay. My maiden name was Boldišova.'

'How do you say it?'

'Bol-dish-oh-vah. Erika Boldišova. It's very Slovak.'

'And difficult to say after a couple of rum and Cokes.'

Erika smiled. 'It was easier to keep being Erika Foster. And it's a little piece of Mark I get to keep. What about you and Celia?'

'She's Celia Grainger, and I'm Kate Moss.' She saw the driver glance at her in the rear-view mirror. 'Not THE Kate Moss, obviously.'

'Obviously,' he laughed.

'Cheeky bastard,' grinned Moss. She went on. 'I suppose we both kept our names when we got married for our careers. Jacob is Moss-Grainger, which sounds quite posh I suppose.'

'Let's do some digging on Mariette; find out her maiden name and where it leads us. She could be one of the last people who saw Thomas Hoffman,' said Erika.

They hit the start of the evening rush, so it took almost two hours to drive over to Uxbridge, in west London. Charlene Selby's parents lived in a long, leafy avenue, a world away from the Pinkhurst Estate. At a set of black iron gates, Moss got out of the car and went to a small intercom embedded in the brickwork, and was ready with her warrant card when a woman's voice answered. She sounded wary and didn't want to let her in, but eventually relented, and the gates swung inwards. A long, tree-lined drive took them to a large manor house, and they parked beside a huge ornamental fountain. It had started to rain, and even though it was blurring the surface, Erika could see huge koi carp swimming lazily on the bottom.

A woman opened the front door. She was in her late fifties, elegantly dressed, with overly tanned skin and short bleached blonde hair. She had a very detached manner.

'Good afternoon, are you Daphne Selby?' asked Erika. The woman nodded. 'I'm Detective Chief Inspector Erika Foster, and this is Detective Inspector Moss, may we come in?'

Erika and Moss flashed their warrant cards. Daphne peered at them and nodded. They stepped into a large, double-height hallway with a winding staircase. The rain rattled onto a small stained glass cupola above. She took them through to a large airy living room, where an open fire was burning low; lots of dark wooden furniture and a chintzy sofa and armchairs. A tall, middle-aged man was working with a screwdriver to release a huge pull-down cinema screen. He wore tan slacks and a salmon-coloured V-neck sweater, and like his wife, he had a deep tan.

'The police are here,' said Daphne.

His face dropped when he saw them, and he leaned forward to shake hands.

'It's Charlene, isn't it?' he asked.

'Please, can we all sit down,' said Erika. 'Can I confirm you are Justin Selby?'

He nodded. 'Just tell us straight away, don't lead us around the houses. It's Charlene, isn't it?' he said. His face was turning red and tears were forming in his eyes. Daphne reached out and took his hand.

'Yes, I'm afraid your daughter was found dead,' said Erika.

Justin staggered to the sofa, helped by Daphne. Erika and Moss waited until they were seated, and each perched on an armchair. Daphne and Justin held each other for a long time, sobbing, and then Erika gently gave them the rest of the details.

'Do you feel up to us asking a few questions?' asked Moss softly.

'Like what?' asked Justin, wiping his eyes with the back of his tanned hand. He wore several gold rings and a gold identity bracelet. 'If we know someone who would do that to our daughter? No!'

'Can I ask why you didn't report Charlene as missing?'

A sad, despairing look passed between Justin and Daphne.

'We were estranged,' said Daphne. She had a very soft voice.

'Why was that?' asked Erika.

'Drugs, she was a drug addict,' said Justin. 'There's nothing more destructive than a kid with a drug problem, and an allowance. They destroy themselves, and they attract all kinds of hangers-on. She's been an addict for the past few years.'

'We'd cut off her allowance in the spring,' said Daphne. Despite her voice being soft it was strong. 'She's been to rehab four times. You have to understand, we did it, we did it to try and help her. The doctors said she had to reach rock bottom. We didn't even know her address… You said you found her body near Chelsea Embankment, by the Thames?'

'Yes. Now there's no way of putting this nicely,' started Erika.
'Her body was found inside a suitcase. It had been dismembered.'

Daphne began to cry.

'When did you last see Charlene?' asked Moss.

'Three weeks ago... It was the day when we get new cars in at
the showroom. She came to the showroom on Love Lane.'

'This is your car showroom?' asked Erika.

'Yeah.' He put his arm around Daphne.

'Do you mind telling us what happened?'

Justin laughed bitterly. 'She wanted to take one of the cars on
a test drive. I bet it was that bloke who was with her,' said Justin.

'What bloke?' asked Erika.

He heaved and sobbed and managed to get control of himself.
'When she came to the showroom, there was a bloke with her. A
big dirty bloke with dark hair. She just rocked up out of the blue,
demanding the keys. I said she couldn't take it; she said she was
sober, then he joined in and made a scene.'

'What kind of scene?'

'She was shouting; he was getting up in my face, saying how he
knows all about us, how we don't care about Charlene... Like this
stranger had the right... I would have lamped him, but we had
two clients in that day, both of them do a trade-in every year. We're
talking three hundred grand of business sat there in the showroom,
watching it all...' His voice tailed off. 'So, I let them take the car.'

'What time of day did they come to the showroom?' asked Moss.

'Two, two thirty-ish.'

'Three weeks ago on Tuesday, was the 12th of September, does
that sound right?'

Daphne lifted her head, wiped the tears from her eyes and
nodded.

'Did you get this man's name?' asked Erika.

'No. He was big; he stank of booze. We didn't bring her up to
hang about with people like him.'

Erika took a small photo of Thomas Hoffman from her bag and held it up.

'Yeah. That's him,' said Justin. 'Have you arrested him?'

'No. He's also dead. We also found his body in the river, in a suitcase, and dismembered, just like Charlene,' said Erika softly. There was a long silence.

'Did Charlene say why she wanted to take the car?' asked Moss.

'She just said she fancied taking it for a test drive,' said Justin.

'Is this something she did often? Take out cars for test drives?'

'It was something she used to love doing when she was learning to drive, when she was seventeen… Of course, back then she was, she wasn't drinking or taking drugs.'

'After they took the Jaguar, we didn't hear from her and she didn't return it that day, or the next. We found it abandoned three days later outside the gates of the car showroom.'

'That would be Friday the 15th of September?' asked Moss.

'If she said three days later then that's what it is!' snapped Justin. Daphne put her hand on his arm.

'The keys were left in the ignition. The upholstery was stained. It was a mess; someone had been sick in the back.'

'Did you call the police?' asked Moss.

At this, Justin became angry. 'No! I wouldn't call you lot for my own daughter. We knew she'd bring it back.'

'And you have no idea why she took it for so long, and where they went?'

Daphne shook her head.

'And what did you do with the Jaguar?' asked Erika.

'We had it cleaned, but it's still a bloody mess. We're waiting to have it re-upholstered, in the hope we can still…' said Daphne. She started to sob. Justin waved his hand dismissively at them, dropping his head to hide his tears.

'Let's give you some space,' said Erika.

*

Erika and Moss retreated from the living room, past the staircase, and into a bright, airy kitchen looking out over a beautifully kept garden, with a sandpit and a child's swing set and a slide. Erika filled the kettle at the sink.

'If they cut off Charlene's allowance, where was she getting her money from?' she asked. 'How did Thomas fit into the equation? Was he using drugs? I wish we had the toxicology reports back on their bodies.' She plugged in the kettle.

'On September the 12th Charlene went to the car showroom with Thomas. That's the same day that Mariette says Thomas went to see her,' said Moss.

'He saw her in the morning. So it could just be coincidence, but I don't buy into coincidence.'

They were silent for a moment and listened to the sound of the kettle starting to boil. Erika moved over to the large stainless steel American-style fridge. It was covered in Post-its and a Weight Watchers diet sheet. There were pictures of Daphne playing with a tiny boy and girl on the swings and slide in the back garden, and in another she was pictured hugging the children in a restaurant. Above it was written 'Granny's 60th!'. There was a wedding photo of a thin-haired man in a suit with his bride.

'This must be Charlene's brother? And the grandkids?' asked Moss.

In the top left-hand corner there was a photo stuck on under a smiley face magnet. Erika lifted it off the fridge. It was taken at a party, and it was a family photo with Daphne, Justin, the small kids and Charlene, who was standing on the end. She looked emaciated, with messy hair, and was holding a bottle of beer, but despite her bedraggled state, she was still an attractive woman. The smiley face magnet had been placed over her part of the photo.

'They looked like they'd been expecting to hear that Charlene was dead,' said Moss. 'I can't imagine living like that. Waiting for the call, or the police at the door.'

The kettle clicked off and they made tea for the grieving parents.

CHAPTER 15

AUGUST 2016

Nina and Max were staying above an old-fashioned pub in a small village on the edge of Dartmoor. It was a tall, thin building of granite blocks, perched at the edge of a small village. Nina woke early, and looked over at Max sleeping beside her, and to the window where the sun streamed through onto a threadbare red carpet. Holding a T-shirt to her bare chest, she went to the window and opened it. She hadn't seen much when they'd arrived late last night. The air was fresh and a little chilly, but the sun was already climbing up a clear blue sky. She could now see for miles across a vast expanse of green hills. A group of walkers were passing on the road below, the clacking of their sticks mixing with murmured chatter. As they hit the grassy moor the clacking ceased and they moved away, their chatter receding. The view was spectacular. Nina was a London girl through and through, and she was struck by just how much colour there was, so many vivid shades of green, stretching away for miles to the grey-topped mountains in the distance. She heard a whistle and turned her head. Approaching from the village, in the other direction, was the young dark-haired guy they'd got talking to in the pub last night. He was handsome, but very skinny, and he'd been very flirty with her.

'Hung-over?' he asked, squinting up at her with a toothy grin.

'A little,' she said, twirling a strand of her long hair between her fingers, and smiling.

'You still up for going on a hike?'

'I don't know; Max is still asleep.'

She felt fingers close over her arm, and Max was behind her.

'Who are you talking to?' he snapped.

'Look, it's Dean,' she said, pointing.

'Put some fucking clothes on,' he said, seeing the T-shirt clutched to her chest and pulling her away from the window. He looked down at Dean. 'Wait there. We'll be down in a bit.'

He slammed the window shut. Max stomped off for a shower in the bathroom down the corridor, and Nina sat on the bed, confused. Last night had been fun. They'd had a late dinner in the pub downstairs, and when Max had gone up to get a round of drinks, he'd returned with Dean, who he'd met at the bar.

'This is my Nina, isn't she gorgeous,' Max had said, introducing them.

'Beautiful,' Dean had agreed, ogling Nina's breasts through her T-shirt. Max had seen him do this and had nodded in agreement. Over drinks, Dean told them he was camping a few miles away, and as the night wore on, and they became drunk, he confided that he was in the area to sell drugs at the local folk festivals. Nina didn't say much, and listened to the boys as they bonded over shared experiences growing up in children's homes and foster care.

They stayed until last orders, and then there had been an odd moment when they all stumbled into the foyer. Max was between them, an arm slung over each and he'd pulled them together, their faces pressed against his. Dean had run his hand over Nina's breasts, and then Max's chest, breathing heavily with an intense love-light in his eyes.

'I really want you, both,' he'd slurred.

'Go on, back to your campsite,' Max had said. 'You'll keep.'

Nina wondered now, in the cold light of the next morning, if she had gone too far.

After an awkward breakfast, where Nina tried and failed to make conversation, Max decided that he did want to go for a hike. He told Nina to go and pack their rucksacks and he went outside to see Dean.

When she came back down fifteen minutes later, she found Max and Dean waiting for her on a bench outside the hotel. They were killing themselves laughing, but stopped when she reached them.

'Everything okay?' she asked, handing Max the larger of the two rucksacks.

He pulled it onto his shoulders. 'Sure, everything is tickety-boo,' he said, and they both burst out laughing again.

'Tickety-boo! Who the fuck says tickety-boo!' cried Dean, slapping his leg. When he laughed, it exposed his large teeth and sticky pink gums. Max reached down and picked up a small bottle of whisky from under the bench and took a slug. It was already half-empty.

'Oh, I see what's making everything tickety-boo,' grinned Nina. Max offered her the bottle, but she shook her head.

They set off down from the pub, and over the moor. They had to cross a bridge over a small river, and then Dartmoor spread out in front of them. Max said there was a secluded little waterfall he wanted them to see, and they hiked for several miles. The boys polished off the rest of the whisky, and soon the conversation moved to sex, and in particular, the sort of stuff they'd done to women. Nina felt uncomfortable so she fell back a bit and watched the scenery. The moor was beautiful, and it was hot, but a light breeze pushed banks of cloud across the sky, and the sun kept vanishing and reappearing, casting everything in a bright steely glare.

Just after midday, they came to a deep dip in the moor, and followed a thin path down to where a waterfall seemed to emerge from the rocks and tumble down into a small deep pool surrounded by large boulders.

The boys were now red in the face and sweating from the heat and the booze, and they all drank from the waterfall. Max then took them to a creased seam in the rock, a little way from where the water cascaded. You couldn't see it from the top of the dip. He shrugged off the rucksack and disappeared through a slim gap in the rock, about two feet wide and very tall.

'Come on, you two,' he said, popping his head back out.

Dean placed his rucksack on the rocks and went in after him; Nina reluctantly followed.

A couple of steps into the gap, the light faded and she had to feel her way along, the rock on either side brushing her shoulders. As her eyes adjusted to the light the small passage opened out into a large cave with a domed ceiling. It was very dry inside, and the walls and floor were smooth. It was cool and protected from the heat.

'Can you feel that?' asked Max, putting a hand up to a hole in the ceiling. Nina moved over to them and looked up. The hole in the ceiling was black, and she couldn't see where it went, but she could feel cool air flooding down onto them. 'I think this is where the water used to come in, thousands of years ago, and it made this cave. See how the floor is smooth but full of ripples.'

'It's well cool,' said Dean.

'If I was ever on the run, this is where I'd hide out,' joked Max.

Nina stepped away from the cool air and looked around. There was a pile of sticks and ash where someone had lit a long ago fire, and to one side, where the smooth rock bulged out and created a platform, there was graffiti. She shivered. Max appeared at her side and slung an arm around her neck, pulling her into his chest. Dean was standing a few feet away from them, and stared. Max put out his hand to Dean and pulled him in under his other arm. Nina could feel herself pressed against the two men. Max squeezed them together tighter and she felt a tingle of excitement and allowed herself to be sandwiched between them. Her chest pressed against Max, and she felt Dean's tall wiry body pushing into her back, and a growing hardness pressing against her buttocks.

'You two fancy a swim?' she asked.

'Okay, babe, whatever you want,' said Max.

They broke apart and came back out of the cave into the blazing sunshine. The boys were brazen, and stripped off all their clothes, leaping from a low, smooth rock at one side of the waterfall and into the deep pool of water below. Nina self-consciously took off her trousers until she had on her underwear and T-shirt. Max was doing backstroke in the pool, and Dean broke the surface, his dark hair slick against his head.

'The water feels much better naked,' shouted Max.

'Really?'

'Yeah, it's so cold and fresh,' said Dean.

Nina took a deep breath and stripped off her T-shirt and then her underwear. She moved to the edge of the rock and looked down into the water. It was very deep, and clear, and she could make out several large boulders in the deep blue depths.

'Come on! Jump!' shouted Max, slicing at the water and splashing her.

Nina screamed as the cold water hit her, then held her nose and jumped in.

'It's freezing!' she gasped, breaking the surface a moment later. her long, dark hair slick against her head. She doggy paddled out to the boys, but the water was painfully cold, so she turned and swam back, pulling herself back out and onto the long, flat rock.

'Come on, wimp!' cried Max, splashing her again.

'No! It's fucking freezing.' She shivered, crossing her hands over her naked body. She unrolled a rug from her little backpack and slung it around her shoulders.

'There's more whisky in the side pocket of my rucksack, it'll warm you up,' shouted Dean.

Nina found a small bottle and undid the cap, taking a long sip. She lay in the sun, drinking the whisky and watching the boys splash and fight in the water. She felt a pang of desire as they wrestled, naked, in the water; Max wrapping his legs around Dean, putting him in a headlock. He held him under and then, just as Nina screamed for him to stop, he let go of Dean who came to the surface and launched himself on Max.

A little while later they heaved themselves out and onto the rock, but they didn't put their clothes on and lay naked beside her, forming a neat line: Nina, Max, then Dean. Drops of water pooled on their taut bellies and Nina shrugged off the blanket and tipped her head back. There was a silence as they looked at each other. Max leaned over and kissed Nina. She hesitated, then kissed him back. She could see that, unlike Max, Dean was circumcised, and he put his hand down and started to squeeze his penis.

'You embarrassed, Nina?' asked Max, stroking his fingers across her belly and pushing them down between her legs.

She tensed as she saw Dean was now masturbating. 'I don't know…' She shrugged and sat up a little, crossing her arms over her chest and closing her legs.

'Okay. What if I did this?' said Max. He leaned over and kissed Dean, who responded enthusiastically. Nina's mouth dropped open and she laughed. The boys started to grope at each other, hands exploring each other's bodies, and this excited Nina. Max reached out his hand and pulled her between their writhing bodies.

CHAPTER 16

Nina had sex with Max, while Dean watched them hungrily. When Max pulled away from her, they were covered in sweat. He smiled, and stood, leaping over her into the water. She lay back catching her breath and wiped strands of hair away from her face. Dean was still watching her; he was still hard, and he had a wild look in his eyes. Nina sat up and covered herself with a corner of the rug.

'No. I'm sorry, this was fun, but I don't want to,' she said.

He moved towards her with a predatory look in his eyes. His gangly naked body suddenly seemed obscene. Nina looked over to the pool but Max had dived under the water. There were just ripples spreading out across the surface.

'Sorry, no, Dean,' she said, putting one arm out, and crossing the other over her naked body.

He was masturbating furiously and kneeling over her. His eyes were crazy, unfocused. He placed a skinny knee between her legs. Just before he prised them apart she saw blood pouring out from a cut on his knee.

'No!' she cried, trying to get up. But he pushed himself on top of her, and she felt a stab of pain as he penetrated her and started to roughly thrust in and out. His face had changed, and he was no longer the funny, gangly guy. His lips were curled back showing those pink gums, his eyes were wide and, on his thin face, the veins threaded across his temple were pulsing. His hands gripped her upper arms painfully, and she could feel her hip bones slamming into the sharp rock underneath. Nina tried to see past him to the pool, but she couldn't see Max. Dean pounded into her harder and as she tensed the pain was terrible. What had been daring and exciting a few short minutes ago was now terrifying. Just as he lifted one of his hands off her upper arm and started to squeeze at her throat, Nina suddenly felt the pressure ease as Dean's body seemed to lift away from hers. She thought at first he had relented, but Max had him by the hair, with one arm hooked between his legs and he threw him down onto the rock. Dean leaped up, his face red and eyes bulging and he punched Max in the face. Max staggered back and almost fell into the pool, but he recovered and was on top of him on the bare rock, punching him over and over. Then he reached over, grabbed a rock and hit Dean over the head.

Dean lay still, blood running from his nose. Max took a deep breath and started to batter Dean's head with the rock, reducing his face to a pulp.

Nina was in shock at how quickly it had happened. She didn't cry out. She was frozen, her legs still wide open. Dean was on the rocks, lying very still, and she couldn't see his face for all the blood. Max stood up slowly, still holding the rock in his hands. His face, arms and torso were spattered with blood. Nina glanced down and saw her skin was spotted with blood. She could just hear the sounds of the waterfall and birds singing in the breeze.

Max turned and dropped the rock into the deep water.

'Are you okay?' he asked, kneeling beside her and seeing the blood. Nina went to say something but felt her stomach contract and she threw up over the rocks beside her. Max dived in and washed himself off, breaking the surface and scrubbing at his bloody knuckles. He heaved himself back out onto the rock, dripping wet, and helped Nina up and, holding on to her arms, he lowered her into the water then pulled her back out, perching her on the edge of the rock. She shivered.

'He was hurting you. I did it to protect you,' he said in a matter-of-fact way.

'No, no, no!' whispered Nina. She looked back at Dean. He was still, and underneath all the blood, his body now looked like wax. Max pulled on a pair of shorts, his walking boots, and grabbed Dean by the ankles and dragged his body off the rock and away up the thin path, his head bouncing off the uneven path. Nina leaned over and threw up again, the little she had left in her stomach spreading out over the clear water.

Her next memory was of being dressed and walking along unsteadily behind Max, his bare back now red from the sun. Then she seemed to zone out and the next thing she heard was the sound of running water. Max had stopped by an ancient stone drinking trough beside a high pile of rocks. A metal pipe had been rigged up to catch the spring bubbling up from the rocks and it poured into the deep trough, overflowing onto the grass. Max leaned down and drank, and pulled Nina over to drink too.

'You okay?' he asked.

'I don't know,' said Nina.

He stroked her long hair away from her sweaty face, and kissed her softly, then lifted her up, and placed her in the stone trough. Water slopped over the edges and she felt relief as she sank inside. When her shoes touched the bottom, the water level was at her shoulders.

'Hold your breath,' he said and he pushed her head under.

The cold water hit her scalp and she opened her eyes and could see down to the bottom, to the chisel marks in the rock when it was sculpted hundreds of years before. She felt the pressure of Max's hand on the back of her head, and he lifted her out and sat her on the grass. Next to the trough was what looked like a mossy-shaped doughnut. It was such a vivid green colour, and it looked soft, almost edible. She leaned over and pulled at it, and tugged a piece away to reveal a piece of a smooth white millstone.

'Where is he?' asked Nina, another wave of fear and nausea overwhelming her.

'There's an old well, a deep hole, a little way from the waterfall. I chucked him in with his backpack, and then piled in a load of rocks. No one will find him.'

He crouched down and looked her in the eyes.

'He was raping you, Nina, and he could have killed you... he told me before that he'd killed another lad when he was banged up in young offenders.'

Nina shook her head.

'But you killed him.'

Max grabbed her face in his hands and shook her.

'I acted in self-defence. He was going to kill you! You hear me?' He let go. 'Please, Nina. I love you. I did it for you, to save you.'

They were silent for a long time, and then Max said they should get going, to get back to the hotel before it got dark.

CHAPTER 17

WEDNESDAY, 4 OCTOBER 2017

'Could this be two people, two murderers, working together?' said Detective Constable Brian Temple. He had a warm Scottish accent. Erika turned away from the crime scene photos on the whiteboard. 'You did say there's no stupid questions, ma'am,' he added. His accent made 'ma'am' sound like 'mum'.

'I'm not your mother,' said Erika. 'I prefer boss.'

'Okay, boss,' he said, unfazed.

'But it's true, there are no stupid questions. What makes you think *two* people did this?' Everyone in the incident room turned to look at Temple. He was a big bloke, and he sat forward in his chair, pointing at the crime scene photos with his pen.

'It's hard for one person to overpower two people. Thomas Hoffman was a big guy, Charlene Selby was a woman, no offence, ladies, but you are in some ways the weaker sex.'

There were a few cold looks and snorts from the other women in the incident room: Moss, Marta and DC Knight.

'He's making a valid point,' said Erika and indicated he should continue.

'Thomas and Charlene have no marks whatsoever on their bodies to indicate they were shot, or drugged, or tied up.'

'Charlene was stabbed, but we don't know if this was *before* she was battered to death... Toxicology results show that she had high levels of cocaine and heroin in her blood, which could have made her easier to subdue,' said Erika.

'She was a habitual user. Her parents have confirmed this,' said Moss.

'And Thomas Hoffman was clean, apart from the drugs in his belly, but he wasn't a user,' said Temple. 'So it takes us back to my theory of two people. What if two people picked them up in a car, took them somewhere quiet and quickly overpowered them? A lock-up perhaps?'

'Why would they go willingly to some lock-up?' asked Moss.

'Zada, the woman I spoke to who'd smuggled drugs into the UK said that dealers expect people to drop off their stash immediately after they land,' said Erika. 'They usually meet them and take them to a place to do this. In her case it was a rented office block near Heathrow.'

'That could explain them going willingly to a lock-up,' said McGorry.

'Who says that Thomas Hoffman was smuggling drugs *into* the UK, what if he was all prepped and ready to smuggle them out?' added Moss. 'Then whoever killed him might not have known the drugs were in his body.'

'There's too many ifs, buts and maybes for my liking,' said Erika, moving back over to the whiteboards and looking at the large map of London and the river. 'We need to find out if Thomas and Charlene were booked on a flight in or out of the country.'

'I've put in a request,' said Moss.

Erika paused and sighed. 'Okay. And what about the Jaguar they borrowed for three days? Do we know where they went?'

'I've also put in a request to the National ANPR Data Centre, the number plate would have been clocked by the CCTV in and around central London. I'm expecting the data asap.'

'Good. It seems Moss is doing all the legwork,' snapped Erika, eyeing the rest of the team.

'To be fair, boss, only officers of my rank and above can access records from ANPR. I'm the only Detective Inspector, with Peterson not being here…'

There was an awkward silence. Erika looked back at Thomas Hoffman's passport photo on the whiteboard. He'd renewed his passport eighteen months previously: six months after his wife died. There was a blank, haunted look in his eyes which she identified with. She'd had to have her warrant card renewed when she returned to service after Mark's death. Her photo had that same look. She then thought of Peterson, and wondered what he was doing. She pictured him on the sofa in his flat, his thin frame huddled in a blanket. She shook the thought away and turned and realised that Crane was now talking.

'Thomas Hoffman's Facebook profile was pretty sparse,' he said. 'There were very few updates. All he seemed to do was play games online, but this does give us the link to Charlene Selby. They met through Facebook three months ago, playing the *Candy Crush Saga* game online. They started to communicate through Facebook Messenger. They seemed to share common ground in that they were depressed, unemployed and unmotivated. They discovered they lived close together: Thomas in Dollis Hill, and Charlene was sleeping on a friend's couch in Willesden Green. They exchanged phone numbers and then stopped talking through Messenger. We're still waiting on their mobile phone records so we can access their text messages.'

'Who was the friend Charlene was staying with?' asked Erika.

'Another druggie, a woman and her boyfriend,' said Crane. 'Someone from uniform called around earlier today, but they were pretty out of it and barely remembered her. Some of Charlene's stuff was there, and it's being sent over to forensics before we release it to the family.'

'OK. And Mariette Hoffman, who's been looking her up?'

DC Knight put up her hand. 'Born in 1963 in Cambridge. No qualifications. She's spent most of her life on benefits, with sporadic jobs in retail and a couple of factories. In fact, the DWP is where we got all of her information, going right back to when she was in her early twenties. She's been arrested once for drunken and disorderly, that was in 2004 on New Year's Eve, in King's Cross. She and Thomas Hoffman had a fight at a bus stop and she smashed a shop window. Uniform picked her up, and she was let off with a caution. However, she owns her flat on the Pinkhurst Estate. She was a council tenant, but bought it for £18,000 with the right-to-buy scheme. She had a mortgage for half of that, but paid it off seven years ago. Although, she claims not to have worked full-time for the past twenty years, so I'm not sure how she got hold of a nine grand deposit and was able to pay off the mortgage. She should have declared it to the DWP. Could be a case for benefit fraud.'

'OK, let's keep that to one side in case we need to bring her in,' said Erika. It was late and she could see her team was weary after another long day. 'Okay. Let's finish there, and we'll meet back here at 9 a.m. tomorrow.'

The team started to collect their coats and there was a burst of chatter as they left the incident room.

'You fancy a drink?' asked Moss as she pulled on her coat.

'Thanks, but I've got a few things to follow up on,' said Erika. 'I need to chase up Nils Åkerman over at forensics. I'm still pinning our hopes on the superglue fuming tests.'

'I'm going to carry on tonight, when I get that data through. Try and find where that Jaguar went.'

'Good,' said Erika, starting to sort through a pile of folders on one of the desks.

'And I'm sorry I mentioned Peterson.'

'Why? It was a valid point. You are the only officer on the team with the D.I. rank.'

'Okay, well, don't work too hard. We'll be at the Wetherspoon's if you change your mind,' said Moss.

'Okay, 'night,' said Erika.

*

As the last of the team cleared out of the incident room, she picked up the phone and called Nils. He answered immediately.

'Hi, Nils. I'm just chasing up the superglue fuming test on the piece of concrete.'

He sounded disappointed to hear her voice. 'Oh, hello, Erika. I'm actually just about to set up the test. One of my lab assistants is prepping as we speak.'

'Great. When do you think you'll…?'

'Erika, I've told you already, this takes several hours, and even then I don't know if there will be enough fingerprint residue to give us anything!' he shouted.

She was surprised at the outburst. He always seemed so calm and collected.

'Okay,' she said. 'Can I remind you that this is the first time I'm enquiring about this, and you did say—'

'I know what I said,' he snapped. There was silence on the end of the line. Erika resisted the urge to argue back.

'Are you okay, Nils?'

'Yes. Yes. Fine. I'm just a little stressed. Budgets, workload. I'm sorry, Erika.'

'Okay. Well, I hope the test goes well,' she said.

'I will contact you the second I have anything,' he said, then hung up.

Erika replaced the receiver and looked around at the incident room. *Resources must be stretched if cool, calm, unflappable Nils is flipping out,* she thought.

She decided to go for that drink after all. She grabbed her coat, switched off the lights, and headed out of the station to join Moss and the team at the pub.

CHAPTER 18

Nils Åkerman stood in his office for several minutes after the phone call with Erika, taking deep breaths. He gripped the side of his desk as a wave of dizziness and nausea passed. He was shivering, and a sheen of sweat covered his skin. His nose began to run, and he moved to the sink in the corner of his office, yanking out a length of blue paper from the dispenser, blowing his nose and wincing at the pain. He was shocked at his reflection in the mirror. His skin was sallow and he had dark circles under his eyes. The small stainless steel soap dispenser glinted in the light, and he went to open it, but there was a knock at the door.

One of the CSIs, Rebecca March, was waiting in the corridor. She was a small woman, with long, mousy hair, plaited at the nape of her neck.

'Everything is set up to start the superglue fingerprint fuming,' she said and then frowned. 'Are you okay?'

'Yes,' he said.

'Allergies still bad?' He nodded and retrieved his ID card from his desk. 'It's very strange you're still getting symptoms; shouldn't the pollen season be over now?'

'I have a very high sensitivity. Pollution is also a problem for me. I've just taken another antihistamine,' he said, pulling the lanyard over his head.

They came out of the office and headed down the corridor, past a glass wall looking into one of the laboratories where members of his team worked. They came to a set of double doors at the end. Nils glanced across at Rebecca as she used her access card to open them, but she seemed focused on the upcoming job. They emerged into another corridor and Nils used his card to access a door on the left. It led into a small prep room, with a large sink, storage cupboards and a window looking out into a testing lab. In the centre was a large square Perspex chamber. They washed their hands at the sink and then pulled on fresh crime scene coveralls, face masks and latex gloves. When they were ready, Nils nodded from behind his mask, and Rebecca opened the door into the testing lab.

Nils moved to a bench along the side wall and picked up the large evidence bag containing the piece of concrete. He checked the adhesive seals hadn't been tampered with. Rebecca opened one of the Perspex panels of the chamber and prepared a tiny silver foil tray, adding several drops of superglue. She placed it on a trolley, along with a small plastic container of water. Nils joined her and stood the piece of concrete on a three-pronged frame beside the silver tray of superglue, so that all areas would be exposed to the fuming process. Several dark patches showed where blood had soaked into its porous surface.

'Let's hope we get something off it,' said Rebecca.

'It's been in the water for a long time, but I always live in hope,' agreed Nils.

They backed out of the chamber and closed the Perspex panel. Nils bent down and set a timer on the side of the chamber to thirty minutes. When he straightened up and turned, he saw Rebecca was staring at him, her eyes narrowed above her mask.

'I think you're bleeding,' she said, indicating the mask around his nose with a gloved finger. They left the lab and came back out into the small prep room. Rebecca removed her overalls, mask, and gloves and placed them in a plastic evidence bag. Nils pulled off his face mask and saw it was spotted with blood. He wiped his nose on the sleeve of his coveralls, and it left a smear of blood. Rebecca was now watching him with a concerned look on her face.

'Are you okay?'

'The allergies, they make my nose bleed,' he said.

'I'll have to write a note about this in the file when we submit our overalls in the evidence bags,' she said.

He moved to the sink and pulled out a paper towel, wiping his nose. Her eyes moved from the bloody spotted tissue to his face, watching him closely. 'You look really ill.'

'I told you, I'll be okay!' he snapped, binning the tissue.

She held out a fresh plastic evidence bag and watched as he stripped off the coveralls and placed them inside with the gloves and bloodied face mask. She was about to seal it up when Nils said: 'I can finish off here.'

'I'm supposed to record and bag these up…'

He took the evidence bag from her.

'Rebecca, I'm sorry to snap at you. We're all working so hard. You didn't get a full lunch break, did you? I can do this, go and grab twenty minutes.' A flicker of concern passed over her face. 'Please, help me be a good boss,' he said, smiling and trying to remain calm.

'Okay, thank you,' she said, still a little unsure.

He kept the smile on his face until she'd gone. When he heard the double doors outside buzz and click shut, Nils removed the bloodied face mask from the evidence bag and stuffed it in the pocket of his trousers. He grabbed a fresh mask from the packet, scrunched it up a little, and stuffed it in the evidence bag. He peeled off the plastic on both bags and sealed up the adhesive labels, signing Rebecca's name across both seals.

The corridor was empty as Nils hurried to his office, shaking and sweating. When he got inside he locked the door. He checked the blind was down covering the small strip of window in the door, locked it, and went to the soap dispenser above the small sink. He lifted off the metal housing, and in the cavity where the liquid sachet of soap usually sat, there was a small bottle of pills. He took the bottle and a sheet of paper from the printer and sat at the marble coffee table. His hands shook as he took the lid off the bottle, folded two tablets in the sheet of paper and crushed it with the Murano glass paperweight. He funnelled two bumps of powder onto the back of his right hand and snorted them with each nostril. He slumped in the chair, tipping his head back, allowing the familiar rush to come over him. Dizzying euphoria, threatening to overwhelm him, and make him black out.

CHAPTER 19

Early the next morning, and Erika, Moss and McGorry were in one of the viewing suites at Lewisham Row, watching a tape from the CCTV cameras outside the showroom of Selby Autos. The black-and-white image on the screen showed a view from the main entrance. The camera was mounted high above the gates, and a chain-link fence entwined with bunting stretched away, lining a quiet road surrounded by trees.

'So here we are, road is quiet, it's 9.03 a.m. on the 15th of September,' said McGorry. A moment later, a small Jaguar came weaving along, briefly mounted the grass verge before it passed the camera and came to a stop beside the chain-link fence. Charlene Selby emerged from the driver's side, unsteady on her feet and scruffily dressed in a long skirt. She stopped to reach inside and pull out a large handbag. A figure emerged from the passenger side wearing shorts, trainers, and a hooded top with the hood up, but whoever it was kept their head down.

'Shit, we can't see the face. Is that Thomas Hoffman?' asked Erika.

'No, he gets out behind,' said McGorry. On cue, a large lumbering man got out of the back seat, finding it difficult emerging from the small, low car. The wind blew his wispy hair, and he caught his foot in the seat belt and almost went flying, but managed to right himself. He turned and looked up and down the road.

'Okay, that's Thomas Hoffman,' said Erika. He wore shorts, a dark T-shirt and he bent back down inside the door to get a carrier bag.

'And who's this?' asked Moss as a fourth figure got out of the rear door. It was a woman in a sleeveless top and sarong, with a baseball cap pulled down over her face. Long, dark hair spilled from underneath. She also kept her head down, and under the baseball cap her face was in shadow. She moved round the car, and jogged a little way to catch up with the figure in the hoodie who was walking up the road. They put a hand on her backside as they walked away. Charlene hung back and waited for Thomas. They moved off to join the woman in the baseball cap and the figure in the hoodie who were now waiting up the road.

'Okay, they all stand here for two minutes,' said McGorry, and they watched the tape.

'But no view of their faces,' said Moss.

He shook his head. 'We can't enhance; the tape is too blurred.'

'Blurry CCTV seems to be a running theme on our investigations, doesn't it, boss?' said Moss.

Erika nodded and rolled her eyes.

On the screen, a minicab sped past the abandoned Jaguar, and came to a stop beside the four of them waiting. The figure in the hoodie leaned in to the car window, seeming to say a few words to the driver, and then got in the passenger side. Charlene hurried over to the back door and got in followed by the woman. Thomas was left to limp round to the back door on the other side of the minicab.

'Can we run it back to when Thomas Hoffman gets out of the car, and show us a close-up on his face?' asked Erika. McGorry quickly rewound the tape. 'Yes, freeze it there, and zoom in.'

The image was blurred, but they could see on the close-up Thomas Hoffman had bruising to his face.

'Who are these other two people?' asked Moss.

'A young woman, and perhaps, well probably a young man,' added McGorry.

'It's the first we've seen of them,' said Erika. 'And they look like they could be friends with Thomas and Charlene.'

'And it adds weight to Temple's theory that two people could have bumped them off,' said Moss. Erika gave her a look. 'Sorry, killed them.'

'That minicab driver would have got a good look at them all,' said Erika. 'Check out minicab firms in the local area and see who was driving that car.'

CHAPTER 20

Nils Åkerman arrived at work late the next day, telling colleagues that he had been to the doctor about his allergy problems. They feigned concern, and some tilted their heads in sympathy, but no one questioned him further. Did they really buy it that his terrible appearance, trembling hands, and sweaty face were plant allergies, in central London, in October? There were no allergies. He had been a functioning drug addict for several years. It had started ten years ago, during his gap year in America when he'd hurt his back in a surfing accident and a doctor had prescribed the highly addictive painkiller Vicodin. This had been the beginning of a long and slippery slope to where he was today.

He went straight to his office, locked the door and flipped up the silver soap dispenser. He shook out three pills into his hand and went to one of the easy chairs at the marble table. He crushed the pills and snorted two huge bumps of the white powder off the back of his hand. Nils slumped back in the chair and wiped his nose. It felt red raw inside. He stood, swaying a little before chucking the scrunched up paper into the bin. He put the pill bottle back into the soap dispenser and saw it was almost empty. He grabbed his phone off the desk and called Jack, a young guy who had been his dealer for the past few years.

'It's Nils, can I come by later?' he asked.

'To pay me?' said Jack.

He hesitated. 'Not today, I need more stuff. I have until the end of next week as per our arrangement—'

'Things have changed. I need the money today,' he said, his youthful voice full of disdain.

'Jack, we go week by week, you know this.'

'Yeah, well, my boss is withdrawing credit, and calling in what's owed, after a couple of customers defaulted, well, defaulted is the wrong word. Overdosed. Dead junkies can't pay their debts, so I'll need you to pay up.'

'I'm not a junkie,' said Nils through gritted teeth.

Jack laughed. It was a hollow, mocking laugh.

'You owe me two grand.'

'I'm good for it,' said Nils.

'You better be…'

'Jack!'

'No, you listen, Nils. You are a fucking junkie, and shit has got serious, so I need that money by the end of the day.'

'But…'

'I know you earn good money, Nils. So it shouldn't be a problem. Should it?'

Jack hung up and Nils stood there shaking, staring at the phone. He felt a warmth flooding in his nose, and grabbed some of the blue tissue from the dispenser just in time to blot the blood trickling from his nostrils. He tipped his head back to try and stem the flow, but after a few minutes he had to resort to packing his nostrils with tissue.

Nils grabbed his ID pass and left the office. He walked out of the underground car park and into the cold air. The Thames was quiet and sparkled in the weak sun. It only took a few minutes to walk round to Vauxhall bus station, which was busy, and he lined up to use the cash machine. When he got to the front of the line, he tried to withdraw £500. The screen flashed up that he didn't have available funds. He tried his other two credit cards, but they were also declined. He could hear tutting, and saw there were a couple of builders in mud-splattered overalls waiting behind.

'Mate, you gonna be long?' scowled one of them, his hands shoved deep in his pockets against the cold.

'Sorry, just one more moment,' said Nils. The builder rolled his eyes. Nils inserted his bank card, keyed in his PIN and requested £500. The cash machine seemed to mull it over for a long time. A cold wind blew around the wall of the station, and people hurried past. The machine beeped, and it flashed up on the screen that he didn't have available funds.

'What?' he cried. He pressed the option to check his balance; £1,000 had been debited, on top of his mortgage payment and the minimum payments for his credit cards. How could he have forgotten his loan repayment was coming out? With shaking hands he took his card and staggered back to work, not noticing the looks on people's faces as blood dripped down the front of his white shirt.

When Nils got back to his office, he changed his shirt, splashed his face with cold water and re-packed his nose with tissue. He searched through his wallet, but he had nothing. He did some quick maths to work out how long it was until pay day, but a huge chunk of his salary would be swallowed up with loans and repayments. There was a knock at the door and he opened it, still holding tissue to his nose. Rebecca was outside.

'Afternoon, sir,' she said, her eyebrows furrowed. 'Still having problems?'

He forced a smile and blotted his nose.

'Yeah.'

'I have the superglue fuming results back on the murder weapon. The test didn't give us anything. There were no fingerprints.'

CHAPTER 21

There was a depressed atmosphere in the incident room when Erika relayed the news that Nils hadn't been able to lift any prints off the piece of concrete.

'It was a long shot, but I thought that they could work with such minute amounts. I thought there would be something left on it...' Her voice tailed off.

'What about blood residue on the concrete?' asked Moss.

'They'll run further tests, but the blood is soaked into the porous surface of the concrete. It's going to take time. It's a complicated process. What else do we have?'

'Thomas Hoffman booked two flights to Jersey, one in his name, and one for Charlene. They were due to depart on Sunday 17th September from Gatwick,' said McGorry. 'Obviously, they never boarded the flight.'

'When did he buy the tickets?' asked Erika.

'Thursday 14th September.'

'So there's a chance he was going to smuggle cocaine over to Jersey, or on to some other destination.'

'I'm following up on everything, boss. I've put in a request for CCTV, in case they showed up at the airport.'

'I doubt someone would be stupid enough to abduct them from the departure lounge, but it's always worth checking,' said Erika despondently. 'Moss, how are we doing with the number plate data from National ANPR Data Centre?'

'I've been sent a vast spreadsheet which I'm having to work through,' said Moss. 'It's good and bad. Good because the Jaguar was driven all around central London during the three days it was taken from Justin Selby's car showroom, and its number plate was caught on hundreds of cameras, bad because I have to collate the data and put together a route and a pattern, but I'm on it.'

Erika looked around at the faces of her team and tried to think of something, anything, that would rally them and keep things moving, but she couldn't. Her mood was as low as theirs. They had also tracked down the minicab driver who'd picked up Thomas, Charlene, and the unidentified man and woman outside Selby Autos, identifying the cab company from a logo on the side of the car. The driver was a Samir Granta. A woman who worked in the dispatch office said he was on holiday to Australia with his family and she didn't know when he would be back. She was also unaware of where Samir had driven the four passengers, as they didn't keep a record of addresses. She'd given them Samir's mobile phone number, but it was the middle of the night where he was staying in Melbourne and he wasn't answering.

Erika looked at the clock. It was almost 6 p.m.

'Okay, let's leave it there, everyone,' she said. 'Go home and get some rest. We'll meet back here at eight thirty tomorrow morning.'

The team started to make their way to the door, coats in hands, saying good night. Moss stopped by Erika's desk.

'Seeing as we're finishing early, boss, why don't you come over for dinner?'

Erika looked at her watch.

'Thanks, but I'm going to stop here. In a few hours it'll be morning in Australia, and this Samir could be our lead on this unidentified man and woman seen with Thomas and Charlene.'

'You look pooped, boss. Come back for a bite to eat, and then you can carry on working. I have to crack on with the number plate data. We eat early, and Jacob would love to say hello to his aunt Erika.'

'He calls me Aunt Erika?'

'Yes, he's always asking about you. He drew a picture of you last week at school…'

'That's sweet.'

'Well, you know the score. Kids' pictures aren't the most flattering. You had nine fingers on each hand and you were as tall as our house, but the thought was there.'

Erika laughed. She checked her watch again, and was tempted to get out for a few hours, but she knew tonight she wouldn't be the best company. She couldn't stop thinking about the case.

'Thank you, but maybe next time. If I come over, I'll get stuck into the wine and the night will be gone! Let's do it soon though, and say hello to Celia and Jacob.'

The handsome twen 'OK, take it easy, and I'll let you know when I've cracked the data.' She smiled and, picking up her coat, she left the incident room.

Erika went over to the whiteboard and drank in the silence for a moment. She looked over the photos and the maps, and once again, she had that familiar feeling that it was all getting away from her. If she didn't make some headway soon, there was a person, or people, who were going to get away with murder.

'Can I have a word, Erika?' said a voice. She turned and saw it was Superintendent Hudson, and she was holding Starbucks. She joined her at the whiteboard and handed her one of the cups.

'Thanks,' said Erika.

'I saw the report from Nils Åkerman. No prints or partial from the concrete block.'

Erika shook her head and took a sip of her coffee, savouring the taste.

'I'm hoping to talk to the minicab driver later and find out if he can tell us anything about the two people with Charlene Selby and Thomas Hoffman. We're also sifting through CCTV data of the Jaguar's movements.'

Melanie nodded. 'I know you work on instinct, Erika, and I respect that, but I need to keep this investigation moving. What are you pursuing with the drugs found in Thomas Hoffman's stomach?'

'I keep saying the person who killed Hoffman wasn't involved in drugs,' said Erika.

'I've been in touch with DCI Steve Harper over at narcotics…' Erika went to protest but Melanie put up her hand. 'Last night his team raided a drug factory in Neasden. They seized equipment for drug manufacture, raw chemicals and materials used in packaging drugs and smuggling. I need you to submit the drugs you found in Thomas Hoffman's stomach to forensics, to run tests on the drug packets.'

'They did run tests on the packets.'

'They just ran the basics. I need them to do specific batch tests on the materials used to wrap the drug packets and see if we can match them with the materials seized from this drug factory. DCI Harper's team made four arrests last night. These men are now in custody, and we could have a shot at proving the drugs in Thomas Hoffman's stomach were cooked up and packaged by them.'

'Are you taking me off this investigation?' said Erika.

'Of course not, but I have to open it out; we have to share this evidence as there is a potential overlap with your murder investigation.'

'*Double* murder investigation.'

Melanie took a deep breath and tried to stay composed. 'That is something still up for debate. Can you please arrange for the drugs found in Thomas Hoffman's body to go over to forensics in Vauxhall? I have called ahead. Nils Åkerman and his team are aware they need to be fast-tracked.'

'If you've arranged it all, why are you asking me?' snapped Erika. 'I wondered why you'd shown up with the good coffee.'

'It's called professional courtesy,' said Melanie. 'You should practise it. Enjoy your coffee.'

She went off, leaving Erika alone again in the incident room.

CHAPTER 22

Nils had been pacing his office for hours. He'd watched through the small window in his office as the sun sank down the sky, and then as the stars came out above the Thames.

He was shocked at the turn of events with Jack. When he'd first started buying gear, it had almost been like he was making social calls to Jack's flat in Camberwell. They would chat about politics or sport. He'd sometimes have a cup of tea before they exchanged cash and merchandise, but now that kid had called him a junkie.

Nils had called Jack back to try and appeal to him, and ask for more time, but Jack had threatened him.

'Nils. I know you work in the forensics unit in Temple Wharf, fourth floor. I know who your boss is, and I know his direct number. And I know where you live.'

'What? You're going to barge in here and break my legs?!' Nils had cried, horrified, wondering how Jack knew this information.

'If you don't pay me, Nils, I'll do worse stuff than break your legs. I'll leave your legs, cos you'll need to run away from the fucking chaos I cause you. I will destroy you. I will destroy your reputation,' he'd said calmly, before ending the call.

Pacing his office, Jack's final words echoed around his head. Two thousand pounds wasn't a huge amount, but it was money he couldn't find quickly. He owed money to two friends already, and as he sat, sweating, his heart pounding, he realised they probably wouldn't be in his life much longer; he had been avoiding their calls. Could he ask one of his colleagues? No way. You borrowed a fiver at most from colleagues, and that's colleagues you know quite well. He opened the fridge, pulling out the stale remnants of the carrot cake. He shoved a piece in his mouth and began to chew, hoping the sugar would do something for the terrible cravings, but no sooner had he swallowed, he had to rush to the sink, where he threw it up.

As he was running the tap and rinsing it away, his phone rang. It was Erika Foster, explaining that she needed to deliver the narcotics taken from the stomach of Thomas Hoffman for further tests.

'What time were you thinking?' he asked.

'This is urgent, so I could be there in the next hour, hour and a half, depending on the traffic,' she said.

Nils gripped the phone; an idea had pricked the back of his mind.

'If you make it two hours then the lab will be ready to put them through immediately.'

'OK, thank you.'

'My shift will be over,' he lied. 'But one of the team will run the first round of tests. There's a safety deposit box just inside the underground garage. Put them through the slot.'

'Thanks, Nils,' said Erika.

He came off the phone with the plan fully formed in his head. It was terrible and bold. Narcotics came in and out of the lab every day. They were strictly controlled when they came in, and had to be accounted for when they went out again. However, it wasn't unusual after hours for narcotics to be dropped off in the safety deposit box downstairs. He looked at his watch. In two hours, Erika would be dropping off a bag of cocaine wraps with a street value of £30,000. She would be driving up to the safety deposit box. What if someone came along on a motorbike and snatched them from her? The location of the forensics lab wasn't widely known to the public, but the location of the safety deposit box had been flagged before as being far too open and public.

He put his head in his hands and gave a low groan of despair. Had it really come to this? For the first time he realised, deep down, that he was a junkie. He needed to get help, but he needed to do this. He could clear his debt and move on. Turn over a new leaf. Start again. He grabbed his phone and called Jack.

'About fucking time! This better be good or—'

'Please, listen,' said Nils, his voice shaking. 'If you do exactly what I say, you'll get your money back with a huge profit. But you have to promise me that this is done without anyone getting hurt.'

CHAPTER 23

It was late when Erika went down to the evidence room. It was housed in the basement of Lewisham Row, on the opposite side of the building to the cells, and even after so many years in the force, it gave her the chills.

She spoke to the young officer working the small desk by the door, who took the serial number from her and vanished off down the rows of shelves. The low room was lit harshly from above, and the lights shone off the young officer's brown hair as she moved along the crammed shelves. They were crammed with evidence bags in all shapes and sizes, containing knives encrusted with blood; clothes neatly folded and spattered with bodily fluids; lengths of rope; blunt, heavy objects; delicate items of jewellery; there were even children's toys. The toys affected Erika most, along with all the evidence bags stuffed with women's underwear: the different sizes and styles rendered all the more sinister by their ripped and soiled state. The evidence room contained the answers to so many crimes, the scientific link between victim and perpetrator.

The officer located the clear plastic bag of drug wraps on a shelf at the back, and returned to the desk. There were two labels stuck over the opening of the bag which had been signed by Erika, and Isaac Strong, their signatures overlapping the adhesive sticker so that if the bag was opened and tampered with it would be impossible to re-seal and line up the complex web of writing.

Erika checked it was intact and spent a few minutes filling in forms before she left the evidence room.

She emerged into the main corridor housing the canteen, staff locker rooms and weapon store. She passed Sergeant Woolf coming out of the canteen with a steaming cup of tea.

'You're not on the hunt for a digestive biscuit, are you? I nabbed the last of them,' he said, holding a little packet.

'I've got something much stronger,' she said, holding up the evidence bag of drugs.

Woolf cast his eye over them. 'I'll stick to digestive biscuits.'

Erika passed another couple of uniform officers coming off shift, and then reached the door of the weapons store. She pressed the bell and looked up at the camera mounted above it. A second later the door clicked and opened. She had her warrant card ready, and requested a baton and a taser. As a weapons trained officer, Erika was registered to operate a taser. She signed for both and checked that the taser was charged before slipping it into a leather belt with the baton.

The traffic was light as she drove from Lewisham, through Peckham and Camberwell. She could have easily sent a junior officer to drop off the evidence bag, but delegating wasn't something that came easy to Erika. She wanted to keep on at Nils to make sure her face was fresh in his mind. She was going to put in a request for a complete forensics test on the Jaguar from Selby Autos. Charlene's parents said they'd had it cleaned, but it could still give her fingerprints and DNA. The problem was time and resources. Forensics was overworked and lacked the resources to process evidence quickly, and keeping herself on Nils's radar could help.

There was a little traffic at a junction near Kennington, and she came to a halt behind the line of cars. Erika checked that the central locking was activated. The narcotics were in a Tesco Bag for Life on the passenger seat, the jaunty picture of fruit and veg at odds with what was inside. The lights turned green, and she moved off again, past Oval tube station, following the road around the high walls of the cricket ground. The few cars in front peeled off just before the one-way system, cutting behind Vauxhall train station to Nine Elms Lane. When Erika emerged onto the road beside the Thames, she didn't notice the black Range Rover with tinted windows, which was parked up in the shadows next to the high curved wall separating Nine Elms Lane from the Thames flowing past below.

She slowed and indicated to turn left, where a slip road led down to the underground car park and drop-off for the forensics lab.

The headlights of the Range Rover lit up on full beam, and it lurched forward with a squeal of rubber, crossing the opposite lane and appearing up close in her rear-view mirror.

'What the hell?' she said, as the Range Rover came level with her bumper and blinded her with a flash of headlights. Instinctively, she accelerated, and missed the turning for the slip road. The Range Rover accelerated and with a jolt made contact with her rear bumper. Erika grappled with the steering wheel trying to remain in control of the car. The road hurtled past on each side, and she reached for her radio on the seat next to her, but the Range Rover fell back and then increased its speed, ramming into the back of her car. Her radio and the taser belt slithered off the seat and landed in the passenger footwell. Whipping past in a blur on either side were warehouses and a chain-link fence and a lane busy with traffic and the high wall separating road from river. The Range Rover fell back a little, so she floored her accelerator in the hope of putting distance between them, but as the speedometer moved from eighty to ninety, the Range Rover kept pace, hitting her again.

'Shit!' she cried as a line of red lights appeared ahead, where traffic was waiting at a junction. The Range Rover dropped back and then started to overtake with a honking of horns from the opposite lane. It rammed into her right side, pushing her to the left. Erika gripped the wheel as the car bumped and bounced into an uneven slip road. It was a single lane leading down between two chain-link fences. There were no streetlights, and the Range Rover kept on at her, ramming her from behind, and she had to grip the steering wheel to keep control. Her mind was whirring, trying to keep up with what had happened in the space of sixty seconds.

The single lane road banked sharply and curved to the left. A large corrugated building with a loading bay loomed up ahead, and in front of the large roll-up door was a raised concrete platform around six feet high. The Range Rover braked and dropped back. Erika slammed on her brakes, coming to a screeching halt a few feet from the concrete platform. She reached down for the radio in the passenger footwell, but before she could get hold, she heard the engine roar and her head hit the dashboard as the Range Rover slammed into the back of her. It pulled back with a squeal of rubber, and rammed into her again. The bonnet crumpled like cardboard as it hit the low wall of the loading bay. Erika was dazed, and she could hardly move her head after the impact. Blood was pouring from above her left eyebrow.

The Range Rover stopped a few feet behind her, its engine idling. Then the headlights went out, plunging her into darkness.

'Shit, shit,' she whispered, trying to move quickly, gritting her teeth against the pain. The loading bay was surrounded by warehouses, blocking out much of the surrounding artificial light. She felt in the passenger footwell and her hand closed around the radio, but when she tried to call in for backup, there was no signal. 'What?' she said, pressing frantically at the buttons. She tried again, switching between signals but there was nothing but dead air. She turned her head and winced. The Range Rover's headlights were off and she couldn't see any movement inside. She pulled at the door handle, but the front wing had been pushed back over the driver's door, preventing her from getting out. Erika tried the radio again, and felt around for the leather belt with the taser and baton.

'Control, are you reading me?' she hissed. She saw the button just under the steering wheel and pressed it, activating the blue lights and high-pitched sirens of her unmarked police car. The Range Rover was still and dark. Erika clambered over to the passenger side, her long legs and long dark coat becoming briefly entangled with the gearstick, and she tried the passenger door, but this too was jammed. She shouldered the door, feeling pain shoot through her body, but it still wouldn't budge. She was about to squeeze through to the back seats, but remembered the doors and windows were disabled for carrying suspects. She reached through, wincing at the pain and tried both doors, but she was right.

Erika was now panicking, and sweating under her thick coat. She leaned forward and tried to open the electric windows in the front, but they weren't working; the door frames were bent inwards. She looked to the back window and it was now steaming up. Her mind was working fast. *Did they know she was due to drop the evidence bag?* The lab's location wasn't known to the public. *Why else would someone force her off the road?*

Through the steamed-up back window, Erika saw the doors on the Range Rover open; two tall figures in black slowly got out. They approached the car carrying crowbars, and both wore full-face balaclavas. Erika looked around and saw the buckle of the leather belt containing the taser and the long baton poking out from under the passenger seat. The car rocked as one of the black-clad figures tried to lever the boot open with the crowbar. Erika reached under the passenger seat as the driver's window burst inwards with a shower of glass. The cold air and the sound of the blaring siren rushed in. She turned to the figure at the window. His eyes glowed beadily through the holes of the balaclava.

'Show me your hands,' he said, pointing a gun at her.

CHAPTER 24

OCTOBER 2016

The events on the holiday in Dartmoor changed Nina. Max had helped her back to the hotel that night, confiscated her phone, and given her tablets which made her sleep. When she woke late the next day, she still wanted to go to the police.

'I was defending you,' said Max incredulously. 'Nina, he could have killed you. And in return you'd have me put away?'

'They wouldn't put you away if we told the truth!' she'd argued.

'And what is the truth, Nina? It's something that we know, me and you, but what about the police who'll look at my record? The DNA evidence left on him. The fact I dumped his body, and we walked away. Would a judge and jury believe the truth, or would they look at me and just see a murderer?'

'But… That's how things work…' she replied weakly. 'You tell the truth, and it will all be okay. My mum always says that if you speak the truth then things will all work out.'

Max shook his head and took her in his arms.

'You need to open your eyes to how the world works, Nina. It's not just my DNA is on him, yours is too. Do you think the police will believe you, any more than they believe me?'

'He tried to rape me.'

'You had sex with me as he watched. And you were draping yourself all over him the night before in the pub. They'll hear you were acting like a slut. And a judge and jury would think the same…' She buried her head in his chest and began to sob. 'Do you know what prison is like for young, pretty girls like you?' he said, rocking her like a baby. 'He's lying at the bottom of a deep, deep well. They'll never find him. He was a loner, a drug dealer, and a rapist. You remember his hands around your neck, don't you, Nina?' She'd pulled back and looked up at him and nodded, her face red with tears. 'He could have killed you.'

'If he had killed me, would you have gone to the police?'

''Course I'd have fucking gone to the police,' he snapped, pushing her away. 'I did this for you,' he leaned in, whispering. 'I killed a man with my bare hands for *you*, and *you* want to turn me in to the police, and then you ask if I would chuck your body down that well?'

'No, Max I didn't say tha—'

'You're so fucking stupid. Here I am, standing before you, a man who loves you. Who would die for you. Who has *killed* for you…'

'Max, I'm sorry,' she sobbed, now hysterical, going to him and grabbing at his clothes.

'It's obvious that's not enough for you, so then fine, go to the police. Walk away. Good luck out there in the real world. All they'll see is a slutty little bitch.'

'I won't go! I promise, please, I can't cope. I need you; I love you. Let's just deal with it. I'll deal with it…' Nina gave a lurching sob and had to run to the sink in the bathroom so she could be sick. Max followed and held her hair back.

'It's okay,' he said, soothingly. 'You just bring it all up. We'll move on. Stuff like this happens in life and you have to move on. Move forward. We have each other, don't we?'

She'd wiped her mouth and looked up at him through bloodshot eyes.

'Yes,' she said.

'It's just you and me, Nina; you and me against the world. Say it.'

She nodded. 'It's you and me against the world.'

When Nina arrived home, she just wanted to curl up in her bedroom and shut out the world. However, her mother informed her Paul had moved his stuff in, and he would now be living with them. The house immediately took on a different feel. It had been Nina and her mother for as long as she could remember, but she found Paul creepy, and the way her mother desperately fawned over him was embarrassing. The house felt alien with his belongings everywhere, hearing the low murmur of his voice when she was upstairs in bed, and the smell of his cheap aftershave aggressively filling the house.

On the first morning, Nina had emerged from the bathroom wrapped in a small towel, almost bumping into Paul who was waiting to go in. He wore just boxer shorts and an old white T-shirt.

'Morning, Neen.' He smiled, his eyes lingering over her body.

'Morning,' she'd replied and went to move past him, but he'd blocked her way.

'You don't mind if I call you Neen, do you?' he said, his eyes moving down to the curve of her body under the towel.

'I suppose not…' she'd said, avoiding his gaze and clinging on to the towel, wishing it was longer.

'I won't ask you to call me daddy,' he'd laughed.

Mandy had appeared at the top of the stairs with a stack of fresh towels, and Paul had immediately dropped the sleaziness, stepping back. But Mandy had seen the tableaux, and decided it was Nina who was overstepping the mark.

'Go to your room and put something on!' she'd snapped. Nina had hurried off, her blushing cheeks not helping her cause.

That day she'd visited Max's bedsit for the first time. It was at the top of an old terraced house near King's Cross, looking out over the train tracks. It was tiny but clean with a kitchenette in one corner and a tiny bathroom in another. His collection of books took up one wall, a mixture of titles about philosophy and history. He had made them egg on toast with hot mugs of tea. They had eaten it on their laps in front of the glow of a three-bar electric fire, listening to the rain hammer down on the roof, and Nina had felt safe next to Max. She felt as if she'd been spat out into the world. She no longer had the routine of school, she felt like the cuckoo in the nest at home, and all of her close friends had gone away to university. All she had was Max.

Over the next few weeks, as the weather turned bad and the nights drew in, Nina spent most of her time at Max's bedsit. Despite what had happened in Dartmoor weighing heavily on her mind, it was a blissful time, and they grew very close. Nina was shocked at his intelligence, and how articulate he could be. She realised that she might have more qualifications, but in comparison she was uneducated and ignorant of the world. Max talked about world governments, and history. He talked about conspiracy theories, and his obsession with the Illuminati.

'We're all just pawns in a huge game. No one cares about us, Nina. No one cares about you... apart from me. We're all just maggots writhing around in the shit, and a small group of people, the corporations, the elite, they control us.'

He went into more details about his childhood, of being abandoned by his mother when he was tiny, and the terrible time he'd had growing up in children's homes, and how he had been sexually abused by several of the staff when he was nine years old.

'You have to fight for everything in this life,' he'd said. 'I fought for you when Dean wanted to rape you, and take your life. So is me killing him wrong or is that right?'

'I suppose, if you look at it like that, it's right,' Nina had replied in a small voice.

''Course it is. Think of all those politicians who start wars. What are wars?'

'It's when one country does something bad to another.'

Max had shaken his head and stood, pacing the room, animated. 'Nina. Wars are about money. About selling weapons and gaining power. Do you know how many politicians own companies which manufacture products for war? I can show you examples in so many books. Those same politicians declare wars for personal interests. They kill thousands if not millions of innocent people, and they are never held to account. We're all brainwashed to think that war is noble. That soldiers who go up and fight are doing it for their country. Poor bastards. The soldiers are noble, sure, but what they are fighting for isn't… And I defended you, Nina, I took one miserable life to protect you, and I could be locked away for twenty years and left to rot in prison? How many other women might Dean have raped and killed? No, there is one rule for the elite and another for us the fucking maggots. I refuse to be one of the maggots. I refuse to writhe and be subservient!'

At the end of October, they were fired from their jobs at Santino's for not showing up on several occasions. Nina had been fed up of working there for some time, but she'd kept the job, partly because her mother insisted on her now paying housekeeping.

It was another turning point for their relationship. Max invited her to move into the bedsit and they both started to claim the dole. Nina felt free and happy for the first time in months, and she believed that she and Max had a real future, that she had found the one.

And then they went to Blackpool.

CHAPTER 25

FRIDAY, 6 OCTOBER 2017

Erika could see that the gun pointed at her was a Smith & Wesson with a home-made silencer. The sirens on her unmarked car continued to blare, and the small loading bay was lit up by the flashing blue lights.

'Hands in the air!' he shouted. His full pink lips poked obscenely through the hole in the balaclava.

Erika raised them slowly from her crouching position in the passenger seat.

'Open the boot,' shouted the voice. It was male and well spoken. 'Do it or I shoot you!'

'The button is next to the steering column,' said Erika, not taking her eyes off him. 'You want the drugs?'

'Yeah, now open the boot!' he shouted, his voice shrill.

They've just assumed I put them in the back, she thought. She was crouched in an awkward position on the seat, and the Tesco Bag for Life containing the narcotics was underneath her legs. There was a squeal of metal as the other man used the crowbar on the boot. *Who are these two?* she thought. *This is amateurish stuff, all for thirty grand's worth of gear. Even if they cut it with baking soda, they could sell it for a few grand more, but they were risking a lot.* They were wearing balaclavas, and she couldn't identify them; this meant there was a chance they would leave her alive.

'Come on, quickly, open it, and shut off the sirens!' he shouted, twitching the gun to the steering wheel.

'I need to bend down to get to the button underneath the steering column,' said Erika.

'Fucking do it!'

The scraping of the crowbar continued at the back, and in the split second that the man in the balaclava glanced back to the other man and let the gun drop a little, Erika lifted the taser she'd concealed behind her and fired it at his neck. The sirens masked the bang and the charge as the wire hooks shot out and caught in his skin. He went rigid and hit the floor. Keeping hold of the taser, Erika moved across to the driver's seat and climbed through the window. The man lay on the floor, and she removed the magazine from his gun and pocketed it, limping around to the back of the car where the second figure was now in a panic, clawing at the boot with the crowbar.

'Hands in the air!' she shouted. He looked up, dropped the crowbar and reached for the back of his trousers.

'Hands where I can see them,' she said, pointing the taser at his chest.

'You fucking bitch!' he said through the balaclava.

Erika angled the taser down to his crotch and fired it at his balls. He screamed and went rigid, hitting the ground.

'That'll teach you to call me a fucking bitch,' she said, rolling him over onto his front, retrieving the Smith & Wesson handgun tucked under his belt, and pulling out the magazine. She searched his pockets and found a small black key fob. It was a close-range signal jammer used to block radio and mobile phone frequencies. She then moved to the rear passenger door and smashed the window with the butt of the gun. Reaching in, she pulled out two sets of cuffs. She went to the first man, cuffing one of his hands, and dragged him over to a long low metal railing by the loading bay where she cuffed him to the lowest bar. She pulled off his balaclava. He had sandy blond hair and a smooth round face. He stared up at her, dazed. She did the same to the second man, dragging his limp body over to the railing and cuffing him to it. She also yanked off his balaclava. She was surprised to see how young he was; he barely looked out of his teens.

She then found her radio and called in for backup, moving to the Range Rover to check that it was empty. She pulled the keys out of the ignition. She came back and flashed her warrant card at the two men.

'You are both under arrest. You do not have to say anything. But it may harm your defence if you do not mention when questioned something which you later rely on in court. Anything you do say may be given in evidence.'

It was only then, when the adrenalin began to leave her body, that she started to feel the extent of her injuries.

The older man with the sandy hair attempted to spit in her face, but he didn't have the energy. Erika had to resist the urge to beat him with the baton. She knew if she started she wouldn't be able to stop.

CHAPTER 26

OCTOBER 2017

Nina had fallen out with her mother, and as a result of this, they no longer had a car. Max heard from a mate of his in Blackpool who had a car going cheap, so they decided to make a holiday of it.

As Nina suspected, Blackpool in late October was very cold and very windy. The guest house they stayed in was a bit rough, and even with the windows shut the curtains in their dingy room gently billowed in the draught. But it didn't matter. They were on the Golden Mile, and at night the illuminations shone through the net curtain, playing coloured lights over the ceiling above their bed. Nina loved to be by the sea. They woke early on Saturday and spent the day on the Mile. They played the slot machines, ate hot fish and chips out of the paper, and ventured down onto the beach to paddle in the freezing sea.

They were due to pick up their new car that evening, and before they left, Max paid for them to go all the way up Blackpool Tower and see the glass walkway. It was shortly before closing, and they were the only ones to go up on the last tour. It was quiet at the top, and Max took Nina's hand when they walked out onto the clear glass walkway. People moved on the promenade far below, and the sea stretched out to the horizon, with the pier reaching out from the prom.

'It's like we're floating above it all,' said Nina, gripping the railing and crouching down to her knees. She lay face down.

She could feel the wind buffeting the tower, and far below, the dragging sound as the breaking waves pulled shingle back from the shore. Max knelt down and joined her, and they lay with the tops of their heads touching. Directly below, two women walked with empty pushchairs, and their three small children ran around them like tiny satellites.

'Look at them all down there,' said Max.

'Like tiny toy people,' said Nina.

Max turned his head to her. 'Writhing like tiny maggots is what I think. Teeming, blindly wriggling, blindly breeding. Just about surviving. Insignificant. They're all oblivious to how the world really works... Take those two women. If they knew how the world *really* works, they wouldn't have given birth. Do you ever wonder if your mother considered aborting you?'

Nina turned to him.

'No! And I know she wanted me, despite the fact we're not talking. I know she loves me.'

'You do?'

'Yes.'

'My mother wanted an abortion, I'm sure of it, but she was too far gone when she found out she'd fallen...'

Nina looked at the top of his head, the weak sunshine catching in his golden hair. She felt so many emotions for him: lust, pity... fear. But her love for him always floated above these, making them seem insignificant, like white noise.

'You don't talk about your mum much,' she said. 'I'd love to hear about her.'

'She was a cunt. That's all you need to know,' he said. 'I'd piss on her grave, if I knew where it was.'

'Max, we could find out, I'm sure. Not that I want you to piss on it, but we could leave some flowers...'

Max turned his head to her so their foreheads were pressed together.

'That's why I love you, Neen, you see so much good in things. And even though I know you're wrong, it's nice to see the world hasn't yet destroyed you.'

'The world is a good place, Max,' she said, kissing him. He kissed her back and turned to look down at the swarming crowds far below, the tops of their heads still pressed together.

'I imagine being up here with a big red button,' said Max. 'And I can press it at any time and it will drop a bomb on the lot of them, put them out of their misery. A nuclear bomb would vaporise them all.'

'What about us?' asked Nina.

'You're with me, Neen. I've got the red button. I rule the world, and you're my queen.' He grinned. It was a malevolent grin, devoid of warmth.

Nina went to say more but was interrupted by a young lad coming to tell them that the tower was about to close. Max rolled over onto his back and checked his watch.

'I make it four minutes to, so we've still got four minutes,' said Max.

'My watch is set by GMB,' said the lad. He was young and slim with bucked teeth.

Max got up. 'GMB?'

'Yeah,' said the lad.

'And what does "GMB" stand for?' asked Max.

'I dunno, all I know is that it's time for you both to go. We're closing.'

Nina got up from the glass walkway.

'It's GMT, you moron: Greenwich Mean Time,' said Max.

'Come on, let's go,' said Nina, pulling at his arm.

Max eyeballed the young lad, who noted the crazy look in his eyes. His head shrank back into his neck and he smiled awkwardly.

'What are you smiling at?'

'Nothing,' said the lad. He now looked scared.

'Come on, Max...'

'You think something's funny?'

The lad shook his head.

'And for the record, dickhead, we're still on British Summer Time. *BST*,' said Max.

If Nina hadn't been so afraid of him kicking off, she would have laughed. Did it really matter that this lad, who was probably on minimum wage, didn't know the difference between GMT and BST? And Max's watch had been running slow, so the lad probably had the correct time. She finally pulled Max away, and they took the lift down to ground level and joined the teeming masses.

They walked back to the guest house to collect their bags and then took a bus out to an estate where Max's mate lived. Nina had been nervous about meeting Max's friend, worried what he might think of her, or if she might come across as stuck-up or uncool. But it was a quick transaction. A tall, scally looking lad with yellow teeth and bad skin met them outside a terraced house, and took them to a small Renault, which looked a treacly brown colour in the dark. Max peered through the windows, and then he climbed into the inside with the lad and revved the engine, their faces elongated in the shadows cast by the interior light. Then they came around to the bonnet and the lad shone a torch as they peered in. And that was it.

'Take it easy, love.' The lad winked at Nina as he loped back to his house with a wedge of folded over £50 notes.

'How much was it?' asked Nina, as they put their bags in the boot.

'Fifteen hundred quid,' he said.

They got in, and she saw it was clean and neat, and there was a CD player.

'It's nice.'

'It's more than nice, it's a fucking bargain.'

'Why was it a bargain?'

'Ask me no questions and I tell you no lies.' He grinned and leaned across and kissed her.

It was a long journey home, and there was heavy traffic on the M40, so they came off the motorway and took the back roads. They were on a quiet country lane near Oxford, with no streetlights or cat's eyes in the road, nothing but the outline of the tarmac in front. Nina was dozing off, lulled by the motion of the car, when suddenly a dark figure stepped out from the side of the road. They hit it at full speed, and in a blur it rolled over the bonnet, up the windscreen then off the back of the roof. Max hit the brakes and the wheels screamed. The car skidded to a halt in the opposite lane, stopping close to a ditch.

'You okay, sweetheart?' he asked.

Nina said she wasn't sure. She'd hit the dashboard and her nose was bleeding. Max took the corner of his T-shirt and he dabbed her nose.

'You're bleeding too,' she said, pointing to a cut on his chin.

They climbed out of the car, and it was so dark and quiet, just the sound of the engine ticking over. There were no houses or buildings, and trees and undergrowth lined the road. Their tall, black shadows loomed ahead in the light cast by the headlights. A hundred yards up the road a man lay on his back. Max took out his phone and activated the torch. He had a beard and was wearing black, a big coat with baggy trousers and plimsolls. His body was twisted at a funny angle, with his right arm under his back. His face was bloody, and he was wheezing, blood sputtering over his lips. Nina went to help him, but Max put out his hand to stop her.

'Can you hear me?' he asked.

The man swallowed with difficulty. 'Yes,' he finally croaked.

'You were waiting for a car, to kill yourself?'

He nodded and winced, tears forming in the corners of his eyes.

'We need to call for an ambulance,' said Nina, taking out her phone. Max grabbed it from her and slid it into his pocket. 'What are you doing? He needs help! Max, this man needs an ambulance!'

The man on the road was now making a terrible whining, gurgling noise. Max crouched down and put two fingers to the man's neck.

'His pulse is pretty strong,' he said, patting down the man's body, searching under the folds of the long coat for his pockets. 'Jeez, his hip bone is poking through his trousers,' said Max, pulling a face. Nina saw the flash of white and red poking through the material of the man's trousers. He screamed and blood oozed from his mouth as Max reached under him, into his back pocket, and retrieved a battered black wallet.

'Give me my phone; we have to call for help,' said Nina.

Max stood and circled the man, who started to plead in gurgling whispered tones. Max went to the grass verge and scrabbled around for a moment. He came back holding a large flat rock.

'You can make it stop,' said Max, holding it out to Nina. 'He wanted to kill himself, but he couldn't even do that properly. If we were to call an ambulance, that's not really what he wants. He looks pretty screwed. Probably won't walk again. They'll keep him alive but he won't have the strength to end it. I respect him for calling it quits. I wish I was going faster...' He hefted the rock from one hand to another and started to laugh. 'The one time I stick to the speed limit!'

Nina was confused, and in pain from the whiplash. The blood on her chin felt cold. The man tried to sit up, but the oversize clothes bundled around him and his injuries gave him a disturbing jerky movement. He was watching Max through wide, bloodshot eyes. He shifted onto his side with a scream and started to crawl and pull away towards the grass verge.

'Oh, no, no,' said Max. He placed the rock down on the road, and grabbed one of the man's legs and dragged him back.

'Please no! NO, NOOOO!' shouted the man, and he vomited blood.

Max pulled out a packet of cigarettes from his pocket and lit one; he exhaled and started to go through the man's wallet, pulling out his driving licence, peering at it.

'Derek Walton,' he said, reading. 'Walton. So they were the Waltons growing up. Wonder if it was a big family? Wonder if they care about him. Probably not.' He fished around in the wallet. 'No money though, and he's got a card to say he's diabetic.' He put the cards back in and stuffed the wallet in his pocket. Nina was rooted to the spot. The man had pulled himself a few feet away from them again. Max went over and pressed his heel into the ankle on the same leg that the hip bone was poking out. The man howled.

'Max, Stop this!'

'Nina. He's a maggot, a pathetic little maggot. You're just watching him. And you've sat there and listened and agreed with me all this time, about how the world works. You've agreed to live a life free of rules and bowing and scraping. You need to prove to me that you want to live a life by my rules. Put this man out of his misery. Think of it as a test.'

He held the rock out to her and pressed his heel down harder. The man gave another gurgling wail.

'No, Max, no… Please. You have to see that the world is a good place. I agree with what you say, but there is light and dark. There has to be. I love you, you know that.'

'Do you? Is there an "us" or do you just humour me? I can find someone else, some other girl who wants to be with me…'

'Please, Max,' she whimpered, but he fixed her with those caramel eyes burning with orange and pushed the rock into her hands.

'It can be over in a second, and you'll be helping him, Nina. You'll be shining some light into the darkness. If I'd hit a deer, you wouldn't think twice about putting it out of its misery. You'll be his saviour. He wanted to die, Nina; he wanted to end it all. And the longer you wait, the longer *you* keep him in misery and despair.'

Nina took the rock. It was heavy and smooth in her hand. Cool and smooth. She looked down at the man reaching out towards the edge of the road, his head turned to her, wincing, eyes full of fear and face smeared with blood.

'Max, I…'

'Go for the face, bridge of the nose, hold it high and bring it down fast,' said Max insistently. He came to her and smoothed the hair away from her face. 'You can only talk the talk for so long. You can't just be a spectator, Nina. I killed Dean to protect you, and you accepted that. You accepted that the rules don't apply to us. I took a risk for you. I risked my life. Do you believe that?'

'I do believe that.'

'Good, then look at this. I had a drink earlier. If we call the ambulance, the police will come. I'll be tested. They'll look at how much booze I have in my blood; they can see if I was speeding, which I was. This man stepped out of nowhere and used us to end his life. Or he tried. You can save him and you can save me, Nina.' Nina was now crying and the man was frantically trying to pull his leg free from Max's foot. 'Do this, Nina. Do it now. As an act of compassion, and humanity. An act of love. Step up. Be with me for ever.' He pulled Nina down to her knees beside the wailing man with eyes wide open, and he turned the rock over in her hands. 'Lift it high and bring it down fast. Here we have a maggot who knows what he is, and has tried to end it. Don't take that from him, Nina. Be a good person, stand high with me. Above the petty rules. End him. END HIM!'

Nina suddenly cracked and raised the rock high in the air. She brought it down on the man's face with a crunch. She lifted it again, a wail bursting from her mouth, and hit his head with a wet thud. The man was still. Max lifted his foot away and stepped back.

'Look at him, Nina. Look how you saved him,' he said.

As Nina looked down at the man's ruined face, the moon sailed out from the clouds and made the blood black. He took the rock from her shaking hands.

'Go back to the car,' he said softly.

Nina stumbled back along the road and stopped to throw up on the grass verge. She wiped her mouth with her sleeve and climbed into the car. She put the heater on and sat shivering for a few minutes. All she could see was her reflection from the interior light. Her face seemed long and grotesque, like she was in the hall of mirrors at a funfair. The door opened a few minutes later and Max was covered in blood. It spattered his T-shirt, his face and arms.

'What did you do?' she croaked.

'I made sure no one will find him. There was an old drainage pipe in the ditch. I pulled him in there.'

He led her out of the car and around to the boot. There was a large bottle of water, and he heaved it out, stripping off his T-shirt. Something in Nina took over and she held the bottle high and poured the water all over him as he washed the blood away. He shook his long wet hair and grinned. Then he took the bottle and washed her face, so tenderly. She took off her bloody T-shirt and he poured the water over her body.

'I baptise you,' he said with a smile.

They found a towel and change of clothes in their bags. When they were back in the car, Nina had an odd, disturbing feeling. It was a rush, a high. She had proved herself. Proved to Max who she was, and that she was his. He looked across at her and smiled.

'I love you even more now,' he said. He started the engine, and they drove away.

CHAPTER 27

SATURDAY, 7 OCTOBER 2017

Erika knew she was dreaming; this was the first time she'd been aware of being inside a dream...

She was back in her home town in Slovakia, and it was late on a summer day. The heat had lost its fierceness, and the sun was setting in her direct line of vision. She brought a hand up to her face, shielding her eyes from the golden light, and she saw a young girl a little way ahead of her, running across a huge expanse of concrete. The girl stopped and turned back, smiling. She wasn't more than eleven or twelve. She was barefoot, and wore a thin blue summer dress, covered in mud and grass stains from playing. Her long, blonde hair was in a plait, and she had strong, pretty features. At first Erika thought it was her sister, Lenka, or her niece, Karolina, but it was another girl, a young girl she had seen often over the years in her imagination. Erika's body was aching, her face felt swollen, but when she put her hands up to feel her skin, it was smooth and youthful. Her blonde hair was long and tied at the nape of her neck.

The girl smiled and beckoned for Erika to catch up with her, then turned her head and started running. The sun dipped down behind a large building opposite and Erika could now see that they were on the wide flat roof of the theatre in town. The girl reached the edge of the roof and sat with her bare feet dangling down. Below was the town square, paved in a mosaic of grey and white stone, and in the centre, a group of children played by a fountain. Handsome buildings lined the edges of the square and, painted in pastel, blues, greens and pinks, looked almost edible, like sumptuous icing. Erika and Lenka had often played on the roof of this theatre, and it had been a building site for most of their early years. She reached the edge of the roof and reached out to touch the girl's hair, which sparkled in the sunlight.

'Watch me jump, Mum,' said the girl.

'No!' started Erika, but the girl gripped the edge and pushed herself off, hurtling towards the square below, arms and feet flailing, hair flowing out.

Erika moved forward and peered over the edge; the drop was a dizzying eighty feet, but there was no little girl lying broken on the mosaic stones in the square. There was just the sound of laughter as the children played below and the gentle spatter of the water in the fountain. She searched the square and found the girl paddling in the fountain, unhurt, and waving up at her.

'Mum... she called me Mum,' said Erika. She knew it was a dream but the words felt real in her mouth. She could smell the summer air, and the little girl, the way she smiled, it was the combination of Mark's face, and hers.

It was the baby, the girl she had decided not to keep, and even though she knew she would wake up soon, she just had to see her; she had so much to say to her. The golden light blurred as her eyes filled with tears, and a terrible sob worked its way up from her chest. Erika hurried to a doorway to the side of the roof. She wanted to say sorry and hold the girl. She hurried down the bare concrete stairs inside; the half-built theatre was just as she remembered growing up, playing in the concrete building site.

When she emerged out into the square it was winter. There was a foot of snow covering the ground, and the Christmas market was in full swing. Erika looked back. The theatre was now complete with glass in the windows and a poster for the Christmas show. She turned back to the fountain and saw it was now covered over with wooden boards, and a nativity scene, and beside it was a huge Christmas tree. The little girl was dressed in a bright red winter coat, standing by the nativity scene. A group of people moved in front of Erika blocking her view, and she pushed through them,

'I'm here! Mum's here!' she shouted, but her voice couldn't carry across the noise and crowds. A Christmas carol was playing, 'In the Bleak Midwinter'. The crowd parted just a little, and Erika saw the girl again, looking around lost. Erika pushed her way through the people laughing and drinking mulled wine and approached the nativity scene. The girl now had her back to Erika, and the hood was up on her red coat.

'It's okay, I'm here, Mum's here,' said Erika, but as she put her arms around the girl, the coat crumpled. There was nothing inside. Erika gripped it harder, but all she had in her hands was an empty red coat. She put the material close to her face, and breathed in, but all she smelt was antiseptic. Everything began to fade. The square, the Christmas market, the music and the smell of hot food, and it was replaced by a cold numbness.

Erika opened her eyes and the inside of a hospital cubicle came into focus. She didn't feel pain, and she was lying on a soft bed, almost floating. Her vision sharpened and the soundtrack of the A & E filled the air: feet moving past; the low murmur of voices; the swish of a curtain; pills rattling in a tray. She lay for a few minutes, breathing, tears flowing, aware that she had been dreaming, but shocked at what her subconscious had inflicted on her.

The curtain opened and a tiny doctor came in. The woman couldn't have been more than four feet tall and she looked washed-out, with grey hair and a stern face. The only colourful thing about her was the hot pink stethoscope around her neck.

'How are you?' asked the doctor, unhooking the clipboard containing her notes from the end of the bed.

Erika put up her hand to wipe tears from her chin. 'You tell me,' she croaked. She saw there was a drip in the back of her hand. 'Shit, why's that there?'

'Morphine,' said the doctor, leafing through the notes.

Erika saw that her other arm had a plaster cast from the hand to the elbow.

'You've broken your right wrist, fractured a rib, and you'll probably start to feel the severe whiplash when the pain meds wear off. You also had a nasty gash above your left eye. I'm a dab hand with my butterfly stitches, so any scarring will be on the line of the eyebrow.'

Erika put her hand up to her neck and the brace she wore.

'Where am I?' she asked. Her voice sounded thick and strange, and she touched her face. She couldn't feel where she touched but the skin was puffy and misshapen.

'UCL Hospital, in London…'

'I know where UCL is.'

'I see you're a police officer, Detective Chief Inspector Foster,' she said, looking at her chart.

Erika remembered the wreckage of her car, and the two guys trying to take the bag of drugs.

'I have to talk to my boss. Where's my phone?' she asked, sitting up.

'Please, lie back,' said the doctor, gently putting her hand to Erika's shoulder. 'You won't be able to work for some weeks. And we need to keep you in under observation… You have a nasty concussion.'

A nurse came through the curtain and nodded to the doctor. He checked the drip; the doctor went on: 'You haven't put anyone down as your next of kin?'

'My family, my sister is in Slovakia; they don't speak English.'

'What about in the UK. Anyone you want us to call?'

Erika briefly thought of Peterson, but shook the idea away. 'Yeah, Kate Moss.'

The doctor and nurse exchanged looks, and the nurse moved over to consult the chart. 'Pressure is normal, temperature slightly elevated,' he said in a low voice.

'We do need to monitor for any signs of hallucination. She has had a battering,' agreed the doctor. She turned to Erika again. 'Why do you want us to call Kate Moss?'

'No, not *Kate Moss*. Detective Inspector Kate Moss, she's a colleague on my team in the Met,' said Erika.

The doctor took down the phone number, but still didn't seem convinced.

'Now, please, I just need my phone; I need to talk to my superintendent. There's a murder case I'm working on.'

'I'm sorry, you have to rest,' said the nurse.

'I want my bloody phone! I can lie here and look at a phone!'

The doctor cocked her head and stared at her.

'I don't want to have to sedate you.'

Erika lay back and grimaced. 'How long am I stuck here?'

'Another twenty-four hours, at least. We'll be moving you to a ward when a bed is available.'

The doctor and nurse left the cubicle, swishing the curtain back round, and Erika looked up at the ceiling, her head spinning. Despite her frustration, she drifted off to sleep.

CHAPTER 28

Erika slept fitfully until the morphine started to wear off, and the remaining hours until she was allowed to leave hospital seemed to stretch with only the ceiling and a ward full of sedated old ladies for company.

The doctor gave her a final check-up and a stern reminder that she had to rest for at least four weeks, and then Moss appeared in the ward.

'Jeez, boss. You look beat up,' she said.

'Thanks,' said Erika, wincing as she picked up her coat and the large paper bag of medication. 'I saw my face earlier when I went to the loo.'

'I'm not going to lie. The right side of your face does have a look of the "Bride of Wildenstein".'

Erika smiled. 'You're a bitch. Ow. It hurts to move my face.'

'Good job, cos you're not known as a smiler,' said Moss, helping her with the coat. She tried to put it over the hand with the plaster cast, but saw it was too thick. 'I think we're going to have to drop this over your shoulders.'

They moved slowly along the ward and out down the corridor. When they got to the double doors at the end, Moss held one open and Erika gingerly slipped through, and they reached the lift.

'It's the broken rib, isn't it?'

Erika nodded. The lift doors opened, and they squeezed in next to a bed carrying a small old lady propped up on pillows who stared at them. They travelled down two floors in silence until the lift stopped and the orderly wheeled out the bed.

'Tell me what's happening,' said Erika. 'I was too out of it when the first responders arrived at the scene. How long was I in for?'

'Two days. It's Monday morning. Superintendent Hudson is sending someone to get a statement from you tomorrow. You'll have to account for handling the two firearms belonging to your attackers, and why you removed the ammunition. You also have to give clear reasons why you fired your taser.'

Erika gingerly turned her head in her neck brace to look at Moss. 'Are you kidding me? The firearms were being pointed at me, and they targeted me, I think, because I was carrying thirty grand worth of narcotics.'

'I think it's because you deviated from the rule book, and tasered one of them in the balls. It was apparently quite a dicey procedure, removing the barbs from his ball sack.'

'You didn't have to do it, did you?' grinned Erika, wincing.

'I'm not the best person to navigate a ball sack.'

The lift came to a halt and they got out, making their way slowly across the gloomy car park. Moss helped Erika inside the car, and she yelled out in pain when her seatbelt was strapped across her. She drove out very slowly, but she could see Erika grimace when they went over the speed bumps. When they were out on Warren Street and heading back to Lewisham, Moss started to fill her in.

'The two men you arrested are Eduardo Lee and Simon Dvorak. They are a couple of middlemen in one of the central London drug networks. They were tipped off that you'd be delivering the narcotics.'

'Who tipped them off?'

Moss paused, a pained look on her face.

'Kate. Who?'

'Nils Åkerman,' she said.

'What? No. Nils?'

Moss nodded. 'Sorry, yes. Melanie has been on it like a dog with a bone. She was looking at everyone who knew you were going to forensics in Vauxhall. Nils made a call to two people ninety minutes before you left for Vauxhall. One was to a Jack Owen, a student whose flat in Camberwell was raided yesterday afternoon, and a large quantity of cocaine, cannabis resin and ecstasy was seized. He in turn had called Simon Dvorak, who you tasered in the balls. Simon is further up the chain of supply, well, was, before he lost his liberty, and narrowly lost his right…'

'Okay, Moss, I get the idea.'

'Sorry, they are all now in custody and being questioned.'

'How was Nils mixed up in all that?'

'There's still a lot we don't know, but he was screened positive for opiates, cocaine and alcohol when he was arrested. One of his colleagues came forward about an incident in one of the labs when he bled onto a forensic face mask and he switched it for a clean one. Obviously, it would have been screened to rule out contamination and his drug taking would have shown up. Nils is deep in debt. The bank is about to repossess his flat. He owed £2,000 to Jack Owen. Jack has been his drug dealer for the past two years…'

Erika was glad that they hit the Blackwall Tunnel. The dim light allowed her a moment to wipe away her tears.

'I'm sorry this happened,' said Moss.

Erika shook her head. 'Nils has worked with us on so many cases: the disappearance of Jessica Collins, the Darryl Bradley case… He was someone I trusted, someone who had been a big part of our team.'

'I know,' said Moss. 'And I don't want to be the bearer of bad news, but the Met is freaking out. He was responsible for key testimony and evidence in so many cases.'

'It was his testimony that put away Simone Matthews, for fuck's sake!' cried Erika, wincing as she put her head back against her seat.

Simone Matthews was a case Erika and her team had worked on two years previously. Matthews had been an unassuming geriatric nurse who had gone on a revenge killing spree in London, breaking into the homes of four men and suffocating them with a plastic bag. Despite confessing to all the killings, her defence ruled that she was suffering from paranoid schizophrenia. Nils and his forensics team had pulled off an extraordinary forensic examination so they could link Simone Matthews to every crime scene. Simone was currently being held indefinitely at Broadmoor psychiatric hospital.

'It's still early days,' said Moss. 'On a positive note, we have Jack Owen, Simon Dvorak, and Eduardo Lee all in custody. We have their vehicle, mobile phones, and we're hoping that some kind of deal can be done to implicate people higher up.'

'What about Nils?'

'He's in custody too, at Belmarsh. Looking at ten to twelve years, and of course he'll never work again in forensics.'

Erika stared out of the window as the traffic slid past in the darkness.

'Nils must have known what they would do to me. He knew that they might kill me for those drugs,' she said.

'You think you know people,' said Moss. 'People are mostly put on this earth to disappoint us.'

'But he must have been desperate. Drug addiction, it changes people. Their personality gets lost. What about the case?'

'It's being assigned to one of the larger teams in Murder Investigation in West End Central, and DCI Harper is also now pursuing the drug angle with Thomas Hoffman's death.'

'What about you?'

'I'm off the case too, along with the rest of the team...' She looked over at Erika. 'How long are you signed off for?'

'I don't know. I've been told I can't work for a couple of weeks.'

'Seeing how you look, boss, no offence, but you'll need longer than a couple of weeks to get better.'

Erika looked at her face in the small mirror. One side was puffed up, as well as her bottom lip, and a large black bruise was starting to form. The gash above her eye was covered with a blood-spotted bandage, and her eye was red with burst blood vessels. 'You need to take it easy. I bet you're gonna be signed off for at least a few weeks. Enjoy some much needed time off.'

'Time off,' said Erika with a shudder. The words were alien to her.

'Yeah, take it easy, acquaint yourself with morning telly… I also let Peterson know, I hope that's okay?'

Erika looked at her reflection in the mirror again.

'Fine.'

'He wanted to come with me, but I thought that you could do with some space.'

Erika felt an overwhelming tiredness flood over her, and she tipped her head back and closed her eyes.

'I just need to go home. I just need to sleep, and I need more painkillers,' she said.

CHAPTER 29

FRIDAY, 11 AUGUST 2017

Me and Max are living together. Cohabiting, my mother would call it. If me and Mum were speaking.

We've got a council flat on the ground floor of a tower block in Kennington. I've never lived this side of the river. It's dodgy. Loads of lads hang around, selling drugs, but I feel safe when I'm with Max. I don't know if he's had words with them, or if they know him, but they give us a wide berth. There's black iron bars on all the windows, all the ground floor flats have bars, but ours has been re-done inside. The sofa and chairs in the living room are new, so is the kitchen and the bathroom suite. The front door opens out over the car park, and when I'm washing up at the window, people walk right past in the corridor. The bedroom window looks out over a main road, but there's a little bit of the London skyline; I can see Big Ben. Our mattress isn't new, though. I don't understand why the council made the effort to redecorate the place but gave us someone else's mattress? There was a brown stain on it. I hope it's tea, but Max turned it over and the other side was pristine.

After everything that's happened, it's a big step to properly live together. I'm happy. I have to be. We haven't had any visitors as I'm not talking to Mum, or Kath, or anyone else. I used to think I saw Max all the time and knew him, but living together is different. Most days he's out from early until late. 'Doing business', he says.

I've never asked him what he does. That sounds crazy, doesn't it? Even as I've written it down, and I'm looking at the words, it's... it's naive of me not to have asked him. When we worked at the chip shop, I assumed that was his job. But it was part-time, and he always seems to have cash, like the big wedge of cash he had to buy the car in Blackpool. It's drugs, I'm sure of it. He's involved with drugs, but he doesn't take them. He's proud of the fact he doesn't take them. He doesn't really drink, either. His only vice is his books. It took five car loads to get all his books into the flat, and he wouldn't let me unpack them from the boxes. They are all stacked around the walls of our bedroom, right up to the ceiling.

There was only one set of keys when we got the flat. I did ask Max to get another set cut, but he said he doesn't trust handing over our key to anyone. He said he'd been on the list for a council flat for years, but he'd turned one down in the past. He loved this one because it had bars on the windows.

When he leaves the house, he takes the key. I can't go anywhere. I have to stay in. It's fine. I know he loves me.

He wants me here for him.

CHAPTER 30

SUNDAY, 20 AUGUST

I was loading the washing machine this morning, and I heard Max shout my name. I came through to the kitchen, and the front door was open. The little mixed-race boy who lives upstairs was standing on the step by the kitchen door with his hands in the pockets of his jeans. He can't be more than five years old.

'This kid wants a piece of toast?' said Max.

'She made me some the other day,' said the little boy, pointing at me. He had chubby cheeks and a towering mass of Afro hair which was a rich, shiny brown. He was confident and well dressed for a five-year-old, in jeans, a bright blue Adidas T-shirt, and an expensive little pair of trainers. 'Can I have that jam?'

'So this kid, who has nicer shoes than me, eats my food?' said Max.

'I can see a whole loaf of bread on the counter. You can spare a piece, man!'

Despite their age gap, Max and the little boy were squaring up to each other, chests puffed, chins up, and hands outstretched.

'Does it look like I run a fucking canteen? Go on, piss off,' said Max, kicking the door shut. I could see the outline of the little boy through the frosted glass, and then he moved away. Max shook his head and sat back down, picking up the newspaper.

'It was just the once,' I said. 'The kids on this estate. I see them hanging around in the car park all day. Some of them can only be three or four, their mothers must chuck them out in the morning…'

He looked up from the paper with his angry eyes and my voice tailed off.

'That's cos their mothers are on the game, Nina. You think they should be indoors, with a Disney video playing, and the sound of Mum getting fucked in the background? And should I bust my arse all day to feed their bastard spawn?'

He took a bite of his toast and sat back, waiting for an answer. My legs started to shake.

'It was only when I took out the bin the other day. He was waiting at the door when I got back. He asked for a drink of water, and he cried, saying he was hungry…' I didn't tell him that I gave a little girl and another little boy some toast too.

The outline of the little boy appeared again through the door, and his small palms slapped against the frosted glass.

'Please, I want some toast… pleeeease,' he whined.

Max threw down the newspaper and got up. I flinched, but he moved past me to the door and yanked it open.

'Changed your mind?' he said, looking up at Max with a smug little grin.

Max grabbed the washing-up bowl from the sink, which was full of dirty water, and he dumped it over the little boy's head. All his cockiness vanished and he burst into tears, tea leaves, coffee grounds and some of last night's noodles sticking to his wet hair and T-shirt. The washing-up bowl clattered as Max chucked it in the sink, and he leaned down and hit him round the face. The boy fell back with a nasty thud on the concrete.

'Knock on my door again, and I'll fucking kill you. Then I'll kill your fucking whore mother,' said Max and he slammed the door. He wiped his hands on the dishcloth and sat down at the kitchen table with his newspaper. I could hear the little boy crying. 'Why did you do that to me?' he said in a voice so full of confusion that

I wanted to open the door, scoop him up, and give him a cuddle. But I was frozen, too scared to do anything.

'Don't just stand there. Make me another cup of tea,' said Max, his voice dangerously quiet.

I did as I was told.

The cries finally subsided outside, and I poured him some fresh tea. I wanted to put the radio on, but I knew that when Max was in one of his moods it was best not to do anything or make sudden movements. It was safer to blend into the background. Part of me felt relief that the little boy had borne the brunt of his outburst, and not me. Is that cowardice, or survival? Lately I'm wondering if they are the same thing.

There was a scrape of his chair as Max got up, and without looking at me, he picked up his keys, wallet and phone and left, slamming the door. I watched his outline through the frosted glass as he turned the key from the outside. Locking me in.

CHAPTER 31

TUESDAY, 10 OCTOBER 2017

It was a grim afternoon, the sky was almost black and rain was lashing against the window. Melanie Hudson had called on Erika with a uniformed officer, who had just taken a formal statement. The officer had just left, and Melanie decided to stay afterwards for a more informal chat, and check everything was okay.

'You know you have my full support,' she said, perching on the edge of the sofa in her smart skirt and jacket, her blonde hair sleek and neat. 'Taking a statement from you is a formality, Erika. I know you were in a terrible situation, and that your life was in danger. I am proud of how you dealt with the situation.'

'I was just doing my job. Am I under investigation?' asked Erika. Her voice was thick and a little slurred. The lights were all on in the living room, despite it being early afternoon, and the brightness seemed to intensify the bruising that had blossomed across her face. She shifted uncomfortably in her armchair. She was finding it hard to sit, lie, walk and pretty much do everything else.

'No, you're not under investigation,' said Melanie. 'We're signing you off for a month, that's to begin with. You'll need to keep us posted with what the doctor says. But I've been informed that you may need longer to recuperate. And I just want to say to you, that's fine. There will be no pressure to return until you feel able. Moving forward, let's keep communicating.'

'I'll need a couple of weeks,' said Erika, putting up her hand with the cast to wave the suggestion away. Melanie nodded sympathetically, deciding not to press the issue further. She looked around Erika's flat, at the sparse furnishing, the mess in the kitchen, piles of dirty dishes, an overflowing rubbish bin. 'Do you need any help?'

'What? Home help? Like some old biddy?'

'That's not what I meant...'

'You're offering to wash up?'

Melanie's eyes shifted back to the sink, and Erika wondered mischievously for a moment if Melanie would actually do her washing up if she asked. 'No, I'm fine. You could take the cellophane off this,' she said, pulling out a packet of cigarettes from the side of the armchair.

'Of course.' Melanie took the packet, peeled it off and opened the box, handing them back.

'You want one?' asked Erika, teasing one into the corner of her swollen mouth and lighting it with her good hand. For a moment, Melanie looked like she was going to say yes.

'No. Thank you. I gave up six years ago. Willpower and cold turkey.'

'Lucky you,' she said, exhaling with a wince. 'Who has the case? The double murder?'

'It's been passed over to DCI Jackson,' said Melanie. She saw a teacup on the coffee table overflowing with cigarette ends. She got up and went over to the kitchen.

'Never heard of him. What are you doing?'

'Looking for an ashtray.'

'Try one of the drawers.'

Melanie opened the top drawer with the photo of Mark. She paused for a second, but didn't say anything, closing it quickly. She carried on searching until she found a cut-glass ashtray in the bottom drawer. She came back and Erika took it, balanced it on the arm rest, and tapped the ash off her cigarette.

'You need to make sure DCI Jackson has the ANPR data that Moss was working through. The traffic cameras… I don't want it getting lost in the cracks.'

'The case files, and everything to do with the investigation, are all being passed over,' said Melanie. 'I will supervise the handover.'

'Okay… And there's a cab… a minicab…' Erika paused, losing her train of thought. She took another wincing drag on her cigarette. Melanie waited patiently for a moment as she put a hand to her forehead trying to remember.

'Have you ordered a minicab?'

'What? No, it's the bloody pills they've got me on, they're making my brain fuzzy. I'm still talking about the case. There was the cab driver, minicab driver who picked up Thomas Hoffman and Charlotte.'

'Charlene.'

'Yeah, Charlene. I was trying to get in contact with him, before, but he's been away on holiday… Australia. That needs to be followed up by the new team. He could be the only witness to…'

'Please. You need to rest. You need time to recuperate. You were involved in a nasty attack. Have you got anyone coming in to help? Friends or family?'

'Course I have,' said Erika defensively.

Melanie nodded. She knew Erika didn't have much family, and that they were in Slovakia. She was aware of a relationship of sorts with Peterson, and that Moss was a friend, but the rest of Erika's life was a bit of a mystery. Although, looking around the sparse flat, she wondered if Erika had much of a private life outside work.

Erika could see Melanie sizing her up, and the pity on her face was worse than the pain she was feeling.

'Are we done?' she said. Melanie picked up her bag and stood up.

'Yes, Erika. Phone me if you need anything, any time. If there's an emergency. If you need a lift to the hospital or to get some shopping. I can be your friend as well as your boss…'

Erika fixed her with a hard stare. She hated being pitied.

'But you're going on holiday next week?'

'Well, yes. I am.'

'For two weeks.'

'Yes.'

'So, you're just being polite?' There was an awkward pause, Melanie opened and closed her mouth. 'And where are you going? Yekaterinburg, in Russia?'

'Yes.'

'It's a cold and miserable place. Why aren't you taking him to Disneyland like every other normal parent?' Erika exhaled and fixed her with a cold stare. Melanie retrieved her coat from the back of the sofa.

'I'm just going to pretend that's the pain medication talking,' she said, and she let herself out of the flat, slamming the door.

Erika tipped her head back and flinched as her swollen face hit the side of the chair.

'Shit,' she said.

CHAPTER 32

MONDAY, 28 AUGUST 2017

Max has been locking me inside the flat for the past week. I should have said something the first time he did it, but I didn't, and when he came home, I'd made a big effort with my hair and make-up, and got dressed up. I served him dinner and then we had sex, and I felt an all-consuming lust and love for him. Nothing feels right without him. I need him. There's a voice inside me which disagrees, but it seems to be growing fainter by the day, a voice which tells me this isn't right.

I've been rationalising it in my mind, why he locks me in the flat. I keep telling myself I have all the food I need, clean clothes, a TV, computer. We've even got Netflix.

I've been watching the kids outside the window, playing in the car park. They give our front door a wide berth, and I miss them. I only gave them food and drink that one time; there's something healthy about talking to little kids. They see the world in such a pure, honest light. I'm sure if Max had locked them in, they'd have piped up: 'Why have you locked me in this room?' Just like the little boy asked Max: 'Why did you do that to me?' I've heard them knocking on the door of the old lady at the end. She's not very friendly, but she gives them water.

Last night, Max came home and actually made a joke about locking me in but I didn't realise at the time. He had a flower, a white lily, and he tucked it behind my ear, saying, 'You're my little Aung San Suu Kyi…' I didn't know who that was, so I just laughed, vacuously, hoping that this was the correct response. Later in bed, after we'd had sex and his breathing had settled down to a slow rhythm, I noticed one of the books piled up around the walls was written about Aung San Suu Kyi. I got up and slipped it out from its place between books about Nazi Germany. I flicked through it, and realised why he'd used that name. She was a political prisoner, who spent a long time under house arrest. Does Max think I'm dangerous, that I'll talk about things? That he has me under house arrest? He shifted in bed, so I quickly replaced the book and came back to lie beside him. I spend so much time running back over conversations we've had, and if we row, I try to work out how it happened. And what I did wrong.

I don't really sleep much at night. I like to watch Max sleep and feel his body close to mine, but I can't relax. I also have nightmares. I see the old man who stepped in front of the car. The man I killed. There. I've written it down. I killed a man. That's what I did. I killed him. He might have lived, and he probably would have died, but I took his life at that moment. I also have nightmares about that walk we did across Dartmoor to the waterfall. In the nightmare, Max and me are on the run and we've come to his hiding place, the cave under the waterfall. In my dreams, it's just like I remember it; the smooth half-hidden entrance, the high ceiling of undulating rock, but when we go inside, Dean is there, waiting. He's dead and rotting. Bits of flesh are hanging off his body. Max holds me down as Dean comes towards me, the veins pulsing in his forehead. Luckily, at that point I've always woken up. His body must still be there, buried deep in that well.

I've buried everything so deep in myself that I worry, one day, it's all going to come spewing out. For months after that journey home from Blackpool, I worried I would blurt it out to a stranger, or in a shop, or when I was on the phone with my mum.

I don't have to worry about the last one any more. That's why I decided to write this diary. I have to put that voice down on paper, the voice in my head that's slowly diminishing.

I'm terrified, but I'm in love, and this person who I put my soul into, who I can't live without, is someone I don't understand. Someone who wants to keep me, like a possession.

There's a huge mirror screwed to the wall in our bedroom, and I keep this diary hidden between the back of it and the wall.

CHAPTER 33

WEDNESDAY, 30 AUGUST 2017

Max arrived home with two people tonight. He didn't offer any explanation as he unlocked the door and they filed into the kitchen after him. There was a big, scruffy, dark-haired guy and this pretty blonde woman. The guy introduced himself as Thomas. The woman said she was Charlene. Thomas was lanky and a bit sweaty, but he had a rugged handsomeness. Charlene was pretty with nice clothes, and she had a Mulberry handbag, which I assumed was a fake. Max took them through to the living room and told me to make some drinks.

'What kind of drinks? Tea?' I asked.

'No. Something stronger. That Black Label Smirnoff with Coke, in the decent glasses.'

I fixed four drinks and stuck in some ice, then came through to the living room. Max had the TV on VH1, and they were watching Lady Gaga's 'Poker Face' video. Thomas was sitting next to Max, and Charlene was in the armchair. They were all smoking. I put down the drinks and as I reached down to get the ashtray from the shelf under the coffee table, I smelt the leather of her Mulberry bag. The rich fragrance of supple leather.

'Is that real or fake?' I asked.

'Real,' she said, absentmindedly sipping at her drink. She swallowed and did that gurning thing with her chin that druggies do.

'Can I hold it?' I asked.

Charlene shrugged and nodded, then her eyes sort of rolled back in her head for a moment. Thomas didn't seem to be on drugs, and was talking to Max about his ex-wife, Mariette.

'She's getting worse with her cleaning. When I saw her the other day, her hands were red raw from all the bleach. It hurt me to look at them…' he was saying.

My attention went back to Charlene's bag. I picked it up. It was soft and luxurious, a beautiful dark blue, and it had a buttery coloured lining. 'I've always wanted a handbag like this. They're crazy expensive.'

'Yeah, they are…' she said, but her eyes were on Max. He had placed a long wide wooden box on the coffee table. It was old, with a two-tone pattern of light and dark wood.

He lifted the lid and nestled inside, in neat rows, were bags of white powder, pills, a block of something brown which looked like muscovado sugar, but I knew it was cannabis resin. Lady Gaga's 'Paparazzi' was now playing on the TV, but the atmosphere in the room was almost studious. Max took out eight little bags of cocaine from the wooden box.

'I need my handbag back,' snapped Charlene, grabbing it from me. She started to rummage around inside for her wallet and took out a credit card and a £10 note.

Max opened one of the little bags and tipped a small amount of the white powder onto the glass tabletop. Charlene knelt down and cut two lines of the powder. Rolling up the note, she snorted one and then offered the note to Thomas, but he declined. She sat back on the carpet, and wiped her nose and snorted.

'Told you it was good shit,' said Max, watching and smiling as the effects washed over her. Thomas rubbed at his sweaty face with a huge hand.

'You alright, love,' he said, reaching out and touching her shoulder. He had a kinder face. Hers was pretty but pinched, and a bit mean.

'How long have you two been together?' I asked. Max shot me a look.

'A couple of months,' said Thomas proudly, getting up off the sofa and sitting on the carpet next to Charlene. Her eyes rolled in the sockets and her head flopped back. He pulled her into him for a hug. She farted loudly. It stank, and a moment later I got up and opened the window. Max shot me another look, but there was mirth in his eyes.

'Doing a line always gives her a bit of wind, especially after the purer stuff,' said Thomas, as if she'd had nothing more than a couple of slices of brown bread with a high fibre content. There was something a bit creepy about the way Thomas protectively held Charlene, like he owned her. Like she was a possession. After a few minutes and a couple more Lady Gaga songs played on the TV, Charlene seemed to come back to her senses.

'That is such good shit, Max,' she said. Leaning forward, she swept the six bags of cocaine off the coffee table into her Mulberry. 'I do have to owe you…'

There was a long silence. Max looked at them for a long moment.

'You know she's good for it, Max,' said Thomas, putting his arm around her again, but she shrugged it off, and got to her feet.

'He knows I'm good for it,' she said confidently.

''Course,' said Max.

She licked her finger, and pressed it against the last of the white powder on the table and rubbed it into her gums.

When they were gone, I started to clear away the cups and clean the table.

'How long have you been a drug dealer?' I asked, spraying multi-surface cleaner on the coffee table and wiping it with a cloth. Max was stuffing the box in his backpack.

'Sorry about that. I don't like to do business at home,' he said. He came over to me and I straightened up, shaking out the cloth.

'It's dangerous,' I said, looking up into his eyes, which were glowing with warmth.

He shook his head. 'I'm high up in the organisation. And it's better for you not to know anything, okay?'

I nodded.

'And business has been good lately. I was going to get you one of those Mulberry bags.'

'Really?' I said.

'Yeah, only the best for my girl.'

And the sad thing was, I believed him.

CHAPTER 34

TUESDAY, 12 SEPTEMBER

Just after six this evening, a Jaguar drove into the car park. A small green Jaguar, like the one James Bond drives. It roared up in the shitty potholed car park out back, bouncing along past a few shitty old cars and kids playing. It screeched to a halt outside the window. Max climbed out, tucking his long blond hair behind his ears. He had on jeans and a brown leather jacket and he looked pretty damn sexy. He unlocked the door and was grinning. I hadn't seen him grin for a long time.

'What's this?' I asked.

'Your chariot. Fancy a spin?'

'I was about to cook…'

'Fuck that.' He smiled.

He grabbed my arm, and pulled me over to it. Several of the neighbours had come out to their balconies and were staring, and the younger girls in particular, the pram faces who give me dirty looks, were so jealous.

He opened the passenger door, and I got in. It was so new and luxurious with leather seats and the dashboard was made of a polished wood. We drove through Kennington and up into central London. I was struck by the smell of the leather. Supple leather. It turned me on, and Max too. I could see he was getting hard in his trousers, but when I put my hand there, he took it gently and placed it back on my leg.

'Later. I want to do something first,' he said.

We drove up to Primrose Hill, and the sun was setting as we parked up, looking out over London. He unclipped his seatbelt, and went to the back, returning with a wicker hamper.

'What's this?' I said.

He helped me to push my seat right back and he placed it in the footwell at my feet. Inside was a bottle of champagne with two of those long, thin glasses, there was cheese and olives and crackers, and a lavender-coloured cardboard box filled with cakes – the posh types that glisten with fresh fruit on top. My mouth dropped open.

'You catching flies, Neen?'

'No. I'm just shocked… Happy shocked,' I added quickly.

He squeezed open the champagne with a pop and filled the two glasses. The foam rose quickly in one of them and he leaned forward and sucked it up with a slurp, and then belched.

'Shit, not very classy. You can tell I was never a waiter,' he said, handing me a glass. 'To us, to you, Neen. The best thing that's happened to me.' I clinked glasses with him. 'I know I've been a nightmare, Neen. But it's me and you. Me and you, and I love you.'

'I love you too,' I said. I was reeling inside. I looked around at the car, at him, and at the sun setting golden over London stretching out ahead of us.

'I always wanted to come here. Did you ever read *The 101 Dalmatians*?'

I shook my head. 'No. I saw the film.'

'The book is leagues better. I love how the dogs come up to Primrose Hill for the Twilight Barking, and they talk to each other, they talk to other dogs miles away.'

'That's not true though?'

'I like to think it is. And we don't have a fucking clue what dogs are actually saying when they bark. I like the idea that when dogs bark they are talking to each other. Stupid, though, isn't it?' he said, running his hands through his hair.

'No. It's not. It's magical,' I said. And it felt magical there with him. I felt like I did when I first got together with him that first night when I stopped at the traffic lights near Santino's chip shop and he climbed in my car. He smiled and topped up my glass.

'One day we'll have a car like this, Neen. I promise you.' I smiled and nodded, not wanting to risk breaking his mood with a question, but he answered it for me. 'You remember that couple who came round the other night, Charlene and Thomas?'

'I won't forget her farting. That's etched on my brain.'

Max smiled for a moment, then he was serious. 'She still owes me for the gear she bought.'

'How much?'

'Enough. She's a trust fund kid, her dad owns a car dealership. I've taken this car as insurance: she gets it back when I get my money. And when I get my money, it will be with a hefty chunk of interest.'

'You didn't?'

'What? Beat them up? No. It was her idea, stupid cow. Fucking rich kids are the worst. Daddy has cut off her allowance, but he always relents, apparently. In the long run, I'll make even more money off the stupid bitch.'

I nodded and bit into an olive.

'These are delicious,' I said.

'They better be, they cost enough.' He looked at me and ran his tongue around his teeth.

'What?'

'I wasn't going to do this until later, but fuck it.' He opened the door, got out of the car and went around to the back, returning with a giant shopping bag which he placed in my lap. It was a luxurious grey, and had a bow on top and the Mulberry logo embossed in gold. He saw my shock.

'Go on, open it,' he said.

He took my glass and I undid the bow; inside was another box, and when I lifted the lid and pulled away the tissue, there, nestling inside, was a Mulberry handbag in red. I took it out, pawing the material, the folds of soft fabric. I put it to my nose and inhaled the fresh leather; the lining inside was cream.

'Oh, Max. This is real?' I asked.

''Course,' he said, smiling. I hugged it to my chest and felt such joy. 'And you should look inside, in the pocket.' I dived in and searched the lining, finding the pocket and pulling out a silver key. 'It's for the flat. I'm sorry. I've kind of been a bit crazy lately about sharing everything with you. I don't trust people easily and I trust you.'

I felt a huge wave of love and relief. I launched myself on him, covering his face with kisses. He started the engine and we drove off and found a quiet road with a dead end. He told me to take off all my clothes and get on the back seat. The leather felt incredible on my skin, and as he pressed his warm body onto mine I truly believed that everything would be okay.

I tried to hold on to this feeling for as long as I could.

CHAPTER 35

FRIDAY, 15 SEPTEMBER

The Jaguar has been here for a few days. This is a rough block, but I can tell that everyone is scared of Max. Each morning we've got up and there it is, still shining in the car park, untouched and in pristine condition. As the days have passed, I've felt Max's mood darken. I've wanted to ask how much money Charlene and Thomas owe him, but I haven't dared.

Then they showed up at the door very early this morning, when we were eating breakfast. Charlene looked out of it, and was well dressed as usual, but her eyes were dilated and there was an unwashed smell about her. Thomas was sweating, and his Man United T-shirt had damp patches under the arms.

They sat down at the kitchen table and I got up and busied myself making tea. Max listened with his arms crossed, as Charlene cried, and Thomas explained that Charlene's parents have cut her off.

'They always pay her monthly allowance, even in the past when they've said they'd cut her off, they haven't meant it…'

'So. I get to keep the Jaguar, that was the deal,' said Max.

'Nooo!' cried Charlene. 'My dad would get the police involved if you did that.'

'So that car you left, as insurance against what you owe me, is worthless?' said Max.

'It's from my dad's dealership!' shrilled Charlene, her eyes wide and chin gurning. 'He's minted, a millionaire! Max, I can get the money from him!'

'But they've cut you off…' She was lost for words and turned to Thomas, but he looked at the floor. 'So, what are the chances of them handing over £6,000?'

'Six thousand! The gear was only, only £2,000!' said Thomas.

Max tilted his head, and I could see them both shrink back. He got up, and I moved out of the way as he opened the cutlery drawer and took out a large carving knife. Grabbing an apple from the bowl, he came back to the table. Charlene and Thomas couldn't take their eyes off the blade.

'I need my money,' he said softly, the knife glinting as he sliced and twisted, the red peel growing in a long ribbon from the flesh of the apple. 'Now, you're not going to sit there crying. You're going to come up with a solution. Fast.'

'Max, that's why we came here,' said Thomas, forcing a smile to his lips. He had beads of sweat on his forehead, and his large hands were shaking. He put them under the table. Charlene rummaged around in her bag,

'Max. I have a key to my parents' house,' she said, holding it up. 'They'll be away today at my brother's. Looking after his kids. They always keep money in the house… I know the combination for the safe, and there's jewellery.' Max put a piece of the apple in his mouth and chewed slowly. Her eyes were wide and she gave him a manic smile. 'What if I gave Nina my Mulberry bag?' she added, holding it up. It was now scuffed and a little grubby. I went to say something but Max put up his hand.

'Nina is not having your scaggy old bag as part payment. She's got her own.'

'Yeah. I've got my own bag. In red,' I said. Charlene lowered her head, and looked like a beaten-up dog. She started to cry again.

'I'm immune to druggie's tears,' said Max. 'But we will come and collect the six grand you owe.'

'You will?' said Thomas, taking Charlene's hand in his.

'Yes. Right now, but you two try any funny business and I swear to God, I'll kill you,' said Max. He looked at me, and I nodded in agreement, feeling a surge of power.

Max was in charge, and I was with him.

It took a few hours to get over to Slough, where Charlene's father had his car dealership. We parked the Jaguar outside the front gate and got a minicab to her parents' house. I thought this was all too risky, but Max said that where rich people were concerned the rules were different. Her parents would be out, and we would be letting ourselves in with a key, and as Charlene was the only one with a key, she would be the one to take the blame.

'They can't say we broke in. We've got a key,' he said, adding, 'I want you with me if anything goes wrong, it will look like we're guests. A couples thing…'

I wasn't sold on it, but things had been good between us: he'd given me the bag, and the memory of that picnic on Primrose Hill was still warm in my stomach.

When we got to the house, it was seriously posh. Iron gates, a long driveway. At the top of a driveway was a huge fish pond, and it was a really beautiful garden. I could see how mad Max was getting when he saw all of this.

'She grew up amongst this? Had all this opportunity? I fucking hate her even more,' he hissed in my ear. When we got to the front door she put her key in but it didn't work.

'They must have changed the locks,' she said, looking back at them all.

'What about the back door, babe?' asked Thomas. He was now sweating, and the hair was sticking to his bald patch. 'Wait here,' he added to me and Max, and they disappeared around the back. The minicab driver was waiting in the car, parked up by the fountain, and he was absorbed in his phone. I walked over to the fountain and peered down into its depths where some huge fish swam, covered in blotches of red and white.

Suddenly an alarm went off. I looked up and a blue light was flashing on a box on the front of the house. It was very loud, and it cut through the silence. Max looked agitated, and went to the windows and peered inside. He pulled out his phone and tried a number, but there was no answer.

'Mate, I'm out of here,' said the minicab driver, starting the engine.

'Wait!' said Max. He pulled me around the fountain and we got in.

'What the fuck is going on?' said the driver as he floored the accelerator, spraying up the gravel in the driveway.

'We thought she had a key; it's her parents' house,' I said.

We zoomed down the long drive with the sound of the alarms still ringing behind us. We came to the large iron gates, and he slowed.

'If these don't open automatically,' started the driver, but there was a pause and they swung inwards. We were halfway along the smart avenue when two police cars passed us, but Max didn't look relieved.

'They still owe me six fucking grand,' he growled in my ear.

CHAPTER 36

MONDAY, 16 OCTOBER 2017

Erika sat in front of the TV with a cup of coffee and a cigarette. She was watching it side on, glancing out of the window periodically at the leaves falling from the trees into the car park. It was almost like she couldn't quite acknowledge the fact she was enjoying watching television mid-morning on a weekday. It was a show about botched plastic surgery procedures. She'd seen it last week, and it occurred to her when she was making coffee that the show was on and she was eager not to miss it. She lit up another cigarette and grimaced as on screen a woman was showing the two plastic surgeons how her butt implant surgery had gone wrong, leaving her with one cheek bigger than the other.

A week had passed since she'd been discharged from the hospital, and she was feeling a little more like herself again. The swelling had gone down on her face, and she was able to manage the pain. Moss had called around a couple of times with food, and despite Erika's protests, had cleaned up a little, done a load of washing for her, and even been shopping for fruit, ready meals and cigarettes.

'I'm happy to help, but I draw the line at putting you in the shower and washing your naughty bits,' she'd said on her last visit. It had been the first time Erika had laughed, and with her cracked rib, it had really hurt.

The surgeons on screen were about to operate on the woman's vast misshapen bottom, when the front door bell buzzed. She heaved herself out of the chair with a wince, and shuffled through to open it. She was surprised to see Peterson outside.

'Hello,' he said. He was holding a casserole dish.

'Hi.'

'Ouch, Moss said you'd been in the wars.' He peered at the bruising on her face and she put her hand with the cast up self-consciously.

'Did she?'

'Yeah. She's been keeping me in the loop. You broke your wrist?'

'And fractured a rib.'

He was dressed in blue jeans and a smart black winter coat with a red scarf. He was clean shaven, and his face was still thin, but he seemed to have more energy.

'Come in,' she said, standing to one side.

'Are you going somewhere?' he asked, stepping into the hallway and seeing a suitcase by the front door.

'Yeah. I'm going to see Lenka in Slovakia. Stay with her for a bit, see the kids. The baby is now walking, well, she's not a baby anymore. I've been signed off for a few weeks, and I'm going a bit crazy, so I thought it would be a good time to go.'

They came through to the living room. The woman on screen was lying face down on the operating table and the surgeon was pulling a large silicone implant from one of her buttocks. Erika picked up the remote and switched it off. The flat was silent, and they could hear the wind whistling around the building and the rustle of the piles of dry leaves being whirled around the car park. 'I've never spent so much time in this flat. I didn't realise how dead and quiet it was during the day.'

'Tell me about it. When are you off?'

'This afternoon.'

He put the casserole dish down on the kitchen counter. 'So this is no good?'

'I can freeze it.'

'Mum made it. She sends her love…' There was an awkward pause. 'Can I make you a coffee?'

'I'm fine, do you want one?' she asked.

'Still can't have it…' he said, patting his stomach lightly. They were both still standing, and Erika indicated for him to sit.

'I've thought about you over the last week, in the silences in this flat…' She shook her head. "That sounded more morbid and weird than I meant it to. I've been thinking about all those weeks and months you were stuck at home.'

'Now you see how it feels.'

'Yeah. Even though I saw what you were going through, I didn't *get* it. I'm sorry, James.'

'Erika. We've been through this.'

'But I want you to know how sorry I am, about everything.' She gave him a smile and then winced. The side of her face was still sore. He smiled back.

'Can I just get a water?'

'Sure.'

He got up and moved to the kitchen, finding a glass and filling it. She thought how different he was from the last few weeks. He was moving normally, and had a spring back in his step. He sat on the sofa, took a sip of the water, and then had to push aside a pile of books and magazines to find a spot on the coffee table for the glass.

'You seem better,' she said.

'I am. The doctor says I've turned a corner. I've started eating properly. My appetite came back with a bang a few days ago, and the difference is remarkable. I'm sleeping again… *Having regular bowel movements*,' he added, jokily putting a hand to the side of his mouth and pulling a face. 'I never realised how important these things are to your wellbeing and happiness, until they were gone.'

'That's great. When do you go back to work?'

'Still a few weeks, but I'm still taking it easy. I hope to start training in the gym soon. Low impact stuff.'

He noticed her arm in the cast resting on the side of the armchair.

'I didn't come here to… to gloat, or anything. I came to repay the favours.'

'What favours?'

'You came to see me all those times, you brought food, and you dealt with my bad moods.'

'Those weren't favours, James. I came as, well, it doesn't matter now.'

'My girlfriend,' he said.

'Yeah. Although, I think I stopped being that to you long ago.'

Peterson didn't say anything, and he looked past her out of the window. Erika wished she'd left the TV on. The wind moaned and wailed as it blew around the corners of the building.

'You don't want to…' he started.

'Get back together?'

He swallowed and rubbed his hands awkwardly. 'Erika. I thought we were just friends?'

'We are. But thanks for the update. I now know how you feel,' said Erika, recoiling at his tone, which indicated that he was letting her down gently.

'Did you think we were getting back together?'

'No!'

'Then what?' he asked.

'I don't know. You're British. I thought it was part of the deal that as a British person you never talk about your feelings. I thought we were just going to let it fizzle out.'

He nodded. 'OK. Good.'

'OK, good? Did you come here to put the official stamp on things? To dump me?'

'No! But you brought this up.'

'No. I didn't,' she said.

'Erika, you just did, I was coming here just to give you some food and say hi.'

'Well, you brought the food. You said hi. You can fuck off.'

He shook his head. 'You can be such a bitch.'

'Yeah, well, I've been called worse.'

He got up, and went to leave then stopped.

'Erika. We are going to have to work together, and I want to put on the record that I don't blame you for what happened. Things have changed between us, that's all. Our relationship just wasn't meant to be. Can we just move on, be friends?'

'You just called me a bitch and now you want to be friends.'

'I said you can be a bitch. I didn't say you are one.'

'Well, seeing as we're putting things on the record, you are an arsehole to come here when I feel like shit and start this!' She felt tears prickling her eyes and she put a hand up. 'Just go... GO!'

He stood his ground for a moment longer, went to say something, but then changed his mind and left.

Erika looked at the clock and willed the hours to pass. She wanted to get away, to leave everything behind for a while. It was all too much.

CHAPTER 37

SATURDAY, 16 SEPTEMBER 2017

Max has heard nothing from Charlene and Thomas. He came home late last night, drunk, and demanding food. I gave him a plate of pasta. I'd made it earlier in the evening, but after a few hours in the pan it had dried out. He shoved a forkful in his mouth and then spat it out.

'What's this?'

'I made it earlier. I didn't know when you'd be back,' I said. I was sitting opposite him at the kitchen table, and I had that familiar sinking feeling of dread when I knew things were about to turn bad. It's like the air starts to buzz around my ears, and a cold trickling feeling starts in my stomach. I begin to sweat and shake, because I know, whatever I do, however I answer, it will be wrong.

'This is fucking dog food,' he said, stabbing at it with his fork. 'You think it's okay to feed me food not fit for a fucking dog?'

I tried to catch my breath as I started to cry.

'Oh, turning on the tears now, are we?'

'You're scaring me!' I cried.

He threw the plate of pasta at the wall behind me. I felt the sauce splatter my back.

'Why are you just sitting there? Clean it up.'

I pushed back, the chair scraping as I slowly got up.

'Clean it UP!'

I flinched as he came around the table, grabbed the back of my hair and turned my head to the wall. A streak of red was smeared down it. 'What is this shit? I work my arse off and you make this shit.'

I squeezed my eyes shut. Trying to clamp down my emotions, but tears escaped and ran down my face. I thought things had been getting better, but then this shit had happened with Charlene and Thomas, and now he was taking it all out on me.

'Would you eat this?' he said, still gripping my head and picking up a handful of the cold pasta.

'I did eat it...' I didn't get the rest of the words out because he shoved a handful of the pasta into my mouth and rubbed the rest over my face. I tried to spit it out, but he kept his hand on the back of my head and the other pushing the sloppy mess into my mouth. I could feel it slipping to the back of my throat, and I couldn't breathe. The sauce was in my eyes and it stung and I couldn't see. Max suddenly let go and I dropped down on the floor heaving and trying to get my breath.

I heard the back door slam and the lock turn. I cleaned myself up, and the mess, and it was then that I saw he had taken my phone.

This can't continue. I'm going to leave him. When he comes back, I'm going to have a knife ready, and I'm walking out.

CHAPTER 38

MONDAY, 18 SEPTEMBER

I sat at the kitchen table all night, facing the door with a huge carving knife on the table in front of me, but Max didn't come back. In the early morning sunlight, I got up and made some tea, and saw the neighbours outside starting to go about their business. The old lady down the hall went past with her shopping bags. The kids started to play, and my panic eased.

Sunday went by so slowly, and then the sun began to set. I worried how I would get out if there was a fire. How I would escape. The iron safety bars are screwed outside each window, like a cage. The back door is made of stout wood with safety glass in the window. There is no way out.

At three in the morning, I woke up with a gasp. I felt about in the bedsheets and found the handle of the carving knife. Rain was slapping against the window, and I jumped as thunder cracked and rumbled. I came out of the bedroom with the knife held out in front of me. The living room and bathroom were empty. I came into the kitchen and got a drink of water. I sat at the table in the dark, listening to the storm. The lightning flickered, illuminating the walls.

Then I heard the sound of a car pull into the car park, it bounced over the water-filled potholes and the headlights shone through the blinds, casting a grid of light above my head, before it slid along the wall. It was replaced by a dim red light. The car had turned around. The red lights intensified and the hum of the engine got louder.

I got up, thinking that the car was going to reverse through the kitchen wall. I poked my finger through the blind and saw the car was parked up with the boot inches from the back door. Max got out. He was drenched. I let go of the blind, and stood braced with the carving knife held out in front of me. My hand was shaking as I heard the key scrape in the lock, and the outline of Max appeared through the frosted glass. The key turned and the door swung open. Thunder cracked loudly, and the rain echoed on the concrete walkway. I moved towards the door, and Max had his back to me, opening the boot.

He turned.

'Jeez! What are you doing, Neen?' he whispered, seeing me with the knife. He looked genuinely confused as to why I would be pointing it at him. His clothes were soaked through, his long blond hair hung wet around his shoulders and he had a smear of earth on his cheek. His eyes had lost the psychotic coldness from the other evening, and he looked scared.

'What are you doing?' I said, keeping the knife pointed at him.

'I need your help, please,' he whispered, putting up his finger to his lips. 'Put your coat on and give me a hand.'

I was so weirded out by his change of mood, so relieved to see him, that I came back inside and pulled on my long coat, belting it up over my pyjamas. I put a baseball cap on my head and, still holding the knife, I came back towards the kitchen.

I stopped in the doorway. I could see the boot of the car was open, and Max had his arms under the shoulders of a man's body, and was dragging it into the kitchen. He dropped it in the middle of the floor, and went back through the door. The head bounced off the lino, and the arms flopped out. I recognised the grubby jeans and football T-shirt before the face. It was Thomas.

Max put his head around the door as there was another crack of thunder and lightning.

'I need a hand,' he said, as if it were shopping bags he had in the car.

I walked past the body, and outside into the corridor. The windows along from us were dark. I joined Max at the rear passenger door of the car where he was pulling out the body of Charlene.

'Help me with the legs.'

'No,' I said, shaking my head, and came back inside.

A moment later Max followed and dumped Charlene's body beside Thomas.

'I'm just going to put the car back where it normally goes,' said Max. He closed the door and left me with the two bodies. I felt like I had experienced death and trauma over the past few months but nothing prepares you for the surreal experience of having two dead people laid out in your kitchen. I wanted to laugh. It wasn't funny, but a laugh escaped my mouth. It didn't sound like a laugh though. It was a strange panicked sound. Charlene's clothes were torn. She wore a long skirt and a blue blouse, but the buttons were open and one of her breasts was showing over the cup of her bra. Her blonde hair was matted with blood, and her nose was completely flat. Thomas's face was a bloody mess, and his arms were flopped out at a funny angle.

The back door closing snapped me out of staring. Max was inside with two large suitcases which he'd propped against the counter. He checked the blinds were closed and tied back his hair, pulling an elastic band from his wrist. He went to the sink and took out the big roll of black bin liners. He tore one off and shook it open.

'Can you hold it, Neen?'

I shook my head. I still had the knife; I was gripping it, but it was like it wasn't there. He gave it no more than a glance, and took off Thomas's then Charlene's shoes and dumped them in the bin liner. As he bent down to do it, I saw the butt of a gun poking out from the back of his jeans. I saw myself moving over, pulling it out and shooting him. It would take no more than a few seconds.

He now had a pair of scissors and, with a whistle of fabric cutting, he slit Thomas's football shirt up the front and one of the arms. He caught the skin at the top of Thomas's right arm and swore, but cut the rest of it off and then dropped it in the bin liner. There was a thick layer of dark hair across Thomas's chest, but his skin didn't look real; it was a pale yellow. Max turned and started to cut off the jeans, which wasn't as easy.

'You killed them?' I said.

'Yes. They were gonna leave the country. They'd booked flights to go to Jersey.'

'How did you find out?'

'I've got mates. I know people who keep an eye out for these things, when people owe money.'

'Jersey? Why Jersey?'

'I dunno, something to do with her dad. What a couple of fuckers. They were clearing off, leaving for good…'

He was now cutting off the right leg of the jeans. Charlene's body shifted on the kitchen floor and she sat up. I was too afraid to move, but finally I screamed as she reached up with a strange misshapen arm and lifted the gun out of Max's trousers.

'Jesus Christ!' he said.

Charlene was sitting up, and trying to move her legs. One of her eyes was swollen shut, and she transferred the gun to her unbroken hand, which shook as she pointed it at Max. There was a deafening bang. I'd never heard a real gun go off, and the force of it threw her arm back, but she made a strange moaning sound and held the gun up again, pointing it shakily at Max's chest.

He looked at me, and I realised I still had the knife. I knocked her arm away and sank the long blade of the knife between her breasts, up to the hilt. She struggled under me, but I pushed her back onto the kitchen floor and sank the knife in deeper, twisting it until she was still again.

'Jeez, Neen,' said Max, looking at me in awe as he retrieved the gun and checked the bullets.

I ran to the bathroom and threw up in the sink. I locked the door and took a shower, staying under the water for a long time, until I was numb from the cold. When I went back in the kitchen, Max was mopping a vast pool of blood off the floor, and there was a meat cleaver in the sink. A bin liner by the sink contained Thomas and Charlene's clothes, and by the front door sat two bulging suitcases. Blood was oozing from the bottom of both.

'We need to clean this up, then dump the suitcases in the river before it gets light,' said Max.

I was shocked at how in control I now felt.

'Okay,' I said. 'What about the gunshot. It was loud...'

'The police would have been here by now. And this is a rough estate.'

I nodded and took the mop from him. I had killed Charlene to save Max's life. She would have shot him in the chest. I no longer felt like a victim. I felt in control, and for the first time I felt I was Max's equal. Things had happened to me that I would never be able to come back from. I would never be able to go back. I had to move forward, and I had to survive.

'I know a place by the river. It's quiet and there are no cameras,' I said.

It was almost four in the morning when we loaded up the suitcases and drove out to a run-down industrial estate in Battersea Park. It was an old printworks I used to visit with Dad when I used to go with him on his deliveries during the summer holidays. Dad delivered fizzy drinks all round London.

We parked at the side of the crumbling office blocks and heaved the two suitcases to a small jetty next to the river. There was very little light and the water was an expanse of black.

We dumped the suitcases with Thomas and Charlene's bodies in the river, throwing them as far out as we could, and with a splash they were gone, sucked down into the water rushing past.

Max put his arm around me and we stood there for a long time, watching the water. It looked black, like ink.

CHAPTER 39

WEDNESDAY, 1 NOVEMBER 2017

It was early evening as Erika climbed down from the back of her brother-in-law's Jeep Cherokee. It was high up off the ground and stepping down from it seemed to aggravate her cracked rib, which was almost healed. With her good arm, she helped out her niece, Karolina, and nephew, Jakub. Despite the dark, cold evening, the car park outside the cemetery was busy and she told them to keep close.

They were dressed in their best clothes, as was Erika. A group of old ladies walked past in smart black coats, gold jewellery and coiffed hair. They each held a large plastic green wreath with vivid coloured flowers and joined the end of the line waiting to file in through the cemetery gates. Hundreds of tea lights and votive candles blazed next to a statue of the Virgin Mary embedded in the wall beside the gates, and Erika could see a carpet of candles glowing inside.

The first of November was celebrated as All Saints Day. It was an important day in Slovakia, and in the early evening, the crowds were pouring into the cemetery. Erika's sister, Lenka, appeared around the car pushing the buggy with two-year-old Evka, who was dressed in a smart black winter coat and black bobble hat.

'Look at your face!' cried Lenka to Jakub, who had a smear of chocolate on his chin. She pulled out a hanky and spat on it.

'Mamiiiiii!' he shouted, pulling away.

'My face is clean,' added Karolina.

'Jakub, come here. You are not going to Grandma's grave with a messy face!'

'Here,' said Erika, pulling a packet of make-up remover wipes from the pocket of her coat. 'These don't have spit in them.' She crouched down and Karolina helped her open the pack, and pulled one out. Erika still had her right wrist strapped up in a plaster cast. She gently wiped her nephew's cherubic face, and he crossed his eyes and stuck out his tongue, making her laugh.

Erika's brother-in-law, Marek, came out of the car to join them, talking on the phone. He was a huge imposing man, with a shaved head, but he had kind brown eyes. He'd put on a black suit for the occasion and Erika thought how well he scrubbed up. Just as he ended the call, his phone rang again. The ringtone was 'Gangnam Style' and it cut through the sombre mood.

'*Ty si sedlac*,' hissed Lenka.

'It's business!' he said, rolling his eyes, but he took the call, and moved off up the car park.

'This is one of the most religious days of the year, and he's doing business beside a graveyard!'

'Yes. He's selling a lot of ice cream in November,' muttered Erika, giving Lenka a look. She finished wiping Jakub's face, and he gave her a gummy smile with his two front teeth missing.

'Don't you start,' said Lenka.

'I like you being here, Auntie Erika,' said Jakub. 'Please can you stay for ever?'

Erika had been staying with them now for a couple of weeks, and she had been made to feel part of the family. Of course, she *was* part of the family, but she'd forgotten how things worked in Slovakia. Families rubbed together, often arguing, but were always honest with each other, and that honesty was underscored with love and loyalty. Erika thought back to when Mark's relations would come to stay. It was always a time where everyone was on their best behaviour, and it was exhausting.

Jakub and Karolina were looking up at her, waiting for an answer,

'I can't stay for ever, but I'll be here a little longer, until I'm all healed up.' She smiled.

'Tell us again how you fought those two men with guns!' cried Jakub, grabbing her hand.

'How did it feel to shoot them?' asked Karolina.

'It was a taser I shot them with. It's not a gun, it fires an electric shock into...' started Erika, but a couple of old ladies walking past gave her a funny look. 'Maybe we should talk about this afterwards when we go for hot chocolate.'

'Daddy's got a gun; he keeps it in a Batman lunchbox,' said Jakub.

'That's enough talk, let's get moving,' said Lenka as she took a wreath of flowers and a packet of tea lights from the back of the jeep. She shoved the wreath at Marek, who was still on the phone.

'Have you seen her belt,' mouthed Karolina. Erika looked at the belt on Lenka's coat. The buckle was emblazoned with the words 'GOLD DIGGA'. 'She doesn't know what "Gold Digger" means,' added Karolina.

'Take these candles,' said Lenka, handing the tea lights to Karolina. 'It's a brand. A very exclusive brand. I got it from Bratislava.'

'A Gold Digger is a woman who sleeps with a rich man just for his money,' piped up Karolina. Erika stifled a smile. Lenka wasn't listening. She went over to Marek and told him to get off the phone, then they made their way into the cemetery.

It was the biggest cemetery in the town of Nitra, and stretched away for several acres with a carpet of lights twinkling into the far distance. It was crowded with people moving amongst the gravestones, and Erika looked at the candles in coloured jars and ornate glass holders as they passed each stone. The trees above still had the last of their autumn leaves, and the light from the mass of candles was reflected with a warm orange glow. They walked in silence for a few minutes, and then found the gravestone for Erika and Lenka's parents. It was simple with grey marble and gold lettering.

FRANTIŠEK BOLDIŠ   IRENA BOLDIŠOVA
       1950–1980   1953–2005

Lenka lay the wreath of flowers on the marble, and the kids set to work clearing away the candles which had burnt down and replacing them. As Erika helped Jakub light a small tea light and drop it into one of the votive candleholders, she looked at the names written in gold on the stone. She had been eight, and Lenka six when their father died. He was a distant memory, and Erika could only recall snapshots of him in their childhood; when he came home from work at the plastics factory with a pocket filled with sweets; a holiday when they went camping beside a lake and they took it in turns to sit on his shoulders as he walked out into the deep water.

The memory was still vivid in her mind of the night there was a knock at the door of their flat. A policeman was outside with the building manager. Erika could still hear her mother's wails when they informed her that he'd been killed in an accident at the factory. Lenka had been too tiny to understand, and Erika had taken her to their room and they'd played with dolls for hours and hours, not knowing what to do.

Over the next ten years, Erika and Lenka had watched their mother descend into alcoholism…

Erika shook away the memories she didn't want to dwell on. She looked over at Lenka and Marek, holding hands, Jakub and Karolina standing in front of them next to little Evka who was looking at all the candles in wonderment. They were the picture of a happy family, all bathed in the soft glow.

Erika left Slovakia when she was eighteen, running away from her unhappy childhood, and the terrible relationship with her mother, to find a better life – a new life in England. In the light of the flickering candles, she thought about her life in England over the past few years, of losing Mark, how she had to fight every day at work to get the job done. Then she thought of the case she'd just been working on, of her last meetings with Melanie and Peterson. She knew that she and Peterson were over, but hearing it from his lips made it concrete. And what had it been, their relationship? It had been a minefield in many ways. She was his senior officer, they worked together, and it had been such a big thing for her to commit to another man after Mark. And she hadn't fully committed, she knew that now.

Looking at Lenka, so happy with her family and her life in Nitra, Erika wondered if running away had been worth it. And what had she been running away from? Lenka stayed and made a life. Erika was heading towards fifty as a widow with no children, a career teetering on the brink of failure; Nils Åkerman's betrayal had cut her deep and the ramifications of what he had done were still yet to come to light. She had friends in London, Isaac and Moss, but she always kept them at arm's length. She struggled to see anything positive in her future.

'You look sad, Aunt Erika,' said Jakub, his little brown eyes glowing with concern.

'It's a sad time of year,' she said, wiping away a tear.

'Do you miss Uncle Mark?'

Erika nodded.

'He was nice. I don't remember him too much, but he smiled a lot.'

The tears were running down Erika's cheeks now, and Lenka crouched down beside her.

'It's okay,' she said, putting her arms around her. Erika sobbed into her sister's shoulder, and she gripped her arm and buried her face in the soft material. Marek beckoned to the children and he took them for a walk to give them privacy. Erika cried for a long time. She cried for the people she'd lost, and for the life she felt she'd wasted.

'It's okay, *moja zlata*,' said Lenka, stroking her sister's short hair. 'It's okay, you're not alone.'

Erika's tears finally subsided, and she felt better. No one was staring because this was the one place where it was acceptable to cry.

Lenka gave her a tissue.

'You know you can stay for as long as you like.'

'I know. Thank you, but my life isn't here anymore. I have to go back at some point.'

'Come on, let's get these candles lit and go for some hot chocolate in town,' said Lenka. 'And then I'll get Marek to take the kids and we can have a few drinks.'

Erika nodded and smiled, and they lit the rest of the candles.

CHAPTER 40

I haven't written this diary for ages. I think I've needed time to adjust and process everything that happened. When I stabbed Charlene, it changed me. It was like I stepped out of myself and into a different person. It's not that I don't feel guilt and horror for what I've done. But I feel like I'd been beaten down, and taking the initiative, and taking control has given me the awakening that Max is always talking about. I understand him. The world isn't skewed in our favour. You have to take what you need; you have to fight to survive. It's like I just decided I no longer wanted to be a victim. The voice in my head used to say, *why don't you like me? Why are you doing this to me? What am I doing wrong?* I felt empowered when I pushed that knife into her chest. The lying, cheating, druggie bitch.

When we arrived back from dumping the bodies, we stayed up talking. I asked Max what he wanted from life, and how we could make it happen. He was taken aback at the question. He told me he wanted to get out. He said that his dream would be to emigrate, and leave this shithole of a country. Save some money, and go to Spain or Morocco and run a bar or a farm.

'In this country I'll always be scum,' he said. 'I'll always be the kid with the criminal record. The whole class system is stacked against me. I could hang around and wait to win the lottery, and even then I'd be seen as vulgar and undeserving, or I could make it happen for myself.'

'We could make it happen. Let's work together, stop thinking I'm against you. We're in this together. I've killed. I've got blood on my hands. We're equals. Let's make it happen,' I said.

Our talk was transformative. The whole nature of our relationship changed, and we settled down to something approaching normality. In the weeks after we dumped Thomas and Charlene, we've kept our heads down. There has been very little made of them going missing. Their bodies washed up a couple of weeks after we dumped them, but the police are clueless. There was a little flurry of activity online and a sidebar in one of the newspapers, but then it all went quiet. In the meantime, we've been making plans. And to make our plans a reality, we need money.

Last night we went out in Soho. Max has been dealing to this gay guy who works in the City, who recently let slip that he owns a penthouse flat in Drury Lane. I thought this would benefit from more investigating. A penthouse flat in Drury Lane would be worth millions, and he might have a few of those millions lying around at home.

We started the night in Ku Bar and got a table in the corner. Max got a lot of attention from the lads behind the bar, and I could see how he stood out. He had on a new shirt we'd bought that afternoon and it was quite tight and showed off his muscles. His hair was now long and fell past his shoulders. He has that kind of hair which looks good without anything being done. He had on a brand new baseball cap, and where his hair hung down from the cap, it shone under the coloured lights in the bar. It was getting busy, and a couple of guys had offered to buy him drinks – which he accepted. As far as I knew Max was down the line straight, but he was happy to lead these guys on with a bit of chat in return for some seriously expensive drinks. It was strange to see things work the other way. I'm so used to panicking in clubs and pubs when I'm with Max, trying not to appear too flirty or make eye contact with anyone for fear of his jealousy. We'd been there for an hour when a really tall, handsome guy came over, and Max introduced him to me as Daniel. He was very polite and beautifully dressed. He went to the bar and returned with an ice bucket with Cristal champagne and three glasses. I waited until he'd poured us each a glass and taken a sip, and then I excused myself and went to the ladies' loos, giving Max a chance to ply Daniel with drink. When I came back Max was pouring them the last of the bottle.

'You boys are thirsty.' I smiled.

'We can get another bottle if you like?' said Daniel.

'Fuck yeah.' Max smiled, downing his champagne in one. We drank the next bottle just as fast, and then Max and Daniel went off to dance. I was a bit shocked as they hit the dance floor and Max ground himself up against Daniel. I sat there and drank the rest of the champagne feeling jealous. After a couple more songs, the guy went off to the toilets and Max came back.

'You seem to be enjoying yourself,' I said.

'This is the only place I ever want to stick my cock,' he said, reaching down and grabbing my crotch. I opened my legs slightly.

'Don't you forget it,' I said.

'He's invited us back to his place, Neen. The fucking penthouse apartment!'

'How far do you think you'll have to go?' I said. 'What are you going to do with him?' I wasn't normally this forthright with him, but I was jealous. He was mine. He belonged to me. For so long I felt like I belonged to him, that it was nice for a change to realise that he also belonged to me.

Max leaned close across the table, and took my hand. He pulled it down to his right pocket and rested my hand on the bulge of his gun. It felt bigger in his pocket, and I could feel him getting hard underneath it.

'We're going to make ourselves some serious money tonight,' he said with a grin. 'This is what we've talked about.'

'Don't go crazy, Max.'

'He'll live.' He grinned.

A moment later, Daniel came back from the toilets. He was swaying on his feet and his eyes were a little glazed. He downed the rest of his champagne and we left the bar.

We took a cab the short journey to Daniel's apartment. I have never been in such a beautiful place, like a posh hotel. Daniel barely noticed me when we arrived, and after he'd fixed us all drinks, I excused myself and went to the bathroom. He had framed photographs along the walls in the hallway, I think they were his family, they shared his dark looks. One woman featured in almost all the photos, and there were several of just her and Daniel. I think it was his mother. She was very tiny and well dressed, with an Imelda Marcos-style haircut.

The bathroom was vast and beautiful, with white marble and gold taps. Stuck to the huge mirror above the sink was another picture of that woman, much younger and cradling a tiny dark-haired boy that must have been Daniel. I stared at it and my reflection for a long time. I wanted to have a tiny baby to hold on my lap, and I missed my mother. She was never overly affectionate, and we were never close like those Mediterranean families, but I would have given anything to go back in time to before all this, before things changed, before I changed.

I looked at my reflection in the mirror. I ran my fingers through my hair, which now fell past my shoulders, and I adjusted my cleavage. I thought how good she looked, the woman in the mirror staring back at me. I didn't recognise her as 'me' anymore.

When I came back into the living room, I found Max sitting astride Daniel on the floor beside a huge L-shaped sofa. They both had their shirts off, and I thought they were getting it on, then I saw Max's nose was bleeding and he had his hands tight around Daniel's neck. It was all happening with very little noise, just a few soft gurgles and gasps from Daniel.

'Jeez, help me here, will you?' said Max. I froze. 'Neen! Get the gun out of my pocket.'

I moved closer, and one of Daniel's legs thrashed out and flipped a huge silver bowl of potpourri from the glass coffee table. The red pieces scattered all over the blue carpet. I pulled the gun from Max's pocket, and as I had it in my hands, I thought, what if I shot Max? What if I shot him, and then told Daniel all about my life, that I've been the victim? He had money; he might reward me for saving his life.

'What are you waiting for!' shouted Max. He was thrown back and Daniel got to his feet, his face purple, and the belt from Max's trousers wound around his neck. He staggered back and landed on the glass coffee table, which cracked underneath him. Max lunged forward, picking up a large ashtray and hitting him over the head. Daniel went limp after the first blow, but Max kept on hitting him, over and over. The blood started to spray up the walls and it glistened off the ashtray and spattered the ceiling in graceful arcs.

'Enough! That's enough!' I shouted. Max hesitated, the bloody ashtray held above his head. He turned and looked at me. I pointed the gun at him. 'That's enough. Now we need to move fast. Put the ashtray down.'

Max obediently did as he was told and placed it down on the pale carpet. He came towards me and his hand closed over the muzzle and he lifted it from my hands.

'Find me a knife.'

I went to the kitchen and found a meat cleaver in the drawer. I took it back to him. He had pulled Daniel onto the floor and was stripping off his clothes.

'I'm going to get washed up,' I said.

I took a shower in that amazing bathroom, but I placed the photograph of the baby and the young mother face down on the sink. I came out of the shower and wrapped myself in a huge towel. The master bedroom had its own balcony and terrace with a view out over the city. There was a walk-in wardrobe with a polished wood floor filled with elegant clothes and shoes, winter coats, hats and even gloves. I started to search through the closets, looking in the drawers, through the clothes. Then I saw where the shoes were lined up along one side of the walk-in closet, and underneath there was a tile in the wood floor shinier than the rest.

It came up easily, and underneath was a cavity with a little black safe. The safe was open, and inside were blocks of cash, £50 notes, all neat and pristine with those little paper sleeves keeping them together. Written on each was £5,000. There were four in total: £20,000.

Max appeared at the door, covered in blood. He saw the packets of money laid out on the floor, and his eyes lit up.

CHAPTER 41

SUNDAY, 19 NOVEMBER 2017

The atmosphere in Westminster CCTV Control Centre was quiet and studious. Along one side of the room was a video wall where vast screens displayed the live feeds from CCTV cameras all over London.

At 4.15 a.m. two figures reached the top of Covent Garden in central London, and made their way up to the tube station, heads down, faces obscured by baseball caps. They walked with purpose, ignored by a few drunk people passing by. The taller of the two figures was pulling a suitcase on wheels.

The first CCTV camera, close to the Apple Store on the top end of Covent Garden, caught them as it made its sweeping arc, moving from King Street, where a hunched-over tramp shuffled along with a shopping cart, over the cobbles between the pillared St Paul's Church and the giant arches of the glass-covered market, and then came to a stop with a view of the Royal Opera House. Covent Garden is never completely empty, even at 4.15 a.m.

As the two figures in the pulled-down baseball caps passed over the computer screen of a young officer, he noted them and peered closer. They were white and well-dressed, pulling a suitcase. It was freezing cold, and they were moving fast, walking with purpose. The officer on duty in the control room passed them off as people travelling, on their way to catch an early flight, and he turned his attention to another of the live video feeds.

The two figures carried on walking up the cobblestones towards Covent Garden tube station. The shutters were down on the ticket hall, and it wouldn't open for another hour and a half. Two indistinct humps of material and clothes indicated people sleeping rough against the grille.

The officer in the control room had seen the two people bed down at 2.30 a.m., when the pubs and clubs had kicked everyone out, and it was safe to find a spot to grab a few hours' sleep. He had checked back on them over the past few hours, peering at them on his screen, but they remained still. The temperature had dropped below zero every night in the past week, and he had watched two days ago, as an ambulance had been called by a member of the tube station staff when she had found a young woman frozen solid in her sleeping bag.

He sat back in his chair. The couple with the suitcase were now near the entrance to the tube station, moving fast with their heads down. *They must be eager to get inside,* he thought, and then turned his attention to a group of lads who had appeared in the video feed at the bottom of his screen, weaving drunkenly up King Street. He missed the moment when the couple dumped the suitcase. They did it fast, leaving it beside one of the sleeping homeless. Then they kept walking and carried on their journey up towards Charing Cross Road.

Halfway up Long Acre, the two figures left the young officer's computer monitor; he was now concerned about the young lads weaving their way up to Covent Garden tube, and they appeared on the computer monitor of another operator in the control room. She peered at them over her coffee, but only saw two people in a hurry to get home in the cold. Her attention was diverted when the young man called her over. The lads were now trying to force their way into the front entrance of the Apple Store. She left her computer; on the screen, the two figures reached Charing Cross Road and boarded a night bus.

CHAPTER 42

Cat Marshall had been homeless since the summer. She was only in her forties, and this time last year she'd been in arrears on her rent and facing unemployment. She'd thought then that the wolf was at the door, but it was nothing compared to losing your home. She'd spent six months sofa surfing and drinking heavily, until, one by one, her friendships started to tank. At the end of June an acquaintance had reluctantly let her sleep in her old second-hand car in the driveway. It had been the last thread connecting her to the real world, and an address she could use to claim benefits. A few days later, the house burnt down, and her second-hand car was caught in the blaze. Cat was pulled out by paramedics, and spent the night in hospital for smoke inhalation. She was discharged the following day with nothing. She'd lost her bank cards, her phone, passport and most of her belongings. She'd spent several days in hostels, but as each day passed she became filthier and more despondent. She'd often walked by homeless people on the street, and wondered why they drank filthy cheap alcohol, and now she found out. It was the only means of escape. That night she vomited spectacularly in the reception of the hostel where she'd been staying, and was swiftly ejected, beginning her life on the streets.

Cat was frozen when she woke by the shuttered doors of Covent Garden tube station. She could hear shouting, but she was used to shouting. When she opened her sleep-encrusted eyes, there was a police officer in protective gear pointing a gun at her head.

She shifted and felt the cold jolt through her body and she felt she was wet.

'This is the police, get up and put your hands in the air!' shouted the voice, projected through a loud hailer. 'Keep your movements slow.'

She did as she was told, bringing up two filthy hands from the warmth of the sleeping bag. The cold air stung. She didn't fear the gun, nor was she scared that police vans were parked up on the cobbles, and the area around the station had been cordoned off. She instinctively looked for where the wetness had come from. She'd made the mistake in the past of bedding down out the back of one of the big hotels, close to a heating vent which pumped out hot air. One of the hotel workers had doused her with filthy washing-up water. This had been back in November and the cold had nearly killed her.

'Get up, NOW!' said the voice through the loud hailer. It was eerily quiet, and just starting to get light, but there was no one around.

Cat started to move, easing her aching body up and out of the sleeping bag. The rags she tied over her head and under her chin were coming loose. Then she saw the big black suitcase parked beside her. A large pool of red was seeping out from underneath and it was all over her, all over her sleeping bag, and had soaked through to her legs. She screamed.

CHAPTER 43

The taxi dropped Erika outside her flat in Forest Hill, and she paid the driver and pulled her suitcase across the car park. When she'd left to go to Slovakia she had barely been able to open the taxi door, but now she was almost healed. Physically, at least.

It was very early on Sunday morning. She'd caught the 4 a.m. flight from Bratislava, and with a clear road from Luton Airport she was home just before 9 a.m. The last of the autumn leaves had fallen, and she noted how grey everything looked. When she opened her front door, she was greeted by a pile of post on the mat, and it was very cold inside. She parked her suitcase by the bedroom door and moved through the flat, opening the windows a little to let the air in, and she cranked up the heating. She opened the patio door. An icy breeze flooded in as she stepped out onto the small square of patio. The air felt different in London. The cold was cruel and damp. She took a pack of cigarettes from her pocket and peeled off the cellophane with her house key. Her plaster cast was now a little grubby, but it bore the scrawling signatures of Jakub, Karolina, Evka and Lenka. She ran her finger over the felt-tip pen and the smiley face Jakub had drawn, the little squishy heart from Karolina and the tiny squiggle from little Evka. For the first time, she hadn't wanted to come back to London, and she'd been having crazy thoughts of retiring early, buying a small house with a garden and living on her police pension in Nitra – for once, letting life take her where it wanted to lead.

But the case, the bodies in the suitcases, had been niggling at her, and as she recovered her health and started to feel well again, that restless niggling feeling had returned.

She teased a cigarette from the packet and lit up. The two small trees in the tiny communal garden were now devoid of leaves. She heard the sound of the patio door unlocking in the flat above, and she quickly darted back underneath the small veranda. She had been away for a few weeks, and her neighbour Alison above was chatty at the best of times, but she'd have weeks of pent-up questions, and Erika would never get away. She heard Alison moving about above her, the sound of the plastic chairs being dragged across the balcony, and a clothes dryer being opened out. Alison had the nose of a bloodhound and probably smelt her cigarette, but if she did, she took the hint and went back inside. Erika relaxed and lit another. She was halfway through it when she heard her door buzzer.

'Shit,' she muttered. Alison had decided to come down and get the gossip. She debated answering, when it buzzed again. Stubbing out the half smoked cigarette on the bottom of her shoe, she slipped it back in the packet.

When she opened the front door, she was surprised to see Commander Paul Marsh, dressed head to toe in Marks & Spencer menswear, and holding a box of chocolates.

'Bloody hell, it's you!' she said.

'Thanks. Is that all you can say?' He smiled. Erika and Mark had met Marsh when they were all police trainees back in Manchester, but Marsh had always been a career policeman and had risen rapidly in the ranks. He was a handsome man, and at six feet three inches, he was one of the few men who was taller than her.

'Sorry, I thought you were my chatty neighbour, come in.' He leaned over and gave her an awkward peck on the cheek, and she stood to one side to let him in.

'Can I get you a drink?' asked Erika, taking the chocolates. 'I have black coffee, tap water.'

'You got anything stronger?' he asked as they came through to the living room.

'Vodka, but it's not even ten o'clock on a Sunday morning.'

'I have news,' he said. 'I've been reinstated.'

Erika stopped rummaging in the freezer and stood up.

'Did you go to tribunal?'

'No. There was no evidence, well, nothing concrete. So my gardening leave has come to an end after nearly a year. Reinstated with a clean record.'

'What an excellent use of taxpayer money,' said Erika, locating an ice-encrusted bottle of vodka in the back of the freezer and filling two shot glasses. She handed him one and they clinked and took a sip. 'Congratulations.'

Marsh had been suspended by the Met's new Assistant Commissioner, the much feared Camilla Brace-Cosworthy. During his time as borough commander, he had turned a blind eye to the activities of the Gadd family who ran an import-export business in London. In return for this, the Gadd family would share valuable information about criminal networks in the capital. Marsh had merely been following the lead from his predecessors, who had all found the arrangement to be beneficial, but Camilla had seen an opportunity to flex her muscles in her new post, and Marsh had been suspended.

'I'll be coming back to Lewisham Row. Working out of there as borough commander of Lewisham, Greenwich and Bromley,' he said.

'Wow, things change so quickly. I'm pleased for you.'

'How about you?' he said, looking at the cast on her wrist.

'I don't know. I have to see the doctor tomorrow.'

'I heard about Nils Åkerman…' He shook his head. 'You were lucky to get out of that carjacking alive.'

'Well, I did and that's a good enough reason to have another to celebrate,' she said, downing the rest of her vodka and grabbing the bottle, refilling their glasses. He smiled and they clinked and took another drink.

'That tastes good…Why didn't you take the promotion, Erika?' he asked. The change of subject took her by surprise. 'I could have used you as my superintendent. This Melanie Hudson seems a bit wishy-washy.'

Erika thought back to her last meeting with Melanie and felt guilty. 'She's not wishy-washy.'

'Why didn't you take it?'

'I didn't join the force to fill in paperwork and get stuck in an office. I know you did.'

Marsh let that comment roll off his back. 'You have to play to your strengths, Erika. You could have had real influence. Top brass aren't all the corrupt bastards that you think we are.'

'Says the man who's been reinstated due to lack of evidence.'

'Ouch,' said Marsh, draining his glass.

'Sorry. It's just, I've seen the reality of life,' she said, holding up her plaster cast. 'I've spent years trying to change things, trying to fight against the system. Where does it get you?'

'This doesn't sound like the Erika Foster I know and… and call my friend.'

'It won't be long before the murder cases I worked on with Nils are reopened, and I'll have no control over it. And there was a double murder case I was working on before I got carjacked, and I've no doubt some other team is making a pig's ear out of it. Anyway, nothing I can do.'

She took another sip of vodka and looked at Marsh over her glass. He seemed to be back to his old self. He had been through a lot with the suspension, and he was separated from his wife and two small girls. 'What's happening with you and Marcie?'

'We're getting back together, making another go of it,' he said, his face breaking into a smile. 'She wants to try again. So do I, and I think it's best for the girls. Officially, I'm moving back in tomorrow. Tomorrow is the day when we start afresh.'

He held out his glass.

'One more, tiny one,' he said.

She nodded and topped them up.

'I need a cigarette,' she said. They took their drinks out onto the small patio. Erika lit up a cigarette and was surprised when he accepted one. 'I didn't know you smoked?'

'I'm just enjoying myself before…'

'Before you go back to your wife?'

Marsh closed his eyes. 'The situation is so fucked up. I love Marcie. You know I love her…' Erika nodded. 'And my girls, they mean the world to me, but it was Marcie who went off and slept with that bloke. The handsome twenty-nine-year-old art student with the floppy hair. I could have coped with her and any other guy… I think she's come back to me because of the money. The moment I got reinstated she wanted me back.'

'Do you know that for sure?'

'I don't know… I'm not young like him. I can't make her laugh like he does. He encouraged her with her hobby, painting, they even did a joint exhibition.'

'Paul, I don't want to speak out of turn, but Marcie's paintings are bollocks,' said Erika.

He looked at her in surprise.

'Really?'

'*Really.* All that modern bollocks, stapling soiled nappies to a canvas, selfies at the Saatchi Gallery. It's very easy just to splatter a canvas with paint and call it art. Did she sell any of it? That one she did in red reminded me of a crime scene.'

'Her dad bought that one for £500.'

'Five hundred quid? Jeez. Don't artists have to earn the right to charge the earth? Until then it's just bollocks with a hefty price tag.'

Marsh started to laugh. She picked up the bottle of vodka and filled his glass. They looked at each other for a long moment, and Marsh leaned over and kissed her. She put the bottle down; he pulled her close and she responded, kissing him urgently. His hands moved across her back and pulled her T-shirt from her jeans, and he ran his fingers up her back. She felt his chest muscles against her breasts, and her nipples hardened. They moved inside, still kissing, and they collapsed onto the sofa, their hands all over each other, and she unbuckled his trousers.

The front door buzzer cut through the silence. Marsh pulled back and they looked at each other, breathless and shocked. It rang out again, longer. Erika put a hand to her mouth, stunned at what had happened, and how she had been lost in the moment.

'Shit, shit,' he said, jumping up, doing up his trousers and smoothing down his hair.

'It's probably my neighbour.' The buzzer droned again. 'Paul, I don't know what just happened—'

'I should go,' he said, moving to the hallway. Erika followed, tucking in her clothes. Marsh pulled open the door and Moss was outside, in her long black coat. Her freckled cheeks were flushed from the cold.

'Boss, you'll never guess what has just happened…' she started, then she saw Marsh. 'Oh, hello, sir.'

'I was just heading off,' said Marsh. 'I'll see you, Erika.' He nodded at Moss and he was gone.

She looked after him as he hurried out of the communal entrance to his car, then turned back to Erika. 'It's really good to see you.'

'Good to see you too,' said Erika, trying to regain her composure. 'You want to come in?'

'I heard you were back, and I just had to come and get you.'

'Get me?'

'Yeah. I've just had a call. Another body has been found stuffed in a suitcase outside Covent Garden station.'

Erika gripped the doorframe. 'What?'

'I know we're not on the case, but I figured you'd want to check it out?'

'Of course.'

'Good. I've got my car.'

Erika's eyes lit up. She grabbed her coat, and left the flat.

CHAPTER 44

Erika and Moss were waved through the police cordon in Moss's car, and they had the novelty of driving across the cobblestones of the deserted Covent Garden. The huge Christmas tree outside the covered market swayed in the wind, and they drove past a small crowd that was gathering at a police cordon by the Royal Opera House. They parked the car opposite the Boots store, and walked up to the police cordon. Further up towards the tube station they could see the pathologist's van and a large Met police support vehicle. They showed their warrant cards to the officer at the cordon, and they were signed in. They walked up to a second cordon, where they were met by a young woman who gave them paper coveralls. As they were suiting up, Erika saw it was Rebecca March, one of the lab assistants who worked for Nils. They recognised each other at the same time.

'How are you doing?' she asked, helping her to pull the sleeve over her plaster cast.

'I'm doing fine,' said Erika.

'I thought it was allergies, his strange behaviour,' she said. 'How stupid was I?'

'You're not stupid,' said Erika. 'You were being a good colleague. Good colleagues trust each other. It was Nils who broke that trust.'

Rebecca nodded, and Erika and Moss headed up to the crime scene. A white crime scene tent had been rigged up to the left side of the grilles covering the entrance to Covent Garden tube station.

They were met by a forensics officer they had never met before. She was very short with piercing green eyes. She had a broad Irish accent which sounded very jolly through her face mask.

'I'm Cariad Hemsworth,' she said, her eyes crinkling with a smile. 'I'm Nils Åkerman's replacement. Your timing is impeccable. We've just had to take swabs from the poor lady who got mixed up in all this.'

'The homeless woman?' asked Erika.

'Yes. We're going to have to make sure she's given new clothes and looked after. All her worldly goods are now bagged up and on the way to the lab.'

She took them into the crime scene tent. It was tight inside and underfoot was the mosaic tile of the tube station concourse. Isaac was working with a crime scene photographer to document the scene. A hard-shell black suitcase lay open on the tiles, and inside, packed in, were the bloody limbs of a naked male. The victim's head was severed from the torso and stuffed in under the arm. The face was a bloody mess, with matted black hair. Beside the case was a vast slick and smear of blood, now congealing and glistening under the fierce lamps clipped into the roof of the tent.

'Hello,' said Isaac, seeing Erika and Moss and standing.

The photographer took a last picture and then skirted around the blood slick and squeezed past them out of the tent.

'What a strange place to see you again after being away.'

'Yeah. We'll have to have coffee,' said Erika, adding with a smile: 'Good to see you.'

Isaac smiled in return and then turned to the body in the suitcase. 'We believe the victim is twenty-eight-year-old Daniel de Souza.'

'How do you already have an ID?' said Moss.

Isaac passed them a couple of evidence bags. Inside was a bloodstained driving licence with a picture of a handsome olive-skinned young man with jet black hair.

'Face is smashed in. Body has been chopped up. And this time, whoever did this, packed in his ID, wallet, keys and mobile phone,' said Isaac.

Cariad retrieved a piece of paper in a clear plastic evidence bag and handed it to Erika.

'And he left a note,' she said.

It was a single sheet of paper, which had some blood spatter on one corner. It was written in a crazed scrawl:

This is OUR fifth victim. Do you CLOWNS even know that WE'VE killed four people? You know of Thomas Hoffman and Charlene Selby, but what of the others? It's getting boring, at least you could make things interesting and attempt to track us down. Or have you all just been sitting around snorting the blow I left in Tommy's tummy? Ta ta.

'Jesus,' said Erika, looking up at Moss. 'There's two of them.'

CHAPTER 45

Erika and Moss arrived at Lewisham Row just before lunch. As they walked into the reception area, Sergeant Woolf was helping one of the support workers decorate a small fake Christmas tree by the door.

'Long time no see,' he said, giving her a smile. 'How are you feeling?'

'Alright, unlike that fairy,' she said, indicating the knackered-looking Barbie doll with a silver star sticky-taped to its head.

'Yes, she does look like she's spent a few hours in the cells,' grinned Woolf, and pulling open her legs he plonked her on the top branch of the tree. He moved around the desk and buzzed them through the door. 'Good to see you back,' said Woolf, giving her a wink. Moss hurried along behind Erika as she started up the stairs towards Melanie's office.

Erika knocked on the door, but didn't bother to wait and walked right in. Melanie was sitting at her desk and looked up from her computer.

'Erika? What are you doing here?' she said, surprised. 'And hello, Kate.'

'Hello, ma'am,' said Moss awkwardly, joining Erika.

'We've just come from a crime scene,' said Erika. 'A twenty-eight-year-old male, found chopped up and dumped in a suitcase outside Covent Garden tube station, and this time the killers left a note.'

'Killers?'

Erika took a copy of the note from her pocket, smoothed it out and slid it across the desk. Melanie took it and started to read, then turned it over in her hand.

'Bloody hell…Hang on, hang on, when did you get back from being away? You're still technically on sick leave… I was going to ease you back in, and I wanted to talk to you.'

'Consider me eased back in. I'm ready to work, and I want back on this case, please, ma'am.' Erika smiled at her hopefully.

'Okay. How do we know this is genuine?' asked Melanie.

'We never released anything in the press about the drugs we found inside Thomas Hoffman,' said Erika. 'This is genuine, and they are still way ahead of us. What is the progress of the case? How far have the team got with it over at West End Central?'

'I don't know. I think it's been kicked into the long grass.'

Erika rolled her eyes.

'Well, I'm here, and I want the case back. There are still two killers out there.'

Melanie looked at the note again and nodded. 'Okay. Let me know what you need.'

A few hours later, Erika approached the incident room in the basement of Lewisham Row and saw through the glass partition that the team was assembled. The chatter died down when she entered.

'Afternoon, everyone, it's good to see you again,' she said.

'And good to see you back on your feet, boss. How are you doing?' said Sergeant Crane. All eyes in the room looked at the plaster cast on her arm, and she saw looks of pity. She took a deep breath and held up the wrist with the cast.

'I'll just say that sticks and stones may break my bones. But nothing will stop me from finding this killer.'

'Nice one, you should put that on a bumper sticker,' said Crane.

'Now, I'm sure you'll all be aware of what happened with Nils Åkerman, but we have to move on. We can't dwell on the betrayal of a former colleague. It won't stop us doing our jobs to the best of our abilities. Each and every one of you are valuable to this investigation.'

There was silence in the incident room as everyone nodded, sombre expressions on their faces.

'Okay, I'll bring you up to speed with what we have,' she said, scratching at the edges of her plaster cast. 'This morning the body of twenty-eight-year-old Daniel de Souza was found chopped up and dumped in a suitcase outside Covent Garden tube station…' She indicated a photo from the crime scene next to a photo taken of Daniel on a beach holiday; he was smiling into the camera with blue sky and sand behind him. 'A note was left with the body. In it the killers state they killed Thomas Hoffman and Charlene Selby, Daniel de Souza and two others.'

'Was he a model? He's a handsome lad,' asked McGorry, peering at the photo of Daniel. McGorry had been called in from a walk in the park with his girlfriend, and was still wearing his Sunday clothes, jeans and a Chelsea football top.

'Fancy him, do you?' said Crane.

'No. It's a statement.'

Crane pulled a face.

'Alright, alright. It's a valid point,' said Erika. 'Everything is up for grabs, but no, he wasn't a model, he worked for a hedge fund in the City.'

'Didn't I say early on that I thought this was two people working together?' said DC Temple in his soft Scots accent.

'Yes, and that was duly noted, well done, but we need to do more than guess correctly,' said Erika. She moved to another image on the whiteboard. 'We've had this through from a security camera on the entrance to Daniel de Souza's apartment. The image shows

Daniel in front, and behind him are two other people. The woman's
face is slightly blurred, but I think she's a young woman. The man
behind her has his head down, wearing a baseball cap, so his face is
obscured. The timestamp on this image is just after ten p.m. yesterday
evening…' Erika pointed at an image next to it. 'Then almost six
hours later, at 3.47 a.m., you can see the man and woman leaving,
pulling a black suitcase. John, can you kill the lights?'

McGorry went to the door and turned off the lights. Erika
nodded to Sergeant Crane, who turned on the projector. A black-
and-white CCTV video feed showing Covent Garden appeared
on the whiteboard.

'This is taken fourteen minutes later, 4.01 a.m. Here we have
the two figures with the suitcase, making their way up to Covent
Garden tube station. Daniel de Souza's flat is just a few minutes'
walk from this location.'

The angle changed to a view of the tube station, and Erika
pointed at the video the moment that they left the suitcase by the
row of sleeping homeless people and carried on walking out of
shot. The video on the whiteboard went blank and was replaced
by the footage taken from the CCTV camera at Selby Autos.

'Now, if we revisit the CCTV footage from the 15th of September, when Charlene Selby dropped off the Jaguar at her parents'
car dealership, again we have these two unidentified people. The
male with long blond hair, and a similar build to the male seen at
Daniel de Souza's, and the same with the female.'

'They've gone to vast lengths to conceal their identities from
us,' said Moss. 'But now they've left the victim's ID in the suitcase,
along with a note.'

Erika went to the light switches and flicked them on; the team
winced as the fluorescent lights came back on.

'Okay. I want a full profile of our victim, Daniel de Souza. And
we need to find out the identity of these two people. I'm going to
get hold of the Cyber Team and see if we can enhance this blurred

image of the woman taken in the entrance to Daniel de Souza's flat. I also want that Jaguar from Selby Autos tested for DNA from top to bottom. Cariad Hemsworth is our new contact over at forensics; let's make it our mission to get her fully invested in this case. Now let's get to work.'

The rest of the afternoon passed in a flurry of activity, and Erika was surprised at how quickly she had slipped back into work mode. Just before five o'clock, Moss came over to Erika's desk with a case file.

'Got a moment?'

'What?'

'I've been inputting case file details into Holmes, and something came up. There was an unusual case of a body found ten days ago, in a drainage ditch on farmland. A few miles from Oxford off the M40.'

'Why is it unusual?' asked Erika.

'It was the body of a male in his late fifties, and he was partially mummified.'

'What does being mummified have to do with our case?'

'It's the manner in which the body was killed which flagged as a match with our other victims. His face had been smashed in with a rock. Now, apart from the suitcase, this is the one thing which links Thomas Hoffman, Charlene Selby, and now Daniel de Souza. The killer smashed in their faces, obliterating their identity. This body found in the drainage pipe still hasn't been identified, but the police managed to recover several large bloodstained rocks from the drainage pipe, and some hair samples on the victim's clothes. The forensic pathologist in Oxford is an old colleague of mine. I can get in contact with her.'

Erika took the file from Moss and scanned the paperwork.

'This could be our missing fourth victim,' she said. 'Yes, give her a call.'

CHAPTER 46

Erika returned home late from work, and details of the case were whirling around her head. It was one of those grotty November evenings, dark and damp. She was unlocking her front door when she ran into her neighbour, Alison, a large blowsy woman with a mass of dark curly hair. She wore a long army print coat and with her was her huge Rottweiler on a lead.

'Alright, love, I thought I heard you were back,' she said. She had a soft Welsh accent.

'I just got back…' said Erika, putting her key in the lock.

'Was it Slovenia?'

'Slovakia.'

'Oh right, is that different?'

'Yeah, Slovenia is a different country…'

Erika opened the door, but Alison went on. 'I've always wanted to travel, but Duke's getting on now, and I can't be arsed with all the faffing to get a pet passport.' The dog looked up at Erika with a mournful face and lay down on the carpet with a sigh.

'Okay, well, have a nice eve—' started Erika, going to move through the door.

'I haven't seen your feller around for a while, Erika. The one who looks a bit like Idris Elba. Such a dish, he is.'

Erika tried to come up with an excuse which didn't too much information away; she also didn't know how Peterson was doing. It had been several weeks since they'd spoken.

'He's been, erm, ill. Off sick from work.'

'Oh, that's terrible. What was it? My late husband used to have terrible kidney stones. I'm telling you, kidney stones can knock you right back, and he had such a terrible time when he went for a piss. He kept passing them into the toilet. Poor bugger. One was so big it cracked the lavatory pan.'

'It wasn't kidney stones…'

'Oh, that's good. And how about you? I see you've buggered up your wrist. How did you do that? Do you play tennis?'

'No. The cast should be coming off soon.' There was a microsecond lull in the conversation, and Erika tried to dart indoors, but Alison went on again.

'We had a right problem when you were gone. Fiona, the landlady, needed to get access to your place to have the gutters cleaned. But we didn't have a key. Have you met Fiona?'

'No.'

'She's a hard-faced cow, I tell you. And she looks worse now she's lost weight. Did you know they hypnotised her to think she had a gastric band?'

'Did they?'

'Yeah. They tricked her subconscious into thinking that she had one, even though she knew she didn't. She lost six stone. I'm thinking about doing it myself. I've been back on the Ryvita for a fortnight and not lost a pound.'

'Alison, I've got to go,' snapped Erika.

'Oh, OK,' she said, blinking in surprise at Erika's tone. 'I'd better be off myself, I'm late for my pole dancing class.' Erika looked between Alison in her winter coat and the dog lying on the floor. 'I do the class where we can bring our pets. It gets me out of the house. I don't have anyone who can look after her. I'm all alone in the world…' The perpetual smile which had been on Alison's lips during the conversation fell for a moment. 'I'll see you, Erika, ta ra.' And she went off with Duke loping behind her.

*

Erika went inside and closed the door behind her. She rubbed her face and went through to the living room. The two shot glasses from that morning were still on the coffee table. It seemed like days ago that Marsh had been over. She thought of what had happened between them and cringed, and then she thought of what Alison had so freely admitted. That she was all alone in the world. It made Erika feel uncomfortable. She thought about herself, and how good it felt to be back at work. Work was an addiction, something she couldn't do without, but she had a little voice at the back of her head, asking what she would do in ten years' time, when she'd be under pressure to retire.

She took off her coat and poured herself a drink. When sat down on the sofa, she pulled out her phone and went to call Peterson. She stared at his number for a long time, then put her phone down, opened her computer and carried on working on the case.

CHAPTER 47

The next morning Erika's buzzer rang shortly after seven and she went out into the car park. It was still dark and the potholes were filled with icy puddles. Moss was waiting outside in her car, and Erika hurried over and climbed in, savouring the warm air.

'I hate early mornings this time of year,' said Erika as they pulled away into the empty, dark street. 'It feels like the middle of the night.' She scratched at the edges of the plaster cast.

'When's it coming off?' asked Moss.

'It was meant to be today, but I cancelled my appointment. It's so itchy,'

'You should use a knitting needle to get at the itch.'

'Do I look like someone who owns a knitting needle?' said Erika.

'You make sure you go to see the doctor.'

'I re-booked it. One day won't hurt.'

Moss shrugged.

'Health should come first.'

Erika shot her a look, and changed the subject.

'How do you know this forensic pathologist, what's her name?'

'Patty Kaminsky. We dated for a time when I was training and she was in medical school,' said Moss.

'Did it end amicably?'

'Kind of. I ended it, but it's all water under the bridge. I've arranged for us to go to the crime scene first.'

'So the perfect location to meet an ex,' said Erika. Moss grinned and rolled her eyes. 'Talking of exes. Have you heard much from Peterson?'

'No. Not since before I went away.'

There was something in the way Moss was avoiding eye contact which made Erika think there was something else.

'Have you seen him?'

'Yeah. Is that okay?'

'Why wouldn't it be?'

'You're my mate, he's my mate. I just want us all to be mates, or for me to be mates with you both.'

'It's fine. I'm not one of those people who'll ask you to choose,' said Erika.

'Good.' She grinned, looking relieved.

'Do you know when he's coming back to work?'

'Could be soon, he's going in to talk to the superintendent this week. He's put on lots of weight, he looks good. Well, I mean healthy-good… Do you fancy the radio on?'

'Yeah.'

Moss leaned forward and switched it on. The *Today* programme blared out, and they spent the rest of the journey listening to the news.

It took them a few hours to drive up to Oxford. It was just getting light as they came off the motorway and started to weave their way through the surrounding villages. So many of the cottages already had Christmas lights in the windows, and there were nativity scenes dotted around the ancient churches. It always struck Erika how England changed when you escaped the boundaries of the M25 motorway. It was a world away from the hustle and bustle of London.

'I think it's just coming up here,' said Moss, looking at the GPS on the dashboard. 'Yes, here's the church she mentioned.'

They pulled off the road into a small car park by an ancient stone church with a round tower. A small red Porsche sat in the corner, and it flashed its lights. Moss's phone rang on the hands-free and she answered.

'Good to see you're on time!' came a plummy voice. 'Don't get out of the car, it's fucking freezing. I'll take us in convoy.' Then she rang off.

The Porsche's engine roared to life and it pulled out past them. Behind the wheel, Erika could see a woman with a chalk-white face and scarlet lipstick. She lifted a finger from her steering wheel.

'She sounds posh,' said Erika.

'She comes from old money,' said Moss.

'I hate that expression, old money and new money. So a person who works their arse off and becomes rich is vulgar, but someone who is bone idle but inherits wealth from a distant aunt is thought of as superior?'

'Sounds about right.'

'This bloody country,' said Erika, shaking her head.

Moss found it hard to keep up with the red Porsche which roared off along the road. They passed fields and a couple of derelict outbuildings. The road then banked down, and when they turned a corner the fields spread out around them in several shades of brown and black in the winter sun.

The Porsche was parked up by a ditch next to an old-fashioned white road sign, and Moss pulled in behind. When she turned off the engine, they felt the wind buffet the car.

Patty was a tiny woman, with jet black hair scraped back and kept in place by a dark green velvet headband. She wore black leggings and welly boots and a huge brown fur coat and gloves.

Erika towered over her, and had to shout above the noise of the wind roaring across the fields. Moss and Erika put on wellington boots, and they followed Patty as she climbed down the bank of the grass and into a deep ditch, hidden from view up on the road.

It was very dry and there were leaves deep underfoot. It was also very quiet as the wind stopped screaming, the walls of the ditch sheltering them.

'A couple of road workers found the body,' said Patty, leading, with Moss behind her, and Erika brought up the rear. She pulled out a torch and flicked it on as they approached the lip of a huge concrete pipe. Inside, it had a dry, peaty smell, and underfoot there was a layer of leaves and the soil was cracked.

'I wanted to show you the inside of the pipe,' said Patty, playing the torch over the curved walls. 'It was built to take the run-off from the surrounding fields, but another pipe was built over the field for a bypass, which means all the rainwater gets re-directed away and it's extremely dry down here. When they discovered the body, it was almost covered in leaves. It had lain down here for several months, but the low moisture content, added to the amount of nitrogen produced by the slowly rotting leaves, meant that the rate of decay dramatically slowed.'

'He was mummified?' asked Erika.

'No, there was purification, but the body had also dried out. It's quite remarkable how the rate of decay can slow in the right conditions. You can see that there is very little in the way of insects in here.'

'Did the police find any evidence of a murder weapon?'

'They spent a long time down here sifting the leaves away and they found several large stones and rocks around the body which they took away.'

Erika walked further into the pipe which extended away for fifty feet. The light dimmed, and Moss and Patty's voices receded. There was a strange atmosphere, as if the air was pressing down on her, and it was so dry. She swallowed a couple of times, and there was a metallic taste on her tongue. She took out her phone and switched on the torch, playing the light over the dry peaty soil. She spied something on the earth next to the pipe, and knelt down, directing the light on her phone towards it. A small twist of brown thread was tightly bundled around something. Erika pulled on a latex glove and carefully pulled it from the soil. It was a lock of dark hair, around four inches in length and it had been fastened with the thread at the end. Erika placed it in a small plastic evidence bag, and sealed it up.

Their next stop was the morgue, where Patty showed them the remains of the man who had been found in the pipe. She pulled out the steel drawer and unzipped the black body bag. His skin was a strange, leathery, brown colour, almost like beef jerky.

'He's Caucasian,' said Patty, seeing Erika's face. 'Internal organs were fairly mushy, but I could see he has internal injuries, and he has a broken leg and ribs, a cracked pelvis. If you note, the right femur in the leg is protruding from the skin. These are injuries consistent with him being hit by a vehicle, and his close proximity to the roadside would support this theory. However, if you see the face, he has been hit repeatedly with a rock or stone. I found fragments of rock in the skin. The cheekbones, nose, jaw and skull are all broken in several places. The cartilage in the nose had been forced up into the brain.'

'And that's not consistent with a car or vehicle impact?' asked Erika.

'No. The force of the impact is centred on his ribs and leg, which would mean he was standing in the road when the vehicle hit him. He could have suffered some injuries to the face if he was thrown into the road, but there is no one impact point on his face. The kind of injuries he has are from being repeatedly smashed with a hard, blunt object.'

'And there's no ID,' said Moss.

'As yet, no. He didn't have anything on him. His wallet was empty.'

They looked back at the mangled body of the man lying on the steel table.

'I think someone hit him with a car, and then finished him off to put him out of his misery,' said Patty as she slowly zipped up the body bag and pushed the body back into the refrigerated drawer.

'Put him out of his misery, and then stuffed him in the drainage pipe,' added Erika. 'What's happening with forensics?'

'Everything has been sent off, along with several pieces of concrete found with blood spatter around the body,' said Patty. 'If you're saying we have a link to another case, I'm sure we can have things fast-tracked.'

'Do you think we're clutching at straws?' asked Erika on their way back in the car.

'Do I think we want to link that murder with the others, yes, but the psychology of smashing in that bloke's face, it could be our killers. If we can match forensic material from that crime to DNA or bodily fluids found in Justin Selby's Jaguar, we could hit the jackpot.'

Erika nodded and stared out of the window into the blackness. 'A man and a woman. The psychology of that is just too disturbing. The dynamic of a dysfunctional relationship added in with committing murder.'

'And why do you think they're doing it?'

'Fun, power, revenge, lust… money. Pick any or all of them. Everyday emotions bring out the worst in people.'

CHAPTER 48

The next morning, Erika was called into a briefing with Superintendent Hudson and Commander Marsh in the large conference room at the top of the station. It was the first time she'd seen Marsh since he'd come to her flat the other morning, and he gave her a curt nod in greeting. Erika briefly outlined the case so far, and then shared some new evidence.

'We now have an enhanced image of the woman who came back to Daniel de Souza's flat,' said Erika, holding up a CCTV image which clearly showed the young woman's face.

'And there's nothing workable from the CCTV of the male?' asked Marsh.

'No. The Cyber Team were able to enhance the face of the woman, but he seems pretty savvy, or just lucky. He kept his head down. There was nothing to enhance. However, we have him wearing the same blue Von Dutch branded baseball cap in the footage taken from outside Selby Autos, and when he arrives at de Souza's flat, and later on in the CCTV footage when they dumped the case in Covent Garden. They then walked down Long Acre, and took the N155 night bus which goes towards Morden, through Westminster, Elephant and Castle, Clapham etc. We've put in an urgent request with TFL for any camera footage they can give us.'

'Have we had anyone from the family identify the body of Daniel de Souza? It would be ideal to have that in place before we put out anything in the media,' said Melanie.

'Yes. Daniel de Souza's mother identified his body an hour ago. She lives close to his flat. He bought her an apartment nearby, in Marylebone, two years ago.'

Marsh picked up the photos taken from the crime scene, of the blood-spattered body parts in the suitcase, and of his bloodied, smashed-in face.

'Erika, how can we be sure that this is Daniel de Souza?'

'His mother has formally identified the body.'

'The body was heavily mutilated and left unrecognisable. Do we need to run any DNA? To be sure?' asked Marsh.

'We had a Family Liaison Officer visit Mrs de Souza yesterday. Daniel de Souza is of Cuban heritage, and he had the *mariposa* flower tattooed on the inside of his left arm.' Erika held up a post-mortem photo of the tattoo. It was a white flower with four petals, and the pale ink used in the tattoo had a ghostly sheen on his dark skin. 'His mother was aware of the tattoo, and this formed part of the formal identification,' said Erika, a little more brusquely than she needed to. 'Now, I would like to release details of his murder. We've discovered Daniel was gay, and I would like to focus our appeal on the social networks, targeting the gay community first.'

'OK. Let's get in contact with Colleen Scanlan about this,' said Melanie.

'You think this is a gay bashing?' asked Marsh.

'I don't know; the previous victims are from different social groups. I just think there's a lot of noise out there, and focusing this as a gay interest story will highlight the case more in the press, make it stand out,' said Erika. 'I've got uniform asking around bars in Soho, and we're looking into several leads where de Souza was seen on Saturday night.' She paused. 'I also have an unidentified body found in a drainage pipe close to the M40 in an Oxfordshire village. It wasn't dismembered, but it shares several characteristics with these other murders.'

A look passed between Marsh and Hudson, and then Marsh spoke.

'So you think we have a Bonnie and Clyde thing going on here?'

'I don't know. I want to keep our cards close to our chest. I need to be sure I can link all the murders before we go public, and I want to play down to the media that it was two people. I want to lead with the photo of the woman. I'm waiting on forensics from the Jaguar, taken by Charlene Selby from her parents' dealership. I also want to talk to a minicab driver who picked up all four of them in Slough. It seems that during my absence, when this case was handed over to DCI Harper at narcotics, nothing was done. It was kicked into the long grass.'

'But the case did give them a valuable break on a sizeable drug network,' said Melanie.

'No, me being attacked by two low-level drug dealers gave them a valuable break,' snapped Erika, holding up the plaster cast on her arm. There was an uncomfortable silence in which Marsh and Melanie busied themselves in the paperwork strewn out on the desk.

'Yes, well, I'm sure all things are in hand to do with that,' said Marsh. Erika had to stop herself from rolling her eyes. 'And Erika, just make sure that your team doesn't get involved in nicknames, talking about Bonnie and Clyde… Thelma and Louise. The press love to pick up on these things.'

'I think you need to give my officers credit, sir. I have no leaks in my team, and you're the first person who's used these names. And the press will be more than capable of coming up with something on their own, and we'll have no control over it,' said Erika.

'Just remember that stupid names stick,' said Marsh. 'They stoke fear in the public and they put the spotlight back on the police, and we always come out in an unfavourable light.'

Erika looked at him, and saw he was using his old tactics of deflecting and attacking.

'If the police were properly funded, and not obsessed with PR and what people think of us, we could just get on with doing our jobs—'

Melanie interrupted. 'Erika, can I remind you that the commander has taken time out of his schedule to meet with us at very short notice.'

'And I thank him for making time for us,' said Erika with a hint of sarcasm. 'Now, I'd like to get going with putting out an appeal for the ID on this woman, if that's okay with you, sir?'

Melanie looked at Erika and Marsh who were almost squaring up to each other.

'Is there anything else you would like to say?' asked Hudson, turning to Marsh. He locked eyes with Erika and she could see his emotions bubbling away behind his eyes. He had lots more to say, but it wasn't to do with the case.

'That's all, thank you, Erika. Keep us posted,' said Marsh.

And she left the office.

CHAPTER 49

Later that afternoon Erika and her team were working in the incident room when McGorry said she had a phone call. Erika took it at her desk. It was Cariad Hemsworth from forensics.

'Erika, hi. Our tests are now complete on the Jaguar. We've identified five sets of fingerprints: Charlene Selby, Thomas Hoffman, Justin Selby, as I would expect, him being the owner of the car showroom. There were also two other sets of prints which could be consistent with the two other people seen exiting the car.'

The atmosphere in the incident room was very rowdy and Erika waved her arm for them to quieten down.

Cariad went on. 'Forensics also took prints from Daniel de Souza's apartment. The same two sets of unidentified fingerprints were present. We got a partial thumb, and index finger.'

Erika punched the air with her plaster cast, and the incident room went quiet, watching.

'I've also had a call from Patty Kaminsky, my colleague working in Thames Valley Police, Oxford. You met with her yesterday concerning an unidentified body.'

'Yes.'

'Her colleague did a superglue fuming test on two of the large rocks recovered with the body of the unidentified male in the drainage pipe, and it yielded a usable thumb print. It matches one of the prints that is present in the Jaguar and at Daniel de Souza's apartment.'

Erika gripped the phone. 'Would the prints stand up in court?'

'We have a twelve-point match on all of the prints. We're also running additional tests for DNA on fingerprint residue and swabs, but this will take a little longer.'

'Thank you…' started Erika.

'There's more,' said Cariad. 'We had a DNA match back from the lock of hair you found in the drainage pipe. It's a woman called Rachel Trevellian. She lives here in Oxford. She's forty-five years old, and was arrested for ABH back in 2009. She was swabbed for DNA when she was arrested, but the charges were dropped. I'm sending all of this over in an email. Her address is in there too.'

Erika came off the phone and relayed the information to the team. There was a whoop and a cheer.

'You were right, boss!' said McGorry with a huge smile on his face. 'You had a hunch the murders were linked and they are.'

Moss punched the air, and Crane nodded and gave her the thumbs up.

'Okay, this is a very strong development—'

'Strong development? That's fucking brilliant,' said Detective Temple, his Scottish accent somehow making the F-word more palatable.

'I say *strong development* because we still need an ID on our two main suspects,' said Erika.

'Colleen Scanlan has just emailed,' said Moss. 'She's now got everything ready to release the CCTV image to the media, and hopefully they will go with it on the early evening news bulletins. She's also posting on social media. She's leading with the information that Daniel de Souza was gay. It's not explicitly stating this was a hate crime, but the details are compelling, and should hopefully grab people and get them sharing and commenting on their newsfeeds.'

Erika and the team stayed in the incident room until the report had gone out on the BBC London early evening news. A contact team was ready on the telephone switchboard at Lewisham Row, but the phones remained quiet.

*

Erika decided to call a short break to get some food, and made her way down to the reception area, where Sergeant Woolf was just finishing up his shift and handing over to another officer.

'What happened to the Christmas tree?' asked Erika, seeing it had vanished from the corner of the reception area. 'Don't tell me someone complained about us having a religious symbol on display?'

'No,' he said, shaking his head and pulling on his coat. 'They brought a crackhead in for questioning the other day, and this crackhead was left in reception. He started eating the baubles.'

'You're kidding.'

He shook his head. 'He ate two and half a string of tinsel before I noticed, and that was only because he was choking. Luckily I pulled the tinsel out before he lost consciousness.'

Erika bit her lip. 'Sorry. It's not funny.'

'It is, but it's a shame, the tree really brightened things up in here,' he said. 'It seems like anything nice in this world is destroyed or taken away from us.' They emerged from the station onto the steps. It was freezing cold, but the sky was clear. 'Ah well, good night,' he said.

'Haven't you got a car?'

'No, I take the train. It's much easier on the DLR.' He wound his scarf around his neck and went off to the station.

Erika started walking across the car park, past a large blue Space Cruiser in Marsh's parking space. As she looked in the window, she saw Marsh's wife, Marcie, inside. She waved awkwardly, and went to carry on but Marcie wound down her window.

'Hello, Erika. It's been a while,' she said. Marcie was a similar age to Erika, but oozed an almost ethereal beauty with her creamy, blemish-free skin, long, dark hair and beautiful face.

Erika moved over to the car and saw two young girls in the back seat, arguing over an iPad.

'Can you two share? You both want to watch *Peppa Pig*, so I don't know what you're bickering about,' snapped Marcie over her shoulder. The little girls were identical twins, with long, dark hair and the beginnings of their mother's good looks. 'Sorry, Erika. It's always a bit of a madhouse. How are you? I heard you had a run-in with some nasty men.'

Erika bristled a little at the way Marcie reduced what had happened to her to Enid Blyton proportions. Erika forced a smile on her face.

'Yeah, a cracked rib, whiplash and stitches, and a broken wrist,' she said, holding up her arm.

'Didn't they offer you a promotion? You should have taken it, it's much safer behind a desk.' She turned back to the girls, who were staring at Erika in awe. 'Do you remember Auntie Erika, girls? She's a friend of Daddy's.'

Both girls obediently squinted through the window at Erika, and then in unison said: 'No, Mummy.'

'I remember you both when you were born, and I've been to your house a few times,' said Erika.

'The girls probably don't remember you, because you usually bang on the door late at night.'

There was an uncomfortable silence and they stared at each other. Marsh then appeared, coming down the steps of the station.

'Daddy, daddy, daddy!' the girls cried and started to wriggle around in their seats. Marsh came to the rear passenger door, opened it and started to unbuckle them.

'Hello, you two!' he said as they climbed out of the car seats and put their little arms around him. They wore matching pink coats with blue trousers and pink trainers.

'Bloody hell, Mummy has you strapped in tight.'

'I don't want them to get in the habit of clambering around in the car,' said Marcie.

Erika noted how her nostrils flared when she spoke to Marsh.

'Marcie, you've got the child lock on the doors. You should let them out of the belts when you're parked,' he said, adding: 'You'll keep me posted on the appeal.' He didn't look Erika in the eye.

'Of course, sir. I'm just off to grab a sandwich…'

'Well, if you're off to grab a sandwich can we give you a lift?' said Marcie.

This was one thing Erika didn't get about British people: they would cut you to the quick one moment with a barbed comment, but then would offer you a lift so as not to appear rude.

'No, thank you. I was going to drive,' replied Erika. It had started to rain and she pulled the collar up on her coat. 'Nice to see you, Marcie, and you too, girls.'

They all ignored her, too caught up in bickering about getting the girls back in their car seats. Erika sprinted to her car and got inside, relishing the silence. She waited until Marcie had driven away and then started the engine. Just as she pulled past the front entrance, Peterson came out onto the steps. He wore jeans and a thick black jacket, and he had lost the thin gaunt look in his face. Erika slowed and wound down her window.

'Hey, how are you?' she said. 'What are you doing here?'

'I've been to see Superintendent Hudson about coming back. To work.'

'She didn't mention it.'

He shrugged. 'I think stuff like that is confidential.'

Erika could see he was getting wet in the rain.

'Haven't you got your car?'

'No. I came on the train.'

'Let me give you a lift to the DLR.'

He pondered it for a minute and then came down the steps and got in. They both hesitated, and then he gave her an awkward peck on the cheek.

'How are you doing?' he asked, looking at the plaster cast.

'This is coming off any day now, and I'm as good as new, doing great. You look almost back to your old self too.'

'Yeah, I turned a corner when—'

'When I went away?' Erika shot back.

'No, I was going to say when they got my meds right, and I've been able to eat and sleep. I've put on almost two stone.'

'Are you coming back to work full-time?'

'In the next few weeks, yes.'

'And where have you requested to be placed? Murder Investigation?'

'Yes. Is that going to be a problem? It's going to be desk work for the first few weeks,' he said.

'I won't make it a problem if you won't. You know I think you're a brilliant officer, and a valuable part of the team, any team.'

'Thanks for the review.'

'It wasn't a review.'

The rain was now pounding on the roof and they had reached the station. He thanked her for the lift, and got out.

'James, wait,' she blurted. He ducked down in the rain, peering through the car door. 'Um, can we be…'

'We can be friends,' he said, the rain rapidly turning his coat a darker shade. 'That's what you were going to ask? Can we be friends?'

'Yeah. I think it will be easier. It's easier to just let things go. And I know Moss will be pleased.'

He nodded, and blinked against the falling rain. 'Look, I have to go.'

'OK, bye.'

He slammed the door and ran off to the awning of Lewisham Station. Erika watched until he went inside. She was pleased to see him looking like his old self, and was pleased they had agreed to be friends. But that was easier said than done, working together with all their baggage.

Her phone rang, making her jump. It was Moss.

'Boss, where are you? We've had a positive ID on the girl.'

'I'm just around the corner. Who is she?'

'A Nina Hargreaves, aged nineteen.'

'And you think it's right? That the ID is reliable?'

'It should be. It was her mother who called the hotline number.'

CHAPTER 50

It was very late when Nina Hargreaves's mother, Mandy, arrived at Lewisham Row. Erika and Moss took her up to the conference room on the top floor of the station, and they got one of the uniform officers to go out and buy some decent takeaway coffee.

'Thank you for coming in to talk to us, Mrs Hargreaves,' said Erika. There was a large sofa in the corner by the window, and she indicated for Mandy to sit. Erika and Moss turned two of the chairs around from the long table and sat opposite. At this stage they wanted the chat to be as informal as possible. Erika hadn't yet ruled her out as having valuable information, but the best way to get people to talk was to have them relax. The officer arrived with cappuccinos and handed them out.

'Thank you,' said Mandy, taking the cup and cradling it in her hands. She was a small woman, in her fifties, but she wore her dark hair very long, past her shoulders. She had clear olive skin and was very beautiful. She wore blue jeans and a tight black jumper and looked much younger than her years.

'What made you call us?' asked Erika.

Mandy took a sip of her coffee.

'Because I think my daughter will be safer in custody.'

A look passed between Erika and Moss.

'You saw the details of our enquiry?'

Mandy nodded. 'My neighbour saw it on her Facebook page. The picture from a CCTV camera. She knocked on my door and I went over, watched it on the BBC London news with her.'

'Your daughter is wanted for questioning in relation to a murder.'

'I know.'

'Now, you positively identified her from this image,' said Erika, pulling the image from a folder.

Mandy took the printout and bit her lip. 'Yes. She looks thin.'

'We also believe that Nina has been involved in the deaths of two other people, and may have been involved in, or witnessed, a third.'

Mandy gave a gasp and then broke down. Her hands shook so badly that her coffee spilled out onto the floor.

'I'm sorry, so sorry.'

'It's okay,' said Moss, grabbing some napkins and helping her clean up. Mandy took one and wiped her eyes. Her mascara had started to run.

'I've been estranged from Nina for almost a year now… It's not like she went off the rails… Her dad, my husband, died when she was eleven. Heart attack. He was a delivery driver, and I'm sure it was all those long hours and fast food… Nina was my little tower of strength. I was the one who crumbled to pieces, and she was there to look after me, perk me up… She's my only child.'

'How did you become estranged?' asked Erika.

'After she left school, all her friends went to university, but she was lost. She didn't know what to do with herself. I wanted her to go to university, but we couldn't afford it, and she wasn't that keen so I thought what's the point of her getting into debt with loans for the next twenty years. She got a job at a local chip shop. There was this guy working there, older guy, who she got obsessed with. His name's Max Kirkham.' She sniffed and wiped her nose with the napkin.

'And are they still together?'

Mandy picked up the printouts from the CCTV camera. 'I'll bet you anything that's him,' she said, pointing to the image of the man wearing the blue Von Dutch cap with his head down.

Erika looked at Moss, whose eyebrows had disappeared into her hairline.

'How can you be sure this is Max Kirkham?' asked Erika.

'It looks like him. The hair, the nose, even though it's blurred, and because the only way she'll escape him is if they get caught, or if one of them dies. And then that would be the only way she would come back to me...' She shook her head and the tears started to flow again.

'What do you know about Max Kirkham?'

She took another napkin from Moss and wiped her eyes. 'Very little. No parents that I know of. He says they both died and he was sent to a children's home. No other family. He's obsessed with weird stuff, like conspiracy theories and the Illuminati, guns and weapons. He tried to join the army but he was refused on psychological grounds. He keeps hunting knives; I know he got into building air rifles.'

'How old is he?'

'He's in his thirties. We went to his birthday drinks.'

'We?'

'Me and my ex-partner. We broke up six, seven months ago. That birthday party was an education. If you can call a bunch of angry white young men going mad in a pub a party. That was the night that the rot set in. I hadn't been happy about her and Max, and then things kicked off.'

'Which pub was it?' asked Moss.

'I think it was The White Horse on Carradine Road, in Crouch End. Filthy, violent shithole. I tried to get her to come with me that night, just to come home, to get out of that place and let Max sleep off whatever he was taking and drinking... but despite all the drink and the people, it was like he had eyes in the back of his head and was watching her. He came over from the other side of the bar and started hurling abuse at me. Called me the C-word.' She shook her head. 'Nina took his side, said I'd been the one who was confrontational. She told me to go home and calm down. She said I'd upset him. *I'd* upset *him*.' Mandy shook her head again. 'It was after that they moved in together, or she moved in with him.'

'Do you know where they moved?'

'No.'

'You don't know her address?' asked Moss, sounding a little incredulous. Mandy looked up at her.

'Do you have children?'

'Yes, I have a little boy.'

'Being estranged from your child is one of the most awful things in the world. I tried to keep in contact. But she blocked me from Facebook; she deleted me from her phone. She dropped all her friends. She dropped off the face of the earth. I did hire a private investigator at one point, but he was hopeless and cost me the earth. He couldn't find her. Her friend Kath managed to find her through a friend of a friend and look at her Facebook profile, but she'd stopped updating it. Does that satisfy you that I'm not a heartless bitch?'

'I'm sorry,' said Moss. 'I know this must be hard.'

'Yes, and we're very grateful to you for coming to talk to us, especially so late. Do you have a photo of Nina?' asked Erika.

'I've got loads of her, and I've got one of her and him,' said Mandy wearily. She picked up her handbag and took out a small plastic Snappy Snaps album. 'The photo of him is in the back. I only kept it cos… Cos I thought I might have to give it to the police.'

'You thought Max might murder someone?'

'No, I thought Max would kill Nina.'

Erika and Moss took the album and flicked through the photos. They showed Nina from when she was ten years old, wearing a Brownie outfit beside a Christmas tree. She had her mother's dark good looks and smiled cheekily, her hands on her hips. She was an active young girl, and another photo showed her with a blonde girl in a swimming pool, another sitting on the sofa cuddling a cat, and then the photos moved to when she was in her late teens, and Nina was sitting in a restaurant, blocking the camera lens with her hand, a smattering of acne on her jawline. As they reached the back of the album, the final photo was of Nina behind the counter in a chip shop, wearing a white coat, hat and hairnet.

'I took that one without her knowing,' said Mandy. 'Her first night working at Santino's chip shop. That's where she met Max.'

'When was this?' asked Erika, holding up the photo.

'August, last year.'

'How long did she work there?'

'A couple of months. They both got fired for not turning up. Then they signed on, although Max deals drugs on the side. That's his real income.'

Erika found a photo tucked in the back of the album. It was taken by a car in a sunny street with terraced houses. Nina sat next to a handsome lad with long blond hair. She wore small pink shorts and a white T-shirt. Her feet were bare and her long hair tied back. She had her arm hooked through his, and her head was turned to him. He wore football shorts, a sleeveless T-shirt and a baseball cap.

'Can we use this photo?' asked Erika.

'Yes. That's why it's there.'

There was silence for a moment.

'Officers, what's going to happen to Nina? She's not herself; she's been brainwashed by him. She's scared and I think he's been asking her do things under duress. I just want her to be safe. Do you take that kind of thing into account if you catch him and her?'

'Yes, it is something we will take into account,' said Erika. Moss glanced at her and they both knew that she was telling Mandy what she wanted to hear.

There was a knock at the door and a young female officer entered.

'Mandy, this is Detective Constable Kay Price,' said Erika. 'She'll take you home, and will be our point of contact.'

'That's it?'

'Yes, it is for now. We'll let you know as soon as we have any more information.'

'Nice to meet you,' said Kay, smiling and shaking her hand.

'There is one more thing,' said Mandy, as she got up to leave. 'One of the last times I spoke to Nina, she was on holiday with Max. They were in Devon, and she called me from a phone box. I don't know if her phone was dead. She said she'd been attacked, and Max had done something about it.'

'How do you mean, "done something"?'

'She hung up and I called back. I called 192 to try and find out where the number was, and it was just a phone box by the motorway which leads to Okehampton. When she came home, she laughed it off and never spoke about it again. She said they'd been drinking, but it didn't sound like she was drunk. She sounded—'

'How did she sound?' asked Erika, putting a hand on her arm.

'In the grip of terror. Absolutely terrified...' She started to cry again. 'I haven't slept properly in months, I stopped living my life. My relationship crumbled... I saw on the news what they did to that bloke. So I'll either see my daughter across a table in a prison visiting room, or on a mortuary slab. Either way it will be some kind of resolution.'

Erika looked across at Mandy, and thought how sad and defeated she must feel to say this.

CHAPTER 51

The armed response team arrived in Kennington very early the next morning, just after 5 a.m. Erika and Moss were stationed in a support van around the corner from the front entrance to the high-rise block of flats. It was a grimy 1970s building, tucked away in the maze of houses stretching away from the tube station and The Oval. It made up the Wallis Simpson Estate and three other blocks rose up to form a grid of four. They had traced Nina Hargreaves, and in turn Max Kirkham, through the benefits office to a one-bedroom flat on the ground floor of Baden-Powell House, and Erika had rapidly put together an armed response team to arrest them both. Neither of them had been named in the media coverage the previous night, but there was still a chance they could have seen it and run.

It was freezing cold in the support van, and Erika and Moss were watching on a screen as the firearms team moved into place, surrounding the building. The team was twelve strong, and headed by DI Parkinson, a determined woman with red hair.

'She's like a thinner version of me with a rifle,' Moss had joked, after Erika had conducted the 3.30 a.m. briefing at Lewisham Row.

'We're in position. There are no signs of anyone inside the flat, no lights are on,' came Parkinson's voice through the radio.

'Just be on the lookout from above,' replied Erika.

'Above, below, our eyes are everywhere. This is a bloody rough estate…' There was some interference and the radio fell silent. Erika wasn't directly in command: it was down to DI Parkinson, but this was the first armed response team Erika had been closely involved with since she was an officer in Manchester, and she was extremely nervous.

There was another burst of interference and Parkinson's voice came booming through. 'We're activating our cameras.' There was a monitor set up on the desk in front of Erika and Moss, and it lit up with six screens.

'Jeez, the wonders of modern technology,' said Moss.

Each video feed was being beamed wirelessly from the lapels of the armed response team. The night-vision footage was tinged with green and a little grainy, but they could see three slightly different angles of the large floodlit car park filled with a smattering of parked cars. Another feed showed the doors of the first floor flats stretching away along a concrete hallway, and the fourth and fifth were being beamed to them from a little way along the street and looking at the opposite side of the building.

This was a new development for policing. Body-worn camera technology had only been rolled out to the Met's front line officers six months previously, and this was the first time Erika and Moss had seen it in action.

'Okay, we're moving in,' said DI Parkinson. The grainy footage on the top row of images shook as the team stealthily moved forward.

The front door moved closer towards them on the screens. Two other video feeds showed a view along the concrete hallway, where two officers were stationed either side of the communal staircase. As well as night-vision cameras, two members of the armed response team had been equipped with night-vision goggles.

This had been questioned earlier in the evening during an emergency meeting with Marsh and Superintendent Hudson.

'This is a busy block of flats. The flats are very small with communal lighting,' Marsh had argued. 'There are floodlights in the car park, and London is heavily light polluted.'

Erika had then told them about the interview with Mandy Hargreaves, and how she had told them about Max's obsession with the army and weapons.

'We don't know what we're going to find, and we can't wait to go in until daylight,' Erika had argued. 'You do realise that night-vision goggles have been approved for some pretty crazy stuff. Staffordshire council have used them in the past to catch dog walkers who didn't pick up after their dogs, and police in Swindon used them to catch a gang of allotment robbers. This is a multiple murder investigation!'

Marsh had relented and authorised the use of night-vision goggles.

On the monitor, Erika and Moss saw the team approach the front door of the flat, the images steady as they moved slowly. But on another feed from the bottom of the communal stairs there was the sound of footsteps and then two lads in tracksuits and baseball caps rounded the corner. They were very young and their eyes opened wide with fear at the sight of the armed response team.

'Go back up, and get back inside,' hissed the officer. On the screen they saw a gloved hand signal for them to go back up the stairs. The lads turned and dashed back up the steps.

'Oh, here we go,' said Moss, indicating another video feed showing an officer at the front window of the flat.

'The kitchen opens out straight onto this main corridor,' said Erika. The image on screen went dark as the officer peered through the window. There was a long pause, and a burst of static and murmuring. The four video feeds at the front door suddenly pulled back, and they saw the building rapidly receding through the video link.

'What's going on?' asked Erika. 'Can you hear me?'

'Everyone fall back immediately,' came DI Parkinson's voice through the radio. 'I repeat, fall back immediately. It looks like an explosive device has been rigged up in the kitchen, on a large table. It looks like a small explosive grenade, and it's connected to a wire.'

'Shit,' said Erika, turning to Moss.

'We need to evacuate the building, and get the bomb disposal unit down here fast,' said Parkinson.

CHAPTER 52

It was just after 7.30 a.m. when Mariette Hoffman entered Bunhill Fields cemetery and walked towards the gravestones. The sun was just coming up and lighting the sky with blue and gold. The tall trees were now bare, and her white trainers looked grubby against the carpet of orange and red leaves covering the grass. She carried a bag of shopping and another small carrier bag with cloths and cleaning supplies. It was a calming place amongst the surrounding chaos, and the sounds of the traffic were muted. Mariette loved the early mornings, when the day was fresh, new and full of opportunity. She'd bought a scratch card, and it sat in the shopping bag with milk, butter, and nice wholemeal bread. The thought of it filled her with hope. She was going to pay her respects, and then go home and make herself a nice cup of strong tea and a couple of rounds of hot buttered toast. Then she'd try her luck with the scratch card. Last month at the Tesco Metro, she'd watched as a woman had won £500 on a quid scratch card – and she'd looked pretty well off in the first place. It was now a new month, and surely it was time for someone else to have a chance. Even a hundred quid would be a gift from God.

The cemetery was tucked away less than a mile from Mariette's flat on the Pinkhurst Estate. She was a regular visitor and liked to lose herself amongst the moss-covered gravestones. There were even some ornate tombs with carved marble and topped with angels and cherubs, and she'd often stop to read the inscriptions dating back to the 1800s. There were young women who'd died of consumption, babies who'd only lived for a few days and then succumbed to yellow fever.

She'd scattered Thomas's ashes a couple of weeks back, on the grass by a row of benches. She was too poor to afford a plot or a headstone, and she'd had to ask the council for financial help just to have him cremated.

She didn't give the benches more than a glance, then took a left, down a gravel path. At the end of a long row, next to a thick oak tree root pushing up underneath the path, was a square headstone of simple black granite. Embossed in gold letters were the names of her mother and father. They had bought one of the last family plots before the cemetery was closed for new burials. It was full up, like the rest of London.

Mariette put her bags down and took out a small dustpan and brush; unclipping the brush, she set to work, sweeping away the wet leaves covering the base of the headstone. Then she took out a cloth and wiped it down, running it carefully over the gold lettering.

MAY JEAN KIRKHAM	DEREK KIRKHAM
DIED 1/2/1981	DIED 23/03/1982

'There, all clean and tidy.' She straightened up and rested the cloth on top of the headstone for a moment, breathing in the cold morning air. She'd assumed she'd be alone this early in the morning, but she saw a flash of colour behind a tree in the next row.

Max appeared from behind it with a young brown-haired girl in tow. They both wore baseball caps pulled down low, and Mariette thought how skinny and exhausted the girl looked. Max hurried towards her, ducking through the headstones. He was carrying a rucksack, and so was the girl.

'Alright, Mum,' he said.

Mariette pursed her lips and chucked the cloth back in the bag.

'This is my girlfriend, Nina.'

'I saw her photo on the news last night,' said Mariette, looking Nina up and down. 'You look fatter in your picture. It suits you.'

Nina didn't know how to reply to that.

'Hi. It's nice to meet you, I didn't know…'

'Didn't know he had a mother?'

'He never told me,' said Nina.

'I gave him up, did he tell you that? Had him adopted. And then all these years later he found me… Though he should have stayed lost if you ask me.' She picked up her bags and walked off.

Nina gave Max a pained look.

'Now what the hell are we going to do?' she hissed.

Max shook his head and smiled, and then ran to catch up with Mariette. He walked alongside her, and unhooked one of the straps on his backpack.

'I can give you five grand now, in cash, and another five when we leave,' he said, taking one of the bundles of fifties out. Mariette stopped. She slowly put down her bags and took the bundle of cash, flicking it through her fingers, and then, almost comically, smelling it. She looked at Nina, who was hanging back at the end of a row of gravestones.

'What does she know?'

'Everything. She knows about Thomas and Charlene. She's the one who finished off Charlene.'

Mariette pursed her lips and tilted her head, looking Nina up and down.

'She looks a bit wet to me. Posh spoilt girl. Likes a bit of rough, does she?'

Max leaned in close to her face. 'Listen, you bitter old cunt. That money is real and so is this,' he said, holding up another bundle of £50 notes. 'In return we need to hide out at your place for a few days. I have a plan, and we'll be out of your badly dyed hair before you know it.'

Mariette seemed to take more offence at Max saying she dyed her hair badly than by him calling her the C-word.

'Fine,' she said.

'Aren't you curious where I got the money?'

'No,' she said, taking the bundle of notes and stuffing it into her coat pocket. 'Where's your car?'

'It's outside the lock-up.'

Mariette took a bunch of keys from her other pocket. 'You go now and park it inside. I'll take her back to the flat. We'll meet you there.'

Max took the keys and darted off towards the trees.

'And you can take these bags,' said Mariette, holding them out. Nina came over and took them. 'Come on, I'll put the kettle on.'

Nina looked around, and reluctantly followed Mariette out of the cemetery.

CHAPTER 53

It took several hours for the bomb disposal squad to clear and search the building, and ensure it was safe. They removed a small device they found sitting on the kitchen table, and took it away for further analysis. Shortly before midday, Erika and Moss, with the forensics team, entered the flat shared by Max and Nina. As they walked through the small flat, Erika was struck by how sparse their possessions were. There was very little food in the fridge, some out-of-date milk and a small tub of spread. The bathroom contained nothing but a single bar of soap, a razor and an empty box of tampons. The living room had some generic furniture and a small TV. There were no magazines or DVDs.

'You think they cleared out all their stuff when the media ran the picture of Nina Hargreaves?' asked Moss.

'I don't know. Unless they were minimalists?' said Erika.

One of the CSIs in protective gear appeared in a doorway at the end of the hallway.

'You should see this,' he said.

Erika and Moss followed. It was the bedroom, and it took a moment for Erika to work out what was different. On all four walls, piled from the floor to the ceiling were books, hundreds and hundreds of books of all shapes and sizes. A small wardrobe sat on the opposite wall to the bed, and the books had been stacked around it and on top of it. None of the wall was visible, apart from a small piece above the door. The bed was unmade and the room smelt musty.

'I wonder if they ran a book club,' said Moss. Erika heard the CSI stifle a chuckle behind his mask. She moved to the wardrobe and opened it. There were a few pieces of clothing hanging up: cheap women's stuff from off the market and a couple of pairs of old jeans, and a pile of underwear. There was also a stack of porn in the bottom. Erika pulled on a pair of latex gloves and pulled one of them out. It was extreme stuff. There were bondage scenes; in one of the pictures, a young woman lay strapped to a table with a gag ball in her mouth. Her eyes were wide with fear, and the skin across her breasts and stomach was red raw and mottled with blood. A man, naked apart from a black leather hood, stood over her with a riding crop. Erika flicked through and the images got progressively worse. She counted twenty-seven magazines in total and saw beside them was a stack of re-writable DVDs. Moss appeared behind her.

'Boss. You should look at this.'

Erika replaced the stack of magazines and went over to the right-hand corner of the bed. At first glance, the books looked like they were stacked in blocks of colour, but on closer inspection, she saw that the books were duplicated many times.

'He has seventeen copies of *Mein Kampf*, all stacked together; there's another twenty-five copies of *The Gates of Janus*,' said Moss.

Erika pulled one of the copies out and looked at the cover. '*The Gates of Janus: Serial Killing and its Analysis by the Moors Murderer Ian Brady*,' she said, reading. The cover had a hand-drawn image of Ian Brady. His intense, glowering stare always gave her chills.

'In each version, he's made notes on every page,' said the CSI, thumbing through another two identical copies. 'There are books here about the Holocaust, psychology, hypnosis, philosophy. The whole wall on the left side of the wardrobe is stacked with copies of the Bible; the Old and New Testaments, the Hebrew Bible, The Qur'an. And there are sixty-four copies of *American Psycho* …'

Erika looked around the walls and saw that despite the volume of books, there were maybe a hundred or so original titles. The rest were duplicates.

'There's no law against hoarding the same copy of one book over and over, or reading religious texts,' she said.

'Yes. My wife has the Famous Five books, old and new editions,' said the CSI.

'The original books are completely class-ridden, aren't they?' said Moss. 'I was quite shocked at how different the modern versions are when I read them to my son.'

'What's that got to do with anything?' said Erika.

'Well. Owning books and reading isn't a crime,' said the CSI. 'One can read widely and explore different opinions. It doesn't mean they agree with them. Despite the extreme nature of this particular library... I'm more concerned with the hardcore pornography in the wardrobe than words written on a page. Those women are real, and the terrible things that happened to them when the photos were taken are real. All these books, it's just a jumble of letters on a piece of paper.'

'True,' said Moss. 'But what's that saying? The pen is mightier than the sword?'

Erika was about to change the subject, when another CSI appeared at the door.

'We've found something in the hallway,' she said.

They followed to where a full-length mirror had been lifted off the wall. The CSI held up a small exercise book in her gloved hand. Erika took it and leafed through page after page of diary entries in neat blue ink.

'This is her diary,' said Erika, scanning the pages.

'It was jammed in the cavity behind the mirror,' said the CSI.

The hallway went dark as the blinds were lowered and the light turned out in the kitchen.

'Can you close the doors to all the rooms?' asked a voice. The CSI who had discovered the diary moved to close the doors to the living room, bathroom, and bedroom and the interior of the flat went dark.

Still clutching the diary, Erika moved to the entrance of the kitchen; it was in darkness. There was a click and the room was bathed in violet UV light. One of the CSIs knelt on the floor beside the back door, holding a flat UV lamp. He started to play it slowly from the edge of the door towards where Erika and Moss were standing. The light dispersed in an even layer until he hit the centre of the room and the UV bulb picked up the brightly glowing residue of a massive pool of blood; it extended several metres out across the middle of the kitchen, and there was blood spatter residue all up the cupboards, over the fridge, and up part of the wall.

'Jesus, it must have been a bloodbath in here,' said Moss.

CHAPTER 54

Later that afternoon, Erika was unexpectedly called into a meeting at the New Scotland Yard building in central London. She arrived alone and was shown straight up to the conference room on the top floor.

When she entered, everyone was assembled. At the head of a long, polished table was the assistant commissioner of the Met Police, Camilla Brace-Cosworthy. She was dressed for battle in a beautiful powder-blue designer suit and a chunky gold necklace. Her nails were painted red to match her lipstick, and her blonde hair had recently been cut very short, and parted to one side. Moss had coined this haircut 'The Machiavellian Bob'. Beside Camilla, her assistant was poised to take notes, and to Camilla's right and left were Commander Marsh and Superintendent Hudson. They had both dressed up for the occasion. Colleen Scanlan sat next to Melanie. Next to Marsh sat a man and a woman. They were a similar age to Erika and were dressed in very expensive suits.

'I'm sorry I'm late. I didn't have much notice we were going to meet. I had to come from the crime scene,' said Erika, looking down at her plaster cast, scruffy black trousers, creased blouse and long black coat covered in fingerprint dust. She smoothed her hair down and took the seat next to Colleen. She nodded at the man and woman opposite, but they ignored her.

'Don't worry, Erika. You're right on time,' said Camilla in her usual patronising tone. 'Now we can get started.'

Erika looked to see if the man and woman opposite wore name badges, but there was nothing. She wondered why Camilla hadn't introduced them. She thought they must be important because tea and coffee had been provided in china cups, with a milk jug and sugar lumps in bowls. Brown *and* white. After being up all night and most of the day, Erika was parched so she poured herself a steaming cup, and dropped in two lumps of sugar.

Melanie opened the meeting and outlined what had happened in the early hours of the morning with the raid on the block of flats in Kennington, and she confirmed that the device found in the kitchen wasn't a terror-related explosive.

'Thank you,' said Camilla. 'Now if I can firstly address the events leading up to the armed response unit going in…The problem I'm having with all this, Erika, is that you went in there, perhaps, with insufficient intelligence?'

Erika put down her cup, surprised. 'We did speak with the counter terrorism unit beforehand…'

'I am here representing counter terrorism,' said the man, speaking for the first time. He had a smooth, and rather high voice.

'Then you know,' said Erika.

'And we told you the current threat level for terrorism was severe.'

'Sorry, can I ask who you are?'

'I told you, I represent counter terrorism.'

Camilla then interrupted. 'I think what we're all concerned about is that this device could have been triggered, and if it had been it could have resulted in catastrophic loss of life. We're just concerned, Erika, that procedure is followed to the letter. Are you aware of the disruption this caused? The resources that had to be deployed to evacuate not just the building but the surrounding area?' She cocked her head and stared at Erika.

She felt anger rising in her stomach.

'Ma'am, we had a positive ID on Nina Hargreaves and Max Kirkham. There was nothing to suggest that they would plant an explosive device. As I said I contacted counter terrorism to share intel, there are no known terror cells operating in that area. Max Kirkham has a previous conviction for petty theft as a teenager, and Nina Hargreaves has a clean record.'

'Nina Hargreaves's mother stated that Max Kirkham was obsessed with air rifles,' said Camilla, looking down at her notes.

'She did, yes. That's why we had the armed response team who went in prepared with assault rifles and body armour. This operation was done by the book, ma'am. But there are often things you just can't plan for. I think that the team headed by DI Parkinson should be commended for how they dealt with this safely and efficiently...' Erika turned back to the woman opposite. 'And if you don't mind me asking, what's your role here?'

She shifted uncomfortably.

'I'm a representative from the Home Office. If this had been a terrorist attack, we would have had to convene a meeting of COBRA. Of course, all this kind of stuff is well above your pay grade.'

Erika smiled and tried to remain calm. 'With respect, I repeat again, it wasn't a terrorist attack.'

'It was a home-made explosive device found in a central London location,' said the woman, spreading her hands and looking around the table with amusement. 'Kennington is a densely populated area of the capital. What if it had been a chemical weapon, or a nuclear device? We would have been looking at an exclusion zone including the Palace of Westminster. *Millions of people affected*.'

'All valid points,' said Erika. 'But I don't know why I've been called to this meeting?'

'Erika,' started Marsh, fixing her with a grim stare, but she went on: 'Which has taken me away from a multiple murder case. Now, if you all want to talk about the nuts and bolts of what happened last night, fine. I'd like it on the record that I had to fight for two of the officers on that armed response team to be issued with night-vision goggles.'

'Erika, this is not the forum to start dictating requests for police equipment and budgets,' snapped Camilla.

'With respect, ma'am, perhaps it is. I feel that the officers who work the beat don't have the opportunity to voice these concerns. Night-vision goggles retail at around three hundred quid a pair, and there is a shortage of these in the force. Now if those two officers hadn't been equipped with night-vision, they would have battered down the door to that flat, detonating the device, and most likely, they would have been killed. And as the unnamed lady opposite me states, the device could have been anything: a dirty bomb, or a nuclear device. So my point is that officers need to be properly equipped. No one wants to read in the newspaper that for want of six hundred quid, the centre of London is now a nuclear exclusion zone and no longer habitable. But, of course, as you say, this is far above my pay grade.'

She sat back, shaking. There was a nasty silence.

'Paul? Melanie? You are Erika's line managers? Any thoughts from you?' asked Camilla, breaking the silence.

CHAPTER 55

Marsh looked furious as he headed down in the lift with Erika and Melanie.

'I'm sorry. I stand by everything I said in there,' said Erika.

'You put my arse on the line.'

'You put your own arse on the line!'

'Erika…' warned Melanie.

'Sorry, no. I am not going to be blamed for telling the truth. You think I'm stupid. I was called in there as a scapegoat. They were looking for someone to pin the blame on for this morning's expensive evacuation.'

'You don't understand how budgets run the force, Erika,' said Marsh.

'No, people run the force! Officers! And who were those two suits? They were Home Office, weren't they? Why couldn't they have the decency to tell me their names? All this cloak-and-dagger stuff is so boring. Don't come to a bloody meeting and sit there with a face like a slapped arse. Why can't we work together instead of causing divisions and power struggles. It's exhausting.'

'It was only on Superintendent Hudson's recommendation that you were even allowed to attend!' snapped Marsh.

'I appreciate that, Melanie,' said Erika.

'She is your senior officer and you will address her as such!' shouted Marsh.

'Thank you, ma'am,' said Erika. She knew she was winding Marsh up by staying calm, so she carried on. 'I felt like I was the only one in that meeting who genuinely cared about this case, and about catching Nina Hargreaves and Max Kirkham.'

'You've never grasped how government departments work, and how we have to work hand in hand with the civil service,' said Marsh.

'There is no one more committed than me to this case,' said Erika. 'And this meeting was a waste of time. I should be back at the station. There was blood spatter residue all over that flat. Forensics found four different blood types. We also have a diary written by, we think, Nina Hargreaves which goes into some details about their crimes.'

'Do you have any leads on their whereabouts?' asked Melanie.

'No. And that's what we should be having meetings about. They've killed four people, that we know of, and I think we only found out who they were because they wanted us to. And that's something very dangerous for us to deal with.'

They came to the ground floor and the lift doors opened. They walked out into the street, and it looked like it was threatening to rain. Marsh still looked furious.

'I want you to supervise Erika on this case, Melanie. It seems, as usual, she needs reining in. And in future, Erika will not attend meetings with senior management.'

'Yes, sir.'

Marsh stalked off to his car, waiting by the kerb, and got in without inviting them to join him back to the station.

As it drove away, Erika turned to Melanie. 'Okay, I hear what everyone is saying. And I will work with you on this case. We've always got along, and I respect you.'

'It's okay, Erika. Between you and me I quite enjoyed seeing you have a go at them about the budget cuts. Although you need to be careful with these Cabinet Office types. They are woefully cut off from the real world.'

'Thank you,' said Erika.

'And Marsh really squirmed when Camilla gave him a bollocking.'

'I think Marsh misses the old assistant commissioner. He knew how to flatter and manipulate Oakley.'

'Okay, so what is your next move, Erika?'

'I want to work forensics, dig more into the background of Max and Nina. We need to find them.'

'They have to have someone who is working with them or sheltering them,' said Melanie.

'We've put a hold on Nina Hargreaves's passport; Max Kirkham doesn't even own one. All airports, ports, and train stations are on high alert, and we've got all the nationwide crime agencies on board with their photos.'

'Why didn't you say all of this back there in the meeting?' said Melanie. 'That's the officer I know who has her head screwed on.'

Erika shrugged. 'I know, I'm stupid. But I'm sick and tired of dealing with top brass who have no clue how policing works.'

'I hear you. Now, I don't know where Marsh has stormed off to, he needs to be back here in an hour.'

'Why?'

'The two of you are going to make a formal statement to the press,' said Melanie.

CHAPTER 56

It was early evening, and Nina and Max were in front of the mirror in the cramped bathroom of Mariette's flat. Max was perched on a stool, and Nina had just finished shaving his head with clippers.

'Jeez, my head feels cold,' he said, rubbing his hand over the short stubble and leaning in to the mirror.

'You look good. You've got a nice shaped head.'

'And you, my darling, give very nice head,' he said. He stood, unzipped his flies and started to push her down.

'Max! No. No, I keep hearing your mother walking past the door. And there's no lock.'

'It would probably give her a thrill,' he said, stripping off his clothes and jumping into the tiny shower cubicle.

Nina started to pick up Max's long locks of blond hair and, checking if he was watching, she slipped one into her pocket. She looked around at the grubby bathroom with the avocado suite and the Spanish señorita knitted toilet roll holders. She found Mariette, and her flat, grubby, and a little creepy. When they first arrived, Mariette had made her some tea and toast and pulled out all the old photo albums. Nina had assumed this was to show her some baby pictures of Max, but every one of the ten photo albums contained pictures of Mariette as a majorette in marching bands and competitions.

'Help yourself to what you want in the flat, love,' she'd said, touching Nina's knee lightly. 'But if I see you touching that hat or that baton, I'll break your fucking legs.'

Nina had waited for Mariette to laugh or say it was a joke, but she hadn't. She'd followed Mariette's gaze to the hooks above the sofa where the hat and baton were displayed, and she'd promised not to touch them.

'Good girl, I think we have an understanding,' she said.

Nina looked at her reflection in the mirror. She'd already cut her shoulder-length hair extremely short, and with the aid of a home hair bleaching kit, she was now transformed. She tilted her head and liked what she saw. It was astonishing how different she looked. Max finished in the shower and he opened the door, reaching out for a towel. She handed him one and he stepped out onto the carpet.

'So, what do you think of my plan?' he said, watching her in the mirror.

Nina chewed her lip and looked at herself in the mirror. 'Let's do it. But promise me one thing, they don't get hurt.'

'I promise you; no one will get hurt,' said Max. He opened the towel and pulled her against his growing hardness. This time Nina couldn't resist and she sank down and took him in her mouth.

The plan had started to form early that evening, when two police officers had appeared outside Scotland Yard to make a formal statement about the Daniel de Souza murder case, and that they were officially linking it to the murders of Thomas Hoffman and Charlene Selby.

Max had googled the officers, and read with interest everything about Detective Chief Inspector Erika Foster, how she had lost her husband during a drug raid, and there was a profile about her written in the *Daily Mail* a few years previously, when she had caught the serial killer, Simone Matthews. It painted a picture of a lonely, driven woman. No children, few friends. And Max decided their plan wouldn't work on her. She had no one who would miss her.

When he googled Commander Paul Marsh, something very interesting came up in the search results. It was a small piece in a south London local newspaper, dated 2015, and it told how Commander Marsh had taken part in the Hilly Fields Fun Run, in aid of Comic Relief. He'd run six miles dressed as Lady Gaga, helping to raise £10,000 for charity. The article showed Paul Marsh with his wife Marcie, who had made the costume for him, but it was the picture at the bottom of the article which really lit a fire in Max's mind.

Marsh was pictured at the finish line with his wife, Marcie, and their two small daughters. He'd pored over the picture. They were identical twins called Mia and Sophie. Cute as buttons, the pair of them.

'I bet they would be worth a lot if they were to go missing,' Max had said.

'What do mean?' asked Nina.

'If you abduct just any old kid, the police always say that they don't get into paying ransoms. The police won't pay a ransom in a kidnap situation, but abduct the kid or kids of a senior police officer, and I bet it's a whole different ball game.'

CHAPTER 57

The next morning, Nina and Max started to put their plan into action. Commander Paul Marsh wasn't on Facebook, but Marcie was, and even though her account was locked right down, it still showed the things that she had 'liked'. One of these was The Acorns Nursery, in Hilly Fields, south London. They did a name search online and found Paul and Marcie's address. They lived on Hilly Fields Road, which was less than a mile from The Acorns Nursery.

Another online search revealed that The Acorns Nursery was looking for a part-time childminder. Max knew the advantages of having a nice white girl with a middle-class voice to put people at ease, so he got Nina to phone up and ask some general questions about the job. He crouched beside her and listened in to the conversation. Nina spent the first few minutes chatting to the secretary at the nursery about her past 'experience', and when she had established a rapport, she started to fish for more information.

'A friend of mine's kids actually come to the nursery,' said Nina. 'I didn't want to mention her right away, and put you on the spot. It's Marcie Marsh? She says her twins love it there.'

The secretary gave a slight pause on the end of the phone, and Nina waited to see if she'd guessed correctly.

'Oh yes, they're so cute,' said the secretary. 'Sophie and Mia. And they really are identical, you probably know, Marcie dresses them in the same clothes so we often have trouble telling them apart!'

Max was listening in beside Nina and he put his thumbs up.

'Yes, whenever we go shopping and she sees a little girl's outfit, the first thing Marcie asks is if they have two in stock!'

'Too much,' mouthed Max. Nina nodded.

'Okay, well, I'd love to apply for the job. What days are you hiring for?'

'It's Monday, Tuesday, and Wednesday.'

'That's great,' said Nina. She paused and decided to go for it. 'That would mean I get to see the girls too.'

'Yes, well they're here every day except Thursday. Marcie has them in just the four days a week. She likes to spend Thursday with them.'

'Yeah, yeah she does... Okay. Super. Look, I've downloaded an application from your website, so I'll fill it in and get it back to you?'

'What's your name again?' asked the secretary.

'It's Emma. Emma Potter,' said Nina.

'OK, Emma, I'll look out for it. Good luck!'

Nina replaced the receiver. They were quiet for a moment. They'd taken the phone upstairs to the landing, and they were sitting on the carpet outside the bathroom.

'You, are a fucking genius,' said Max.

'I don't know about this,' said Nina, feeling sick. She was shocked how easy it had been to find out the information. 'Even if we did do it, how the hell are we going to walk up to that nursery and get those twins to come with us? And Marcie will be there.'

'No, she won't,' said Max. 'I'll make sure of it.'

'You said no one would get hurt?'

'No one will. But she's our biggest problem, Marcie. We'll find a way of you pretending to be the new nanny, and you can pick up the kids. We just need to keep being inventive with this. We'll need to get hold of Marcie's mobile phone, and you'll have to find a way to imitate her voice. Good old-fashioned espionage.'

He smiled and leaned in to kiss her, but she pulled back.

'You have to promise me that we just kidnap them. We don't lay a finger on them. I'm serious, Max.'

''Course, Neen. This is two little kids. I'd never hurt kids. We'll take them for forty-eight hours, tops. They'll be safe and warm. And how old are they? They won't remember this in years to come. We'll take some board games, and sweets.'

Nina stared into Max's eyes, which seemed so earnest. He took her hand.

'This is our ticket to a new start. A new life together. Once we have the money, we're gone. I'm done with breaking the law, and living on my wits. I want a fresh start, away from this fucking shithole of a country, with its class system, everything being rigged in favour of the rich. Don't you want to go away and make a new life together?'

Nina gripped his hands and nodded. 'Yeah. But promise me again, no one gets hurt.'

'You have my word. I promise.'

'Do you really think it will work?'

'Yes. We have absolutely fuck all to lose, Neen, and that puts us in a very strong position. It makes us dangerous.'

Mariette came clattering out of the living room downstairs, dragging the hoover behind her.

'Are you two finished on the blower? Can I do the carpet?' she said, peering up at them.

'Bloody hell, yes,' said Max.

As she brushed past the front door, the edge of the hoover pipe caught on the curtain across the front door, and pulled it open. Light streamed in from the corridor outside.

'Watch that fucking door!' Max shouted, pulling Nina further back along the landing.

'No one can see you up there!' said Mariette, chucking down the hoover and making a show of pulling the curtain back. 'No one gives two shits about you.'

She dragged the hoover up the stairs and stopped at the top, catching her breath. Max leapt up and slapped her around the face with the back of his hand. She fell forward onto the landing.

'I'm giving you ten grand, okay? You keep the curtains and your mouth shut!' He kicked her in the stomach and she cried out in pain, then he went to the bathroom, slamming the door.

Mariette groaned and rolled over on her back, holding her stomach. Nina went to her, and helped her up.

'Thanks, love,' she said, leaning on the bannister. 'I don't know what you two are up to, but none of this is gonna end well. Things never turn out how you want it to.'

Nina didn't respond. She closed her mind, and tried to concentrate on the end result.

CHAPTER 58

Very early on Friday morning, Nina and Max drove out to take a look at Marsh's house in Hilly Fields Road.

Mariette kept an old white van in her lock-up, and she still had the old magnetic sign used by the plumber she'd bought it off. Max knew that for the plan to work, they had to keep the first part very simple, so they'd stuck the sign back on the side of the van, and he and Nina had dressed in overalls. It was a crude attempt at them posing as a plumber and his apprentice, but Max had realised long ago that if you acted the part, and didn't attempt to hide, it was astonishing what you could get away with.

They turned into Marsh's street just after seven thirty. The sun was coming up, and the first weary-looking commuters were leaving their houses to go to work. They parked a few hundred yards from Marsh's house, and sat in the van with a flask of tea, pretending to do some paperwork. Shortly after 8 a.m. Marsh emerged from his front door, got into his car parked by the kerb and drove right past them. Nina lowered her head and grabbed at the flask on the floor, but Max stared right at Marsh as he passed.

'Jeez. He calls himself a police commander?' said Max. 'He didn't even see me, didn't even look at us, Neen. He was probably more concerned with where he was going to get his first cup of coffee.'

'You need to be careful, Max,' said Nina, her hands shaking.

'Darling. We now look completely different to our photos. And this is a posh area. We're two low-life plumbers. People won't give us a second glance.'

On cue, a woman came out of the front door next to the driver's window. She was dumpy, and looked fed up, wearing the uniform black of the average London office worker. She locked her door and walked past the van, not even noticing them.

'See?' said Max.

Nina poured herself some more tea, but her hands wouldn't stop shaking.

At a quarter to nine, Marcie emerged from the front door with Mia and Sophie. Nina was shocked at how sweet the little girls looked, all dressed up in identical pink dresses, thick white tights and dark blue coats. The two little girls were chatting away as Marcie lifted them up into the back of the car and strapped them into their seats. Nina noted how beautiful Marcie was, with her long, dark hair and gorgeous figure. When the twins were safely buckled in, Marcie climbed into the front and drove off.

'Here we go,' said Max, starting the engine. They followed after her, keeping a distance of two cars as Marcie dropped the twins off at the nursery, which was housed in a large converted end-terrace house.

'It's very close by, the nursery,' said Nina.

'Yeah, and the fucking lazy bitch still drives them,' said Max.

A few minutes later Marcie emerged from the front door of the nursery and got back in her car. She was fiddling with her mobile phone as she drove, and she passed them without a glance.

'Another one in her own world,' said Max.

They set off again in pursuit, following as she drove towards Forest Hill Station, where she bought a takeaway coffee, and some bread from the bakery. Then she drove home.

They followed her until the turn-off back to her house, and then Nina and Max turned in the opposite direction, towards New Cross.

'Okay. So we have the weekend to make our last preparations; we rehearse and run through everything, and then Monday morning, we do it,' said Max.

Nina looked out of the windscreen and was quiet. This felt real. Seeing the two little girls. Seeing how much they loved their mother.

'I clean out the back of the van, and we'll put blankets in the back,' said Max, seeing her face. 'And you can ride with them, and give them sweets and stuff.'

'Okay, yeah.'

'This is about the money, not about hurting anyone.'

'I know.'

'We just have to hope that the bitch doesn't have any posh pals coming over for coffee on Monday morning.'

'People tend to come for coffee later in the morning. Elevenses and all that.'

'Well, I wouldn't know about that. We didn't get elevenses in the children's home,' said Max pointedly.

They drove the rest of the way back to the Pinkhurst Estate in silence. When they arrived back at the lock-up, Max parked the car inside and when the door was shut, he changed the number plates on the van.

CHAPTER 59

It was very late, after a long and frustrating weekend. Erika sat with Isaac Strong in her tiny living room, and between them they had just demolished a huge curry. Isaac had seen how tired and hungry Erika had looked on the news report a few days earlier. He'd called her on Friday and Saturday evening, saying she should take a couple of hours to eat properly and have some downtime, but she'd told him she had to work. On Sunday, she finally agreed to dinner.

'Now you have some colour in your cheeks,' said Isaac, snapping a poppadum in half and dipping it into a little pot of mango chutney.

'That was really good, thank you. That's what I miss when I go back home,' said Erika, taking a long pull on her beer. 'Indian food.'

'You don't have Indian food in Slovakia?'

'Not really. Slovak cooking is very good, so we haven't gone all multicultural with our cuisine.'

'When did you come to the UK?'

'In 1992,' said Erika.

'So you came just at the tail end of our nation's terrible cuisine.' He laughed. 'You should have seen the stuff I used to eat growing up. Fish fingers, chips, minced beef stews with very little taste. I didn't see my first avocado until I went to medical school… My parents weren't very adventurous with food,' said Isaac, laughing.

'Where did you grow up?' asked Erika.

'In Norfolk, in a small village near Norwich.'

'My mother used to fry everything, and it always tasted good, but after dad died she was more of a drinker than a foodie,' said Erika.

'She was an alcoholic?'

'Yeah, but the only person she harmed was herself. She never got violent; she held down a job… Anyway. Let's talk about something else.'

'Fancy a cigarette?'

'I've been craving one all day.'

She grabbed a packet of cigarettes and a lighter from the kitchen drawer, and they pulled on their coats and went out onto the small patio. It was freezing cold, and threatening snow. The clouds hung low and glowed orange from the light pollution in the city. They smoked in silence for a few minutes, looking out at the buildings stretching away over the tops of the trees.

'If you were a serial killer, and the police knew who you were, and where you lived, where would you go?' asked Erika.

'That's an interesting question, sounds like a game.'

'I asked this in the incident room earlier today, because we're getting desperate. Max Kirkham and Nina Hargreaves have just vanished… When I asked the question, Moss thought the same as you, like it was one of those games, "who would you most like to sleep with?"'

'Definitely, Jason Statham,' said Isaac.

'What?'

'He's who I'd most like to sleep with.'

'Who's he?'

'Oh, come on, Erika. Haven't you seen *The Transporter*? And *Transporters 2* and *3*? Shaved head, excellent body.'

'No. I don't seem to get much of a chance to watch films.'

'OK, who would you most like to sleep with, apart from the people you work with?'

'There's no one I work with who…' She noticed Isaac raising an eyebrow. 'OK. I'd most like to sleep with, um, Daniel Craig.'

'Oh, please, you're such a public servant, Erika. You want to sleep with James Bond?'

'Not James Bond, Daniel Craig. Anyway, shut up about that. I'm being serious about the question. Where would you go if you were a killer on the run?'

'Well, I wouldn't knock on your door, cos you'd slap a pair of cuffs on me quicker than you can say *Octopussy*. I suppose I'd go to my parents, or I would try to get abroad.'

'Max Kirkham hasn't got a passport.'

'Could he get a fake one?'

'Yes, I suppose so… When they killed Daniel de Souza, emptied the safe at his flat, his mother didn't know how much cash he had in there, but she said he would often keep several thousand pounds. And it depends if Max knows people who can get him a good forgery. And then they'd have to get two passports, because we've put a stop on Nina's.'

'It's incredibly difficult to go on the run. There are CCTV cameras everywhere, and this is a small country, let alone London being so densely packed with people. I'd definitely change how I look: I'd go blond. Or ginger. In the movies when people are on the run, very few of them opt to go ginger,' said Isaac.

They heard a creak from above and then Alison's voice came over the top of the balcony.

'Sorry loves, I was just hanging out my smalls and I heard what you were saying…'

'Hi, Alison,' said Erika.

'I agree with whoever you are, the man with the lovely smooth voice.'

'Hi, I'm Isaac,' said Isaac, moving out on to the grass and waving up at Alison. Erika joined him and waved and then they ducked back under the awning.

'Jason Statham is *lush*,' said Alison. 'But if I'd murdered someone, I'd go to me mam's house in the Gower. She'd keep me safe.'

Erika rolled her eyes at Isaac. 'Okay, thanks, Alison,' she said.

'I saw you on telly last week, Erika. I didn't know you'd been working on that murder case. I hope you catch them soon. I don't like the idea of two killers working together. Must be easier for them if they join forces. Ta ra.'

'Night,' said Erika and Isaac. They heard the balcony creak above them, and her patio door close.

'She sounds nice,' said Isaac.

'Just cos she called you "the man with the lovely smooth voice".' Erika grinned.

He waggled his thin eyebrows. She offered him another cigarette, and they lit up again. Erika lowered her voice.

'Mandy Hargreaves came forward and gave us the ID on her daughter, so Nina's not going to go there. We've also had her under surveillance for the past couple of days; there's been no contact. Nina has no siblings or other relatives. We've also got her ex-best friend under surveillance, but nothing there either.'

'What about Max Kirkham?' asked Isaac, exhaling smoke from the corner of his mouth.

'He's an orphan. He grew up in a children's home in West Norwood. Mother is deceased.'

'And just how thoroughly has that been checked?'

'I had someone on my team check, and they gave me the information.'

Isaac waggled his finger comically. 'The Erika *I* know would have checked that out for herself, and made sure she'd seen a death certificate. Max sounds like a man with a chequered past. He's also a man of limited means, but people who grow up poorer can often have much stronger family bonds... Have you seen a death certificate?'

'No, but I trust my team. They're all very thorough,' said Erika.

'You trusted Nils Åkerman.'

'I didn't look at it like that. The trust was implied. Like I trust you, and your judgement.'

'Have you heard any more about him?' asked Isaac.

'No. I'm tempted to go and visit him in Belmarsh. Look him in the eye and… I don't know. I don't know what I'd say. He betrayed me and so many people, but I've worked in drugs units for long enough to see that drugs take people over. They steal their personalities. Maybe it's the wine talking, making me extra forgiving.'

Isaac smiled. 'I don't know if it's the wine talking, and I know he's a vicious mass murderer, but don't you think Max Kirkham is quite sexy?'

'No! You've obviously had more wine than me.' She grinned. They stubbed their cigarettes out and went inside. 'But you're right about Max's dead mother. I need to check it out.'

CHAPTER 60

Nina and Max spent the rest of the weekend planning and preparing for Monday. They cleaned out the white van, filled it up with diesel and filled an extra 10 litre diesel can, stashing it in the back. Mariette was sent out on two trips to the supermarket, and returned with enough canned and dried foods to fill a large rucksack. On Sunday morning, Max sent her out on one last shopping trip to central London with a stack of the stolen cash. She returned late afternoon.

'Can you mind my carpets,' she said as Max and Nina carried all the bags through to the living room.

'Did you get everything?' asked Max.

'Yes. And in return I want my second payment of five grand.' Despite the cold weather, she was covered in a sheen of sweat, which made her make-up run.

'Tomorrow morning. I'll give it you, bright and early,' said Max. He then started to work through the items in the bags, pulling them out as Nina crossed them off a list. 'Camping stove, four thermal sleeping bags…'

'Why do you need four? There's only two of you,' said Mariette, blotting at her face with a tissue, and watching as it was all unloaded onto her carpet. Max ignored her.

'Three pay-as-you-go mobile phones, plus two extra batteries. We should put these all on to charge, Neen.'

'Okay,' she said, writing it all down.

'It took me a bloody age to get all that… And everywhere is teeming with Christmas shoppers. It's not even December.'

'Why don't you fuck off and make some tea,' snapped Max, glaring at her.

'Five grand, that's what I keep saying, five bloody grand,' muttered Mariette, leaving the room and closing the door.

'It's ten grand!' he shouted after her. He turned back to Nina, who was chewing on the pen nervously. He pulled out a big multipack of Haribo. 'Look, these are for the girls. They'll love them, there's all different stuff: Gummi Bears, Cola Bottles…'

Nina smiled weakly and wrote it down. Max pulled out two spare laptop batteries, and then a long yellow and red plastic box. He whistled.

'Jeez, she even made it to the camping supply shop,' he said, opening the box and taking out two long yellow cylinders with what looked like a red screw-on cap on each end. 'And she got it right. Two long-range rocket-propelled distress flares. I thought the stupid cow might come back with a pair of distressed flares or bell bottom trousers.'

Nina watched him examine the long plastic cylinders.

'How do they work?'

'You hold it with this bit at the top,' he said, indicating an arrow. 'And you unscrew this bit at the bottom.' He twisted one end. The lid came off, and a small length of string fell down. 'And you pull. It fires a burning rocket 300 feet in the air…' He carefully replaced the cap and screwed it tight. 'This, Neen, is the key to our escape. And there's another one as a backup. Okay?'

She nodded.

'And your mate. Can you trust him?'

'I trust him, cos he knows he's going to get a big wedge of the ransom money. And that's the best kind of trust.'

Nina looked at everything strewn across the rug.

'I can't believe we're doing this.'

Max carefully put the distress flares back in their box and then turned to her.

'We *are* doing this, Neen,' he said. 'We're doing this for *us*, for a chance at a future together. Not this miserable existence with no money, no hope, and no prospects. The odds are in our favour. This is our time. And we have to take this opportunity with both hands. No one will get hurt.'

Nina looked into his eyes, and for a moment, she almost believed him.

Nina didn't sleep much that night. She watched Max, snoring peacefully beside her, for a couple of hours, then she got up and padded downstairs to make herself a cup of hot milk. As she placed a small pan of milk on the stove and lit the gas, she caught sight of the landline, sitting on its little table in the hallway. She tiptoed into the hall, and listened to the sounds of the building. The clock ticking, the burning gas hissing on the stove. When she picked up the receiver, the dialling tone sounded warm and reassuring. She knew her mother's number off by heart; it hadn't changed since she was a little girl when she used to practise answering the phone, picking up the receiver saying, 'Hello, 0208 886 6466,' like her grandmother used to do. With her heart hammering, Nina started to dial: 0,2,0,8... 8,8,6... 6,4,6... Her finger hovered above the final '6'.

'You bailing on him?' came a voice which made her jump. She turned and saw Mariette, sitting on the sofa in the dark living room.

'No,' said Nina, replacing the receiver.

'Don't shit a shitter.'

'What?'

'Don't bullshit a bullshitter...' said Mariette, heaving herself up off the sofa. She shuffled into the hall. Under the harsh light from above, every line and bag on her face was accentuated. She wore a grubby white towelling robe, and Nina could see the outline of her cigarettes and lighter in the pocket.

'You're scared, aren't you?' she said, putting her arms around Nina and kissing her on the top of the head.

'Yes.'

'Well, let me tell you, girl. I've spent most of my life being scared, and it's done me fuck all good.'

Nina started to cry. Mariette pulled back and slapped her around the face.

'Now stop that. You need to take this opportunity to get out of the country, do you hear me?'

Nina put a hand to her stinging face, shocked.

'I thought you didn't want to know what we were doing?'

'You think I'm stupid? You think I haven't heard? Now, you're going to go with Max tomorrow, do you hear? If you don't, I'll call the police, and I'll tell them everything. Do you know what they do to girls like you in prison? And do you think anyone in your family will give you the time of day? A modern day Myra Hindley, that's what they'll call you.'

'I'm nothing like her…' started Nina.

'You've killed four people. They've got your DNA, and photos of you. They can link you to the crimes. Are you fucking stupid? You'll go down for life. Unless you decide to end it in a police cell with a makeshift noose made out of a bed sheet.'

'You bitch,' said Nina.

Mariette grabbed her by the throat and slammed her into the wall. Her eyes were now cold and hard, like Max's.

'Ten grand might not be much to a stuck-up little cunt like you,' she said, leaning in close so her voice was a low whisper. 'But it's the most money I'll ever see again in my lifetime. Now, you're going to go back upstairs, and then you're going to leave tomorrow morning with my son, and do whatever you need to do to start a new life. We'll never have to cross paths again…'

She stared at Nina, whose face was now turning purple, and then let go. Nina sank to the floor, gasping for breath as she slowly walked back up the stairs. There was a hissing sound and then a smell of burning. 'And your milk's boiled over,' said Mariette.

When they woke up Mariette was out. After breakfast, Max left the £5,000 in cash on the kitchen table and they came down to the van.

With a new set of plates, they drove to Hilly Fields Road and parked a hundred yards down from Marsh's house. They waited and watched as Marsh went off to work, and then forty-five minutes later Marcie emerged with the twins. They wore identical green dresses, with thick blue jackets, hats, gloves and thick green tights. Marcie lifted the two girls up into the back seat of the Space Cruiser, buckled them in, and then they drove away. Nina looked into the back of the van where they'd placed an old mattress and blacked out the windows in the back doors.

'Max, they're only little,' she said in a small voice.

'How many times have I said this? We're not gonna hurt them. If they do as we say, they'll get their kids back within a day or so. You've done far worse, you do realise that, Nina? Cos you're coming over all Mother fucking Teresa, and we both know that isn't the case!'

'I know what I've done.'

'Good, now we need to focus,' he said.

They passed the next half an hour in silence, and just as Nina was giving up on Marcie returning home, her car appeared in the side mirror and swept past them and into the driveway. They waited until she was inside the house, and then Max unbuckled his seatbelt.

'Now, are we going to do this?'

Nina looked into Max's eyes and nodded.

'Yes, we are.'

CHAPTER 61

Marcie Marsh arrived home from dropping the twins at nursery and was unloading a shopping bag from the local organic store into the fridge. She'd bought some lovely ripe Brie, crusty bread, and a bottle of organic white wine. She wouldn't tell Paul that it was organic; he despised 'poncy wine' as he called it. She shuddered when she thought that his favourite wine was Blue Nun, something he hid from his friends and colleagues, and he always made her keep a bottle in the fridge for when he came home from work.

She went to put the wine in the fridge, when she saw his bottle of Blue Nun in the inside door and lifted it out. It was almost empty. She smiled, and closed the fridge door, taking both bottles of wine to the sink. She tipped the last of the Blue Nun down the sink and then opened the bottle of organic white. She was just smiling to herself and putting a funnel into the top of the Blue Nun bottle when the doorbell rang.

Marcie wiped her hands and went to the hallway, checking her reflection in the small mirror on the way. When she opened the front door, there was a lad outside with a shaved head wearing thick black framed glasses. He gave her a geeky smile and showed his ID, along with a black toolbox he was carrying.

'Morning, love, I just need to read your water meter. Won't take me a second,' he said.

Marcie thought he looked a little familiar, but it was nothing more than a passing thought.

'Okay.' She smiled, standing to one side to let him in. 'Your shoes are nice and clean, but do you mind taking them off?'

'Sure, no probs,' he said. He hopped on one leg as he slipped off the right and then the left shoe. Marcie saw he was wearing Bart Simpson socks.

'Nice socks.'

'You think?'

'No,' she said with a laugh. 'My husband has a Bart Simpson T-shirt he can't bear to part with. It's almost disintegrated, but he insists on keeping it.'

'My wife got me these for Christmas,' he said, pushing the glasses up his nose and grinning at her.

Marcie looked him up and down with an almost appraising eye. She closed the front door and showed him down the hallway to the meter cupboard next to the kitchen door. She unlocked it, pulled the door open, and as she turned around, she saw the man was standing very close with a strange look in his eyes.

He moved so fast that she only registered he had punched her when she hit the floor. She felt pain shooting through her face as he grabbed her by the hair and dragged her into the kitchen. He punched again and again, and then she blacked out.

Max stood up and took a few deep breaths. He removed the glasses, which were blurring his vision. He could now see just how attractive she was. She wore tight white trousers which emphasised her curves, and a snug fitting pink pullover. Her nose was a bloody mess, which was a shame. He knelt down and ran his hands over her shoulders and squeezed her breasts. He hitched up her pullover, unfastened her bra and took it off, exposing her breasts. He ran his hand over her smooth stomach, noting the caesarean scar. He unbuttoned her trousers, and pulled them down to her ankles along with her underwear. He stared for a moment at her nakedness, her large pink nipples, dark pubic hair, the stretch marks on her thighs. He ran a finger through her pubic hair, and worked one finger inside her.

'Oh. Mummy, Mummy, Mummy, if only I had more time with you...' he murmured, but saw that time was moving fast.

He came back out into the hallway, opened the black toolbox, and pulled out a length of blue twine. Back in the kitchen he bound her legs at the ankle, flipped her over and bound her wrists behind her back. He shoved her bra into her mouth, and pulled a pair of tights over her head, fastening them at the neck. He stood back. Her face was distorted under the tight sheer material, but he could see the tights were cutting into her neck. He bent over and loosened them a little. He then parted her legs and took a photo of her splayed out and bound on the kitchen floor.

Max dragged her by the ankles towards the open cupboard. He checked she was bound tightly, and pushed her far back, next to the boiler. Then he closed the door and locked it, pocketing the key. He went to the front door where the white van was now parked outside. The road was deserted. Nina got out of the van and came to the door.

'It's all clear. Her handbag is in the kitchen, find her phone,' he said.

CHAPTER 62

Beryl Donahue was the manager and owner of The Acorns Nursery. She was an imposing matronly woman with short, dark hair and a flamboyant dress sense. She had worked for many years as a nurse, and then a back injury had forced her to reassess her options. She was lucky that she'd bought her large end-terrace house in Forest Hill in the early eighties, when property was affordable, and she had decided to take the plunge and turn the house into a day nursery.

It was just after ten in the morning, and she was on her third cup of coffee and wishing that it was later in the day and she could have something stronger. She'd just received an unwelcome letter informing her that Ofsted, the official inspector of schools and nurseries, would be coming next week for an on-site inspection of The Acorns Nursery. It was the last piece of news she needed so close to Christmas. The Acorns Nursery was excellent in many ways, but she had been complacent, and let some things slide. The one nursing assistant on her staff who was a qualified first aider had just quit, and she would have to quickly hire another nursery assistant qualified in first aid to keep with regulations. The Ofsted inspector could come down hard on her, and a bad inspection could result in parents pulling out their children. No children would mean no fees, and no fees meant missed mortgage payments. And her fire safety certificate had to be checked also; she had a nasty feeling she needed to get it renewed.

All this was going through her mind when she received a call from Marcie Marsh. Marcie apologised profusely, and said that today she would have to send her housekeeper to pick up Mia and Sophie.

'The builders next door have been knocking through, and they hit a water pipe! I have to deal with a flooded kitchen!' she said, her posh voice sounding exaggerated and harassed.

Beryl looked down at the caller ID screen, and saw that it was indeed Marcie Marsh calling.

'Oh dear, Marcie, that's terrible. What's her name, please?' asked Beryl.

'Her name's Emma Potter. She's got very short blond hair, and she's in her early twenties.'

'You know our policy, Marcie, and we have to be strict. She'll need to show some ID, and of course she'll need to tell one of the girls the password.'

There was a long pause.

'Marcie? Are you still there? Is there a problem?'

'No. That's fine. I can give her the password, but she hasn't got any ID on her. She doesn't drive, and she's coming round on foot to get the girls… Look, can I give her my ID? So sorry, but if she can't come and get them then I'm a bit stuck! I can't leave the house, with the builders here…'

Beryl saw the Ofsted letter on the desk, and knew she'd have to start moving fast if she was going to sort things out before the end of the week. She knew Marcie Marsh in passing; she always paid on time, and she was the wife of a very senior policeman. The Marshes had also donated £500 to the nursery each Christmas for the past couple of years, and Beryl hoped they would again.

'Okay. That's fine, Marcie. As long as she has your ID and the current password, and I hope you get things sorted.'

'I know,' she said. 'But the floorboards will have to come up, and then I've got the bloody in-laws coming as well!'

'Dear me, I'll speak to you soon. Oh and text me a picture of her, would you? So we know when she comes to collect the girls.'

Beryl hung up the phone and started to scroll through a recruitment website, rapidly forgetting the conversation she had just had.

CHAPTER 63

On Monday morning, Erika asked her team to revisit Max Kirkham and look into his background. Isaac's words had haunted her for most of the night, and she now had a gut feeling that she'd missed something. She took the original birth certificate they had on file for Max Kirkham, and she asked everyone to stop what they were doing and look deeper into his background.

After phone calls back and forth with the national records office, they confirmed it was a genuine birth certificate. Janice Elise Kirkham gave birth to Maximilian Kirkham in 1983 in North Middlesex University Hospital.

'Her name appears on the birth certificate,' said Crane, reading off an email he'd received. 'There's no father listed. I've looked deeper into her history, and Janice gave Max up for adoption in 1986 when he was aged three, and now I'll hand over to Mr McGorry here who has found her in the system.'

'She has a record, shit,' said Erika, shaking her head.

McGorry stood up. 'Janice Kirkham bounced around the benefits system, working sporadically, but was arrested for possession of cocaine with intent to sell in November 1988. She was given bail, and at the time she was living in a council house: 14 Wandsworth Street, in the East End. Shortly after she was bailed, the bedsit was devastated by fire. A woman's body was found in the bedroom, badly burnt and lying in the remains of a bed. The fire was caused by a faulty heater, and as Janice Kirkham lived alone, it was ruled that she perished in the fire.'

Erika looked at the photo of Max.

'And there's nothing about a father?'

Crane shook his head.

'Bloody hell,' said Erika, putting her head in her hands.

Moss volunteered to do the lunch run, and she returned half an hour later with sandwiches and a shopping bag from a toy shop in the One Shopping Centre. She tried to stash it under her desk before anyone saw, but McGorry cried out across the room: 'Lego City Volcano Response Helicopter!'

'Um, yes,' she said as Erika glowered across the incident room. 'My son is desperate for one, and everywhere is sold out. I just had a tip-off from my wife that they had some in the One Centre.'

'My nephew is desperate for one too,' said McGorry. 'Can I?' He didn't wait to be asked and slipped the colourful box out of the plastic bag.

Moss sloughed off her coat and rolled up her sleeves.

'I worked during the London riots, in full protective gear, and I wish I'd just worn the same in the bloody toy shop! You should have seen it. Yummy mummies can be violent.'

She started to pass out the sandwiches. Erika took one and started to unwrap it.

'You've got one lucky little boy,' said McGorry. 'I used to love playing with my Lego.'

'Don't tell us when you used to play with Lego. It probably wasn't that long ago,' said Crane, unwrapping his sandwich.

'It was twelve years ago, that's a long time, isn't it?'

Some of the older staff members in the room smiled, but Erika remained stony-faced and was getting visibly irritated by the chatter.

'Oh, my lord. Twelve years ago I was having my fiftieth birthday party,' said Marta.

McGorry shrugged his shoulders. 'I used to buy Lego men and pimp them up and sell them at school. I did punk Lego men, and gay Lego men, probably not very PC.'

'I use my son's Wolverine Lego man as a keyring,' said Temple, pulling it from his pocket. 'And my wife likes to change the hair on him every day. You know you can take off the hair and put different ones on. Look, today he's got a little black bowl cut, yesterday he had Gandalf's flowing locks. Same face, different hair.'

'I wish I could do that,' said Crane, stroking the top of his head, which was now bald. 'Although with long hair I'd look like my sister!'

Erika was about to snap at them all to shut up, when she looked over at the whiteboards and did a double take. She rushed over to the wall and grabbed the picture of Max Kirkham they'd lifted from his Jobseekers Allowance file. She moved along and grabbed the small driving licence photo of Mariette Hoffman. She came back to the team and held them up side by side.

'What is it?' asked Moss.

'Have any of us considered how similar Mariette Hoffman looks to Max Kirkham? The Lego man thing you were just talking about, imagine her hair on his head and vice versa.'

'Shit,' said Moss.

'Crane, you've got access to facial recognition software which does a point by point match of facial similarities. Can we compare Mariette and Max's photos?'

It took a little while for Crane to load up the two photos and run the software and there was silence in the incident room as everyone ate their lunch and waited.

'Okay. It's obviously not a match, but it's flagging up similarities in space between eyes, length of nose and spacing on cheekbones,' he said.

'But that doesn't mean anything; so they look alike,' said Erika. 'You say that Max's mother, Janice Kirkham, died in a fire, but her body was so badly burnt they couldn't identify her, yet they ruled that it was her body on the grounds that she lived alone?'

'Yes,' said Crane.

'I want to see Janice Kirkham's birth certificate, and Mariette Hoffman's birth certificate,' said Erika.

It took a few more hours to find the relevant records office and track down the birth certificates. Erika saw it was very quiet in the incident room and everyone was watching with rapt attention as a series of documents came out of the printer. Erika placed them on one of the desks, and everyone gathered around.

'OK, this is the birth certificate that Mariette Elise Hoffman has been using on applications for housing benefit, Jobseekers Allowance, and when she applied for her mortgage,' said Erika. 'It states that she was born Mariette Elise McArdle, on the 1st of March 1963 in a small village near Cambridgeshire. Mother was Laura McArdle; father was Arthur McArdle... Both now deceased, died in 1979 and 1989. The records office in Cambridgeshire has also sent over the same birth certificate. You can see the official registrar's stamp is identical and so is his signature. There's also an ink smudge on the paper, a few centimetres to the right of the stamp... The only problem is that on this version Mariette Elise McArdle died on the 4th of March 1963. Three days after being born.'

'Look here, on the birth certificate Mariette has been using, there's a faint outline of black in the box where the date of death is displayed,' said Moss.

There was silence in the incident room.

'So, when Janice Kirkham was on bail for cocaine possession, and facing a hefty prison sentence, her bedsit burnt down, but it wasn't her who got caught in the fire,' said Erika.

'But whoever's body it was, they assumed it was Janice and she was certified as dead,' said Moss.

'And Janice used the opportunity to steal the identity of a dead baby and start again as Mariette McArdle, eventually becoming Mariette Hoffman,' said Erika.

There was a stunned silence.

'I want her flat searched ASAP, I'll bet you anything that's where Max and Nina have been hiding out.'

CHAPTER 64

It was late afternoon, but the light was already fading as the white van bumped along the dark roads, and there was just the sound of the windscreen wipers dragging across the glass.

Nina sat in the back of the van, on the mattress, with Mia asleep cuddled up under her left arm, and Sophie her right. They moved with the bumps and sways. She could see the back of Max's head in the cab at the front, lit up by the car headlights coming from the other direction.

It had shocked Nina how easily the girls had come with her when she turned up at the nursery just before lunch.

It had helped that Beryl Donahue, the manager, was unwittingly in on the lie.

'Ah yes, Mummy called earlier to say Emma here would be picking you up, and sent us through a lovely photo of her,' she said, smiling at Nina. Nina smiled back and the girls seemed quite in awe of Beryl, and the authority she had over them. They obediently took Nina's hands and followed her down the road and around the corner. What they were most bewildered about was walking. Nina could tell that they were the kind of kids who didn't walk anywhere, and Marcie ferried them everywhere in the car.

'This is my car,' said Nina as they reached the van.

'It's tiny,' said Sophie, shifting on her feet.

'Don't be rude,' whispered Mia, giving her sister a stern little stare. Max had emerged from the driver's side, and his presence had scared the girls a little, even though he'd done his best to smile.

'Alright,' he said. Then looking around he added: 'Come on, Neen, there's bloody houses everywhere, let's get them inside.'

When Nina had opened the back of the van and asked the girls to get in, they'd hesitated, but when sweets were added into the equation and Max had said they were going on an exciting trip, and meeting Mummy and Daddy there, the girls had climbed in and over the mattress.

They were now four hours into the journey, and Nina was starting to feel a deep gnawing fear.

'I need the toilet,' whispered Mia into Nina's neck.

'Me too,' said Sophie. Nina could smell their hair, such a sweet, innocent smell.

Nina looked at the back of Max's head, silhouetted against the glare of the oncoming headlights.

'Max, the girls need the loo, and I could go too,' she said. There was no response. 'Max!'

He glanced back. 'We're not stopping, we need to get some distance.'

'Max, you said this would be… You said… Max let them go to the bloody toilet. Just pull over.'

He eyeballed her in the rear-view mirror, and moments later pulled into a small lay-by surrounded by trees. It was now cold and very damp, and Max came round to open the back doors, waiting until two lorries had passed before opening the left-hand door and shielding them from the road as they climbed out.

'Quickly, go on, in the trees,' he said.

Nina pulled the two girls around a bush, until they were out of sight, but he heard branches cracking and little girls whining about not having any loo roll, about the nasty mud, and how cold they were. A few cars sped past, rocking the van in the gusts of wind. He smoked a cigarette while he waited.

'You took your time,' he said when Nina came back holding the little girls' hands. He could see one of them had ripped their tights. Max opened the left-hand side door as a lorry sped past, its lights on full beam. He shoved Mia inside the van and picked up Sophie and dumped her on the mattress.

'Hey! You don't touch them like that,' said Nina. She poked her head inside and saw the two girls in the dark van, cowering on the mattress. It was dawning on them that something was wrong.

'I've never seen you before, but you told Mrs Donahue that you were Mummy's friend,' said Mia.

'I am Mummy's friend, just hang on…' said Nina, shutting the door. As she turned to face Max he punched her in the face and she went down on the wet tarmac.

'You don't fucking talk to me like that. And you keep those two little shits in line.'

He walked off, and got into the driver's seat. Nina felt water seeping through her jeans and pushed herself up off the tarmac. She wiped her hands on her jeans and felt her face. The left side was numb, but there wasn't any blood. She took a deep breath and wiped the tears away with the back of her hand. Then she got back into the van.

The two little girls reached out for Nina in the darkness as the van pulled out onto the motorway, and they clung to her. She could smell their hair again, and felt their warm shaking bodies against hers. An overpowering feeling of guilt, shame and maternal love hit her like a tidal wave, and she knew that whatever happened to her, she had to try and reverse this situation. She had to make sure these two little girls survived.

CHAPTER 65

Erika was waiting for the vending machine to finish pouring her coffee when she bumped into Marsh on his way down the stairs from his office. It was coming up to six p.m.

'Paul, can I just have a word?' she said.

'Erika, I'm just on my way home. I haven't stopped.'

'I have Max Kirkham's mother, Mariette Hoffman, in custody,' she said. 'We've also got forensics conducting an exhaustive search of the flat. She was alone when they arrested her, but we believe she's sheltering Max Kirkham and Nina Hargreaves. They found long pieces of brown and blond hair in her rubbish bin, and a large amount of cash that we think is from the Daniel de Souza murder scene.'

'Do you have any leverage on Mariette Hoffman?'

'Yes, there is an outstanding arrest warrant for cocaine possession, identity fraud, and benefit fraud. She used a lump sum to buy her flat in the right-to-buy scheme when she was signing on. Technically she should have declared it.'

'Bloody hell, that's a nice amount of leverage. You keep me in the loop. I'm on my mobile…'

'Also. I'm sorry about the other day,' said Erika, lowering her voice.

He nodded and looked at the floor. 'I was the one who made the first move,' he said, lowering his voice too.

'What? I was talking about the meeting at Scotland Yard.'

'Oh, right,' he said, blushing. There was an awkward silence. He looked around and went on. 'Now I've broached this, erm,

I just want to tell you that me and Marcie have this thing now, where we talk about everything. After the break-up, and her affair, we decided to be more open, to have a more open relationship.'

'Okay…'

'Do you see what I mean?'

'Do you mean a "more open" relationship or an "open relationship"?'

Marsh hesitated, unsure of how to frame his next words. 'This is embarrassing to talk about…'

'You don't need to,' said Erika, holding up her hands.

'I just want you to know that I told her about me and you, kissing, and I told her that I put my hands on you.'

Erika looked at him with wide eyes. 'Are you fucking mad?'

'It's fine. She was… okay, about it… I told you, we're talking to each other about this stuff. It turns out she's had a couple of other affairs, ones that I didn't know about…' He looked at the floor. He was now crimson.

'Paul, stop.'

'Just thought you should know that it's alright. It won't happen again and you needn't feel odd when you're around her.'

'I don't see Marcie that often.'

'I'd already told her when you bumped into each other the other day, in the car park. Marcie was fine with things.'

That was Marcie being fine with things, thought Erika.

'Look, it was silly what happened and it…' Erika went to say more, but one of the support staff, a young girl with huge glasses, came up to the vending machine.

'Evening, sir, ma'am,' she said, and she fed in some loose change.

'Right, well, I'll see you tomorrow and keep me posted with the suspect's interview,' said Marsh.

'Yes,' said Erika. He went off and she watched after him for a moment, still shocked, and then made her way down to the interview room.

*

Marsh stopped off at the supermarket on the way home, and scoured the buckets at the entrance displaying fresh flowers and found a lovely bunch of lilies for Marcie. At the self-serve till he saw a display of Haribo Gummi Bears and bought a couple of packets for the twins. He was back out at his car by quarter to seven, and he thought that if there wasn't much traffic through Sydenham, he would make it home before the twins' bath time.

The house looked dark when he parked outside. He'd expected to see lights on in the upstairs bathroom and the hall. He got out of the car with the flowers and sweets, and frowned as he approached the quiet house. It was gone bath time, and Marcie was always punctual. The water would usually be sloshing down the drainpipe; he had just missed it so many times before.

He put his key in the lock and opened the door. The hallway was very cold, and he switched on the light, calling out to Marcie and the girls. There was silence. He put the flowers and sweets down on the hall table and moved through the rooms, first the living room, then the kitchen, where two bottles of wine and a funnel had been left out on the counter. He ran upstairs, now starting to really panic. The rooms were all dark and empty. On the landing, he pulled out his phone and called Marcie's number, but it rang out and went to voicemail. Then he heard a muffled banging. He came back downstairs, through to the hallway and listened for it again, moving from room to room until he realised it was coming from the cupboard under the stairs. When he reached the door it was locked, and there was no key in the lock. The muffled banging came again, from inside the cupboard.

'Marcie! Marcie, what's going on? Are you in there?' he shouted, hammering on the door. There was a banging, again and a faint moan. He rushed upstairs to his office, and scrabbled around in a drawer of spare keys, bringing a bunch down with him. He tried several in the door, the thudding, and moaning got louder.

'Shit, shit. I'm here, honey. Dammit!' he shouted, dropping the keys on the floor. He finally found the right one, turned it and got the door open. He looked in shock at Marcie lying on the floor, sprawled out under the boiler, stripped naked, with her hands bound and a nylon stocking over her head. He rushed in to help her up, gently peeling away the stocking and pulling her bra out of her mouth.

'The girls!' she croaked and sputtered, panting and gagging. 'Where are the girls!?'

CHAPTER 66

Interview Room 1 at Lewisham Row Station was bare, with just a table and chairs. Erika and Moss sat opposite Mariette Hoffman and her solicitor. Mariette looked hideous under the bright lights of the interview room. Her long, dark hair was a mess, and her skin pale and dry. She had a cold sore on her lip, and had a fading bruise on her left eye. A nasty whiff of bleach and stale sweat hung around her.

'For the recording, it's 6.57 p.m., on the 26th of November. Present in Interview Room 1 is Detective Chief Inspector Erika Foster; Detective Inspector Moss; duty solicitor, Donald Frobisher; and Mariette Hoffman.'

Mariette shifted and looked up at the camera mounted in the corner of the room.

'Can I smoke?' she said.

'No, you can't,' said Erika. She opened a file.

'Can I vape? I've got one of those electronic...'

'You can't do that either.'

'Well, what can I do then?'

'You can confirm that your real name is Janice Elise Kirkham and you were born in Little Dunshire, near Cambridge, in 1963.'

Mariette held up her head defiantly.

'But Janice Kirkham died in a fire on the 29th of November 1988...' Erika opened a folder and pulled out two documents. 'For the video, I'm showing the suspect items 1886 and 1887. These are the birth and death certificates for Janice Kirkham. Can you look at these, please?'

Mariette leaned forward and glanced at the documents in front of her. 'Never heard of her, never met her, don't know her.'

Erika nodded and took another document from the folder. 'For the video, I'm now showing item 1888. This is your birth certificate?'

Mariette glanced at it. 'Yep.'

'You were born Mariette Elise McArdle on 1st of March 1963, and then died three days after being born, on the 4th of March 1963?'

'What? Hang on.'

'You just confirmed that this is your birth certificate,' said Erika. 'This is an original document from the records office.'

'No, no, there's some mistake.'

Erika then took out the fake certificate and placed it in front of Mariette.

'So, who are you?'

Mariette leaned in to speak to her solicitor, who recoiled a little as they conversed in hushed tones.

'I'm Janice, Janice Kirkham,' she said.

'Okay, we also know that Max Kirkham is your son,' said Erika. 'The same Max Kirkham who in conjunction with Nina Hargreaves is wanted for the murders of your ex-husband, Thomas Hoffman, Charlene Selby, Daniel de Souza, and a man whose body was found in a drainage ditch close to the M40. We are close to having an ID on that body…'

'Is there a question in there?' said Mariette.

'Why did you lie to us when we interviewed you back in October? You said you didn't know anything about your ex-husband's death. Didn't you try and find Max over the years?'

Mariette shook her head.

'NO. I didn't.'

'Why?'

'I'd been raped. I didn't want to keep a kid who'd been forced inside me by violence. I was raped by the devil and I spawned his child...'

A look passed between Erika and Moss.

Mariette leaned in close. 'Oh, sorry. Am I not saying what you want to hear? It could happen to either one of you. They say that maternal instinct can overcome any hurdle, but no. I wanted rid of him. So I gave him up. That's not a crime.'

Erika leaned forward so their faces were inches apart.

'But cocaine possession is a crime, Janice. Benefit fraud is a crime. And so is sheltering known criminals. You were happy to take Max's stolen money when he showed up.'

'I did it to survive,' spat Mariette, leaning across the table. 'You would know nothing about that!'

'Oh spare me the bloody violins!' snapped Moss, talking for the first time.

There was a knock at the door, and McGorry opened it.

'Sorry, boss. I need to talk to you urgently,' he said.

'I'm suspending this interview at 7.05 p.m.,' said Erika. She and Moss got up.

'Can I have a fag?' asked Mariette.

'No,' said Moss and they left the interview room.

Outside in the corridor, McGorry outlined what had happened with Commander Marsh when he arrived home.

'Is Marcie badly hurt?' asked Erika.

'She has a broken nose, and is badly concussed. Her clothes were removed but she doesn't think that she was assaulted.'

'She doesn't think?'

'She says it was a young man with a shaved head who asked to read the meter. He looked the part, he had Thames Water ID…'

'Oh my God,' said Moss.

McGorry went on. 'It's more serious, because their twins, Mia and Sophie, were collected from the nursery at lunchtime by a young woman with short blonde hair. The nursery manager says that Marcie phoned her shortly after ten this morning, to say her housekeeper would be picking up the girls. The call came from Marcie's mobile phone, and the girl who came and collected Mia and Sophie knew the password that parents or guardians have to quote…'

Moss shook her head and had tears in her eyes.

'Marcie said that they have the password pinned to the fridge in the kitchen, because she keeps forgetting it…'

'That's what me and Celia do with our nursery. When we pick up Jacob,' said Moss, wiping her eyes.

It was the first time that Erika had seen Moss cry. She moved forward and gave her a hug.

'Do the staff at the nursery know if the person who picked up the girls had a vehicle?'

'No, they said she was on foot.'

'And no one has any more information?'

McGorry shook his head.

Erika looked at her watch.

'Shit, that was almost eight hours ago. Whoever took them has a hell of a head start. So we have a man with a shaved head who attacked Marcie, and then a woman with short blonde hair who abducted the girls…'

'They found two types of hair at Mariette Hoffman's flat,' said Moss. 'They've changed their appearance.'

'Find Superintendent Hudson. We need to start the procedure for calling in the Kidnap Unit,' said Erika.

CHAPTER 67

It was ten thirty in the evening when Erika knocked on Marsh's front door. She was with Colleen Scanlan, a young Family Liaison Officer, and Detective Superintendent Paris, a specialist officer from the Met Police Kidnap and Hostage Unit, who in turn had two of his officers, a man and a woman. In the dark street behind, a team of uniformed officers were moving between the houses, knocking on doors, and conducting a door-to-door with the neighbours.

DS Paris was in his late fifties with a head of thick white hair and a portly frame. He had a calm, authoritative presence; what he'd said during their first briefing still rang loud in Erika's ears: *We have to assume that a kidnap is a murder waiting to happen. Violence is used routinely – often extreme violence. The clock is ticking now, and it's ticking fast. The longer it takes us to find the kidnap victims, the less likely the case is to have a successful outcome.*

Marsh's front door was opened by an overly tanned man in his seventies with immaculate grey hair. He was dressed a little rakishly, in tan slacks, a golfing jumper, and he sported a blue spotted cravat poking out from the neck of his open shirt.

'Good evening, I'm Marcie's father, Leonard Montague-Clarke,' he said, introducing himself and stepping to one side to let them in.

He led them through to the living room. Marsh sat on the sofa beside Marcie, who had two black eyes and a plastic splint over her nose. She was weeping heavily. Beside her a young male paramedic was taking her blood pressure. A large, elegant woman in her late sixties sat on the opposite sofa. She wore a smart, pale-blue trouser suit, lots of jewellery, and her short grey hair was immaculate.

'Darling, you have to go to the hospital. Your nose is broken, and you could have other injuries,' she was saying.

'No, Mummy,' said Marcie hoarsely. 'I'm not leaving.'

They all looked up when the team of officers entered. Erika thought how devastated Marsh looked, a shell of the man she had seen just a few hours earlier.

'NO!' cried Marcie, looking up and seeing Erika. 'NO! That bitch is not coming in here.'

The officers turned to look at Erika in surprise. Marsh put his head in his hands.

'Marcie, this is Detective Superintendent Paris, a specialist officer from the Met Police Kidnap Unit—' started Erika.

'Get her OUT OF HERE!' cried Marcie, pointing a finger at Erika. 'Get her out of my house! She's been fucking my husband!'

'That's not true,' said Erika. Despite the situation, and the anger rising in her, she added, 'I am here to help with these officers to do my job, and—'

'DO YOU HEAR ME?' shouted Marcie, standing up and launching herself at Erika. The blood pressure cuff hung off her arm, and the rubber hose whipped back and forth as she beat Erika back into the corner of the room. Everyone froze, and looked on in shock.

'Marcie, stop. STOP THIS!' shouted Marsh, leaping up and dragging her off. The paramedic got her settled back on the sofa. Erika felt her nose to see if it was bleeding, and tried to compose herself.

Detective Superintendent Paris stepped forward. 'I think you need to leave,' he said softly.

'It isn't true what she's saying.'

He put up his hands. 'Okay, that is noted, but you need to leave; this is not conducive to our investigation.'

'Okay, yes,' said Erika, smoothing down her hair. She looked over at Marsh, but he was cradling Marcie in his arms. Marcie's parents were now staring at her with a mix of curiosity and distaste, and even Superintendent Paris and the other officers regarded her coldly. Erika went to say something, but thought better of it and came out of the living room and into the hallway. She stopped at the front door and listened as Paris started to explain in his soft voice that his team had established an incident room working out of Lewisham Row, and they were ready to act.

'How many times have you managed to save… save people who've been kidnapped?' said Marsh, his voice thick with emotion.

'I have a very high success rate,' said Paris.

'They've got my babies, please bring my babies back to me,' cried Marcie, her voice hysterical.

Erika wiped tears from her eyes and quietly let herself out of the house.

CHAPTER 68

Moss was back in Interview Room 1 at Lewisham Row, sitting opposite Mariette Hoffman and her solicitor. It was now late.

'You need to start talking to me, Mariette...' said Moss. Mariette remained stony-faced and impassive. 'Who are you being loyal to? Your son, Max, who killed your ex-husband?'

'Thomas owed him money. A lot of money.'

'So that's reason for Max to bump him off, and Charlene?'

'It was Nina who killed Charlene.'

'So you are talking now?'

'What does it fucking look like? My mouth is moving, sound is coming out...' She turned to her solicitor. 'Aren't you supposed to jump in here and stop her asking stupid questions?' The solicitor sat back and folded his arms. 'I'm talking to you, what's yer name again?'

'My name is Donald Frobisher.'

'Well, Donald. I'm paying you to represent me, and you're sitting there with a face on you.'

He sat back, unwilling to engage, but unable to hide his distaste for her.

'The state is paying for your solicitor,' said Moss.

'Yeah, and I've paid my stamp. In the past,' said Mariette, tapping a grubby fingernail on the edge of the table.

'Is that stamp, or national insurance you've paid? As Janice, or Mariette?'

Mariette scowled and sat back.

'Who do you lot think you are?'

'I'm a detective inspector,' said Moss.

'And a lezzer, by the look of it.'

'Yeah, I am,' said Moss, leaning in close. 'I'm a Big. Fat. Lezzer. But you're not my type, Mariette. I'm not into low-rent low-lifes with poor personal hygiene.'

'I clean my house every day!' she shouted, showing emotion for the first time. 'It's spotless,' she added, sitting back and trying to calm down.

'You've been sheltering two multiple murderers, Mariette. You've withheld information from the police, accepted stolen goods; you faked your own death; you're wanted under a different identity for possession of a class A drug. No wonder you haven't had time to look after yourself. And push the hoover round. I remember your place when we first visited. It was a tip.'

'It bloody wasn't,' she roared, slamming her hand down on the table. 'It was immaculate! Tell her, Donald, stop her!'

The solicitor gave Moss a concerned look and shook his head. 'Please keep your line of questioning to the facts of this case.'

'Of course,' said Moss, trying to hide her glee. She waited for Mariette to sit back and calm down. 'Okay, as we've already gone over, we've found receipts in your flat for camping gear, tinned goods, parachute rocket distress flares, three pay-as-you-go mobile phones, spare batteries, and ammunition for a Glock handgun. We've confiscated £9,000 in cash. We've also found the registration details of a white Berlingo van in your name, and several fake number plates in a lock-up, also rented in your name. The van is missing. Where is it, Mariette? Where have they gone? And what are they intending to do with what you bought them?'

Mariette was now back in control of her emotions. 'Hand on my heart, I don't know.'

'Do you know where it's headed?'

'No.'

'The number plates are now being fed into the Automatic Number Plate Recognition system, so if Max and Nina drove or are driving the van using any of those plates, they will have been captured by ANPR cameras.'

'But you won't know the number plates they're using now,' she said with a small smile.

'Do you know the plate numbers?'

Mariette folded her arms.

'Whatever happens in this interview, Mariette, you are going to prison for a very long time. So you can speak, and a judge might view you with more lenience. Tell me where Max and Nina are going with those two girls. What they are planning?'

Mariette clamped her mouth shut childishly.

Moss slammed her hand down on the table. 'Goddammit, Mariette, you can at least tell me where they've taken Mia and Sophie Marsh!'

She cocked her head and gave Moss a nasty smile. 'I think I'd like to go back to my cell.'

Moss signalled to the camera, and two officers came into the interview room and removed Mariette. Her solicitor picked up his paperwork and followed.

Moss waited until she was alone, and then yelled out in frustration, kicking the large table across the room.

CHAPTER 69

Nina was jolted awake. At first, she didn't know which day it was or where she was, she just felt warmth and a lulling motion. Then one of the twins moved. She opened her eyes and found she'd fallen asleep propped up against the side of the van. Mia and Sophie were under her arms, sleeping with their heads on her chest.

She realised what had woken her up. The van had stopped moving. It was very dark inside; the glow of the display on the car radio gave them a little light, but she couldn't see anything through the front window.

'Shit,' she said under her breath, as she shifted awkwardly. Her leg was curled under her and it had gone dead. A glow of light appeared outside and got brighter, and the driver's side was pulled open. Wind came screaming through the doorway, and flurries of snow. Max poked his head through the door. He was wearing one of the black woolly hats Mariette had bought them.

'You need to wake them two up and we need to get moving,' he said. He threw a carrier bag with the other hats and gloves at her, flicked the interior light on, and slammed the door. The grubby inside of the van came into view. One of the girls stirred, and Nina couldn't tell if it was Mia or Sophie. She opened her little eyes, and then remembered what had happened.

'Oh. Where are we?' she asked, her eyes quickly filling with tears.

'It's okay,' said Nina. She leaned over and poked her sister. 'Mia, Mia, wake up.'

Mia opened her eyes and when she realised, she was scared, but appeared a little more stoic, reaching out with a tiny hand to comfort Sophie. Nina looked down and found their interaction heartbreaking.

'It's okay. It's cold outside and I think it's still late. Just stay here for a moment,' said Nina. 'Look, there's some hats and gloves in here, can you put them on for me?' she added, handing them the carrier. She managed to extricate herself from them and climb through the front seats. Her leg was completely dead and she tried to wiggle her toes to get the blood moving. The girls were staring over at her.

'You're leaving us?' said Sophie.

'No. I'm just going outside to see where we are. I'm not leaving, I promise. Now please find yourself some hats and gloves in that bag and put them on...' Nina forced a smile on her face, but didn't think the girls were buying it. She opened the door and a gust of wind blew in with a whirl of snowflakes. 'Girls, please put on hats and gloves. I'll be back.'

She got out and slammed the door, emerged into a wailing storm, and it was pitch-black. There were no stars or moon in the sky. She started to stagger back to Max, trying to inject some feeling into her dead leg, when he shouted.

'Watch out! There's a huge drop!' He was a little way behind the van with a torch. He directed it down to the ground beside her, and she recoiled and grabbed the side of the van. The arching beam of the powerful torch showed she was standing on a strip of grass less than three feet wide, with a steep drop down to a water-filled quarry.

'Jesus! Where are we?' she shrilled, gripping on tight and inching along the strip of grass to the back of the van where the grassy platform opened out.

'On the edge of the moor. It's about five miles over that way to the cave,' he said, pointing to the left. She joined him at the back of the van, where he had a rucksack on the grass. He was pulling on a thick winter coat, and he pulled another one out, and two smaller ones for the girls. 'Put this on.'

She pulled it on, feeling the warmth immediately.

'These are thermal, no cheap shit,' he shouted.

'What time is it?'

'Just after 3 a.m. We should hang here until first light, okay? Can you keep them quiet?'

'They need water, and I think one of them has wet herself.'

'Deal with it, then,' he said. He took out a pack of cigarettes and crouched down, cupping his hands around it, trying to light up. 'Don't just fucking stand there, help me, Neen.' She crouched down and held open her coat until he got his cigarette lit. He took several deep puffs, and the tip glowed bright. 'Go back in and get some sleep. It won't be light for a few more hours.'

She could see snow was lying on the ground around their feet, and she took the two little coats and inched her way around the steep drop and got back into the van.

Max didn't return for several hours. They sat in the dark as the van shook in the wind, and Nina sang to the twins. Nursery rhymes she remembered her own mother singing to her. She also told the girls that this would soon be over, and they would be going back to their mummy and daddy later in the day.

'But why have we come here?' asked Mia. Nina was now able to tell them apart by their voices. Mia had a slightly higher, more questioning inflection, whereas Sophie spoke with more certainty and confidence.

'We're here because Mummy and Daddy are having builders in—'

'What are they building?' asked Sophie.

'A brand new bathroom and kitchen.'

'But we've got a new one.'

'This is a brand spanking amazing new one,' said Nina.

'And who is that grumpy man driving the van?' asked Mia.

'He's my boss. You know what bosses are like.'

'Yes,' said Mia. 'Daddy has to be a boss. Are bosses called bosses cos they're bossy?'

'Yes. They are.'

Nina was appalled and strangely comforted that the girls accepted this explanation. The night seemed to go on forever, but finally she started to see the sky through the front window of the van moving from black to dark blue and then becoming lighter.

As the sun came up, the swirling mist of the snowy moors came into view. Nina watched it for some time, marvelling at its beauty. Then abruptly the door was yanked open, and Max poked his head back inside.

'It's time to make the call,' he said.

CHAPTER 70

Erika slept in the incident room at Lewisham Row Station, along with Moss. They had attempted to question Mariette Hoffman again in the early hours of the morning, but it yielded nothing, until her solicitor told them they had to give her eight hours of sleep in the cells before they could resume.

Erika opened her eyes. One of the officers from Detective Paris's Kidnap Unit, who had set up base in another of the incident rooms in the basement, was shaking her awake. She'd been sleeping in a chair, and using her coat as a blanket.

'We've had a call come through the switchboard that we think is Max Kirkham. It's just being checked before it comes through to us,' said the officer, a young lad with a kind face.

'OK, thanks,' said Erika. She shook Moss, who was sleeping in a chair on the opposite side of the desk and they followed the officer over to the incident room.

Everyone had congregated around a group of desks, wearing headsets and cradling cups of coffee. Superintendent Paris was sitting at a desk in the middle, and putting on a headset. Erika and Moss were given a spare headset each and they pulled them on. An officer sitting to the side of Paris gave the thumbs up.

'We're recording,' he said.

Paris nodded and pressed a button, opening the microphone.

'Who am I speaking to?' asked a male voice. It was confident and sounded working class yet cultured.

'This is Superintendent Paris,' he said calmly. 'I'm head of the Metropolitan Police Kidnap and Hostage Unit. Can I ask who you are?'

'This is Max Kirkham,' said the voice. A look passed between Erika and Moss as they were finally hearing the voice of their suspect. There was a pause on the end of the line, and they could hear wind and interference in the background. Superintendent Paris wrote something down on a piece of paper and held it up:

TRACING?

One of the officers looked across and shook his head.
Paris nodded.

'You still there, cocker?' said Max.

'Yes, I'm here, Max.'

'Okay. Well, I'll cut to the chase. I can confirm I have the girls.'

'Can you please state the names of the two girls you have with you?'

'Yeah, it's, um, Sophie Marsh and Mia Marsh, and they are the spawn of your very own Commander Paul Marsh.'

'Okay, thank you,' said Paris.

'What the fuck do you mean *thank you*?' said Max. 'I feel like I'm calling up to complain about my electric account, and you're giving me the customer service chat.'

'I want nothing more than a peaceful conclusion to this. I am here to talk without judgement.'

'I don't give a shit about your judgement, and I'm not gonna keep on chatting here so you can trace me. However, this is a disposable phone so good luck.'

Erika scrawled something on a piece of paper and held it up to one of the officers:

WE HAVE RECEIPTS 4 PAY & GO PHONES. CHECK IMEI.

The officer nodded.

'Can you confirm that Mia and Sophie are alive and safe?' asked Paris.

'Yes and yes. And they will stay alive and safe as long as you do exactly what I say. So here's what I want. Have you heard of bitcoin?'

Paris looked up at the officers in the room.

'Yes, we are aware of how bitcoin works.'

'I have a brand new bitcoin account,' said Max, the line crackling with the sound of the wind. 'What I want is £200,000 put in my bitcoin account in the next twenty-four hours. Now, I know that dear old UK PLC don't cough up ransom payments. But I bet Commander Marsh and his wife have a few quid. I'm sure he can re-mortgage that beautiful house or rent out that fine pussy of hers, which I'll add is as smooth as velvet, and it's nice to see that the Brazilian wax hasn't taken over the suburbs of south London. She's certainly a woman who suits looking wild.'

Erika closed her eyes and had to grip her headset. Superintendent Paris, however, was unmoved.

'If Paul and Marcie Marsh decide to comply, and deposit £200,000 into this bitcoin account, you will return both girls safely to their family?'

'Yes, I will. I'll know the moment that the money arrives, and in turn I will text you the location of where I'm keeping the girls. As you probably know, I don't value human life, but I don't have the appetite to kill these two little shits. I just want my money and then they can be free to roam in the world again. Free to go to their private schools and grow up to be bourgeois little cunts. I'll give you five hours, and then I will call back. I won't answer this number, so don't try to call.'

The line then went dead. There was a pause as the team removed their headsets, and they watched Paris as he carried on writing on a piece of paper.

'Okay,' he said. 'We want to get a trace on this phone. We'll have to triangulate with the nearest mobile phone masts. This needs to be a level one priority. We also need to put out a nationwide search for all white vans with the make and model we have from the person in custody. Again, level one priority. We also need to have people on the ground; we should conduct a door-to-door in the immediate houses around the day care centre where these girls were abducted. I want all resources diverted away and this becomes our number one priority.'

'The second two are already underway,' said Erika. 'I also have Nina Hargreaves's diary, which was recovered from their council flat. The entries could prove useful.'

Superintendent Paris paused, and didn't look thrilled to see her.

'Thank you, DCI Foster, but I am making a recommendation that you are not involved in this case from here onwards. You have been welcome here as an observer, but after the events of last night, I think your involvement has crossed over into personal territory.'

'With respect—' started Erika.

But he put up his hand. 'That's all I'm saying on the matter; please can you leave my incident room.'

CHAPTER 71

It was now light, and Nina stood with the girls, shivering in the cold. They watched as Max retrieved the last of the bags from the back of the van and slammed the doors shut. There were two large rucksacks filled with their supplies, and another two bags of food.

Now it was light Nina could see they were standing on a low ridge of rock and heather, and the road had finished a hundred yards further up behind them. In one direction they could see across Dartmoor, the weather was clear, but the green landscape was speckled with snow. To the side of the van was the rocky lip of a large water-filled quarry with a layer of ice. Large wisps of low-hanging cloud drifted past, and the twins, who now had their coats on and their hoods up, gazed at them, momentarily distracted by the sight of clouds that you could reach out and touch.

Max went over to the front of the van and leaned in to the passenger side and undid the window, then moved around and did the same with the driver's side. He turned the wheel until the front wheels were angled towards the frozen water, then took off the handbrake and slammed the door. He leaned into the back and gave it a push. Nina and the girls moved closer to the edge of the quarry and watched as it rolled over the edge, gathering speed before it hit the ice. It stayed there for a moment, bobbing up and down, with the back half poking up out of the water, and then it was still.

'Come on,' said Max as they watched it for a couple of minutes. Nothing happened. Then, slowly, there was a creaking, sucking sound and bubbles floated up as it slowly started to sink through the hole in the ice. As the lip of the front windows reached the water, it filled rapidly and sank fast, disappearing through the ice.

Max came over to the girls and crouched down. He pulled a little bag of the Haribo sweets out of each pocket and handed them to the girls.

'Now, these are for you, okay?' he said. The girls nodded with wide eyes and each took a packet. 'If you keep being good, and quiet, and do exactly what you're told, you'll see your mummy and daddy again. If you misbehave...' He turned and pointed to the bubbles still floating up through the hole in the ice. 'You'll end up in there, with the van... And you know something?' He leaned forward and whispered: 'If you go in there, you never stop sinking. You just keep going down, and down, and down into the dark. And you'll never be found.'

The two girls began to cry, silent tears running down their faces.

'Max, you don't have to—' started Nina.

'Shut up! Now. We need to get moving.'

Max pulled on a large rucksack, and he gave the other one to Nina. They set off down the bank opposite the quarry, towards the green landscape stretching out ahead and speckled with snow.

CHAPTER 72

Paul and Marcie sat on the sofa in their front room. They hadn't slept, and they wore hollow empty stares. Marcie's mother came into the room with a tray of tea, looking a little less coiffed than she had the previous day. She handed out cups to Paul, Marcie, Marcie's father Leonard, Colleen, the Family Liaison Officer, Superintendent Paris and two other uniformed officers. Paris had just outlined what had happened on the phone with Max.

'We've got how much in our joint savings? Fifty-five, sixty thousand?' said Marsh, standing up and talking to Marcie.

'Fifty-six thousand,' she said, cradling her steaming cup of tea. Her nose was still bandaged and the bruises on her eyes were blooming now to a bright purple and green.

'We can make up the rest,' said Leonard.

'Yes, we have the rainy day account, and this is…' started Marcie's mother. 'This is…' She broke down and put a hand to her mouth. Marcie's face crumpled and her mother took her in her arms.

'I'd just like to reiterate that we want to resolve this without you having to send such a large amount of money,' said Paris.

'That's easy for you to say!' shouted Marsh. 'Have you seen our two little girls, they're just… angels… they've never even spent the night away from home, and now they're… Where are they? You're supposed to be the bloody crack team for kidnapping. They've been missing for almost twenty-four hours!'

'We are still attempting to work that out. We are working on several leads. I can assure you that our officers are highly trained and—'

'Don't give me that bullshit! I'm a bloody police officer. I'm your senior bloody officer! So you start giving me some answers.'

Superintendent Paris remained passive and stared at Marsh.

'Paul, I'm sorry I can't share specifics with you at this stage.'

'What do you mean, "Paul"? Didn't you hear me? I outrank you… I outrank you all. You address me as sir and you bloody well tell me what's going on!'

'Paul!' shouted Marcie, standing unsteadily. 'These officers are the only hope we have of getting Sophie and Mia back safe. So you can keep a civil tongue in your head. Right now you are not a police officer, you are on the other side.'

There was silence. Marsh broke down and sank into the sofa. Marcie stood and went over to Paris.

'I know someone who works at the bank, our local branch. We have our account there and Mum's and Dad's are there too. We can get this money together as fast as possible…'

'As I said, I want to try and resolve this without parting with any money,' said Paris.

'And if this was one or even two of your children, would you be so bloody calm and confident? Tell me that, Superintendent Paris?'

He was quiet. Marcie went on. 'So I'm asking you, when you next talk to this… person… you tell them we are ready to pay. And we are serious.'

Paris took Marcie's hand in his and nodded. 'He says he will call back in four hours. So you have some time. Keep in contact and let me know when you have it.'

'Thank you,' she said. He went to take his hand back, and then Marcie asked: 'Do you have children?'

'We had a daughter, but she died when she was nine; she was knocked off her bicycle. It was a long time ago.'

'I'm sorry,' said Marcie.

'Let me know when you have the money,' he said, and then the officers left to go back to the station.

CHAPTER 73

They walked for almost three hours, laden down with the rucksacks. The two little girls slowed things down as they went across the rough ground, up hills and down slopes, and once or twice they had to negotiate stiles across deserted farmland.

Then a farmhouse appeared on the horizon; it grew larger as they walked, and they passed very close, and Nina slowed down, scanning the building, trying to work out if anyone lived there. Max carried on walking ahead. She wasn't sure if he had seen it.

'There's a…' started Mia, pointing at it, and Nina put a hand over her mouth, but it wasn't fast enough. Max stopped and walked back to them.

'That farmhouse, you mean?'

'Yes,' said Mia, squinting up at him. Sophie shot her a look to be quiet.

'It's an empty farmhouse. It's a haunted house, isn't it, Nina?'

'Yes, it is,' said Nina. Inside, her mind was whirring. She hadn't remembered it from when they'd walked on Dartmoor with Dean last summer.

Max leaned over to kiss her, and whispered in her ear. 'Don't think of doing anything stupid.'

''Course,' she said. When he pulled back, she saw something behind his eyes: the malevolence which scared her.

'Good, now come on.'

They carried on walking, passing the farmhouse in the distance, and now Max watched her closely. Nina kept hold of the girls' hands and didn't glance at it again.

A little while later, they came to a depression in the moor, where the grass dipped down. Nina had to stop and collect herself when she saw it again. The thin path was less green than it had been the previous year and the waterfall seemed to be flowing much faster, and the water was a dirty brown colour. The pool surrounded by large boulders looked the same, but then she saw that the water level was higher, and the rocky platform was now half submerged.

Nina gripped the girls' hands and closed her eyes. She was taken back to that hot sunny day, the smell of Dean as he bore down on her, and how his blood was so warm she didn't notice at first that it splattered her naked body.

'What are you doing?' shouted Max.

Nina opened her eyes and saw that he was at the bottom of the slope, close to the water's edge. The girls were now tired and tearful, and she had to drag them down the slope. They followed Max up to where he disappeared into a creased seam in the rock, and then stopped dead.

'Come on. It's a place we can shelter,' said Nina. She could see how grubby their once smart little outfits were, and where their noses were running, dirt had stuck to their skin. Nina took out a tissue and wiped their noses. 'This is a cave, and it's very safe,' she said. 'We can get warm inside and have some food.'

They followed her inside cautiously.

It was the same as she remembered, very dry inside. The walls were just as smooth, and it was a few degrees warmer than the air outside.

'I told you if I was ever on the run, this is where I'd hide out,' said Max.

'Yeah, I remember.'

He was watching her closely again, cocking his head and staring.

'What is it, Max?'

He seemed to snap out of it and sloughed off his backpack, and encouraged Nina to do the same. She went to the rocky platform covered in graffiti, and took it off, relishing the feeling of losing the heavy weight.

They unpacked the blankets and sleeping bags. Max opened some tins of beans and heated them up on the tiny stove, and he found the yellow, blue, and red plastic bowls Mariette bought them and the plastic cutlery. He even had a bit of banter with the girls, asking them which bowl they would like their beans in.

'I want blue,' said Sophie.

'I want blue too,' said Mia.

'Good job I don't like blue,' said Max, and the girls laughed nervously.

Nina was pleased to see them tucking into the food, and that they were warming up, with a little colour spreading across their pale cheeks. As she ate, her mind was racing. Max would shortly head off to make the second phone call, and they would be left alone. She looked at the girls, so young and innocent, eating their food. Could Max be trusted not to hurt them?

'What are you thinking, Neen?' said Max.

She jumped and saw he was staring at her again.

'Nothing.'

'Didn't look like nothing.'

'No, I'm just tired. I'll try to get some sleep when you go. When are you going?'

'In about five minutes, if you'll just let me finish my FUCKING FOOD!' he shouted, and he threw his bowl of beans against the wall of the cave. The girls jumped and looked up from their food as Max's bowl clattered in the silence. Nina saw the girls both had a little orange stain around their mouths.

'Sorry, do you want mine?' asked Nina.

'No… I don't.' He stood up. 'You don't think this is going to work, do you?'

Nina gulped and felt the food in her stomach start to shift. It felt surreal and like it was all getting out of hand.

'No, I mean, no that's not true. I do think it's going to work.'

'Neen, I'm in control. I'm the guy with the plan, the laptop and the phone; I can run everything, and we've planned everything, and if you fuck this up now…'

'I won't, I won't, I promise,' said Nina, jumping up and going to him, pawing at his arms. Mia and Sophie were now staring at her, a mixture of confusion and fear in their faces. 'I'm sorry. I'm jittery and hungry and we wouldn't have this opportunity if it wasn't for you.'

He shook her off and went to the rucksack, pulling out a phone, a map, and the gun.

'Now, I'm going back to the second location on Pitman's Tor to make the second call with the second phone as we planned,' he said.

'Yes.'

'And it will take me a couple of hours. It should buy us some time, confuse them when they try to triangulate the signal. The mobile phone masts are far apart on the moor, and we're safely tucked away here.'

'Yes, I know.'

He came close and looked her in the eyes. 'Because you know there is nowhere to go, Neen. This is a one-way street. A one-way trip. You have to give me your loyalty. I need your loyalty…' He was breathing hard and shaking.

The girls were sitting up on the rock and staring at him open-mouthed.

'Max, I'll be here with the girls, waiting,' she said, trying to smile, trying to look like everything was easy.

He watched her for a moment and nodded. 'Okay. Wish me luck.'

'Good luck,' she said and kissed him. Nina watched as he made his way out through the slit in the cave. She breathed out and waited for ten minutes; the girls were quiet. She turned to them.

'Okay, girls. I want you to keep calm, and in a few minutes, we're going to walk to that farmhouse and we're going to see if anyone is...' Her voice trailed off. Both Mia and Sophie were looking to the gap in the cave behind her. Nina turned. Max was standing in the gap holding the gun.

'Nina...' he said. He looked shocked, almost devastated.

'Max, I was just going to get some...' started Nina, but words failed her, she couldn't think of a lie quickly enough. She took a step back towards the girls.

'I actually trusted you,' he said, shaking his head. 'I had this niggling voice inside that I tried to ignore...'

'Please, Max. Just let us go. We'll start walking. I won't tell anyone anything. I just can't do this. I love you, you know that...'

His eyes narrowed and he suddenly pointed the gun at her left leg and shot her in the thigh. The bang was deafening in the small cave and it echoed and reverberated, drowning out the girls' screams. He took a step closer and aimed the gun at her chest and squeezed off two more deafening shots.

The twins screamed and they moved to Nina's side as she lay there, eyes wide with shock, blood seeping through her trousers and in two spots on her chest. She stared up at Max in utter shock.

'Nina, Nina,' said Mia, her tiny hands cupping Nina's cheek. Sophie turned her head and looked at Max as he moved over to one of the rucksacks and pulled out the small black case he'd used when he posed as the engineer from the water company. He opened it and took out some cable ties. He came back and yanked the twins away from Nina, pulling them over to the soft ledge of rock with the graffiti. Someone had sunk a metal ring into the rock for tethering an animal. He grabbed their wrists and he quickly bound their hands tight to the ring with the cable ties. They were crouched side by side and crying.

Nina was still lying on the floor, gasping and staring up at Max, and she brought her hand to her chest and blood poured through her fingers. Max took the black case and the rucksack with all the supplies, and came back and stood over her.

'You won't be alive when I come back. It should be a quick death,' he said. The look he gave her was so cold and evil, she let out a huge sob.

Then he left the cave.

CHAPTER 74

Back in the Kidnap Unit's incident room at Lewisham Row, it had been almost five hours since Superintendent Paris had spoken with Max. Superintendent Hudson had just arrived and was addressing Paris and his team.

'I'm here to brief you on the ongoing murder investigation and manhunt running in parallel with you here at the Kidnap Unit. We have triangulated a position on the mobile phone used by Max Kirkham this morning.' She indicated the large map pinned up on the wall. 'It's coming from this mast, situated on the north-east corner of Dartmoor National Park.'

'What's the radius of the mast signal?' asked Paris.

'This mast covers a twelve square mile radius,' she said, indicating the vast expanse of the Dartmoor National Park, in Devon. 'The Dartmoor National Park is 368 square miles of rugged terrain, hills, valleys, bogs, and it's November so visibility is poor. An hour ago I gave the order for an Air Rescue search. We've deployed helicopters from London, and they will be working with the Air Operations Unit of Devon and Cornwall Police.'

'He requested a five-hour interval between phone calls,' said Paris. 'The two suspects could have split up, the female...'

'Nina Hargreaves,' said Melanie.

'Nina Hargreaves could be in one location with the girls. That gives Max time to walk. He also has a van,' said Paris. A phone rang out in the incident room. 'Right, this could be our man. Stand by, everyone.'

Melanie and the team took their places and pulled on their headsets. Paris answered the call.

'Do you have my money?' asked Max without any preamble. They could hear he was once again fighting against the elements.

'I can confirm that Paul and Marcie Marsh have the £200,000 available for transfer,' said Paris. 'Do we still have your guarantee that the girls are safe and will be returned unharmed?'

'Yes.'

'OK. Then how can we proceed?'

'I'm going to give you a code; this is the code for my bitcoin wallet. Before you try and trace it, I'll tell you that I'm using TORwallet through the Tor network. It's amazing what a guy can achieve with a mobile phone and a laptop. Here I have you lot at my beck and call, and two hundred grand winging its way to me. Beats working, doesn't it?'

'The code, please?' said Paris, his voice remaining neutral.

Max read out the code and Paris wrote it down.

'I'll expect the money in the next three hours. I'll know I have it in my bitcoin wallet when I receive a text message to say that the money has arrived. Then I will phone you back with the location of Mia and Sophie.'

He hung up. There was silence in the room.

'I don't like the sound of this. Who's to say he won't just kill the girls?' said Melanie. 'I've not worked on kidnap cases before, but this isn't just someone who wants cash...' Her voice tailed off. 'I've been following this case. I know what Max Kirkham and Nina Hargreaves are capable of. Money isn't enough. They want to wreak havoc.'

CHAPTER 75

The hum of the whirring blades was deafening as the Metropolitan Police Air Rescue helicopter flew over a thick blanket of cloud. Rain hammered against the large glass doors either side, as Erika and Moss rode in the back with one of the Air Ambulance officers. The space was cramped, with Moss sitting in the middle. On the floor in front of them was the hoist and stretcher which could be lowered out to the ground, and medical supplies were stuffed in around them.

They were all wearing huge black police radio headsets so they could keep in contact with the pilot above the deafening noise. Erika looked over at Moss clutching at her headset, and saw she was a little green.

'You okay?' she mouthed.

Moss nodded unconvincingly and gripped the seat as the helicopter started to bank down towards the clouds.

'We're heading south at forty knots,' came the tinny voice of the pilot through their earphones. 'We've now reached the edge of Dartmoor and dropping down to a lower altitude for better visibility.'

Moss reached out and grabbed at Erika's hand as the blanket of cloud moved towards them, and they plunged through it, the view outside a blur of white, until they bumped and jolted and emerged above the rolling hills and tors.

Erika had been to see Melanie and had explained she was no longer welcome working with the Kidnap Unit, but she had asked to remain an active part of the murder investigation. She didn't know if Melanie had stuck her in a helicopter to get rid of her or to help.

The helicopter flew low over the vast expanses of green. Over frozen streams and waterways, and fields where cows and sheep dispersed to the four corners at the sound of the helicopter above. But as they flew back and forth, covering the square miles of Dartmoor with six other helicopters, there was nothing to report. No people. Dartmoor, it seemed, was empty.

CHAPTER 76

Nina lay back and felt the hard stone floor tip and sway. Her leg was in agony, but her chest felt strange, like she had a dull ache and it was filled with water. She tried to breathe, but all she could manage were tiny sips of air. It was dark and cold, and she couldn't see very well. She drifted in and out of consciousness several times, but suddenly her mind sharpened and she could hear the sound of the girls sobbing. She tried to say their names, but all that came out was a gurgle, and then she coughed and pain exploded in her chest like a thousand pieces of glass.

'Nina... Nina are you there?' said a little voice through the dark. She put out her hands and felt the rock underneath. It was wet, cold and wet. *Is that my blood?* she thought. Digging in one elbow, she hoisted herself up, unleashing a more intense burst of pain, and she leaned to one side. Blood poured from her mouth and she was able to spit and gasp, and clear her throat,

'It's okay... girls. Girls! I'm here,' she wheezed. She was drenched in sweat, or was it blood? Surely there wasn't that much blood in her body? She tried to sit up, but the pain was so bad that she almost blacked out again.

'Nina, we can't move, and it's hurting us,' said a voice. Nina couldn't tell if it was Mia or Sophie talking.

So much flashed before her eyes. Max had shot her, three times, in the leg and chest. He intended to kill her. Why wasn't she dead yet?

She wished she could go back; she wished that she'd found a man who just made her laugh. She didn't need to feel burning passion: a nice, boring guy who would look after her, who would slob out on the sofa and watch football, and give her babies. She reached down and put her hand to her chest. Blood was pumping out. She could feel it as her heart thumped, rhythmically pushing the life out of her. Her leg was on fire and she tried to reach down, but she couldn't.

There was a low droning sound from outside the cave and, at first, she didn't know what it was, then her mind gave a picture of a helicopter; it got louder and, for a brief moment, she thought it was going to land outside, that, somehow, they knew where she and the girls were hidden… It grew to a high-pitched drone, and then it was gone, passing overhead. It receded into silence, and she was left with just the sounds of the girls sobbing.

CHAPTER 77

Back in the Kidnap Unit incident room in Lewisham Row, the team congregated around one laptop as one of Superintendent Paris's officers went through the steps of transferring the £200,000 into the bitcoin coded account. It was a complex process, and had several steps, and different screens where codes had to be input.

'It all comes down to this: fifteen highly trained police officers peering at a website,' said Melanie, who was next to Paris.

'Gone are the days when we leave holdalls full of cash,' said Paris.

'How do we know he'll release the girls?'

'We don't.'

There was silence. Melanie turned away at the crucial moment when the funds were sent. She didn't want the team to see her cry.

CHAPTER 78

Max hung around on the frozen moor. He had climbed to the top of a tor, and he was standing beside a huge stack of flat stones. They reminded him of the game, Jenga, and he imagined that giants had once walked the moors and had been playing with the stones, leaving this huge pile. The cloud was coming in low, and the air was filling with a cold swirling mist. He heard, far off to the south, the low drone of a helicopter, but looking up the visibility wasn't good. The cloud was giving him the advantage.

He heard the mobile phone beep in his pocket and he pulled it out, and he opened the text message. The code was there. The money had arrived.

He whooped and crowed and punched the air, an ecstatic feeling of euphoria running through his body. He had been confident that his plan would work, but in the back of his mind he'd always thought he could be left empty-handed. He had made a contingency plan to run with the ten grand, which would have cut down his options… but Jesus, he had two hundred grand. *Two hundred fucking grand.*

He didn't wait to celebrate. He set off back to the cave. Now he had the money, he didn't need them anymore. He didn't need to be the good person. He wanted to teach those fuckers a lesson. Those little kids were the spawn of a policeman and his whore wife. He checked his gun. He had two bullets left. One for each of them.

CHAPTER 79

Nina drifted back into consciousness. She wasn't sure how long she had been out; she had tried to sit up but the pain had been too much. The sound of a helicopter droned in the far distance as she came to. The ground was cold underneath her, and she was light-headed.

'Nina?' said Sophie. 'Nina?'

'She's asleep,' said Mia.

'I'm not asleep,' said Nina thickly, her voice slurring. 'I'm not, I'm just hurt and I can't move.'

'Daddy once hurt his back and he had to lie on a plank on the floor in the living room,' said Mia.

'It wasn't a real plank though, was it? It was a piece of wood from Grandad's old sideboard, and he brought it over for Daddy to lie on,' said Sophie.

Nina smiled and swallowed blood. 'My dad hurt his back once, and he had to lie on the ironing board.'

'How did your mummy do the ironing?' asked one of the girls, and, despite the pain, Nina laughed.

'It wasn't upright; he lay on it on the floor. The legs were tucked under.'

Nina saw it for a moment, the image of her dad on the floor, and her mother trying to tuck a cushion onto that wiry bit where the iron sits. It was now so clear in her mind... The smell of the living room, her mother on her knees by her father's head as he moaned for her to bring more cushions. Her father looked up at her and smiled, and she knew she had drifted off again and was dreaming.

Nina had a sudden impulse of energy, and she came back to her senses. She was on the floor of the cave; she turned her head and saw that she was a couple of metres from the entrance. She could try and drag herself outside, and wave at one of the helicopters, but there was a huge slope upwards, filled with rocks and boulders.

She turned her head, and she saw that Max had taken his backpack with all the tools and twine. He also had the black case which was filled with the matches, torch, scissors and wire cutters. They just had the rucksack with the stove and where they kept the rolled-up sleeping bags. She thought about what she could do if he came back. She could throw a tin of baked beans at him, or two. This made her laugh, but it came out as a nasty wet gurgle.

'Are you laughing?' asked a small voice. Sophie.

'Yes, I am,' she said. Nina shifted, and then she forced herself to sit up. The darkness in the cave started to overwhelm her and she saw stars, but she breathed through it. She felt her chest. He must have missed her heart; surely, she'd be dead by now. She tried not to think about how much blood she had lost, the blood seemed to have eased from her chest. Well, the blood that she could see. She had a funny feeling, a fullness which made her think she was bleeding pretty badly inside. It was her leg that continued to pour with blood. What if she made a tourniquet? If she managed to get the bottom of her jeans, and roll them up tight, high above her knee, that could work to stop the bleeding. She reached down, and felt her insides slosh and burn. Her fingers brushed the bottoms of the jeans and she could tell they were too tight for it to work. She wished that the bottoms were wider so she could have rolled them higher.

Shame I'm not wearing flares, she thought, *not that I've ever owned a pair.*

She froze.

Flares.

Distress flares.

In the rucksack, with the stove and bedding, in the side pocket, were the distress flares. *Please*, she thought. *Please don't let him have remembered about it.* He took the stuff that I could use to cut the girls free and the first aid kit, but my rucksack, which had bedding and the maps, that has the red distress flare in the pocket.

She felt another burst of energy and started to drag herself over to the rucksack.

'Nina, are you okay?' asked a small voice. Sophie, she could hear it was Sophie.

'Yes, Sophie, you sit tight, I'm going to get us out of this,' she said. The pain was agonising but she made it across the rough stone floor to the rucksack. She felt around, running her hands over the pockets. *Yes!* There they were in the outside pocket; she could feel the outline. She unzipped the pocket and pulled out the two long red distress flares.

The original plan was that when they received the money, they would leave the girls out on the moor and make a call to Marsh with their exact location. Then they had planned to make their way across the moor to a town on the edge, near Plymouth. Here they would get a cab, and make their way to the port, which was only a few miles. It was then he was going to fire the flare as a signal. Max had arranged for a bloke he knew from the young offender's centre to be waiting to pick them up in a boat. They had been planning to pay him £25,000 to take them across to Europe.

She propped herself up on the rucksack and took stock. It was ridiculous. Everyone was looking for them. Even if Max managed to get the money, their chances... *his* chances of making it were slim.

He shot me. He shot me, and left me for dead, why would he come back? Would he come back?

Nina gripped the two distress flares and unscrewed the base, feeling the pull string drop down. She had been planning to drag herself out to a spot by the waterfall where she could see the sky, wait for a helicopter to come close and fire it into the air.

And then she had a better idea.

CHAPTER 80

Clouds were rushing across the sky in fits and bursts as Max drew close to the place where the ground banked down towards the waterfall. He hadn't heard a helicopter for almost half an hour, but the cloud was lifting, and he would have to wait for dark until he started to hike down the ten miles to the edge of the moor. The boat was due to meet them at 3 a.m.

Not *them, him,* he corrected himself. He figured the helicopters would continue to search until nightfall, so he had time to kill. Time, and other things too.

He stopped at the top of the slope and checked the gun. It was loaded; he felt the weight of it in his hand. He wanted to show that bastard police commander who was in control. He'd avoided hurting the girls in front of Nina, but now she was dead he could do what he liked. It wouldn't be quick. He would strip the girls naked, and cut off all their hair, and torture them a while with his long hunting knife. He had never been into kids, but maybe for the commander he would have to make an exception.

He moved down the slope, through the banks of heather and past the waterfall. It was freezing cold and he thought if the temperature dropped much more it would freeze and suddenly fall silent.

He reached the small slit in the rocks, and stood to one side and listened, his gun cocked. There was no sound from inside. He closed his eyes for a few seconds to get his eyes used to the darkness in the cave. Then he opened them and stepped through and inside.

The twins now looked filthy and dishevelled and were still tied to the steel ring in the rocky shelf. There was a vast pool of blood, but Nina wasn't where he'd shot her. He followed the trail of blood, and saw she was propped up against a rucksack.

'You worthless piece of shit. Eat this!' she cried.

Max only realised that she was pointing the distress flare at him a millisecond before a flash of red came shooting out towards his face.

Nina knew the charge from the distress flare was designed to travel to a height of 100 metres in a matter of seconds, but the force of it detonating threw her back against the rocky wall. The rocket hit Max in his open mouth, and the white-hot temperature of the charge burnt through the flesh of his face and into his brain. At the same time, he was thrown back towards the mouth of the cave, but missed, and slammed into the wall. Nina shouted for the girls to duck down, and she covered her face as the flare exploded in a fiery burst of red, igniting his body and clothes and filling the cave with thick smoke. Nina grabbed the second flare and pointed it in the direction of the mouth of the cave and fired.

CHAPTER 81

The Met police helicopter containing Erika and Moss had been in the air for a couple of hours, flying in a grid formation across Dartmoor.

Erika's hopes of finding Mia and Sophie alive had started to fade a couple of hours into their search. They had listened to the police radio, linking up with pilots flying over other sections of the moors, and they had all reported nothing. They were about to have to turn back and fly back to the base in Plymouth to refuel when Erika saw a thin plume of thick black smoke, and then a red distress flare sailed into the sky in a bright red pinprick of light before arching over and beginning its descent.

'There,' she cried, speaking into her radio. 'We have to go there. We can't turn back yet.'

The pilot turned sharply to the right, and the plume of smoke came closer, clumps of cloud moved past and briefly enveloped them before they seemed to sail apart and give them a perfect bird's-eye view of a small depression in the moor filled with water. As the grass came closer and they descended down towards the edge of the waterfall, they could see down below the blood-spattered body of a woman lying on a piece of grass next to the waterfall.

As soon as the helicopter touched down, Erika, Moss and the air ambulance paramedic jumped out, ducking down under the blades, and they ran down the slope to the woman, who was just barely alive, still clutching the yellow cylinder of the distress flare in her bloody hands.

'In the cave. He's dead, and the girls are there,' she croaked.

Erika and Moss left the paramedic with Nina, and found the entrance to the cave. Erika hurried to the girls and saw them tied to the rock. They were grubby and filthy and crying hysterically. Then Moss noticed the charred figure slumped in the corner, with a burnt-out hole where the face should be.

'He's dead; she killed him!' cried one of the twins.

'Please help us, get us out,' shouted the other.

Erika worked on the cable ties with the sharp edge of her house key, and she managed to cut one of the cable ties and then the other.

'Let's get them out of here,' she cried, and she and Moss scooped them up and ran out of the cave, past the paramedic and up to the top.

Erika left Moss with the girls and came back down to the paramedic.

'Please, leave me to die,' whispered Nina hoarsely.

Erika crouched down at her side and looked at the paramedic, who shook his head.

'Stay with her. I need to run back and get supplies. Hold here,' he said, taking Erika's hand and pressing it onto the blood oozing from Nina's leg. He ran off back to the helicopter.

'There's a boy, buried in the well over there,' said Nina. She winced at the pain.

'What?' asked Erika.

'His name was Dean. Please look in the well, find his body. Give him a proper burial.'

Erika nodded.

'I never got to do so much of the things I wanted…. I never got to have babies… Please make sure they get back safe to their parents… Mia… Sophie.'

Erika could see the life was draining out of Nina, and she looked back at the helicopter, to where Moss was wrapping the girls in blankets and giving them water. Erika could feel the blood slowing from where her hand lay on the wound, and Nina was taking ragged breaths.

'I'm sorry for everything. Tell my mum I love her...' She then looked at Erika. 'I never meant any of this to happen...' With a throaty wheeze, the light left her eyes and her skin rapidly changed from white to a waxy yellow.

The paramedic came running back and reached her side with an IV line.

'She's gone,' said Erika softly. 'She's dead.'

The paramedic looked over at Moss waiting by the helicopter with Mia and Sophie.

'We need to get those girls to a hospital and have them checked over,' he said. 'I'm going to call one of the other helicopters to come and get you.'

Erika didn't have the chance to respond; he ran off up the slope and bundled the girls and Moss inside the helicopter. She closed her eyes against the air pressure as it took off, flattening the grass and heather around her. It sheered up into the sky, grew smaller and then vanished up through the clouds.

Erika looked down at Nina's body and felt an overwhelming sadness. How could a young girl with so much promise stumble down such a dark path? She looked back to the cave, and could just make out Max Kirkham's feet through the gap in the rocks. It was quiet, and the light was fading, and she shivered. With her free hand, she closed Nina's eyes.

The wind whistled across the heather and the air was bitterly cold, and Erika paced up and down to keep warm. She thought how long she had hunted for these two people, and of the trail of destruction they had left in their wake. And now she was alone, guarding their bodies. She was relieved they had been stopped, and even more relieved that Mia and Sophie were safe and would be reunited with Paul and Marcie, but a big part of her wished she could have locked Max and Nina up and thrown away the key. Death seemed too light a sentence for them.

Finally, another helicopter appeared on the horizon.

EPILOGUE

FRIDAY, 15 DECEMBER 2017

It was three weeks later, and Erika was just returning home from a long day which had ended with a doctor's appointment when she finally had the cast on her wrist removed. It was cold, and had been threatening to snow for the past few days, but she doubted they would have a white Christmas. As she put the key in the lock, she saw how emaciated her wrist looked after wearing the cast for so many weeks. She opened the door and stepped inside, picking up a pile of cards on the mat.

She went through to the living room, taking off her coat, and the first thing she did was open the eighteenth door on the Advent calendar Jakub and Karolina had sent her. She popped out the chocolate, and saw behind it was a Santa and Mrs Claus, both fat and jolly with beaming red faces. Santa was holding a piece of mistletoe above Mrs Claus's head, and she was coquettishly leaning up to kiss him.

'You just remember, love, Santa only comes once a year. Make the most of it,' said Erika to the calendar. She popped the chocolate in her mouth, and went to the fridge and poured herself a large vodka. She took it to the sofa and started to open the cards.

There were Christmas cards from Moss, Crane, and McGorry, and even Peterson had sent her one with a rather ambiguous 'best wishes'. She had seen them all that day, apart from Peterson, whose return to work loomed in the new year, so she wasn't sure why they had all posted their cards. She felt a little stingy for slipping her Christmas cards into everyone's pigeon holes.

Erika was about to order a takeaway when there was a knock at the door. When she opened it, she was surprised to see Marsh on the doorstep. They hadn't spoken since the dramatic events on Dartmoor.

'Hi…'

'Hi, Erika,' he said. He looked thin.

'Come in, you fancy a drink?' she said, adding quickly. 'A coffee or tea?'

He came in and wiped his feet, but he didn't take off his coat as she led him through to the living room.

'I won't have a drink, thanks,' he said, tapping his fingers on the back of the sofa nervously. There was an awkward silence.

'How are you… doing?' she asked.

'I don't know. Okay-ish.'

'How's Marcie?'

'She's been better. Taking it one day at a time.'

'And Sophie and Mia?'

'Surprisingly upbeat. They are happy to be home. Very clingy and cuddly. We're going to have to see about getting them some counselling, perhaps, down the line, but they're more upset about Nina Hargreaves… She did so much awful stuff, killed all those people, yet she's the reason my girls are alive.'

'She's also the reason that your girls were kidnapped and that you are now two hundred grand worse off…' Erika frowned. 'Sorry. That came out wrong.'

'It's okay.'

'The Devon and Cornwall Police recovered the body of a Dean Grover. It was where Nina said he was buried, in a well near the waterfall on the moor. His face had been battered with a rock… And Mariette Hoffman is going on trial in the new year.'

Marsh winced at the details of the case, then changed the subject.

'How are you? I heard you went to visit Nils Åkerman.'

'Yeah. I went for selfish reasons, to get closure, but I'm not sure closure works... I could forgive him for what he did to me, but he's jeopardised so many past cases and convictions. And the irony is that he'll probably be out in four or five years, depending on good behaviour.'

Marsh nodded and hovered by the back of the sofa.

'Are you sure you don't want a quick coffee, Paul?'

He shook his head and took a deep breath. 'Marcie wanted to know if you are around on Christmas Day.'

'Me? Why?'

'To come for Christmas lunch.'

'To come to your house for Christmas lunch?'

'Yes. I know you haven't always seen eye to eye...'

'We've never seen eye to eye, and after what happened...'

'She's so grateful to you for your part in saving the girls. She's very emotional about that, and so many other things right now... But she says having you there would be nice, and the girls like you. And you know what she's been through; she can talk to you about stuff. Her mum and dad are going to be there, but they always brush things under the carpet. You could just come for a sherry and a mince pie if lunch is too much... And she wants to apologise to you for what she said in front of all those officers about me and you...'

'Do you want me in your house on Christmas Day?'

'Of course. We go way back, Erika.'

'We do...'

'So is that a yes?'

'Yes.'

They stared at each other for a long time.

'Good lord, look!' Marsh cried, moving to the window. 'It's starting to snow!'

'And I thought it wasn't going to this year,' said Erika.

She joined him at the window. Outside, the snow was whirling in huge flakes and settling on the dry ground. They stared out for a few minutes, watching in silence.

'Well, I should be going back. It's bath time for the girls,' said Marsh.

'Yeah.'

She walked him to the front door, and just as he left he kissed her lightly on the cheek.

'Thank you, for everything. You mean a lot to me,' he said softly.

Erika went back to the window, and watched as Marsh walked across the car park, through the whirling snow, back to his wife and children.

A LETTER FROM ROB

First of all, I want to say a huge thank you for choosing to read *Cold Blood*. As always, this story has been a labour of love. It's always nerve-wracking when a novel I've been working on for months and months goes out into the world. This is book five in the Erika Foster series, and with each book I feel a greater responsibility to readers to keep these characters alive and true to their beginnings. I take this responsibility very seriously, and I hope you enjoy reading.

I will add that while I like to use real locations in London, I have taken a few minor liberties with places and road names; apart from this, Erika Foster's London is as real as the London you live in, or hope to visit. And if you do bump into Erika Foster when you're there, do watch out for serial killers, they seem drawn to her!

So, this is the part when I ask if you did enjoy *Cold Blood*, please could you write a review and tell your friends and family. Reviews and word-of-mouth recommendations are so valuable to me. They make a huge difference, and help new readers discover one of my books for the first time.

I'd also love to hear from you! Drop me a line on my Facebook page, through Twitter, Goodreads or my website, which you'll find at www.robertbryndza.com. There are many more books to come, so I hope you'll stay with me for the ride!

Robert Bryndza

ACKNOWLEDGEMENTS

Thank you to the wonderful team at my publisher Bookouture, and special thanks to my editor, Claire Bord. Working with you is a joy, and as always, your input and suggestions always make my books so much better. Thank you for giving me the creative freedom to write this series the way I want it. Thank you to my brilliant agent, Amy Tannenbaum. Thank you, as ever, to Henry Steadman for the stunning cover, and thank you to Sergeant Lorna Dennison-Wilkins for your help and advice on the effects of human remains being exposed to water.

Thank you to my mother-in-law, Vierka, for her love and support during the writing of this book, and to my amazing husband Ján for your love, support, and for always making me laugh and fighting my corner. And for walking the dogs.

I've talked about word-of-mouth in my author's note, but I just wanted to add a thank you to my mum and dad, Pat and Brian Sutton – there, Mum and Dad, you are now in print! Thanks to them for recommending my books to so many people, friends and neighbours, people on the street, strangers on the train. And thanks for lending my books out to all those people who don't have e-readers. They run the busiest unofficial lending library. Love you both so much!

And lastly, thank you to all the wonderful readers, book bloggers and book groups. Thank you for talking up and blogging about my books. Without you I would have far fewer readers.

Read on for the pulse-pounding beginning
of Robert Bryndza's Kate Marshall series,
Nine Elms

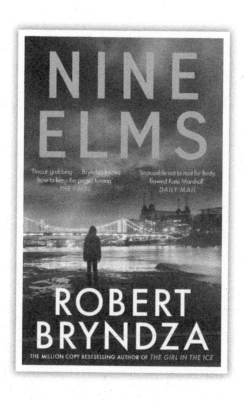

AUTUMN
1995

CHAPTER 1

Detective Constable Kate Marshall was on the train home when her phone rang. It took a moment of searching the folds of her long winter coat before she found it in the inside pocket. She heaved out the huge brick-like handset, pulled up the aerial and answered. It was her boss, Detective Chief Inspector Peter Conway.

'Sir. Hello.'

'Finally. She picks up!' he snapped, without preamble. 'I've been calling you. What's the bloody point in having one of these new mobile phones if you don't answer?'

'Sorry. I've been in court all day for the Travis Jones sentencing. He got three years, which is more than I—'

'A dog walker found the body of a young girl dumped in Crystal Palace Park,' he said, cutting her off. 'Naked. Bite marks on her body, a plastic bag tied over her head.'

'The Nine Elms Cannibal . . . '

'Operation Hemlock. You know I don't like that name.'

Kate wanted to reply that the name had now stuck and was bedded in for life, but he wasn't the kind of boss who encouraged banter. The press had coined the epithet two years earlier, when seventeen-year-old Shelley Norris had been found in a wrecker's yard in the Nine Elms area of south-west London, close to the Thames. Technically, the killer only bit his victims, but the press didn't let this get in the way of a good serial killer moniker. Over the past two years, another two teenage girls had been abducted, each in the early evening, on their way home from school. Their bodies had shown up several days after their disappearances, dumped in parks around London. Nothing sold newspapers more than a cannibal on the loose.

'Kate. Where are you?'

It was dark outside the train window. She looked up at the electronic display in the carriage.

'On the DLR. Almost home, sir.'

'I'll pick you up outside the station, our usual spot.' He hung up without waiting for a response.

Twenty minutes later, Kate was waiting on a small stretch of pavement between the station underpass and the busy South Circular where a line of cars ground slowly past. Much of the area around the station was under development, and Kate's route home to her small flat took her through a long road of empty building sites. It wasn't somewhere to linger after dark. The passengers she'd left the train with had crossed the road and dispersed into the dark streets. She glanced back over her shoulder at the dank empty underpass bathed in shadows and shifted on her heels. A small bag of groceries she'd bought for dinner sat between her feet.

A spot of water hit her neck, and another, and then it started to rain. She turned up the collar of her coat and hunched down, moving closer to the bright headlights in the line of traffic.

Kate had been assigned to Operation Hemlock sixteen months previously, when the Nine Elms Cannibal body count stood at three. It had been a coup to join a high-profile case, along with promotion to the rank of plain-clothes detective.

In the eight months since the third victim's body was found – a seventeen-year-old schoolgirl called Carla Martin – the case had gone cold. Operation Hemlock had been scaled back, and Kate had been re-assigned to the drug squad, along with several other junior officers.

Kate squinted through the rain, down the long line of traffic. Bright headlights appeared around a sharp bend in the road, but there were no police sirens in the distance. She checked her watch and stepped back out of the glare.

She hadn't seen Peter for two months. Shortly before she was reassigned, she had slept with him. He rarely socialised with his team, and during a rare night of after-work drinks they'd wound up talking, and she'd found his company and his intelligence stimulating. They had stayed late in the pub, after the rest of the team went home, and ended up back at her flat. And then the next night he had invited her over to his place. Kate's dalliance with her boss, on not one but two occasions, was something that burned inside her with regret. It was a moment of madness – two moments – before they both came to their senses. She had a strong moral compass. She was a good police officer.

I'll pick you up at our usual spot.

It bothered her that Peter said this on the phone. He'd given her a lift to work twice, and both times he had also picked up her colleague, Detective Cameron Rose, who lived close by. Would he have said *our usual spot* to Cam?

The cold was starting to creep up the back of her long coat, and the rain had seeped in through the holes in the bottom of the 'good shoes' she wore for court. Kate adjusted her collar and huddled into her coat, turning her attention to the line of traffic. Almost all the drivers were men, white, in their mid- to late thirties. The perfect serial killer demographic.

A grimy white van slid past, the driver's face distorted by the rainwater on the windscreen. The police believed the Nine Elms Cannibal was using a van to abduct his victims. Carpet fibres matching a 1994 Citroën Dispatch white van, of which there were over a hundred thousand registered in and around London, had been found on two of the victims. Kate wondered if the officers who'd been retained for Operation Hemlock were still working through that list of Citroën Dispatch white van owners. And who was this new victim? There had been nothing in the newspapers about a missing person.

The lights up ahead turned red, and a small blue Ford stopped in the line of traffic a few feet away. The man inside was a City type: overweight, in his mid-fifties and wearing a pinstriped suit and glasses. He saw Kate, raised his eyebrows suggestively and flashed his headlights. Kate looked away. The blue Ford inched closer, closing the gap in the line of cars until his passenger window was almost level with her. It slid down, and the man leaned across.

'Hello. You look cold. I can make you warm . . . ' He patted the seat beside him and stuck out his tongue which was thin and pointed. Kate froze. Panic rose in her chest. She forgot she had her warrant card, and that she was a police officer. It all went out of the window and fear took over. '*Come on*. Hop inside. Let's warm you up,' he said. He patted the seat again, impatient.

Kate stepped away from the kerb. The underpass behind her was dark and empty. The other vehicles in the line had male drivers, and they seemed oblivious, cocooned in their cars. The lights ahead remained red. The rain thrummed lazily on the car roofs. The man leaned farther over and the passenger door popped open a few inches. Kate took another step back, but felt trapped. What if he got out of his car and pushed her into the underpass?

'Don't fuck me around. How much?' he said. His smile was gone, and she could see his trousers were undone. His underpants were faded and dingy. He hooked his finger under the waistband and exposed his penis and a thatch of greying pubic hair.

Kate was still rooted to the spot, willing the lights to change.

A police siren blared out suddenly, cutting through the silence, and the cars and the arch of the underpass were lit up with blue flashing lights. The man hurriedly rearranged himself, fastened his trousers and pulled the door shut, activating the central locking. His face returned to an impassive stare. Kate fumbled in her bag and pulled out her warrant card. She went to the blue Ford and slapped it against the passenger window, annoyed that she hadn't done it earlier.

Peter's unmarked police car, with its revolving blue light on the roof, came shooting down the outside of the row of traffic, half up on the grass verge. The traffic light changed to green. The car in front drove away, and Peter pulled into the gap. The man inside the Ford was now panicking, smoothing down his hair and tie. Kate fixed him with a stare, put her warrant card back in her bag and went to the passenger door of Peter's car.

CHAPTER 2

'Sorry to keep you waiting. Traffic,' said Peter, giving her a brisk smile. He picked up a pile of paperwork from the passenger seat and put it behind his seat. He was a good-looking man in his late thirties, broad-shouldered with thick dark wavy hair, high cheekbones and soft brown eyes. He wore an expensive tailored black suit.

'Of course,' she said, feeling relief as she stashed her handbag and groceries in the footwell and dropped into the seat. As soon as she closed the door, Peter accelerated and flicked on the sirens.

The sunshade was down on the passenger side, and she caught her reflection in the mirror as she folded it back up. She wasn't wearing any make-up, or dressed provocatively, and Kate always thought herself a little plain. She wasn't delicate. She had strong features. Her shoulder-length hair was tied back off her face, tucked away under the neck of her long winter coat, almost as an afterthought. The only distinguishing features were her unusual eyes, which were a startling cornflower blue with a burst of burnt orange flooding out from the pupils. It was caused by sectoral heterochromia, a rare condition where the eyes have two colours. The other, less permanent mark on her face was a split lip, just starting to scab over, which had been caused by an irate drunk resisting arrest a few days before. She'd felt no fear when dealing with the drunk, and didn't feel ashamed that he'd hit her. It was part of the job. Why did she feel shame after being hit on by the sleazy businessman? He was the one with the sad, saggy grey underwear and the stubby little manhood.

'What was that? With the car behind?' asked Peter.

'Oh, one of his brake lights was out,' she said. It was easier to lie. She felt embarrassed. She pushed the man and his blue Ford to the back of her mind. 'Have you called the whole team to the crime scene?'

'Of course,' said Peter, glancing over. 'After we spoke, I got a call from the assistant commissioner, Anthony Asher. He says if this murder is linked to Operation Hemlock, I only have to ask and I'll have all the resources I need at my disposal.'

He sped around a roundabout in fourth gear, and took the exit to Crystal Palace Park. Peter Conway was a career police officer, and Kate had no doubt that solving this case would result in a promotion to superintendent or even chief superintendent. Peter had been the youngest officer in the history of the Met Police to be promoted to detective chief inspector.

The windows were starting to fog up, and he turned up the heater. The arc of condensation on the windscreen rippled and receded. Between a group of terraced houses Kate caught a glimpse of the London skyline lit up. There were millions of lights, pinpricks in the black fabric of the sky, symbolising the homes and offices of millions. Kate wondered which light belonged to the Nine Elms Cannibal. *What if we never find him?* she thought. *The police never found Jack the Ripper, and back then London was tiny in comparison.*

'Have you had any more leads from the white van database?' she asked.

'We brought in another six men for questioning, but their DNA didn't match our man.'

'The fact he leaves his DNA on the victims, it's not just carelessness or lack of control. It's as if he's marking his territory. Like a dog.'

'You think he wants us to catch him?'

'Yes . . . No . . . Possibly.'

'He's behaving like he's invincible.'

'He *thinks* he's invincible. But he'll slip up. They always do,' said Kate.

They turned off into the north entrance to Crystal Palace Park. A police car was waiting, and the officer waved them through. They drove down a long straight avenue of gravel, usually reserved for people on foot. It was lined with large oak trees shedding leaves, and they hit the windshield with a wet flapping sound, clogging up the wipers. In the far distance the huge Crystal Palace radio transmitter poked up above the trees like a slender Eiffel Tower. The road banked down and ended in a small car park beside a long flat expanse of grass, which backed onto a wooded area. A police tape cordon ringed the entire expanse of grass. In the centre was a second, smaller cordon around a white forensics tent, glowing in the darkness. Next to the second cordon sat the pathologist's van, four squad cars and a large white police support vehicle.

Where the tarmac met the grass, the tape of the first police cordon flapped in the breeze. Kate and Peter were met by two uniformed police officers – a middle-aged man whose belly hung over his belt and a tall, thin young man who still looked like a teenager. Kate and Peter showed their identification to the older officer. His eyes were hooded with loose skin, and as he glanced between their warrant cards, he reminded Kate of a chameleon. He handed them back, and went to lift the police tape, but hesitated, looking over at the glowing tent.

'In all my years, I ain't never seen nothing like it,' he said.

'You were the first on the scene?' asked Peter, impatient for him to lift the tape, but not willing to do it himself.

'Yes. PC Stanley Gresham, sir. This is PC Will Stokes.' He said gesturing to the young officer, who suddenly grimaced, turned away from them and threw up over the police tape. 'It's his first day on the job,' he added, shaking his head. Kate gave the young officer a look of pity as he heaved and threw up again, thin strings of spittle dangling from his mouth. Peter took a clean white handkerchief from his inside pocket, and Kate thought he was going to offer it up to the young officer, but he pressed it to his nose and mouth.

'I want this crime scene locked down. Not a word to anyone,' said Peter.

'Of course, sir.'

Peter fluttered his fingers at the police tape. Stanley lifted it and they ducked under. The grass sloped down to the second police cordon where Detective Cameron Rose and Detective Inspector Marsha Lewis were waiting. Cameron, like Kate, was in his mid-twenties, and Marsha was older than all of them, a thickset woman in her fifties, wearing a smart black trouser suit and long black coat. Her silver hair was cropped short and she had a gravelly smoker's voice.

'Sir,' they both said in unison.

'What's going on, Marsha?' asked Peter.

'All exits in and out of the park are sealed, and I've got local plod being bussed in for a fingertip search and house to house. Forensic pathologist is in there already, and she's ready to talk to us.'

Cameron was tall and gangly, towering above them all. He hadn't had time to change, and looked more like a louche teenager than a detective in his jeans, trainers and a green winter jacket. Kate wondered fleetingly what he had been doing when he got the call to come to the crime scene. She presumed he'd arrived with Marsha.

'Who's our forensic pathologist?' asked Peter.

'Leodora Graves,' said Marsha.

It was hot inside the glowing tent, where the lights were almost painfully bright. Forensic pathologist Leodora Graves, a small dark-skinned woman with penetrating green eyes, worked with two assistants. A naked young girl lay face down in a muddy depression in the grass. Her head was covered by a clear plastic bag, tied tightly around her neck. Her pale skin was streaked with dirt and blood and numerous cuts and scratches. The backs of her thighs and buttocks had several deep bite marks.

Kate stood beside the body, already sweating underneath the hood and face mask of her thick white forensics suit. The rain hammered down on the tight skin of the tent, forcing Leodora to raise her voice.

'The victim is posed, lying on her right side, her right arm under her head. The left arm lies flat and reaching out. There are six bites on her lower back, buttocks and thighs.' She indicated the deepest bites where the flesh had been removed, so deep as to expose the girl's spine. She moved to the victim's head and gently lifted it. The length of thin rope was tied tight around the neck, biting into the now bloated flesh. 'You'll note the specific knot.'

'The monkey's fist knot,' said Cameron, speaking for the first time. He sounded shaken. Everyone's face was obscured by the mask of their forensic suit, but Kate could read the looks of alarm in their eyes.

'Yes,' said Leodora, holding the knot in her gloved hand. What made it unusual was the series of intersecting turns, like a tiny ball of wool, almost impossible to replicate with a machine.

'It's him. The Nine Elms Cannibal,' said Kate. The words came out of her mouth before she could stop them.

'I'll need to conclude more from my post-mortem, but . . . yes,' said Leodora. The rain fell harder, intensifying the thundering thrum on the roof of the tent. She let go of the young girl's head, placing it gently back where it lay on her arm. 'There is evidence that she was raped. There are bodily fluids present, and she's been tortured, cut with a sharp object and burned. You see the burn marks on her arms and outer thighs? They look to be caused by the cigarette lighter from a car.'

'Or a white van,' said Kate. Peter gave her a hard stare. He didn't like being corrected.

'Cause of death?' he asked.

'I need to do the post-mortem, but off the record, at this stage I would say asphyxiation with the plastic bag. There are signs of petechial haemorrhaging on her face and neck.'

'Thank you, Leodora. I look forward to the results of your post-mortem. I hope that we can quickly identify this poor young woman.'

Leodora nodded to her assistants, who brought in a pop-up stretcher with a shiny new black body bag. They placed it beside the body, and gently turned the young woman over onto the stretcher. The front of her naked body was marked with small circular burns and scratches. It was impossible to tell what she looked like – her face was grotesque and distorted under the plastic. She had large pale-blue eyes, milky in death, and frozen in a stare. The look in her eyes made Kate shiver. It was devoid of hope, as if frozen in her eyes was that last thought. She knew she was going to die.